Yours Truly

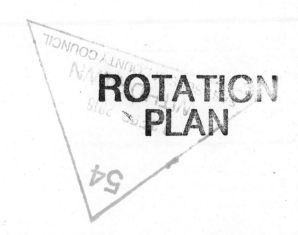

Yours Truly

Kirsty Greenwood

W F HOWES LTD

This large print edition published in 2014 by
W F Howes Ltd
Unit 4, Rearsby Business Park, Gaddesby Lane,
Rearsby, Leicester LE7 4YH

1 3 5 7 9 10 8 6 4 2

First published in the United Kingdom in 2012
by Kirsty Greenwood

A CIP catalogue record for this book is available
from the British Library

ISBN 978 1 47125 689 9

Typeset by Palimpsest Book Production Limited,
Falkirk, Stirlingshire
Printed and bound by
CPI Group (UK) Ltd, Croydon, CR0 4YY

MIX
Paper from
responsible sources
FSC
www.fsc.org FSC® C013604

For Edd. I love you.

CHAPTER 1

In all my twenty-seven years of life, I have never before noticed the astonishing similarities between my own head and a tenpin bowling ball.

Thanks to Barbara – senior stylist at Hair Hackers, Manchester – the resemblance is now uncanny.

In only two hours, this ruthless hair destroyer has managed to enhance my already round face with a Friar Tuck-inspired bob that cups my plump cheeks. Add that to the magic forehead-widening fringe, and the double chin-boosting tuck-under, and the result is nothing less than extraordinary.

'It looks fabulous. Just . . . *stunning*,' Barbara chirps, waving a teeny pink mirror behind my head. 'The colours have turned out gorgeous, don't you think?'

Ah, the colours. I should probably mention that the Luxurious Caramel, Sticky Treacle and Ash Blonde I asked for have somehow turned out to be Felt Tip Orange, Poo Brown and Ash . . . as in cigarette. It's almost as if these particular colours have been specially chosen to enhance the natural ruddiness of my cheeks, making me look like a wind-beaten mountain woman, and to dull the light in my normally quite pretty brown eyes. Also . . . the whole thing is stripy.

I stare into the huge mirror in front of me, bewildered. I'm getting married in a month and my head has just been gravely mistreated.

What the chuff was I thinking?

First rule of getting married: don't go to a brand-new hairdresser mere weeks before your wedding and expect it to be okay.

Hmm . . . that's probably not the *actual* first rule of getting married. I bet it's somewhere in the top ten, though.

Right.

I have to fix this.

I look up at Barbara and give her my most gracious smile.

'I don't think—'

'Do you know, I think I might have these colours myself,' Barbara butts in, beaming. 'They're really complementary, aren't they?'

No. They are not. They're insulting. I look like the love spawn of Ann Widdecombe and . . . a really round-headed tabby cat.

I should tell her.

I'm definitely going to tell her. Right this instant. Barbara's a perfectly nice woman, I'm sure. But what she has just done to my hair is cruel, and I, Natalie Butterworth, am going to have the guts to be honest. I am going to ask her why, when I requested face-slimming, feathery layers à la Jennifer Aniston, she adorned me with a Lego head helmet à la no one since the 1960s.

I will say this. For victims of bad hairdressers here and beyond I will stand up to her. I will tell her firmly that I absolutely refuse to pay for this – the most unflattering haircut in all of England. I will absolutely insist she makes it better. I will . . .

'Yeah, and the cut is brilliant,' I say brightly. 'The condition is *soooo* much better. It's so *smooth* and so *shiny*.'

I am cooing.

Barbara calls over the junior stylists and some of the other clients, who all clamber up to gawp at the monstrosity now sitting atop my horrified face.

Massive balls.

I can't do it. I can't tell her. She looks so proud of her handiwork. And it took her two whole hours. I can't just refuse to pay. That would be terribly rude. Plus, when you think about it, it's not Barbara's fault I have a fat head, is it?

'Would you like to make your way over to the payment area?' she asks, untying the black plastic cape from around my neck and leading me towards a till by the door. One of the hair washers totters over with my denim jacket, her caramel locks flicking flatteringly with every step she takes.

3

See, why can't I have hair like her? Subtle, not scary . . .

'It looks *reeeeally* trendy,' she says, her pretty teenage face turning cherry red. Wait . . . was that a snigger?

Oh man. I want to reach up and ruffle this hair helmet into submission, but I can hardly mess up Barbara's hard work right in front of her.

I'll just fix it when I get home. Maybe I could buy one of those do-it-yourself hair dyes. Yep, I'll do that. Better than causing some dramatic and embarrassing scene.

'Right, flower, that'll be eighty-nine pounds and ninety pence,' says Barbara, 'and I'll book you an appointment for four weeks for a trim, shall I?'

Ninety quid? Ninety quid!

Nooooo!

I cannot pay ninety pounds for this. It's absurd.

'Um . . . look . . .' I say carefully. 'I—'

'You look *stunning*, love,' she cuts in, her expression one of overt pride. 'I'm so glad it's come out so well. You know, I think it might just be one of the best hairdos I've ever done.'

Shit.

I hand over my credit card, tip about thirty per cent, and jog on out of the salon, never to return again.

As the door clicks shut behind me, I'm pretty

sure I hear a burst of laughter from the pre-pubescent hair washer . . .

Can you get married in a hat?

Shuffling through a puddle-soaked Piccadilly Gardens, amongst the final throngs of the day's shoppers, I keep my eyes lowered. The shops have all closed so I haven't been able to buy a hat, and I'm now having to face the general public with my terrifying hair on full show.

I arrive at the bus stop and dig my phone out of my leather satchel. I'll call Meg – best friend since primary school, wannabe pop star, bad hair sympathizer and all-round good egg. She'll know what to do.

While the phone is ringing, a pair of yummy mummies stroll by, perfect, chubby children in tow.

'Mummy,' peeps an angelic-looking girl. 'What is wrong with that lady's head?'

I look around, trying to locate the object of the little girl's interest. But *I'm* the only lady here. Hang on. Is – is she referring to *my* head?

Both mothers squint over before their eyes widen slightly in polite horror. They swiftly grab hold of their respective children's hands.

'Some people are just different, Olivia,' says the taller mum, dragging her daughter away. 'Don't stare at the lady.'

They hurry off, only glancing back when they're

far enough down the road to be safe from my evil-hair-woman clutches.

Excellent.

'Hey, Natty!'

Meg's voice booms out loudly through the mobile, her lush Geordie accent as broad as ever and with no discernible use of the letter T.

'Meg, thank God! I have issues.'

'Didn't we establish that when you were sixteen?'

'Ho ho. Really, I just had my hair done and it's horrible. It's so bad that I'm going to scare people at my own wedding! When I walk down the aisle the guests won't be tearfully moved by my radiant beauty. They'll just be tearful.' I take a deep breath.

Meg's less-than-sympathetic response is to crack up into giggles.

'Cheers,' I huff. 'Your understanding means the world to me.'

'I'm sorry,' says Meg, still chuckling. 'It's just, this is classic Natalie. I bet you didn't even tell them you didn't like it, did you?'

'No, but—'

'Did you pay for it?'

'Yes, of course! I didn't want to cause a scene and—'

'You need to go back and ask them to fix it!'

She's right. That's what any assertive, independent, grown-up woman would do.

But . . .

'I can't,' I sigh, noticing the approaching bus.

6

'It's completely unfixable anyway. It's too short to cut again without me looking like a fatter, more ginger Annie Lennox, and any more hair dye and I'll probably . . . I don't know . . . explode from all the toxic chemicals. Besides, I never want to go there again. They were laughing at me!'

'Were they heck,' she soothes. 'You should stand up for yourself. You *should* tell the truth.'

'I don't want to be rude, Meg. It would have been completely bad manners. Hang on, I'm just getting on the bus . . . Fallowfield, please.' I hand over my fare and find a seat at the back, so no one can sit behind me and take mobile phone pictures of my barnet and spread them viciously around the internet. 'Okay. I'm back again,' I say, once I've taken my seat.

'Look, Olly's not marrying your hairdo, he's marrying you,' she says. 'Don't stress – it'll bring you out in spots. We'll sort it.'

'Yeah . . . I suppose so. It's just, I really wanted to look nice.'

'You will! You'll look perfect, Natty. And I'll be really, really jealous.'

That's true. Meg has wanted to get married ever since she saw video footage of Princess Diana's nuptials when we were fifteen. The desire to be a bride has upped to magnificent proportions since the wedding of Wills and Kate, and finding her very own prince is now a frequent topic of conversation.

'Listen, I've got to go,' she says. 'I've got

7

spinning in ten minutes and I've not done my make-up yet.'

Meg's gym is one of those shiny posh ones, full of *Hollyoaks* cast members and people who wear luminous leotards in a non-ironic way.

'Don't work too hard, will you?' I grin. We both know that Meg doing anything other than look pretty at the gym is about as likely as me ever setting foot inside one.

'Of course not. Unless by "work" you mean ogling the arses of bronzed gods in action, in which case I will work super hard. Ooh, and don't forget the pub tomorrow night. I've got tickets for that hypnotist.'

Ah, the hypnotist. Meg got super excited when she discovered that a real live hypnotist was coming to town. She's been meaning to visit one ever since she read in a Sunday supplement about some woman who was hypnotized into believing she'd had gastric band surgery and lost three stone in as many months. She was all set to get an appointment when she discovered that the hypnosis cost five hundred quid a session. Now, she reckons that if she asks nicely, this pub hypnotist will give her a session for free. I can't see it myself . . . but I'm looking forward to seeing her try.

'Yup, I'll meet you there at around half sixish.'

'Brill. Gotta go. And don't worry, your wedding will be just perfect.'

'Honestly?'

'Honestly. Now bugger off. I have my own husband to find.'

'Germaine Greer would be proud.'

'Who?'

We both laugh because Meg has a Master's degree in Gender, Sexuality and Culture Studies. You wouldn't think it to look at her but she's startlingly bright.

'Bye.'

'Toodle pip.'

I hang up, and make an executive decision not to get so worked up. Meg's right. It *is* only a hairdo. There's always a little disaster before a wedding. It's tradition. This is just my little disaster.

CHAPTER 2

Text from: **Olly Chatterley**
Sweetness, did you manage to pick up my
dry-cleaning? Can't wait to cu later. X

Reply to: **Olly Chatterley**
Of course. Love you lots. X

I'm not a wimp. At least, I never used to be.
Honestly. As a kid I was feisty and assured,
forever bossing around my little sister, Dionne,
standing for student council (which basically
involved making decisions on vital issues such as
themes for the school disco and protesting about
the teachers' ban on friendship bracelets), and
pretty much not giving a shit. But over the years
things gradually changed. Sometimes I think it
wouldn't have been half as bad had my parents
got it together enough to get divorced. Their petty
irritations with each other had turned into full-
scale, noisy rows that continued well into the
night. As they screamed, and cried, and chucked
plates at each other, I'd creep into Dionne's
bedroom and sing her Westlife songs as loudly as

possible, just to drown out the racket. It took ten years of fighting for my father to decide he'd had enough and he eventually left last year for a life of solitude and self-discovery in India. But those ten years took the fight out of me.

While Dionne acted out by drinking vodka/cider/raspberryade cocktails in the park, failing all her exams and becoming a loud-mouthed attention seeker, I went the other way. I kind of became quiet and undemanding, trying my best to keep my parents happy so that they wouldn't argue and studiously avoiding any situation that may end in conflict. After ten years it's become a pretty tough habit to break. Don't get me wrong, my parents didn't 'fuck me up'. I just learned that a quiet life equals an easy one. It makes sense that way.

I've barely stepped through the front porch when Mum calls my name from the kitchen. I've been living with Mum for about a year now. When my dad upped and left for India last year, she had this horrible nervous breakdown. I deferred (indefinitely) on my course in catering, left my flat share with Meg in Chorlton and came back to my childhood home so that I could look after her.

It's not so bad really – outside the city centre, but still close enough to get to Chutney's Deli in Piccadilly where I work as a counter assistant. Of course, I miss living with Meg. The silliness and late nights and . . . well . . . the freedom, I suppose. But sticking by your family is much more important than playing house with your best mate. And my family needs me. Mum needs me. That's why, after we're married, Olly and I are going to move into the flat above the corner shop down the road, so that we're never too far away. It's huge, and has brand-new wooden floors, and Mum managed to convince Irene, the shopkeeper and landlady, to knock fifty pounds a month off the rent. It also means that the whole family will be within a street or so of each other because we'll be living next door to my sister, Dionne. The sister I can now hear calling out to me, along with Mum.

'Natalie! Get a move on. We've got a surprise for you!'

I startle. A surprise? Ooh. Maybe they've ironed my clothes for the week, or moved Dionne's gym equipment out of my bedroom. Let's face it, a cup of tea would have me flailing in shock.

I push open the door and there they are. My family. Beaming proudly and holding up the most horrendous-looking piece of clothing I have ever seen in my life.

Ever.

'Surprise!' they yell in clearly rehearsed unison. 'We got you a dress!'

And then they catch sight of my hair and their expressions of joy melt into ones of shock.

'What the fuck happened to your head?' says Dionne, dashing over to inspect it.

I reach up to touch the pudding-bowl haircut. See? I was right. It really is that bad.

I grimace. 'I asked for caramel highlights and a layered trim. *This* is what happened.'

'Shit . . .' she whispers, her heavily mascara'd blue eyes wide with alarm. 'Why would someone do that to you? Have you pissed anyone off recently? Any gangsters? Is it, like, an act of revenge?'

I tut.

Apparently Dionne's new boyfriend, Bull, has close associates within the Manchester gangland scene. Since they've been dating, she's become a bit obsessed by gangster culture, reading any book about gangs or the mafia that she can lay her hands on and watching all the *Godfather* films back to back.

She glances around furtively, as if at any moment a gangster may pop out from behind Mum's brand-new fridge and deliver the same horrid fate to her long, platinum-blonde hair extensions.

I wonder about the information she's getting if she thinks that mafia retribution involves giving someone an unfortunate haircut.

'It was Hair Hackers in the town centre,' I answer.

'Hair Hackers?' Dionne repeats. 'As in hackers of hair? Erm, I think the clue might have, like, been in the name, sis.' With this she attempts (and fails) to cover a grin, before picking up the dress Mum dropped in shock.

Mum hurries over and stares with narrowed eyes, carefully checking my head from every angle. I feel a frisson of nerves. Mum's a maths teacher at a secondary school and as such I often get the feeling that she's about to grade me below average or send me to the headmaster for punishment.

'Well, I think I like it,' she eventually declares. 'You look exactly like Tracy. May she rest in peace.'

Tracy was our childhood tabby cat. On hearing Mum's observation, Dionne snorts loudly – only this time she doesn't even attempt to cover it.

God.

Maybe I could get a wig.

'Anyway,' Mum continues briskly. 'You've ruined your surprise now. Go on. Take a look.'

Dionne is holding up the dress in front of herself. It's got a corseted top covered in silver sequins and diamantes and a huge puffed skirt held up with reams of stiff netting.

'Is this for the hen night?' I ask, stroking the satiny material. Better than the slutty Moulin Rouge outfits Dionne initially suggested. This isn't so bad. I can wear this. I can have a laugh like the rest of them. The second rule of getting married: everybody looks like a chump on their hen night.

'No, you daft git,' says Mum. 'It's a wedding dress. *For your wedding*.' She rolls her eyes at Dionne.

Whaaaat?

I look hard at Dionne and wait for her to burst into giggles, unable to hold in the joke any longer.

She doesn't. She just sighs lovingly at the dress before bestowing it upon me like a midwife with a newborn baby. 'We were thinking you could wear a muff and all. And maybe a feathery shrug.'

Feathery shrug? And what the pickle is a muff? 'What's a muff?'

'You know. One of those furry mitten things you use to keep your hands warm. They're all the rage at winter weddings.'

A furry mitten thing? Why on earth would my hands be cold at my own wedding? I get a vision of the entire congregation bundled up in colourful scarves and woolly hats. Olly in an expensive, tailor-made balaclava. Dove grey to match his morning suit.

I pull a face of distress.

'Try it on then!' chides Mum. 'We'll have to get it taken in.' Her eyes flicker down towards my stomach. 'Or let out. There isn't much time.'

Is this for real? They haven't actually bought my wedding dress, have they?

'Uh . . . are you joking?' I murmur, my cheeks burning.

They grin at each other, mistaking my question for grateful disbelief.

'Nope,' says Dionne. 'We said we'd pay for your dress. Well . . . here you go!'

They did say they would pay for my dress. I didn't mean for them to go out and buy it. Without telling me. Without letting me choose.

15

Isn't shopping for a wedding dress supposed to be a rite of passage? The free champagne; the seamstress fussing over me and pretending that she knew as soon as I walked through the shop door which dress I was eventually going to choose. Standing on that wooden box and pretending I'm much taller and slimmer than I really am. Picking the dress that I absolutely could not – *not* – wear on my wedding day . . . .

'It's gorgeous, isn't it?' Dionne continues, fingering the hooks and eyes of the corset with her metallic pink talons. 'And look at all the diamante! We thought that diamante could be, like, the theme for the entire wedding.'

Diamante? As a theme? Oh God. No.

I silently curse Olly for proposing last week and insisting we get married as soon as humanly possible.

It was a lovely proposal, mind. He'd whisked me away for a discounted weekend at a health spa in Cheshire and got down on one knee after a delicious meal at the spa's vegan restaurant.

I look down at the ring displayed in pride of place on the third finger of my left hand. A gorgeous heart-shaped diamond on a platinum band. It's very shiny.

I thought I'd have at least a few months to get the wedding sorted, but then Olly surprised me by booking the church for next month.

'Natalie, it was a cancellation. It was either Christmas Eve or 2015. I'm not waiting till 2015!

I want to marry you now! Plus, we get a reason-able discount for taking the space up.'

I've had to rely on Mum and Dionne to help organize everything super quickly. They've even been doing this checklist and emailing it to me each time there's the slightest change to the plans.

I bury the groan bubbling in my throat. I'm being selfish. Their buying me a dress is just their way of helping to get everything sorted in time.

I suddenly spot hundreds of little bows stitched along the hemline of the dress. Bows!

No. This is ridiculous. People choose their own wedding dresses. That's how it's done! When you think about it, it's bloody out of order to choose someone else's wedding dress for them.

But then Mum and Dionne look so pleased with themselves. They genuinely think they've done a good deed. And they *are* planning the entire wedding in only four weeks after all . . .

'Come on then. We want to see what it looks like,' urges Dionne, eyes sparkling like . . . diamante.

Well . . . I suppose there's no harm in trying it on, is there?

'It looks extraordinary!' Mum breathes, as I shuffle into the kitchen to show them the dress. Her dark brown eyes are shining with tears of joy. Wow. It must look better than I thought it would. Maybe, shockingly, they *do* know me better than I know myself.

17

While I was getting changed they brought down the full-length mirror from my bedroom and propped it up against our kitchen table. Dionne pours everyone a glass of wine before gesturing that I should have a look at myself in the mirror.

I warily manoeuvre myself around to the other side of the table, being careful not to knock over the pan stand or the vegetable rack with the massive skirt. Nervously, I glance up at my reflection.

Wow.

Mum's 'extraordinary' is right. Horrendous, horrifying, horrible are also suitable adjectives.

I gawk numbly into the mirror, entranced by the way the diamante glistens under the fluorescent kitchen lights. The flab from my waist is compressed into this iridescent bodice and is now making a bid for freedom by spilling over the top of my corset. I turn around to see the view from behind. Back fat. Definite fat of the back.

'We are so GOOD!' cheers Dionne. 'You look just like Katie Price. Except you've got no tits. Maybe you should buy some tits before the wedding, and then you'll look perfect.' She grabs her own surgically enhanced breasts to demonstrate.

I look down towards my 32Bs and sigh. They're not *that* bad. They'd be improved considerably if I wasn't wearing a dress that flattened them into total oblivion.

And my height! Where has it gone? What little

of it I have, at five foot three, appears to have been squashed by the enormity of this dress. I look like I'm off to see the wizard.

Nope. No. Nuh uh. Noooooooo. This is not what I want to look like on my wedding day. I wanted Audrey Hepburn in *Funny Face*, not Bridal Munchkin Drag Queen in *A Gypsy Wedding Sequin Frenzy*. I take a breath. I must tell them. Meg said to stand up for myself, and that is what I'll do, damn it. I'll tell them that this is just not the dress for me. It's not like they can force me to wear it.

'Mum, Dionne. I don't quite . . .' My voice goes all scratchy. I clear my throat and try again. 'I don't think—'

'You look just like I always wanted to look on my wedding day,' Mum interrupts, welling up. 'I would have done, if it wasn't for your bastard of a dad spending all our money on that stupid motorbike of his.'

Dionne pats her gently on the shoulder.

'Aw, Mum,' I continue. 'I'm sorry, but—'

'Just imagine. Diamante everywhere,' pipes up Dionne brightly, batting her spidery eyelashes for emphasis.

'I'm not sure it's really me,' I eventually get out, turning this way and that in the mirror.

My mother's face hardens, just slightly.

'Look, Natalie,' she says. 'Dionne and I are trying to produce the perfect wedding, in only a few short weeks. It isn't easy.' She takes a shaky

19

breath. 'Do you not want us to be involved with this?'

She looks so sad.

'Of course I want you to be involved,' I soothe.

I do. I can't plan all of this on my own, and Mum and Dionne together are like an unstoppable whirlwind of productivity. When they're around things get done, things get sorted.

'Your dad would have loved that dress,' Mum says again, dabbing her eyes carefully so as not to smudge her mascara.

'I know, Mum. I know.' I neglect to remind her that Dad's not dead, just buggered off to India, and we really shouldn't care whether he'd like it or not. It's just us now. And wasn't she calling him a bastard just a minute ago?

I glance back down at the dress and notice that all the pearls have been stitched on in the shape of little love hearts. Jesus.

'Do you not think I should wear something a bit . . . simpler? I don't want to look flashy,' I try.

'Definitely not,' says Dionne, hands on her teensy hips. 'The idea of a wedding dress is that it makes you look better than usual. Not being funny or anything, but who wants to see the same old boring Natalie rolling down the aisle?'

Mum wipes her eyes and juts out her chin.

'This wedding is not just about you, love. It's about all of us. Our family. God knows we could use a bit of happiness since . . . since . . .' She

20

buries her face into Dionne's silicone bosom and sobs loudly. Shit.

'I'm sorry, Mum. I don't want to upset you. I really don't. But—'

'That is the dress you are wearing.' She looks up sharply. 'A proper wedding dress. Not some flimsy nothing dress you could wear any other time.'

I don't say anything for a moment, just stare into the mirror. I look exactly like a toilet-roll-holder doll. A toilet-roll-holder doll with orange hair and a very round face.

'I'm trying to help you to make the best of yourself, Natalie,' Mum goes on. 'Do you not need my help?' Her voice wobbles again. 'You don't, do you?! You think I'm useless! Your dad thought I was pointless and now you do too!'

She dissolves into another round of tears and presses a hand to her chest, her expression pained.

'Mum, are you all right?' I ask worriedly.

'It's just indigestion,' she sniffs. 'I'll be fine. I'll take a Rennie.'

I don't have any other choice.

'Fine. I'll wear this one.' I plaster a smile onto my face and pat Mum on the arm.

'Fantastic, darling! You'll look like a princess!'

Mum and Dionne grin at each other and clink glasses. I smile weakly, take my glass of wine from the table beside me and neck it in one.

The dress of devastation is hung up on my bedroom door, silently mocking me. I glower at it and frown. A sequin flickers and sparkles under the lights, like an evil spangly wink.

For the past two hours Mum and Dionne have been chattering away about the wedding: how brilliant it's going to be, how gorgeous I'm going to look (if I manage to drop a dress size in the next thirty days), whether there's such a thing as edible diamante for the wedding favours and the probability of our vicar agreeing to wear a bedazzled dog collar. So me wearing a disco ball Barbie dress isn't such a big sacrifice, when you really think about it. Considering how much they like it, and how much of a favour they're doing me, planning the wedding and all. It's the very least I can do.

I glance up at the alarm clock on my bedside table. Eight o'clock already. Olly should be round at any moment. Almost every weeknight he picks me up after he's finished work at Dino's Suits and Ties. We head over to his executive apartment in Deansgate where we have dinner and then snuggle up in front of the TV with a blanket. It's lovely just hanging out with him. Lovely, cosy, quiet and . . . just lovely.

I'm trying to slick back my terrible hair with styling gel when Dionne bursts into my bedroom. She stops before the wedding dress and presses an acrylic-nail-adorned hand to her chest.

'I can't believe you actually get to wear it!'

Me either.

'I know! Lucky me!'

'You are, like, so super jammy. Anyway, I was wondering if you'd do your little sister a massive favour?'

A massive favour. I think back to the other massive favours Dionne has asked of me over the years. Like that massive favour when she got me to break up with her secondary school boyfriend for her. The poor lad snotted and cried on me for two hours before trying to cop a feel. And then there was the massive favour last month when her kitchen flooded and I had to clean it up because she had a vital eyebrow appointment at the beauty salon. Once we're living next door to each other, I suspect the massive favours will be coming thick and fast.

'Go on,' I say wearily.

'Bull just phoned to say he's going to take me for a romantic Madras on Saturday and I was wondering if you'd babysit Jean Paul Gaultier. Please.'

As massive favours go, it's pretty tame. But Saturday night? The night I planned on doing nothing but trying out recipes for the perfect hollandaise sauce while Olly is out with his mates from the gym.

'I'll pay you,' she pleads.

I wouldn't normally accept money for looking after Jean Paul Gaultier – he's the sweetest little poodle – but a bit of extra cash would not go amiss.

'Fine. No probs.'

'Excellent. Cheers, sis. But do you mind if I pay you next month, rather than this? There's this dress I'm after in River Island and I really want to buy it for Saturday night.' She grabs a lipstick off my dressing table, checks out the colour on her hand and then pockets it. 'But you wouldn't have accepted money to look after him anyway, right?'

Yes.

'Oh, no, no. Course not.'

'Woop. That's that sorted. When's Olly getting here?'

Twenty minutes ago.

'He should be here any minute. Probably driving over here as we speak. I best get on.'

'Right,' says Dionne, flipping her blonde hair so that it lands in a perfect arrangement over her shoulder. 'Well, I've got to go anyway – Jean Paul Gaultier needs a walk and then Bull and I are going to his house to watch *Scarface*. His uncle's cousin was a consultant on the set of the movie. He had to make sure it was all true to life and realistic and stuff. It's very close to Bull's heart.'

I picture Al Pacino and his massive desk mountain of cocaine and wonder how realistic that scene was. And then I wonder how worried I should be about this Bull fella and his murky connections.

'When do we get to meet him then?'

Dionne bites her lip and shrugs.

'Soon. He's shy.'

24

A shy gangster. What next? An interesting accountant? An obedient hairdresser?

On her way out of the room, Dionne grabs my favourite silver and turquoise scarf – the one I intend to wear to the pub tomorrow – from the wardrobe door and flings it around her neck.

'Ooh, can I borrow this?'

'Well, actually—'

'Smell ya later, sis!' She dives out, not bothering to wait for my reply.

Aaaargh!

Fifteen minutes later a horn beeps outside. Olly! I check my lip gloss in the mirror, hop downstairs, and with a quick 'see you later' to Mum, head out of the door and into Olly's car.

CHAPTER 3

Text from: **Dionne**
4got to tell u Bull's mate does wedding cakes 4 cheap. All styles. Even glitter cakes.

Reply to: **Dionne**
Sounds great! Nt sure abt glittery cake tho . . .

After all the noise and wedding stress back at Mum's house it is quite lovely to be in the silence of Olly's apartment. We're snuggled up on his huge black leather sofa watching some kind of sporty programme on Sky Sports. I'm not so much watching as peering at the telly and wondering why the men on the screen are wearing Lycra bodysuits. I *am* thoroughly enjoying the feel of Olly's lovely arm flung around my shoulder, though. He lifts his bum off the sofa in excitement; something apparently interesting is happening on the screen involving weird grunting from the Lycra men. I don't really understand it all, but gasp with feigned interest nevertheless. In response, Olly turns to me and winks before eagerly returning to the Lycra action.

I'm not really into sport and stuff but Olly loves it. Really loves it. He's very into fitness and weight training. Every morning at six on the dot he wakes up and heads to the gym to 'get pumped' for an hour before coming back to pick me up and drive us both into Manchester for work. How committed is that? And then at the weekend he does paint-balling with his friends and plays golf with his dad. His favourite things in the world are his car, me (presumably) and competitive sports. Sometimes I wonder how the heck we're still together. Him a muscled wheatgrass drinker, and me decidedly soft (all right, flabtastical) around the edges. He doesn't seem to mind at all, though. Obviously he thinks I should lose a little weight for the sake of my health. Obviously. He doesn't want me conking out on him when we're married, and that's totally understandable. He's really caring like that.

Olly's gorgeous. I'm not just saying that because I'm about to marry him, but he really is. His tanned, angular face makes Jude Law look like Donald Trump gone to seed, and he has the most gorgeous coffee-coloured hair. He's a little shorter than average, but just about taller than me, and it's not like we spend all our time standing up next to each other, so it doesn't really matter that much. And his body is amazing. All toned and muscled and tanned and trim and firm and honed from the gym. And another good thing: Olly is really neat. Not like neat in a Sixties groovy way, though obviously he is that too. But neat in a really tidy way. I've never seen him in anything that is creased or worn and his house is cleaner than a hospital operating theatre, which makes sense because both of his parents are plastic surgeons. And anyway, it's a great antidote to my natural state of messy and cluttered, something I'm working on improving for when we move in together.

At the next ad break on the sports programme (which I've since figured out is a documentary about the exciting lives of pro wrestlers) Olly jumps energetically off the sofa and bounds around into the kitchen area of his open-plan apartment. He lifts the lid off one of the pans that has been simmering away on the cooker and inhales deeply.

'Voila!' he declares. 'Ready in a few minutes, sweetness.'

See? How great is this? Whenever I stay at his, he cooks me dinner. None of those archaic gender stereotypes going on in this relationship. No siree. I mean, I love cooking. Really love it. For as long as I can remember I've wanted to be a chef. Making people happy with delicious food must surely be one of the most wonderful experiences there is. It's too late in the year to take up my catering course again, but I did Google 'Manchester Evening Cooking Courses' and there are a few night classes which look interesting. I'm digressing now. The point I'm trying to make is that as much as I adore cooking, it's kind of nice to know that I don't *have* to cook should I not want to.

I scoot around the black marbled kitchen counter and take a seat over at the little two-person table in Olly's kitchen. As he dishes up he sings quietly to himself. It sounds like an old Kylie song, but I'm not sure. Bless him. As usual he's set the table with a pristine white tablecloth and a couple of tea-light candles in navy-blue glass holders. A well-chilled bottle of non-alcoholic Bonne Nouvelle Chardonnay has been placed at the centre of the table. I pour us both a glass and take a sip. It tastes a little like apple juice that's past its sell-by date, but it's worth it because it has only a third of the calories tasty real wine has. Plus, no hang-over tomorrow!

'Dinner is served, my love.'

Olly zips my wine glass onto a coaster, places my napkin over my lap and sets down the plate in front of me.

'Ooh, yum! It looks great!' I say.

This isn't strictly true. It's a fish stew and boiled brown rice. It's beige.

Olly sits across from me, lifts his plate up to his nose and takes a big old whiff. He says 'Aaaaaah' before setting his plate down. This is a ritual he has. It's kind of cute really.

He nods towards my plate. Oh yes. That's another part of the ritual. I have to sniff too. Apparently it's possible to get full just from sniffing your food before eating it.

So I lift up the plate and inhale.

I can't really smell anything.

This is often the case. The first time it happened I snuck into the kitchen after Olly had gone to bed and took some pickled garlic out of the cupboard to see if my sense of smell still worked. The pungent, acidic scent of it made my eyes water, which was excellent because I was beginning to worry about the sudden disappearance of my smelling powers, especially as a wannabe cook. I suppose that no discernible flavour is just the way with healthy food, though, isn't it? If it smelt and tasted amazing, then you'd want to eat loads of it and you'd eat more than you normally would need to eat, and then you'd get fat and that would defeat the point of it being healthy.

'Take a bite! Fill your boots!' says Olly excitedly.

I do an eager face, heap some of the fish mush and rice onto my fork and put it into my mouth.

Nothing. It is air-flavoured . . . oh, and there's a bit too much black pepper. Any flavour that may have initially existed has been cooked away. 'Mmm . . . lovely!' I smile, giving my tummy an enthusiastic pat.

'Come on,' Olly admonishes. 'You reckon you want to be a chef? You can do better than lovely.'

I nod and then pretend to be the bald bloke from *Masterchef*.

'Um. Soft . . . grainy rice and, um, sweet, sweet

fish. A fishy explosion! The whole thing is . . . delectable. A cuddle on a plate, if you will.'

'And the best thing is that it's so *good* for you!' Olly contributes, proud of his prowess in the kitchen.

Satisfied with my judgement, he declares that I should 'Tuck in before it goes cold,' and heartily scoffs his own.

I eat up as instructed and, trying hard to ignore all thoughts of a big bloody filet mignon with some French beans and onion tempura, repeat to myself that it doesn't taste that bad and at least I'll look all svelte and radiant with good health on my wedding day.

A couple of hours later, Olly and I are tucked up under the covers of his low platform, Zen-style Japanese bed. Before we go to bed Olly always insists we shower together so that we're nice and clean for making love. It does take the spontaneity away somewhat, but at least neither of us smells or anything, which would be infinitely worse. I used to try and encourage Olly to combine the shower and sex into one sensual, soapy activity, but he takes his showering seriously. So now we take turns to stand under the jet stream and wash thoroughly. It's actually a rather nice bonding experience, though it can get a bit cold when it's not your turn to stand under the hot water.

In bed, Olly leans over me and unties my dressing gown so that I'm naked. I feel slightly self-conscious of my stomach, though he strokes it and doesn't appear to notice that it's perhaps not as tight as the bellies of the women he must see at the gym. He grins at me, his eyes shining, before heading straight for my neck.

'You're so damn cute, Natty,' he groans, dotting little kisses around my ears.

'Thanks. You too.'

'I mean it. Your cute little nose.' He kisses my nose. 'Your cute little freckly cheeks.' He kisses my cheeks. 'Your cute little chubby wubby belly.' He kisses my belly. 'You're . . . almost perfect.'

Wait a second.

Did he just say *almost* perfect? I startle for a moment before mentally shrugging. Almost perfect is pretty good going, I'd say. At least he's not lying. If he said I was totally perfect, then he'd be lying.

I place my hand on his bicep and give a little squeeze. Mmm. He really is delicious. Any girl would be lucky to have him. So, so lucky.

Our lips find each other and we kiss for a while, feeling every inch of each other's bodies pressed up close. It's lovely. Right before we get down to the rude stuff, Olly stops and gazes deep into my eyes.

'I really, really can't wait until we're married, sweetness. I love you so very, very much.'

I sigh with contentment, all thoughts of bad hair, shiny wedding dresses and diamante banished from my mind. Those things really don't matter.

32

I'm getting married to a gorgeous, kind, sexy man who thinks I'm almost perfect. That's what matters.

'Me too.' I grin, grabbing his bottom and pulling him into me . . .

'How was that then?' Olly says six minutes later, climbing off me and catching his breath.

He always asks this. It's another of his rituals. We finish and then examine just how good we are at sex. I love that he's so concerned about whether he's pleasing me.

'It was lovely. Really lovely,' I reply, leaning over to kiss him softly on the cheek. I pat his shoulder in a congratulatory way.

What?

It *was* lovely. Okay, it was a teensy bit quick and I didn't quite, you know . . . *you know*. But one look at his satisfied, eager face and it's impossible not to put a positive spin on my answer.

Anyway, it's not like I'm lying to him. Everyone knows that sex in real life isn't like the animal monkey sex in films. No one actually does get taken roughly in the barn. Although sometimes, I kind of wish they did. Okay, I kind of wish I did. Honestly, though, it's about closeness. We made love and it was lovely. Him cuddling me and snogging me is brilliant. All right, so the snogging was a little bit sloppy, but at least he's enthusiastic. Like an adorable puppy.

Olly gently kisses my hand before hopping off

to get into the shower again. I turn over and stare at the silky black curtains over the window. I try to think about how lucky I am, rather than the fact that I'm still a little bit horny.

I lie there snuggled under the duvet until gone midnight when I eventually fall into a warm and dreamless slumber.

CHAPTER 4

The great thing about staying over at Olly's flat is that I get a lift to work with him in the morning. He technically lives close enough for us to walk, but if we did then Olly wouldn't get the chance to air the shiny red Audi his parents bought him for his thirtieth birthday. He even gets free parking at Dino's Suits and Ties in central Manchester, which is excellent for me as it means I am ferried from flat to work like a celeb.

Turning on the engine, Olly flips the buttons on his state-of-the-art car music system. I feel my body tense in anticipation of the thumping, bassy House music (which Olly loves because it reminds him of the gym, and I hate because it reminds me of being puked on in a dubious nightclub last year) and prepare to stealthily cover my ears until we get to work. Only this morning the music that bounces out of the high-tech speakers at the back of the car doesn't appear to be music at all.

No.

Is it . . . is that . . . happy hardcore?

My eyes widen in horror. The noise assaulting

my ears sounds like a sped-up, souped-up version of the theme tune from *Alvin and the Chipmunks*. Only now Alvin, Simon and Theodore are on speed. And helium. It's terrible.

I look over at Olly and fervently signal for him to turn it down. But he seems to think my hand gesture is some kind of appreciative dance movement.

'Isn't this great!' he yells, speeding out of the flat's exclusive car park and onto the road. 'God, I feel pumped!'

He laughs with glee and begins to drum his hands against the steering wheel. I'm about to shout at him to please turn it off, but just as I'm opening my mouth to say it, I stop. It's his car. I shouldn't really dictate what he listens to. Plus, I *am* getting a free lift into work. And it does seem to make him happy. Did he just flex his bicep in the wing mirror?

I decide to leave him to it and wind down the window, which, while helping to let out the terrible noise, forces the wind to whip up my hair into a short, untamed afro. Though this could in fact be an improvement on Barbara the Hair Hacker's attempt.

Which reminds me . . . Olly didn't say anything about my hair last night. I expected a chuckle, or even a cuddle of sympathy, but he didn't say a thing. That's so much better when you think about it. He treated me exactly the same as usual, which just goes to show that our relationship is about so much more than good looks and normal (or really abnormal) hairdos.

Saying that, though, I have to admit that it was his incredible looks that first drew me to Olly. That Saturday a year ago when he walked into Chutney's is a day I'll never forget. He was quite simply the most handsome man I had ever seen in real life. Until him, I wasn't always so swayed by aesthetics. I promise I was a little nobler than that. For example, when I flat shared with Meg (in the heady days of catering courses and not having to be with my mum all of the time), I had a boyfriend who was, shall we say, a bit unfortunate looking. Meg used to refer to him as Gollum on account of his facial features – which, to be fair, were a bit withered looking – and his greyish pallor. I, however, managed to see past that, all the way through to his wit, kindness and shared love of Aretha Franklin. Besides, I'd done the whole good-looking men thing at university and my experiences had led me to the conclusion that average-looking men were much nicer, funnier and, dare I say it, more grateful. Meg said that that was down to my fear of taking a risk and being rejected, but I knew the truth. Gorgeous men generally weren't very nice.

Gollum and I lasted for eight whole weeks before he cheated on me with a hobbity-looking girl from the local Blockbusters, but I still found myself drawn to the less perfect-looking guys. And then Olly happened. As he ordered a hummus and avocado on wholewheat pitta and a skinny latte, I gazed at his perfectly honed body, shiny blue eyes and haughtily high cheek bones, and realized that perhaps I wasn't so noble after all.

The nicest surprise was that he was actually as kind and as lovely as the unfortunately featured guys I'd been out with. Yes, a modelesque man who was sweet and nervous and had no clue how gorgeous he was. They really did exist and I was in with a shot.

We went out on a few dates (pictures, restaurants, health clubs). He told me all about his wholesome, high-achieving family and idyllic childhood in the countryside; I told him about my not-so-idyllic childhood of arguing parents, a loudmouth sister and pre-braces goofy teeth. This was just after Dad had left Mum for good, and Olly didn't even seem to mind when our fourth date at Manchester Art Gallery was gatecrashed by Mum who couldn't bear to be alone at the time, and who talked about what a bastard Dad was the whole way around the Pre-Raphaelite collection. Olly was a keeper. And still is. Of course we have those little irritations that all couples do. But he looks after me. He's this sweet, sexy outlet from the horrors of family life. And that is just what I need.

At Dino's Suits and Ties, Olly parks up, turns off the music (thank you, Jesus) and we get out of the car. He gives me an extra-long kiss and a tight squeeze.

'Can I stay at yours tonight?' I ask. 'I'm going to the pub with Meg for some hypnotist show and it's much closer to your flat. It'll save me a fortune on taxis.'

He thinks for a moment and looks at his phone. 'Ah, go on then. But don't be too late.'

'I won't!'

'Do you want me to plate you up some dinner? I think there's some stew left from last night and—'

'NO! I mean . . . no, thanks. We'll probably grab something at the pub.'

He pulls a face at the thought of pub grub.

'No chips, Nat!'

'Definitely no chips.'

I wave him off into the shop.

I'll almost certainly have chips.

Trundling my way through the busy streets of the Northern Quarter, I look at my watch. I have fifteen minutes before I start work so nip over to Piccadilly Gardens and into a tiny cafe for my usual latte and toast. This is kind of a secret daily occurrence. Olly, of course, served me a lovely grapefruit, carrot and celery smoothie this morning (okay, it was cack), but nothing beats the taste of an extra-shot frothy coffee and a slice of toasted Hobbs bread (which Olly thinks is the food of the devil), all doughy and sweet and dripping with butter. I look back furtively, as I always do, in case Olly suspects my secret bread-eating habit and has decided to follow me here and put me under carb arrest.

He's not there.

Of course he's not.

I get my order and walk back through the Gardens, munching on the toast. Considering it's winter time, the weather is bright and clear, albeit frosty. I mooch past the fountains and negotiate my way through the streams of busy suits. I pause for a moment, feeling a sudden sense of confusing anticipation. I can't quite tell if it's good anticipation or bad anticipation. Just an odd feeling in my gut, an expectation that something big is going to happen, that everything's about to change. It's the weirdest feeling. And then I remember. Of course everything is going to change. Hello! I'm getting hitched! That's it. I'm just excited about the wedding. Either that or that celery smoothie is playing havoc with my digestion.

I reach Chutney's and knock three times on the huge expanse of locked glass door.

Marie pops her head up from behind the meat counter like a meerkat. She rolls her eyes, as if answering the door to me is the most annoying thing she has ever had to do, ever. She still won't give me my own set of keys, though. Marie is the manager of Chutney's, and a bit surly, if truth be told. She's attractive, in a thin, harsh blonde, hard-nosed way, but old before her time. She reminds me of one of those put-upon characters in a Catherine Cookson book. A weary, young, salt-of-the-earth type, who scrubs potatoes and walks around looking like life has done her in.

I wave as she approaches. She moves her mouth into a smile-like shape. I can't hear it, but I think she is sighing.

Back in the olden days (the nineties), Chutney's was a greasy spoon cafe called Eggs, Beans and Stuff. About seven years ago, it was bought by Stone, who was a drummer in some early Manchester band (that I've never heard of) called Chunky Rug. Rumour has it that he walked in one day with the munchies and a craving for some French chèvre cheese. When the owners told him that the only cheese they had was Tesco's own mild cheddar or Dairylea, he had a strop and announced that he was going to bloody well build a place that would provide the foodies of Manchester with a place to buy chèvre cheese, should they need it. The owners of Egg, Beans and Stuff saw an opportunity for early retirement and offered to sell the cafe for much more money than it was worth. Stone accepted, they signed contracts on napkins and the rest is foodie history. Stone still comes in every day. He barely talks. Just sits at one of the tables, sampling all the food, looking around at all the customers sampling all the food, and drinking herbal tea, occasionally nipping outside for a cigarette (or is it a spliff?). Other than that, there's just me and Marie.

Marie unlocks the door, leaving me to push it

open as she immediately walks back to the meat counter.

'Hello!' I say brightly. 'How are you?'

'Some new spicy Spanish sausages have come in this morning. They're in the big fridge. We need some putting out on display, please.'

'No probs. Lovely and bright today, isn't it?'

'The salad delivery is late again. Don't know why we bloody bother. Have you seen the big bowl? The glass one for the black olives? Have you lost it again? Bloody hell. What are you bloody standing there for? I told you to get on with those sausages.'

I resist the urge to tell her to stop being such a grumpy cow. After all, she is my boss. No one likes their boss, do they?

'Righto,' I sigh, wishing that just for once she would be a bit nicer.

I shuffle through the crowded back storeroom and into the walk-in fridge. Marie doesn't like going in here on account of the fact that it's eight degrees. The rumbling whir of the fans and the steel walls make it creepy like a morgue, but I actually quite like it. When I need to have a think about, you know, life and the universe, I come in here. I look around at all the speciality foods (all right, sometimes I eat them too) and wonder what it would be like to have a restaurant of my own. I sit on the mini stepladder and think about what I'd call it and what I'd put on the menu. And then I imagine myself in the kitchen, dressed

42

in starchy whites with a quirky bandana, creating magical sauces and confidently barking orders at lesser chefs.

I laugh to myself. It's silly really. I know it is. Olly says that I'm hardly likely to have my own restaurant when I haven't even completed a full year at catering college, and he's absolutely right. But I do have my experience in Chutney's and I cook loads at home. Once Mum is feeling better I'll definitely get myself back onto a college course. Maybe even take up an apprenticeship somewhere fancy nearby.

'Natalie! What the bloody hell is taking you so long? I asked you to put out the sausages, not bloody invent them!'

I roll my eyes and load the sausages onto a small trolley. Time to stop daydreaming, Natalie.

CHAPTER 5

Text from: **Mum**
Auntie Jan wants to sing at your wedding. She's been fed up since she was on Britain's Got Talent and Amanda Holden pressed the buzzer after 3 secs. Have added her songs to the checklist.

Reply to: **Mum**
Poor Auntie Jan. Not sure we want a singer, though.

Text from: **Mum**
She's ur auntie! Don't be so selfish. She wiped ur bum when u were a baby.

Reply to: **Mum**
Okay. Will have a look at songs. x

I arrive at the Pear and Partridge to meet Meg for the hypnotist show feeling a bit shitty. It's six thirty and after a long day with moaning Marie I'd love nothing more than to slink away to Olly's for a cuddle and some hard-core viewing

44

of *The Walking Dead*. I consider begging off for a moment. I could feasibly have a terrible tummy ache. Or Mum could need me for something?

No.

Of course I should stay. Meg's too excited about this and I can't let her down. That'd be horrible bestie behaviour.

I open the pub doors and am astonished to see that it's really busy. The atmosphere is electric. It's so buzzing that you'd think Take That were dropping by for an impromptu jam sesh, as opposed to some dodgy hypnotist. Well, it's unlikely he's real, is it? If he could *actually* hypnotize people, he'd be doing shows in Las Vegas, or selling CDs on how to stop smoking – not a Thursday night gig at a dubious Manchester pub.

I politely push my way through the crowd and spot Meg. She's sat at a small table as close to the makeshift performance area as it's possible to get. She looks gorgeous as ever with her baby fine, wavy blonde hair and Jessica Rabbit curves accentuated in a too-tight red tea dress. Sexy yet homely, a bit like a slutty farmer's wife crossed with Blake Lively.

As I make my way towards the table, I notice a load of colourful posters dotted around the walls of the pub.

AMAZING BRIAN.

Hypnotizing, Mind Reading, Spell Casting, etc.

Performing at the Pear and Partridge.
Ticket Only.
No photos. No videos.

'Your hair isn't that bad!' Meg says as soon as she sees me, before kissing me softly on the cheek.

I reach my hand up to my head. I've managed to flick the ends out so that it doesn't look quite so bowl-shaped.

'You're just being nice.'

'You know I don't do nice. We'll have to dye it, though. Totes. It's stripy. Actually, it's a little bit like that cat you used to have when we were kids.'

'Tracy.'

'Yeah, that's it – Tracy the tabby! Aaaah. May she rest in peace. Yes. We'll definitely have to change the colour. But the cut is totally awesome sauce – very Uma Thurman in *Pulp Fiction*. Drink?'

She doesn't need to hear my reply before pouring me a fishbowl-sized glass of Sauvignon Blanc from the bottle on the table and thus reinforcing one of the many reasons why she's my best mate.

'Your hypnotist is called Brian?' I say, after taking a long slug of my drink.

'Actually, it's *Amazing* Brian.' She says his name in a low, whispery voice. Meg is excellent at voices. She's always wanted to be a singer in a band but for the past few years she's been working as a voiceover artist. You've probably heard her. She once voiced a really famous food advert. You know

46

the one. Images of food looking totally amazing, like hot chocolate sauce oozing slowly out of a pudding, while a seductive-sounding woman describes it all? Well, the seductive-sounding woman was Meg. Yes, I know. Celebrity mates. Her normal accent is lush, friendly Geordie, which is perfect for the regular radio ads she currently does at Manchester's Key 103.

'Still. Brian?' I try to raise an eyebrow. I end up raising two, which always happens. Maybe it's time to accept that I'll never possess the skill of the single eyebrow raise.

'So what? Paul McKenna's called Paul. And Derren Brown is called Derren. What's that about? Derren isn't even a real name. Anyway, it's not his name I'm interested in. It's the power he has to make me super svelte! Pop stars can't have muffin tops. Everyone knows that, Natty.'

I look at her, already irresistible with her peaches-and-cream skin and perfectly Rubenesque shape, and wonder, not for the first time, why on earth she thinks she needs to change anything about herself. She's got the kind of wonderfully placed curves that make Salma Hayek look like a malnour-ished ten-year-old boy, but there's just no getting through to her.

As it nears seven o'clock, the atmosphere in the pub charges even more. The table next to us is filled with a group of middle-aged ladies, chat-tering away in excitement, and a crowd has formed at the side of our table. I get the same rush of

47

excitement as I did this morning. That odd antici-pation. Must be the wine. It's a bit of a shock to the system after Olly's non-alcoholic stuff.

'Do I look okay?' asks Meg. 'Is this dress too short? I don't want to embarrass myself on the stage.'

I love that it doesn't occur to Meg that she may not be picked to be hypnotized – which is one of the many reasons I love her. She half stands up from the table to show me her dress. It's short. As short as it's possible to get without being in danger of arrest for indecent exposure. She looks at me expectantly before sitting back down.

Well, I can't tell her, can I? At least not right now. The show's about to start and she'd only feel uncomfortable if I told her, or want to go home and change. It isn't *that* bad. As long as she doesn't move AT ALL.

'No, it's fine. Lovely!' I enthuse, taking another swift gulp of my drink.

A waitress comes over with two bowls of chips and places them in front of us.

'Oh, I ordered us chips,' Meg says, reaching for the salt shaker and sprinkling it liberally over the gorgeously fried potatoes. 'I figured you hadn't had time to eat yet, so I hope you don't mind that I chose? If all goes well with the hypnosis, this might be the last time I'll ever eat chips. Imagine that! We'll have to hurry, though, 'cos I don't want to be scoffing my face when Brian comes on!'

I laugh and tuck into the chips. Meg tells me about her day at work, and then asks how the wedding plans are coming along. When I tell her about the dress of horrors, her face goes bright red with indignation.

'They chose your wedding dress!' she shrieks, attracting glances from the group of ladies next to us. 'They can't do that!'

'They did,' I sigh. 'It's fine. They were only trying to help. It's fine.'

'As if the bridesmaid dresses aren't bad enough!'

Oh yeah. Dionne has insisted on bridesmaid dresses that are black and sparkly with tutu skirts.

'Seriously,' says Meg, angrily stuffing chips into her mouth. 'You can't let them get away with it. They take over everything. Always have done. Why don't you ever tell them?'

This is a bone of contention between Meg and me. The only one that's ever occurred in our life-long friendship. Meg thinks my family need to back off. I don't know. Perhaps I do think that in my deepest thoughts. But I would never say it. And when Meg says it, it bristles.

'Well, it's only one day . . .' I reason.

'It's THE day! God. Can't they ever let you make a decision on your own?'

'I only care about the marriage bit anyway. You know I'm not into all the fancy schmancy weddingy cake and flowers stuff. I'm happy for them to take care of it. It's kind of them.'

'They want you to think they're taking care of

it! What they're really doing is controlling it. Just like they control everything. They keep you so locked in, Nat.'

Meg's tirade is drowned out as a heavily reverbed voice booms out from the speakers in the pub. I'm glad of it, because what she's saying about Mum and Dionne is really out of order. And totally, utterly wrong.

'Ladies and Gentlemen . . .'

I look behind me and see one of the barmen crouched behind the bar with a microphone.

'Please take your seats and give a warm welcome tooooooooo . . .'

Meg quickly dabs around her mouth with a napkin and pushes the remainder of her chips over to my side of the table. It now looks like I've had two bowls of chips to myself. Meg reaches over and squeezes my hand, her eyes shining. Her excitement is infectious, and as the lights of the pub dim, I feel a few butterflies flitting around my tummy.

'. . . Amaaaaazing Briaaaaaaan!'

The crowd clap heartily, and there are a few whistles and cheers. Suddenly, multi-coloured lights begin to flash above us, and a loud noise sounds out through the speakers.

Oh God. It's 'Tubular Bells' – the theme from *The Exorcist*.

Emerging from the door to the tap room and politely excusing his way through the crowd is a short, chubby man of about sixty. He has a white beard, and a beer belly encased in a woolly brown jumper with the letters 'AB' knitted in red. Brian looks exactly like his name. And also a little bit like an accountant.

Meg's head spins sharply towards the man and her dark green eyes widen in bewilderment. I muffle my laughter with my hand. I don't know what we were expecting. A cape? Make-up? Paul McKenna's hotter brother? Either way, it wasn't this.

Amazing Brian half walks, half jogs over to the performance area in front of us and, after catching his breath, signals to the barman to turn off the music. The barman complies and the room is plunged into silence.

'Thank you. Thank you, everyone,' Brian murmurs into the microphone. His accent is pure Yorkshire, like something from *Emmerdale*. Thank yo. Thank yo, everywun.

'Right. Well,' he says, squinting out into the crowd, 'we best get on, like.'

The audience waits. A few of them titter nervously. I look to Meg who is suddenly sat up straighter, like the kid in class who wants to be picked for the lead role in the Nativity.

'I'm Brian. Erm, Amazing Brian,' he says pointing to the initials on his jumper. 'And I am right glad to be here tonight. To, you know, hypnotize some people.'

He pauses to take a sip of ale.

'So, Ladies and Gentlemen. During the course

of tonight's show, strange and magical-type things will happen. I have trained in the art of mind-reading and hypnotic induction for many, many years. And while tonight I use my powers for your entertainment, you need to know that what I do is very real. By agreeing to take part, you are agreeing to open up your mind to my control.'

Meg looks at me, eyebrows raised, before topping up my glass of wine. Something about the way Brian speaks, with such simple belief and conviction, rather than the brash, showy way I expected of a pub hypnotist, unsettles me.

'I will now use my powers to choose an audience member who I sense is the most open to suggestion and persuasion.'

His gaze travels across the room. For a moment it rests on me. My tummy plummets. I put my head down and stare at the empty chip bowls.

When I look up again his eyes are still on me, and when they meet mine they light up.

'You, young lady,' he utters softly, staring at me so intently it's like he can see into the very depths of my soul. It's an unusual moment in my life.

Crap.

'Erm. Sorry. I'm not here to be hypnotized,' I mutter nervously. 'I came with my friend, Meg. She's the one you want.' I nod over towards Meg who smiles at me gratefully.

My heart is pounding at the thought of having to get up in front of everyone. No thanks very much!

'I'll do it,' Meg shouts to Brian, standing up and waving at everyone. 'I'd be honoured!'

The male members of the audience, apparently buoyed by her charm, enthusiasm and dangerously short dress, start to whoop and clap. Their wives throw her daggers.

Brian pauses and squints at Meg. She returns his gaze with an eager smile. 'I'm really easily persuaded!' she pleads.

Brian's dark eyes narrow and flicker back towards me for what in reality is probably a few seconds but feels like a few minutes, and then suddenly he smiles and chuckles lightly to himself.

'Okay then, lass. Up you get.'

Giving a little squeal, Meg flicks her shiny waves and bounds up to the performance area, and (thank you, Jesus) pulls down her skirt as she goes. I giggle as I hear a few of the men sigh with disappointment.

'So,' says Meg, once she's reached Brian. 'I've actually come prepared. I know it's unorthodox, but I know exactly how I want you to hypnotize me.'

Brian looks bemused but says nothing, so Meg continues.

'So, basically, I want you to do a hypno surgery on me. To help me to lose weight. Ideally, I'd like to lose about two stone. Primarily off my arms and backside. They're my problem areas, you see. If you could help, it'd be great. Please.'

'Um . . . no, love,' Brian shakes his head.

53

'I'm afraid that's not something I could do on stage.'

Meg's face falls. She folds her arms. 'Why? Why not?'

'It's not my speciality,' Brian explains. 'That kind of thing is not what I do, petal. Besides, it wouldn't be very entertaining for the audience, would it? I'm here to do something performance-based, love.'

'Oh. Right. Yes, of course,' says Meg despondently.

'Get on with it, for the love of God!' shouts one of the women on the next table, apparently completely pissed.

Brian ignores her. 'I can hypnotize you for fun, and that is all.'

Meg looks over to me and I shrug. May as well, while we're here. To be honest, Amazing Brian doesn't appear to be all that amazing, so this should be a laugh.

'Ah, go on then!' says Meg finally. 'Why not. Just . . . no removing of clothes, okay?'

'Booo!' say a couple of men at the bar. Meg blushes and pulls her dress down again. I give her a thumbs up and, spying the now empty bottle, signal to the barman for another glass of wine.

Brian, frowning as if offended by the very thought that his act would ever include anything as plebeian as clothes shedding, shushes the audience and begins.

'Meg. Young lady. I need you first of all to close your eyes and relax . . .'

Meg shakes her shoulders as if loosening up and, after glancing at me one more time, closes her eyes.

I feel nervous and excited. I'm not sure why, because it obviously isn't going to work. Nevertheless, the hairs on the back of my neck prickle.

'As I speak, the sound of my voice will go with you . . .' Brian takes hold of Meg's small, manicured hand and clasps it between his own. His voice becomes deeper and surprisingly soothing, his Yorkshire burr strong and calm.

'Here. Now. As you feel my energies passing into you, you understand everything I say. You are safe and in control. No, wait, I am in control. Count backwards from twenty. Backwards from twenty. And when you reach one you will be under my spell. My voice will soothe you and you will sleep.'

I stare transfixed, able only to hear the sound of my own breathing. Brian begins to count down from twenty and Meg joins in. Her eyes are still closed so I can't tell if she's faking or not. I count with them in my head.

'Sleep!' demands Brian when they reach one, turning back towards the rest of us. On his command, Meg's head lolls forward and the audience, including me, gasp. Whoa!

Brian's gaze meets mine once again, his eyes

dark and intense looking. I feel a shiver run through me.

'Right!' Brian announces to the crowd, back to his normal, less melty voice.

'Meg is now under hypnosis. For the purposes of entertainment, we're going to try an experiment, so t'speak.'

'What we are going to ask Meg to do is simple. We are going to ask her to be completely honest. To tell us the truth.'

A couple of people make 'huh?' faces at each other. I join them.

'When Meg awakens, we will ask her questions. And when she answers, she will only be able to answer the deepest, darkest truth, however far it may be buried in her subconscious.'

'How is that entertaining? This ain't a shrink's office!' shouts a young lad standing beside the fruit machine.

'Well,' replies Brian pointedly, 'that will depend on the questions you ask.'

As what Brian is getting at dawns on the audience, they begin to laugh. My face burns up as I think about what kind of awful questions this audience, starved of entertainment thus far, will ask Meg. And what will she tell them? I try to catch Brian's eye, but he studiously ignores me.

'When I clap, Meg will awaken. Raise your hands to ask a question. Any question. And let us see if it works.' He touches Meg's arm.

'Meg, when I clap once you will awaken. When

asked any question, you will tell the absolute truth. When I clap three times you will be free of the trance and awaken with no recollection of having been hypnotized. You will be calm, refreshed and fully alert.'

A rather odd fizzy feeling rises up through my body. It's that anticipation feeling again. I totally need to stop drinking.

Brian claps once and Meg's eyes flutter open. She looks a little bewildered, but otherwise okay. I wait with baited breath.

She peers over at me and smiles serenely. Does she know what she's let herself in for?

About fifteen hands shoot up.

This is silly. I should stop it at once. I stand up and—

'Oi, Meg, how many sex toys do you have?' pipes up one of the drunken ladies from the next table before I can do anything.

A huge laugh goes up throughout the room. To my utter dismay, I find myself sitting back down in my chair, horribly curious to know the answer. Okay. I'll just let her answer this one and then I'll get Brian to stop.

I am a bad, bad person.

Meg smiles beatifically at the woman who asked the question before saying, ever so solemnly, 'Ten or eleven sex toys.'

I gasp, along with everyone else. Meg continues, unabashed.

'My collection is impressive. I've got my vibrators,

57

my whips, my love balls, my handcuffs. I have those in standard steel and pink and fluffy . . .'

The whole pub is still. No one knows what to say. Brian is frowning.

Oh. My. God. I have known Meg since we were children and I never knew – shit – did she just say rubber mask?

I stand up immediately and march over towards her. My face is hot with embarrassment for poor Meg. What the hell have I let her do?

I'm about to turn off the microphone when I hear a massive snort.

Meg?

She pauses for a second before doubling over in laughter.

What's going on?

'Meg? What's going on?' I shake her shoulder. Why is she laughing? 'Meg, are you okay?'

She stands straight up and wipes away tears of mirth from her eyes.

Once she catches her breath she says, 'You daft mare! You should have seen your face! Ha ha, ha ha. Oh gosh, your face was a picture!'

'You . . . you mean it didn't work?'

Brian takes another sip of bitter, seemingly unbothered by this turn of events.

'Course it bloody didn't!' Meg guffaws. 'S-sorry Bri-hi-hian! He he he.'

The crowd boos, and I'm not sure if it's directed at Meg and me or at poor Brian, who clearly is NOT amazing. I feel the giggles approach my mouth, and before I know it I'm howling with laughter too.

'Come on, Meg! Let's go,' I chuckle, feeling the atmosphere souring at the fact that people have paid good money for what essentially has been a bit of a wind-up. And there I was, thinking that maybe, just maybe, it might have been real. I'm such a chump!

I hand Meg her bag, and gather mine from underneath the table. What a weird day.

I see Brian begin to pack away, eager to get away from the braying crowd. Before we leave I catch his eye once again. He smiles at me – properly smiles – and then does a little wave. So odd.

Still giggling, I wave back and escort a cackling Meg out of the pub.

CHAPTER 6

I awaken the next morning with – apart from the slightly crusty eye snot – no major symptoms of hangover. Possibly I am still pissed and the hangover will turn up later, smug and brutal. I'll admit, I was a bit (well, a lot) tiddly last night.

After the weirdly disastrous hypnotist show, Meg and I decided, in the middle of our giggling fit, to go for a drink at StarRock, an indie nightclub in Manchester city centre. I was already feeling a bit worse for wear so had only three shots of tequila as opposed to the six that Meg downed. Olly's insistence on non-alcoholic wine has, I fear, led to my status as an utter lightweight.

I spent the remainder of the night dancing conspicuously amongst scruffy, stoned students, and listening to Meg say, 'You big geek! You actually thought I was some kind of secret sex paraphernalia collector!' again and again while doubled up at the thought.

It felt nice to be out in the world after dark. I felt young and fizzy – kind of like I did before I moved back in with Mum, actually.

Olly was far from impressed when I poured myself into his bed, drunk, giggly and horny, at about four this morning. So much for not being late!

I climbed under the warm, white feather duvet and pressed myself up against Olly's back, kissing his neck and telling him how really, really handsome and sensible and perfect he was. Grumpy at having his requisite eight hours interrupted (and maybe by the fact that I was trying to initiate sex without showering first), he told me to bugger off and returned to snoring.

I would have been offended, I think, had I not drunkenly passed out immediately after his snub.

Olly seems to have forgiven me, though, as, fresh from the shower, he begins making the sexy moves on me.

I dash to the bathroom, bleary-eyed, for a quick rinse and tooth clean and then return to bed where Olly is waiting for me, naked and sporting an impressive erection.

'Hop on!' he laughs, reaching out for me. And giggling like a teen (or a drunken person), I oblige.

About five minutes and fifteen seconds later Olly slumps back against the pillows, spent and happy. I join him for a cuddle, less satisfied, but, you know, happy to be close to him. He catches his breath and asks, as usual, 'How was that then, baby?'

I stroke my fingers up his arm, look up at him coquettishly and answer.

'Well, you know. Short. Could have been longer. Longer time-wise, I mean, not willy-wise – though, of course, that would be lovely too. I didn't have an orgasm, but what else is new, hey? You've left me unsatisfied, if truth be told, Olly.'

While I'm speaking, I watch Olly's eyes widen in horror. And then, as if in slow motion, what I've just said replays in my mind and it hits me. My cheeks go all hot.

Oh God! Did I just say that? *Out loud?*

Olly's face is stony. The post-coital flush has drained from his face and a small frown has gathered between his eyebrows.

Why the hell would I say those things? They're not even true. Well . . . maybe they're a *teensy* bit true, but still. Why on earth would I say that to him?

I sit up at once and try to make amends.

'Um, ha ha ha!' I attempt to laugh but it comes out sounding like a cruel cackle. 'Only kidding! It was a joke!'

'A joke.' Olly nods, confused and still frowning.

'Well, you know me, ever the joker!'

I can't remember the last time I told a joke. I sound like an absolute chump.

'Weird joke, if you ask me,' Olly grumbles, hopping out of the bed and pulling on his boxer shorts. 'You don't, like, really think that stuff, do you?'

His face is hopeful.

'Yes.' My answer is loud and clear. 'Yes, I really do think it.'

As I hear what I'm saying I immediately try to close my mouth, but I can't. My vocal cords and my tongue and my lips are all working of their own accord. I continue to blab, like some kind of bitchy, idiot blabbermouth. 'And before, when I said I was joking, I was actually lying. It wasn't a joke. It was the absolute truth.'

Whaaaaaaat?

The words tumble out, unstoppable. Why am I saying these things? Am I having some kind of stroke?

Olly's face has transformed now from pasty white to beetroot red. Anger? Embarrassment? I titter nervously, but to Olly it just sounds like I'm laughing at him. He shimmies into his work trousers and sits on the edge of the bed, hands clasped tightly together.

'I don't get it. Is this cold feet, Natalie? Are you trying to cause a row because you're getting cold feet? Because I—'

'I'm not having an attack of the wedding willies,' I plead, my mouth moving, though I don't ask it to. 'I promise. I don't know what's going on. I honestly didn't realize what I was saying. Oh God. Please forget I said that stuff. Olly, I love you.'

'Sure, only you wish I was better in the sack?'

Say no.

Say NO, Natalie. Just one word, two letters. It's

easy. It's the easiest word ever. I mean, I've said no plenty of times before. Like when Auntie Jan asked if I minded picking her up some Imodium from the chemist – No! Or when the fellow who works at the cake shop asked if I wanted the small chocolate éclair rather than the large one – No! No!

I raise my tongue towards the roof of my mouth and form the word, while sending an angry message to my brain to please, for the love of God, please, please, please do what I say.

But my brain ignores me.

'YES!'

I put my head in my hands, and just to make the whole thing worse I bleat, 'Maybe it's a stamina thing. There are things we can do to fix it.'

Shut UP, Natalie.

Olly stands from the bed and glares at me.

'Stamina?'

'Yes.'

'Stamina?'

'Yes.'

'STAMINA? I have plenty of stamina, thank you very much. I'm the king of stamina. Just look at me.' He gestures to his toned arms and stomach. '*I'm* the very model of stamina. If there were a national contest for stamina, I would come first.'

We pause for a few seconds as the unfortunately worded end of that last sentence sinks in. Olly's face is now the colour of a plum. A vein pulsates in his forehead.

'Jesus, Natalie,' he croaks, running a hand through his hair. 'Any other little nuggets of information to share with me? You know. Just to top off your festival of cruelty.'

My eyes well up. My heart jolts at the realization that I will not be able to stop what comes out of my mouth next.

'You have horrible taste in music. That perfume you got me for my birthday and for Christmas makes me want to puke. I give it to the charity shop and tell you that I've used it all. When you drop me off at work I secretly go to a cafe and eat thick Hobbs toast smothered with butter. I don't like that you're so short for a man. Can't we buy you some stacked heels? And . . .'

Stop this. *Stop this!*

'. . . your cooking is truly awful. It doesn't even have a smell!'

Olly gasps as if I've just sucker-punched him, which, let's face it, I may as well have done.

I begin to cry. What the hell is happening? Have I got a brain tumour? Am I a latent schizophrenic? Oh God, poor Olly. He doesn't deserve this! I am a horrible person.

I can only stare and blink as he angrily shoves on his suit, tying the tie extra tightly. He checks his hair in the mirror before turning to me.

'I knew you were eating behind my back. I knew that. You must have been because you haven't

65

lost any weight for the wedding.' He sighs long and low and controlled. 'I love you, Natalie. But I suggest you sort yourself out if you want to get married. And . . .' he raises an eyebrow as he delivers the final blow. 'I think you should take the bus to work.'

With this he storms out, leaving a trail of slammed doors behind him.

Oh God.

I have never argued with Olly. Hell, I've never argued with anybody! It's deeply unpleasant.

'Aaaargh!' I scream, a wave of sharp frustration overwhelming me. I grab one of Olly's pristine white pillows and chuck it across the room. It bounces softly off the wardrobe and knocks over my handbag.

'What the hell is happening?' I cry to the ceiling.

And then I spot it. Scattered amongst the lipsticks, tissues and two-pence coins that have all fallen out of my handbag, is a small gold card with shiny red writing in a gothic font.

I hurry across the room and pick it up. What is this? Where did it come from?

Amazing Brian – Hypnotist, Mind Reader, Spell Caster, etc.

I flip it over to find a phone number and address scrawled on the back in blue ink.

All of a sudden, mad images of last night flash into my head. Brian's desire to hypnotize me, his attempt to make Meg tell the absolute truth, the fact that it didn't work, all those peculiar, dizzy, anticipation feelings I was getting . . .

Oh balls.

Big balls.

I think it worked. It actually worked. Amazing Brian *can* hypnotize. Only he didn't hypnotize Meg. Somehow he . . . he hypnotized *me*.

Balls.

I'm not panicking. Honestly.

Okay, I'm totally panicking. Running around in little circles of distress, I've phoned the number on Amazing Brian's card about fifty gazillion times, only to get a standard voicemail answer service. I left a series of messages in which I tried my best to sound angry, though it's been so long since I did angry that I'm pretty sure I ended the message with, 'If you could call me back whenever you get a moment, I'd be very grateful, Sir Brian.'

I'm still naked, I'm late for work, my fiancé hates me and I appear to be under some kind of hypnosis spell thingy. Brilliant morning. Really. Just fandabidozi.

I speedily pull on the first clothes that come to hand; these turn out to be a pair of Olly's shape-less grey jogging bottoms and my old, too small 'Goonies Never Say Die' T-shirt. God, why do I not have more clothes here? Olly keeps telling me to bring more stuff over. He's right. I have zero organizational skills!

Fuck it.

After a quick comb through my hair, I make a run for the bus stop, thankfully reaching it just as the bus arrives.

Ignoring the other passengers' glares at my frantic, noisy wheezing, I take a seat, pull my mobile out of my handbag and call Meg.

'Nghhgnh,' she answers after a few rings.

'Meg!' I shout into the receiver, causing a couple of old ladies to tut disapprovingly at my volume. I lower my voice.

'Meg. Wake up!'

'Whathefuuuu?' she groans sleepily.

'Meg,' I hiss. 'Wake up now. I need to see you. Now.'

'S'early, Natty. Ugh. Ew.'

'Meg. I. Am. Serious. Wake up!'

Hearing the sternness in my voice works because after a couple of sniffs and what seems to be the sound of her downing a whole glass of water, Meg is awake.

'Sorry, Natty. Fook, my head hurts. Why are you talking like that? Oh no. Has someone died? Has a celebrity died? *Oh no*, is it Phillip Schofield?'

I want to get to the point and tell her to meet me ASAP, but this bizarre need to immediately answer her questions is too strong.

'Nobody has died. Not a celebrity. Phillip Schofield is fine. I think. I *hope*. Listen—'

'Phew! Wow, imagine if Phillip Schofield *had* died. Then it would just be Holly Willoughby doing *This Morning* on her own. It wouldn't be half as good, would it? They'd probably get someone really shit in as a replacement. Somebody like Paul Ross or Russell Grant. You know, I'm forever getting those two mixed up.'

Speak, Natalie!

I try, but it appears that I cannot leave anything unanswered.

I get a vision of watching a solo-hosted *This Morning*. My answer is swift.

'Yes, it would be shit.'

'Yeah—'

'Meg, listen,' I snap. 'Listen to me carefully. Do not say anything. I am so late for work, I haven't got long and I really need to get this out. Something has happened. I cannot tell you about it now because I am on the bus, and it's really bizarro and I'll sound like a total nutcase. If you understand what I am saying, you will get out of bed and meet me at Chutney's as soon as possible. Do you understand?'

Meg can obviously sense my desperation because she answers with a simple, 'Yes. As soon as poss,' before gently clicking down the phone.

Right. Done. Okay. There is no need to panic. We'll just find Brian, get him to make this hypnosis stuff stop. I'll make things up to Olly, tell him I had low blood sugar and went mental or something. He'll forgive me for being so unnecessarily mean and everything will be normal again. We'll get married and live happily ever after for ever and ever, amen. And until then, I just have to avoid talking to anyone. How hard can that be?

CHAPTER 7

'Why are you so late? Do you value your job at all? And what the bloody hell are you wearing?'

Marie is in a bad mood. I can tell because the frown line in the middle of her forehead is cavernous. She looks like a Shar Pei dog, or Gordon Ramsay. As I make my way behind the Cheeses of the World counter and put on my apron, Marie's questions cause the overwhelming need to speak to fizz through my body. It feels kind of like when you get the urge to laugh, and you know you mustn't. Like when a person trips in the street, or someone is mad at you. You know that laughing would be wildly inappropriate but you can do nothing to control those errant chuckles.

Of course, it doesn't work. Out it comes.

'I'm late, Marie, because I was hypnotized last night. I told my fiancé that I wished he was better in bed. I was still drunk this morning, though I don't think I am now. I do value my job – I'm skint, and I need the money. Though I wish you wouldn't be such a bitch to me, and sometimes I wish I was still at chef school instead of here. My outfit is some saggy-arsed jogging bottoms and a *Goonies* T-shirt, through which I'm pretty sure you can see my nipples.' And then my voice goes all loud. 'So why don't you be quiet and give me a sodding break?'

I take a breath. A strange mixture of relief at having answered, surprise at what I've said and utter embarrassment overcomes me.

The small queue of customers stare at me in shock before looking down towards my breasts, which, thank the Lord, are now covered by my apron.

Oh God.

Marie marches over to me, eyes blazing. Her hands are clenched. This is it. She's going to beat me up. I always knew she would beat someone up. I just never imagined it would be me. I'm the nice girl. The nice, polite girl who shuts up and gets on with it. I close my eyes and wait for the impact of fist in head.

'Ahem.' I open my eyes to see Stone looming large in front of Marie, essentially blocking her path towards me. Where did he come from? Behind him, Marie is shaking a fist at me. Surely only people in black-and-white films shake fists at each other. Now is *so* not the time to giggle. What is *wrong* with me?

My face flushes red.

'I'm so sorry,' I bleat. 'I didn't mean to say that.

Something has happened to me. I have no control over my brain. I—'

Stone puts a hand up to stop me from talking, and points Marie in the direction of the bemused, waiting customers. She bares her teeth at me briefly before following his instructions.

Stone ushers me into the storeroom, runs a hand through his dark, Liam Gallagher-style hair and raises his monobrow in concern.

'What have you been taking, love. Is it 'shrooms? Blow? Cat pee?'

In all the time I have worked here this is the first time I've heard Stone speak. His voice is scratchy and actually rather high-pitched. My shock doesn't get a look in as I feel the urge to answer him at once.

'I'm not on drugs. Of course I'm not. Cat pee? That's horrible. Do people actually do that? Ugh!'

Stone frowns and mutters 'Denial ain't just a river in Egypt' to himself.

'Really. I'm not on drugs,' I try.

'Love, I have been around a lot of drugs, and that little speech you just made in there was not you. Now, will you be honest with me?'

It's so weird that he's actually talking. Like a normal, actual person, rather than the silent, shady figure that sits in the corner all day.

'That's the problem. I can't be anything but honest. I've been . . .' – I can already tell how weird this is going to sound – '. . . I've been

73

hypnotized. Somebody has cast a spell over me. Taken over my mind. I'm sorry. I am trying to get it sorted out and then I'll be back to normal. I promise!'

Out in the shop I can hear Meg's voice as she demands to see me, and Marie snapping at her to wait.

Stone bites his fist and shakes his head sadly.

'It's always the quiet ones. It always gets to them.'

'What does?'

'The lure of hard drugs.'

Suddenly he envelops me in a hug. What is it with this morning? We've never spoken and now there is physical contact?

I pull back and try once again to explain that I'm not on drugs, but Stone is having none of it. I'm between a rock and roller and a hard place. Try to get the owner of my workplace to believe that I am under some kind of creepy mind control, or let him think I'm a drug addict. Either one could get me fired. And I need this job.

I have to make an executive decision. Stone is clearly far more sympathetic to the idea that I've been using drugs. And so . . .

'Yes,' I eventually say. 'It's so hard. This . . . squalid life of drugs. Please don't sack me. I'll get help!'

It seems to work because Stone pats me kindly

on the shoulder, and with tears in his eyes, tells me to take some time off. Go to rehab, whatever, he'll pay. My job will be waiting for me.

Wow. What a nice guy.

He's right. Not about the drugs thing obviously, but about the time off. I simply cannot be in work while this is happening. Better to take a little time off than get fired altogether.

'Thank you,' I say. 'Thank you so much.'

Stone clamps his mouth shut, does a kind thumbs up and lumbers back off into the shop.

After whipping my apron off, I run out from behind the counter (avoiding all eye contact with Marie, who I'm sure I can hear growling), grab hold of Meg's hand and drag her out into the bustle of Piccadilly. Without a word, I quickly march us over towards the oak benches by the fountains and try my best to explain to her what I think is going on.

I tell her everything that has happened since this morning, and apart from a few gasps and ill-concealed giggles, Meg listens with an unlikely calmness.

When I'm finished, she takes hold of my hand, looks searchingly into my eyes and says, 'Are you still pissed?'

'No!' I yell, frustrated. 'Please believe me. No one bloody believes me.' I cross my arms and resist the urge to stamp my foot.

75

'Calm down,' Meg says sternly, surprised by my yelling, which we both know is completely out of character for me. 'Let me get this straight. You think that last night when Brian tried to hypnotize me, he ended up hypnotizing you instead?'

'Yes!'

'And that as a result of that hypnosis you have no control over what you say. That you can't help but speak the truth, and only the truth, even if it's buried in your subconscious?'

'Yes! It just blurts on out. It's terrible. Awful!'

'But Brian was a complete fake. Everybody in the pub saw that. He didn't manage to hypnotize me, so how would he have hypnotized you? Without even trying!'

I shrug. 'I'm not sure he was a fake. I don't know. Maybe I'm extra persuadable. I have a weak mind. Plus, I found this card in my bag.' I hand over Amazing Brian's business card. 'I don't even know where it came from.'

Meg examines the card, frowning, her mischievous green eyes glancing suspiciously from side to side as if trying to find a hidden camera or a psychiatrist or something.

'Okay.' I huff. 'I'll prove it to you. I'll prove that this really is happening to me. I know. I'll try to tell you a lie, but I won't be able to. I'll tell you a lie about something easy . . . I don't know, my age.'

Meg obliges me and waits patiently.

I take a deep breath and prepare to tell the lie. 'Okay. Here goes . . . I'm fifty-five years old,' I blurt.

That's odd. I told a lie. I *can* tell a lie. And that weird bubbling urge to tell the truth wasn't there.

Now Meg looks even more confused and, fishing around in her bag for her phone, announces that she is going to call Olly and get him to take me home to bed, because I'm clearly unwell.

'Wait. No,' I plead. 'It didn't work that time. I don't understand.'

I slump back onto the bench and put my head into my hands. I think carefully back to the events of this morning, over my entire conversation with Olly. And then it occurs to me. The urge to tell the truth only happens when I'm *asked* about something. I'm sure of it.

'Ask me a question!' I demand, grabbing Meg's phone and putting it back into her bag. 'I think it only happens when someone asks a question.'

Meg bites her lip for a second before saying, 'Well, that *was* the point of the hypnotism last night. To get the audience to ask me *questions*. That I was only supposed to tell the truth when someone asked me a question.'

'Go on then. Ask me a question. But make sure it's something I wouldn't really want to answer. That way, you'll know I'm not lying.'

Meg nods and rubs her hands together. 'Right. Let me see . . . Okay. Do you ever pick your nose and eat it?'

'No! Ick,' I state immediately, the desperate need to answer overtaking my brain and my mouth. There it is. That feeling. It only happens when I'm asked a question. I look up at Meg haughtily. 'See!'

Meg huffs and folds her arms. 'Well, that's no good. You could be lying!'

Fair point.

'Okay. Try again with another question.'

Meg purses her lips in concentration, and then her face lights up.

'Fine. Remember that time at the upper sixth disco when you went missing for half an hour and told me you got locked in the toilets, even though I checked the toilets and you weren't there?'

'Yes,' I say, my face beginning to burn because I know exactly what's coming next.

'Where were you really?'

'I was in the art studio.'

Meg gasps, her eyes widening. She bites down on her bottom lip.

'And what were you doing?' she whispers.

'I was snogging Mr Francis!' I cry, before covering my face with my hands. 'And his breath smelt like pipe. It was horrible!'

Mr Francis was the sixth form head of art. He had a beard. It was grey. In my defence, I had

78

had two entire bottles of red wine beforehand. Okay. There is no defence.

Meg yelps and does a tiny jump up and down. 'No! That's disgusting.'

'He had the look of Sean Connery,' I reason.

'Nat, he had the look of Bill Oddie. Ew!'

She's right. Oh God. My skin crawls with the memory of how large and pervy his eyes looked beneath those extra-strength jam-jar glasses.

'That was supposed to go with me to the grave.'

Meg is laughing so hard that tears are trickling down her face. And then she stops and inhales sharply, as the realization of what I've just revealed hits her.

'Oh my God, Natty. You're hypnotized.'

At last.

'I know! That's what I've been trying to tell you. What will I do? If I don't fix it, I'll never be able to make it up to Olly. I'll never get married!' At the thought of Olly, tears spring to my eyes. 'I have to fix it, Meg. I have to.'

Meg's face becomes serious and she examines Amazing Brian's card which she's still holding onto. She runs a thumb over the back before looking into my eyes.

'Well, my weak-brained friend. Looks like we're going to be taking a leetle road trip.'

'What? Where?'

'The village of Little Trooley,' she says, reading from the written address on the card.

'But before we go anywhere, you have to do something, and it's extremely important.'

'What is it?' I breathe.

'Put my flipping cardigan on. I can totally see your nipples through that top.'

CHAPTER 8

Text from: **Dionne**
RU going to have a Brazilian wax before
the wedding?

Reply to: **Dionne**
No.

'I thought Yorkshire was just around the corner from Manchester,' I grumble as we zoom along the motorway in Meg's Beetle. We've been on the road for an hour already. Olly is still not returning my calls or texts or tweets or voice-mail and Facebook messages. Meg is insisting that in order to brighten up the despondent mood our soundtrack for the journey is Disco Fever – *The Best 70s Songs in the Universe, Ever*. And while I'm not a fan of disco music, I must admit that all the songs about 'freaking out' are very apt.

'It's *North* Yorkshire,' says Meg, pointing at the sat nav on the dashboard. 'Which is more than double the distance of West Yorkshire, so it'll take at least another hour.' She shoves one hand down the pocket in the car door and tugs out a battered

A to Z which she chucks at me. 'Here. Find Little Trooley in there. Should keep your hands away from your phone for five seconds. Let Olly calm down. He'll ring you back when he's ready.'

Normally I'd agree. There's nothing creepier to a guy than a trillion missed calls from a girlfriend. Needy McNeedyson. But with Olly, I get the feeling that he'd like how hard I've tried to get in touch with him. He'd see it as a sign that I care, that I'm sorry for what I said. Nevertheless, I put my mobile back into my bag, take the *A to Z* and flick through it.

After five minutes of staring at a page full of green, I spot it. It's a tiny little patch in the shape of a figure of eight. Little Trooley. Running through the lower circle of the figure of eight is a river and then – signposted as a landmark – Truth Springs Waterfall. Sounds pretty.

I'm tracing my finger across the line of the river when Meg turns down the radio.

'Natty, can I ask you a question?'

The yearning to answer appears right away. The effect is like a switch being flicked on. My brain feels like it's humming. I'm super alert.

'Yes, you can,' I reply. 'But watch out. You don't know what kind of secrets I may reveal.' I laugh, but it doesn't quite ring true. I feel a tad nervous at the prospect of another embarrassing question that I won't have any choice but to answer.

'Do you love Olly?' Meg asks simply.

Oh.

'What? Yes, of course!' I say at once.

Intense relief floods through me as the truth makes itself known. Not that I was worried about the answer or anything. *Obviously* I love Olly. I frown at Meg, a sudden feeling of indignation prickling at my chest.

'Why on earth would you ask me that?'

'Ah, no reason,' says Meg brightly, carefully overtaking the car ahead of us.

'Seriously. All the questions you could have asked and that is the first one you choose?'

'It's just . . .' Meg begins. She clears her throat and continues. 'It's just, I thought you might not, you know, really . . . I don't know why. You obviously do.'

I frown at her.

'What I mean is . . .' she sniffs. 'You just seem so . . . *settled*.'

I goggle at her. 'That's the entire point of getting married! Being settled!'

'No, I know. But you went from zero to settled in about a month.'

'I knew he was the one,' I say simply.

'There hasn't been a honeymoon period. The passionate bit. You never argue.'

'Passion is overrated,' I say fervently. 'I want to spend my life with him, Meg. Reliable is *way* more important than passion. Jeez. It's a *good* thing that we don't argue. My mum and dad argued all the time and you know how that turned out!'

83

'Sorry. Ignore me,' says Meg. 'I shouldn't have said anything.'

'No,' I sniff, folding my arms and looking out of the window. 'You shouldn't have.'

Meg leans down into her bag and pulls out a family-sized pack of Maltesers. She opens them with her teeth and passes them over to me.

'I *am* sorry, Nats,' she says. 'Are you still my friend? Here's a peace offering of Maltesers. Will you forgive me?'

I hear a hint of mirth in her voice. What a manipulative bugger! 'Of course,' I answer in truth. 'Yup. Your best friend. And yes, you know full well I'll forgive you.'

She grins at me, mouth full of Maltesers. 'Do you see what I did there?'

'Yes, I did. I'm not impressed. It's not on to take advantage of someone under a hypnotic spell.'

'Cos THAT happens all the time.'

I roll my eyes and pull out my phone again and type another message to Olly.

> I love you. Please just forget what I said this morning. I'll come to yours later. Please ring me. N xx

As the message sends I feel a roller coaster of a lurch in my stomach. What if he can't forget what I said? What if he calls the wedding off? What happens then?

'We'll get this sorted, Nat,' Meg says, interrupting my thoughts as if reading my mind. 'We'll be there soon. We'll get Brian to clap or do whatever he has to do to unhypnotize you. You can stop spilling all your secrets and it'll be absolutely fine.'

'I know,' I say, quickly brushing away a tear from my eye. 'Everything will be fine.'

A while later we come off the motorway and navigate long, twisting roads surrounded by fields and farms. As we drive further north, the weather turns colder, and the roads are laced with a thin coat of ice. Meg slows down, manoeuvring the winding roads with caution.

We pass a sign welcoming us to the civil parish of Apperdale. I begin to feel a lift in my mood. We're near to Little Trooley now. And to Amazing Brian. And with Brian, the return of my mind and mouth control.

It *is* going to be okay. I keep my fingers crossed.

I roll the window down and enjoy the feel of the icy wind stinging my face. Meg flicks the iPod onto some nineties Britpop and blasts it up. Halfway through Blur's 'Parklife' we come across a rickety white post with the words *Welcome to Little Trooley – Home of Hobbs Yorkshire Bread*.

'Ooh, look!' I exclaim. 'This is where Hobbs Yorkshire Bread comes from. I love that stuff.'

'Maybe they'll sell it cheap here,' Meg ponders. 'See? There might just be a bright side to this disaster.'

I tut.

'Yay. My fiancé might call off our wedding and I might never get my job back because my boss thinks I can't get through the day without illegal substances. But at least I'll be able to console myself with carbs. Lots and lots of carbs.'

Meg smiles in sympathy. 'We'll sort it, Natty. We will. We're here now any – oh, wow, look at this place!'

I sit up in my seat and gasp as, quite unexpectedly, we drive through a small, tree-lined clearing and straight into a fairy tale.

Little Trooley village is seriously attractive. I've never seen anything like it in my life. Actual chocolate-box cottages of all colours surround us, dotted in a haphazard semicircle around a large pond that leads off to a narrow river, winding its way through lawns and vibrant flower beds. To the left of us there's a post office and a busy little newsagent's, outside which stands an old-fashioned red phone box. In between the shops, a slender path slopes steeply upwards and is lined on one side with a long row of beautiful honey-coloured stone houses with pointy roofs. It's like something from *Midsomer Murders*, only without the terrifyingly high rate of homicide.

'Ooh, look at the pub!' says Meg, clapping her hands together in glee.

In the centre of the village, directly behind the pond, stands a pretty pub declaring itself 'The

Old Whimsy' with a small black and gold painted sign. Its large, pale bricks and navy-painted bay windows are partly obscured by frost-sparkled English ivy, and on the huge wooden front door hangs a mistletoe wreath twinkling with fairy lights.

Up in the distance behind the pub, portly, pale green hills sit against the wintry skyline. I can see what looks like a massive hotel or a manor house, and further down in the valley a vast church steeple makes for a gorgeous view. There are even some sheep and cows hanging out up there too. Sheep and cows!

It's really stunning. A sharp contrast to the red-brick jungle and kebab shops of Manchester.

'Bloody hell! I cannot believe Amazing Brian lives here,' I say, as we drive down the cobbled road and park in a little car park by the pub. 'You'd have to be loaded to afford one of these houses.'

I dig out the hypnotist's card from my purse.

'It says on here that Brian lives at number forty Lilliput Cottages.'

We look around.

'Lilliput Cottages are those ones up that road. There's a street sign.' Meg points to the sloping road between the post office and newsagent's.

'Brill. Be careful, though, Meg,' I say, looking down sternly at her dangerously high-heeled boots. 'It looks pretty icy.'

I soon find out that old trainers with no grip to

speak of are the absolute worst thing to wear when attempting to walk up an icy road with an incline. While Meg bounds along in her heels with no problems, I slip and slide, my stomach plummeting each time I think I'm about to go bum over boobs.

I grab onto Meg's arm for balance.

'Ew. You're getting all sweaty,' she yells, but doesn't pull away, bless her. I use the arm not clinging onto Meg to surreptitiously wipe my cardigan (Meg's cardigan) sleeve over my damp forehead. Man, I'm unfit. I really should go to the gym.

'I'm actually fearing for my life right now,' I pant, as my legs slide outwards. 'Are we nearly there? Woaaah!'

'We're at number twelve. A bit further. Be strong!'

In concentrated silence, we plough on up the road, Meg almost dragging me as I slide here, there and everywhere like an elephant on roller skates.

We finally reach number forty and pause for breath.

Brian's house is separate from and larger than the others in the row. It's really pretty, with winter roses growing around the front door and a silvery grey thatched roof hanging low over the hotch-potch building.

We knock on the door and wait.

After about thirty seconds I knock again. This time I put some oomph into it.

Bang, bang, bang! BANG!

Nothing.

It's fine. It's totally fine. He's probably in a back room or having a siesta or something.

I crouch down and push open the letter box at the bottom of the door. Then I lie down and peer through. I can see . . . a carpet. A blue carpet.

'Um, Brian? Are you there?' I yell hopefully.

No answer.

Meg crouches down with me.

'Hellooo! Yoohoo! Amazing Brian? We need yooooou!'

Still no answer.

We approach the window and peer inside the house, but our view is blocked by curtains.

'Our investigation is being thwarted by soft furnishings!'

'He's definitely not here,' declares Meg.

'Let's knock again. Just in case. We shouldn't give up so easily.'

'He really isn't there. The telly's not on.'

'So?'

'So . . . when people are at home, they watch the telly. No telly, no one home. That's the rule.'

How do you argue with logic like that?

'He might be in the pub,' Meg suggests.

'You know what? I bet he is,' I sniff. 'Drinking local bitter and laughing about destroying my life. Come on.'

You wouldn't think it, but walking downhill on an icy path is actually tougher than walking uphill on an icy path. I grab onto Meg again, sweating as I tense up my whole body in order to keep my balance. It doesn't seem to be working. We're round about number twenty when I take a tumble.

'Aaaargh!' I screech, as I fall and start to slide down the hill. On my knees.

'Bollocks!' Meg cries, tottering after me, trying her best to stop my descent. But it's no use. I keep on slithering down like an eighties rocker doing an air guitar knee skid. Only I'm not on a stage and this really, really hurts.

'Ooooooooooow! Help, I'm going to die!' I cry, tears stinging my eyes, teeny bastard stones stinging my legs.

And then, as I'm pondering whether you *really* need a priest to do your last rites or whether you could just do it yourself, I stop sliding. Just as suddenly as I started.

I cease all the yelling and look up. And there at the bottom of the hill is a small group of pensioners stood by the pond, looking at me like I've just declared a law against bingo.

'You want to get some walking boots, love,' says one elderly woman, helpfully. She's clutching a bottle of milk to her bosom and shaking her head. 'Slippery buggers, these icy roads.'

'Yes. Yes, you're right. Thanks.'

I'm still on my knees in the middle of the road. Oh God.

Meg catches up.

'Christ, are you okay? Can you move? Are you maimed?'

'I'm okay. I can move. I'm not maimed. But I think my knees are scraped pretty badly. Look, there's a hole in my trousers.' I point down towards the tear in my jogging bottoms, flapping open to reveal a dirty, stone-embedded, grazed knee. 'My legs look like a twelve-year-old boy's! This is a horrible, horrible day.'

I'm sobbing now.

'Oh, Natty, you poor thing. Come on. Let's get inside the pub. Hopefully they'll have some plasters and disinfectant so you don't get gangrene and die.'

CHAPTER 9

As we enter the pub, the first thing I notice is how cosy it feels. There are open fires crackling away on each side of the main room. If I wasn't in such pain, I'd be marvelling at how lovely, and how festive, it is to be in a pub with a real fire. The pub, which is much larger than it looks from the outside, is painted in rich claret. It's kind of kooky: there's an eclectic mix of dusky pink velvet-covered benches, battered-looking chesterfield sofas and even a couple of rocking chairs. The walls are dotted with photographs and vivid abstract oil paintings in gilt frames and in the corner of the room is a chubby Christmas tree, lavishly decorated with traditional red and gold ornaments.

The second thing I notice is that, in spite of the relative quiet of the village green, The Old Whimsy is busy. The place is bustling with people drinking pints and having a natter. All of them are wearing wellington boots. Most of them are old.

The third thing I notice is a boy. A very tall, very crumpled-looking boy, stood behind the bar,

92

wearing a soft white shirt and with flour in his hay-coloured hair.

I definitely don't notice his light stubble, broad, masculine shoulders and glittering slate-grey eyes.

Jesus, Natalie. Get yourself together.

I shake my head to rid myself of such inappropriate thoughts. I'm obviously in deep shock about my accident on the sloping road of doom.

Besides, there's a saying, isn't there, that when you've had a near death experience, all you want to do is have sex? It's a basic human instinct. So it figures that I would find the first guy I clapped eyes on sexually attractive.

We approach the bar, drawing more than a few glances. I notice all the men gazing at Meg in obvious delight, and then looking at me in obvious horror. I'm not surprised. Meg is the very picture of buxom, baby-blonde beauty. She exudes an air of confidence and sex appeal. Me? My orange stripy hair is plastered to my clammy forehead. I'm wearing a *Goonies* T-shirt, and my saggy-arse trousers are flapping about, ripped at the knees.

I exude an air of mental confusion and a faint whiff of sweat.

I look around for Brian, but I can't see him.

'Hello, Mr Barman,' Meg says sweetly to the man behind the bar. 'My friend here has had an accident. She's hurt her knees. Please may we have two large glasses of Chablis, some dry-roasted peanuts and a couple of sticky plasters?'

93

'Meg!' I cry. 'We cannot drink. You're driving back soon. And it's only . . .' – I look at my watch – 'two thirty in the afternoon.'

She does a responsible face. It makes her look weird. 'We'll just have the one. To be polite.'

I puzzle at her.

'I'm really not sure it's the best idea. We've got to—'

'Do you not want a lovely glass of delicious, chilled, crisp white wine?'

She grins wickedly. She's bloody enjoying my discomfort.

My eyes flicker up to the barman, who is studying us with vague amusement.

'Yes. Yes, I do. Very much,' I hiss in answer to her question.

The boy leans over the bar and peers down at my knees. He grimaces.

'Honey, will you serve these two ladies?' he says in broad northern tones. He gestures to a petite, floaty looking red-headed woman sat at the end of the bar, sucking a lolly and flipping idly through a fashion magazine.

'Of course, Riley, darling.' She flicks her hair, gracefully hops off the stool she's perched upon and kisses the messy man long and slow on the mouth before getting our order. It's definitely a statement kiss. Hands off.

Ha, like there's any need for that.

Riley stares back down at my bloody knees.

94

'You.' He points right at me. 'You come with me. I'll find you some plasters.'

Honey momentarily stops pouring our wine into glasses. She examines me with narrowed eyes, but after a few seconds decides that I'm obviously not a threat. She puts the wine on the bar, assess Meg and frowns, before reaching into her pocket and pulling out a candy floss pink lip gloss, which she proceeds to smear over her lips in an almost aggressive manner. Woah.

'I'll be right here. Drinking my one and only glass of wine,' grins Meg, looking around in excitement at all the men.

I shrug my shoulders nonchalantly, and shuffle behind the barman and through a door to the side of the bar.

'Sit there,' he instructs, pointing to a pale wicker chair in the hallway. 'I'll be back in a second.'

I take a seat, and vainly attempt to cover my knees with my hands. Bad idea. Ouch.

Within a minute or so, he returns.

Setting down some wet wipes and plasters by the chair, he kneels in front of me. Without a word, he slowly rolls my jogging bottoms up towards my thighs, being careful not to rub the jersey material over the cuts. He tears open the packet of wipes with his teeth and dabs them gently over each of my knees.

He's nice . . .

Natalie, you chump. He's cleaning your scabby,

grimy knees. Get a grip. Now is so not the moment to be thinking about sexy times.

Olly. Olly. Olly. Lovely Olly, who I love dearly and am marrying.

'I can do that,' I blurt, grabbing the plasters from him, ripping them open and haphazardly plonking one down on each knee.

Riley smiles slightly. I lower my eyes.

'That's you all sorted then,' he says, standing back up.

'Yes. Me done! All better. Um, thanks . . . Riley.'

He smiles fully now, rain-coloured eyes flashing, and holds out a paw-like hand.

'Riley Harrington. Good to meet you. And you are?'

'Oh. Natalie Elspeth Butterworth, aged twenty-seven and a bit.'

What on earth do I sound like? Stupid hypnosis. My face goes red.

Riley helps me up from my chair. 'So, Natalie Elspeth Butterworth aged twenty-seven and a bit . . . what brings you—'

Before he can finish, the sound of my phone jingling loudly from my bag catches my attention.

I dig it out and look at the screen. Crikey, it's Olly.

'Excuse me,' I mutter and I scurry away towards a quiet corner of the main pub and press answer on the phone.

'Olly. Thank God.'

'Hey. Where are you?' His voice is all quiet and dejected.

'In Yorkshire of all places,' I say. 'I've been hypnotized.'

Saying it to him makes it sound all the more ridiculous. 'Can you believe it? I'm trying to sort it out. It's horrible.'

'Nat? The reception is patchy. I can't hear you very well.'

I dash outside, passing Meg, who seems to have made friends with a table full of gentlemen.

'Can you hear me now?' I ask.

'No.'

'Can you hear me now?'

'Almost. Are you okay?'

Well, there they are. The three words that ensure that while I might have just about been okay, I'm not now. Like a bottle of pop that's been shaken and then opened, my emotions bubble up and overflow. I start to cry.

'Oh, Olly. I'm not okay. I've been hypnotized by mistake. I've had to come to bloody Yorkshire to try to get the spell broken. It's been a terrible day. I hurt my knees!'

'What's that? You're not very clear. You're on your knees? I know you're sorry for what you said, but I really don't think there's any need to beg . . . especially when I can't even see you.'

'No, no . . . I—'

Suddenly, a tap on my shoulder.

97

It's Riley, and he's holding my bag.

'You forgot your bag,' he says. 'Not that anyone would nick it. Not round here, but just in case you need it . . .'

I take it from him and nod my thanks before turning back to my conversation.

'Who was that?' Olly asks. I can hear the frown in his voice.

'Oh, that? That's Riley. He's just a barman at the pub.'

The phone crackles again.

'The pub. I'm calling to sort out that stupid row this morning and you're in the pub with some guy? That's great that, Natalie. Really fucking marvellous.'

'I'm not *with* him. I'm with Meg. We're trying to find the—'

'I don't know what's going on with you, but there is no need to lie to me. Hypnotism! That's a good one. You must think I'm a muppet.'

'No, no, Olly, you're definitely not a muppet, I'm the muppet—'

'I'm spending a fortune on this wedding. I thought it was what you wanted. All of a sudden you're acting like this totally different person.' He tuts. 'Enjoy yourself at the pub. Call when you're ready to be honest with me. I love you.'

And with that the phone clicks off.

Honest? Doesn't he get that honesty is *so* not the problem right now?

Shit.

How can things get so monumentally fucked up? In one day? He finally phoned, and I made a mess of it, just like I'm making a mess of everything.

I try to call him back but it rings out.

Right. Stop crying, Natalie. It'll be fine. You are going to sort this. It's just one day. One weird, crazy, stupid, shitty day. You *will* figure it out. You have to.

I wipe my eyes and nose on an errant tissue from my handbag. An icy cloud forms in front of my face as I take a deep breath and then exhale slowly.

Okay. I am sorting this out. I am sorting it out right now and nothing is going to stop me.

CHAPTER 10

I haven't *quite* sorted it out.

In fact, somehow, I'm well on my way to being a little bit pissed. Or a lot pissed.

In the past forty minutes I have discovered the following things:

1. Amazing Brian is not in the pub (neck the remainder of my glass of wine).

2. Amazing Brian is not even in Little Trooley. Apparently he popped into the pub yesterday and told a man called Alan that he was going away for a few days (neck the remainder of Meg's wine).

3. Nobody knows where he went. He only recently moved to the area and keeps himself to himself (order a vodka tonic from the bar – drink vodka tonic).

4. Telling a table full of local men that Brian – who they know to be a quiet, straight-down-the-line retiree with a passion for gardening and local ales – magically hypnotized you last night will make you sound a few slices short of a Hobbs loaf (do two large shots of Jägermeister).

I haven't drunk this much this quickly since freshers' week when the local nightclub was holding a 'Free Till You Pee' night. I lasted for three hours until I had to empty my bladder. I'm still proud of that.

'And you say he called himself Amazing Brian?' says Alan, a local with a ruddy face and a flat cap.

'Yes!' I yell fervently. 'He had the initials AB knitted into his woolly jumper!'

This is the funniest thing the men have heard yet. They roar with laughter, causing a few of the other customers to peer over at us curiously. I sigh and take a hefty gulp of my drink. I'm not even sure what it is. It's local, cloudy and tastes a bit like pear cider. Robbie, a baby-faced, dark-haired James Corden lookalike insisted that Meg and I try it. He also insisted that Meg sit next to him while she drinks it. She doesn't seem to mind. He's not her usual beefcake type, but they're getting on really well. At the very least she's enjoying the attention. They're engrossed in conversation and oblivious to the fact that I'm the brand-new village idiot.

'Look here!' I bang my glass down on the table, not caring as it splashes out over the sides. 'I have a card. Brian gave me a calling card. A card that will prove to you that I speak the truth and only the truth! Hell, I'm not sure you guys could even *handle* the truth!'

I think the beers are making me just a teensy bit dramatic. I feel like Jack Nicholson.

I look through my bag, digging around through unwrapped sweets and old receipts – and, strangely, a plastic fork from the chip shop – for Amazing Brian's card. I can't see it. Frantically, I look in my purse, but it's not there.

Shit. Where the chuff is it?

The blokes at the table are still chuckling, nudging each other and smirking as I bury my head deep down into my bag trying my best to find it.

I pull everything out of my bag and lay it down on the table.

'Look, lads. It's Mary Poppins as I live and breathe,' says one of the men.

'Good one.'

I grimace. The card is not there. I swipe my belongings off the table and back into my bag.

'Meg, have you got Amazing Brian's card?'

She tears herself away from her conversation with Robbie to have a look in her purse but she can't find it either.

Marvellous.

'All right, all right,' I say to the men, holding my hands up in an attempt to stop them laughing. 'Meg, help me out here. These gentlemen don't believe that Brian hypnotized me. Tell them!'

Meg nods her head solemnly, her pretty face serious.

'He definitely did. I was right there. If you don't believe it, just ask her a—'

'No, no!' I interrupt. 'That's all right. Never mind, we'll just forget about it.'

I might have told the men that Brian had

hypnotized me, but I didn't tell them in what way I was hypnotized. I don't want any more embarrassing truth-telling situations. I really don't think I could handle it.

Meg gasps. 'You mean, you haven't told them exactly what he did to you?'

'No.' I fold my arms. 'I don't want to. It's private.'

'You should totally show them.' She breathes, turning to the men. 'Seriously, it's a phenomenon. All you need to do is ask her a question—'

'Meg, shush!'

'—and she won't be able to lie.'

Shit. How much has she had to drink? She definitely wouldn't do this to me if she were sober. Or would she? I frown pointedly at her. She grins back, slightly cross-eyed, jiggling her shoulders and boobs to the sound of Girls Aloud coming from the jukebox.

The men have stopped laughing and are looking at me with renewed interest. Oh, nice. They'll believe Meg. What? Because she's *pretty*?

I close my eyes, take a long, slow breath and brace myself for a barrage of awkward questions that I won't be able to help but answer.

But the questions don't come.

I open my eyes again to find that everyone has disappeared from the table and I'm sat alone. Oh no. Did I fart and not even notice amidst all the commotion? I look around, confused, and then see that everyone is huddled around the bar.

What's going on?

I wander over and notice the barman – Riley – handing out freshly baked tomato and mozzarella tarts to everyone.

'Be honest, people,' he's saying, brushing flour off his shirt. 'Only the best can go on the menu. I won't be offended if you don't like them. I might cry for a short while, drink too much and kick something – maybe someone – but then I shall dry my tears and get on with it. I promise.'

I didn't know they did food here. And why is it free? No wonder the place is so busy.

Everyone's tucking in heartily, including Meg, who – oh God – is drunkenly feeding a roasted tomato to Robbie. A bit of tomato seed has dripped onto his ample chin. Meg licks it off. Christ.

The smell of fresh pastry wafts deliciously up my nose and I realize I'm starving.

I push politely through the crowd and help myself to a tart.

'Hello. I'm turning the place into a gastro pub. You know, bring in some more punters.'

It's Riley. The flour has gone from his hair, but there are tomato splotches all over his shirt. Definitely not adorable. Not one bit.

'Oh,' I say politely. 'I thought you were—'

'Just a barman?' he interrupts, golden eyebrows raised.

Oh no. He heard me say that to Olly on the phone. I've only gone and offended him. Nice manners, Nat.

'Yes. I mean no . . . I mean . . . I'm sorry. Erm, not *just* a—'

'I'm playing with you,' he grins, putting me out of my misery. 'And not that there's anything wrong with being a barman, but in the interest of full disclosure, The Old Whimsy is my place.'

'You own it?'

He looks far too young to own a pub. He looks like he should be running around a forest with a bow and arrow.

'Yup. Well, inherited.'

'And you're a chef?' I say, nodding down towards the tart in my hand.

He laughs, showing a set of nice teeth with a tiny gap in between the front two.

'No. At least not yet. I'm an enthusiastic amateur. I'm hoping that my food will bring people to the pub, stop us from being shut down.'

'Shut down?' I look around at the lively pub. 'But it's dead busy in here.'

'Not busy enough to stop us from being bought out, apparently. Food is where the money is nowadays. If we can just get ourselves into one of those good food guides, we'll be swamped.' He looks downcast for a moment but quickly recovers. 'Anyway, that's all a bit depressing. Sorry. Go on, have a taste.'

I take a bite of the tart and munch away, conscious that Riley is watching me.

I taste the sweet, slightly blackened cherry tomatoes, nicely softened, and the salty, chewy mozzarella, and, ick, far too much black pepper. What is it with men and black pepper?

'Hmm,' I nod politely, still chewing. 'S'okay.'

He leans down, moving his face closer to mine, challenging.

'Just okay? Come on, Natalie Elspeth Butterworth. What do you *really* think?'

Why do people ask so many questions? I didn't notice until today how many people ask questions. Crapbags. Here we go. I look straight into his dark, silvery eyes, the urge to answer fizzing right through me.

I feel my face go hot as I tell the truth.

'What I really think is this: I *really* think that they're bland. All that pepper isn't going to stop them from being bland. I mean, you could have added some chilli, or, ooh, some plump black olives would have been nice. Your pastry is terrible. It shouldn't hurt my teeth when I chew it. And tomato and mozzarella – hello? Hardly going to set the world alight with originality, is it? I don't think Heston's got anything to worry about. I'd stick to bartending, mate.'

I pause to take a breath. Why am I so horrible when I'm honest? Is this who I really am? Have I been faking being a good person all this time? My cheeks burn. They'll probably look even redder than usual now. I notice that the crowd has gone quiet. Honey, the gauche barmaid, hurries over, puts her skinny, lacy shirt-encased arm on Riley's shoulder and shoots me a dirty look. Meg puts her head in her hands.

Oops.

The look on Riley's face is a peculiar mix of irritation and amusement. Jeez. He must think I'm the rudest, scruffiest, meanest person he's ever met. I don't even know him and I've just slagged off his tart. Which he made. And gave out *for free*.

'I'm so, so sorry!' I exclaim, my heart beating rapidly with horror and shame. 'I didn't—'

'Who *are* you?' Riley asks, hands on hips, a look of suspicion darkening his features. 'Are you from Hobbs? Did that bastard Jasper send you to scare us off? 'Cause it won't work. We're staying here.'

'I'm Natalie Elspeth Butterworth, aged twenty-seven and a bit.' Oh man. 'I'm not from Hobbs. Though I am a huuuuuge fan of their bread.' I pat my tummy. 'Their oven-bottom muffins are To. Die. For. The only Jasper I know is Jasper Ian Parker, who I snogged behind the stage curtain during our secondary school production of *Bugsy Malone* . . .'

I can't relax until I've got all the answers out. It's like I've got OCD and Tourette's all at the same time.

Shut up, Natalie! For the love of all that is good and great. Just stop!

'. . . so then he tried to feel my left boob and I kicked him in the shin and he told the entire school I was frigid. It was hideous. I haven't seen him

107

for over ten years, so I don't think he's the Jasper you're referring to.'

Meg hurries over.

'She can't help it. She's been hypnotized.'

'Hypnotized?' asks Riley, looking at us and rubbing his eyes like we're a really weird figment of his imagination. 'Oh, really? Hypnotized how? Hypnotized to insult complete strangers?'

His face is all frowny and full of indignation.

'No,' I explain. 'Just to tell the truth. I can't help but tell the truth.'

The parishioners are still chewing on their tarts, eyes wide in astonishment at my unwelcome outburst as a cut-throat culinary critic.

'You should bar her,' chirps Honey, twirling her deep red hair around her finger. 'She can't speak to you like that. I think the tarts are utterly incredible.'

'You're right,' I mutter. 'We should leave. I'm so sorry, everyone.'

'But I can't drive,' Meg hisses. 'I've had too much to drink. I thought we might, you know, stay and wait for Brian?' She looks over at Robbie coquettishly. He waves back, his dark eyes sparkling with disbelief.

'Fine. I'll ring Olly again. Maybe he'll pick me up, or Dionne might, for twenty quid.'

I grab my phone and slink off through the pub. The crowd of people stare after me, the strange girl with terrible hair, who turned up in their village, fell down a hill, got pissed, told them that

108

their reclusive OAP neighbour had spellbound her and insulted the owner of their local pub.

Just as I reach the door, Meg trailing loyally behind me, somebody calls out.

'Wait!'

I turn around to see Alan, the ruddy faced, flat-capped man from before.

'You're not barred,' he says, with a pointed glance at Honey. 'For whatever reason, you came here to find Brian Fernando—'

'Brian is called Brian Fernando?' Meg nudges me and stifles a snort.

'It's obviously important to you,' he continues, looking serious. 'And we like to think of ourselves as good, kind people here in Little Trooley. So we'll help. Those roads are far too icy to be travelling on now. Tonight you'll stay here.'

'Here?'

'There're a couple of rooms to rent upstairs. I'm sure my nephew wouldn't mind putting you up.'

Riley grimaces but doesn't say anything.

'I'm not sure,' I sigh, my voice wobbling. 'Everything's a mess, and I've insulted you, and now you're being kind and—'

I swallow my tears. I've done enough bloody crying today.

'Please, let's stay,' Meg whispers, eyeing Robbie up drunkenly. 'Please, please, pleeeease. Brian might be back in the morning.'

'Maybe . . .'

109

'There is one condition, however,' Alan says sternly.

'Oh. What's the condition?'

'You get yourself a stiff drink and you tell us this whole bloody story from start to finish.'

I fight a yawn, suddenly exhausted from all the drama and the alcohol and the ever present worry that I might not be able to fix this.

'Okay then,' I sniff, going back to the bar and slouching onto a high seat. Everyone's eyes are on me, eager to hear about my strange, shitty day.

I settle myself in and look around at the faces of the attentive crowd.

'Well,' I begin. 'The whole ridiculous affair started just last night . . .'

'And that's how I ended up here,' I finish. 'And now totally sozzled!'

I drain the last of my whisky, slam the glass onto the bar and nod for Honey to bring me another. She scowls, but I'm too drunk to care.

The locals, who until now have been listening quietly, start to talk all at once.

'That doesn't seem like Brian. He's such a quiet old thing! Are you absolutely sure it was him?'

'What a ghastly day, you poor lass.'

'That's incredible. We could get you on Oprah or Graham Norton or something!'

'So, Natalie, if I ask you a question, you can only tell the truth? Right, well, do you like my new corduroy trousers?'

'Olly sounds lovely. He has to forgive you!'

'And what about my haircut? Is it too short? Oh, I've got one. What's your favourite flavour of crisps?'

'Why don't you googlymajig how to unhypnotize yourself?'

Instantly I find my brain weeding out questions from the crowd, and answering them as quickly as possible, much to everyone's delight and disbelief.

Alan shushes them down. It *is* pretty overwhelming.

'Thank you for being honest with us,' he says kindly.

'So you'll help me sort this out?' I hiccup, taking a sip from my drink. 'You believe me?'

'I believe you, love.' He pats my shoulder.

'I believe you too!'

'So do I!'

'It's too darn odd to be a lie.'

'I'll help you. I used to be on the radio.'

'A drunken man's word is a sober man's word, I always say.'

'That's not the saying, Wonky-Faced Joe. Who are you, George Bush?'

As the crowd chatter away thinking of ways to help me, I get a lovely warm feeling all through my body, like a Ready Brek glow. It could be the whisky, but I'm pretty sure it's the fact that after the worst day ever, all these people are being nice to me, ready and willing to help out an absolute stranger. It's so heartening.

Fuelled with a sudden sense of well-being, I scan the room for Riley so I can apologize once more, and thank him for attending to my knees. He's nowhere around. Instead I spot Meg, leant up against a quiz machine, drunkenly and enthusiastically snogging Robbie, who looks like all his Christmases have come at once. A couple of his mates eye the pair of them with astonishment and envy.

'Do you play football, Bobby?' I hear her shout over the music.

'It's Robbie. Robbie is my name.'

'That's what I said!' she giggles and pulls him back to her.

I resist the temptation to drag her away. Maybe she'll regret this in the morning, and he's certainly not the hunky prince she puts so much sway on snaring, but he seems nice, and it's only one night, and it's her choice. And after we find Brian, it's not like we'll see these people again anyway.

With that thought in mind, I tip back the remainder of my whisky. As it burns my throat and sends a wonderful sizzle straight to my belly, I come to the conclusion that the best way to deal with everything that has happened today is to get so completely drunk that I no longer care. There's nothing I can do right now, so what's the point in trying?

'Sod it all!' I yell to the crowd. 'Sambucas are on me!'

A cheer goes up around the pub. And soon enough, all the worries about Olly, Brian, the wedding and my lack of brain control hazily fade away.

CHAPTER 11

Text from: **Dionne**
UR not answering ur fone. Don't forget
babysitting John Paul Gaultier 2morrow.

Text from: **Dionne**
Hve picked a cake 4u. It is amazing. It's
an exact replica of a sleeping swan. Call
back.

Text from: **Dionne**
If u don't want to babysit, you could just
tell me. Don't have to ignore me. UR soooo
selfish!

I t's Saturday morning and I can honestly say
that I have never, ever before experienced a
hangover like the one that is happening to me
right now.

I was cruelly awakened about five minutes ago
by my own headache. It feels like John McEnroe
is playing tennis with my brain. While my brain is
still in my head. Even my earlobes hurt, and it's

not because of the cheapo Claire's Accessories earrings I've been wearing recently.

I peel back my sticky eyelids and fear grips my heart.

Where the pickle am I?

I blink a few times and take in my surroundings.

I am in a strange bed. I gasp and check the space beside me. No one. Phew.

The room is small and chintzy. It's decorated with pink rose-patterned wallpaper, and across from the bed there's a matching flowery couch, with what appears to be a net curtain draped over the back. It smells like lavender furniture polish. In the corner an open door leads to a tiny bathroom.

I notice a little leaflet lying on the bedside cabinet. I rub my eyes and pick it up. *The Old Whimsy Bed & Breakfast, Little Trooley.*

Oh.

The events of yesterday slam straight back into my head. Ouch.

Oh dear. *Oh dear.*

The last thing I remember was Meg and me acting out a scene from *The Fabulous Baker Boys.* She was lying on the bar singing 'Makin' Whoopee' like Michelle Pfeiffer and I was miming playing the piano on some drip trays. Oh balls. When did I get to bed? *How* did I get to bed?

I delicately turn my head this way and that,

trying to locate my phone and trying not to vom. I notice it lying on the floor on top of my ripped and muddy trews.

Nine missed calls.

Three unread text messages.

One new voicemail.

I scroll through the missed calls list. Three are from Dionne, one is from Olly and the rest are from Mum.

Shit. Mum will have been expecting me back last night. She must be frantic! How on earth could I have forgotten to ring her and let her know where I was?

I dial the voicemail number and listen.

'Hiya, it's your mum. Why is your phone off? Did you get the checklist I sent you? I thought you were cooking tea tonight. You could have let me know you were staying at Olly's. I'm left on my own now. See you tonight.'

Okay, not frantic, per se.

I answer the questions in her message out loud, although there's no one around to hear me. Which brings my thoughts around to the hypnotism and Amazing Brian. I have to find him today if it's the last thing I do. And it may well be the last thing I do considering my inability to process this hangover.

Groaning, I slide out of the bed and – not feeling up to walking just yet – crawl across the carpet into the bathroom. Stepping gingerly into the bath, I turn on the shower overhead and breathe deeply as the hot stream of water massages my poor, dehydrated head.

I pick up a small glass bottle off the shelf beside the bath. Mr Harrington's Homemade Shampoo. Mint & Rosemary, Made From Scratch.

Who in this world is Mr Harrington? And why is he making shampoo?

I unscrew the cap and take a tentative sniff, but my left nostril still isn't working properly and it doesn't seem to have much of a smell.

I shrug my shoulders and squirt the shampoo onto my hair, impressed by how zealously it lathers up.

While doing my shower-type business, I set to thinking. It only hurts a little bit.

I need to come up with a master plan. Not the easiest thing to do when all of my brain power is focused on not dying of a hangover, right here in the shower. But I try my best to make a mental to-do list.

1. Locate Brian Fernando.

2. Shout at him for hypnotizing me without even asking and potentially ruining my life.

3. Make him unhypnotize me as quickly as possible.

4. Get back my ability to lie and make things up with Olly. Not that I want to lie to Olly. I just don't want to be brutally honest with him about things that should be firmly locked inside my mind, like sex stuff and niggly little things that don't really matter in the grand scheme of things.

5. Get married to Olly (all the while ignoring the fact that I'm wearing the world's most horrendous dress).

6. Live a simple, peaceful, happy existence forever and ever. The end.

That seems like a good enough start.

I step out of the bath, dry myself off and just as I'm about to pull on yesterday's torn and bedraggled outfit, I notice a little pile of fresh clothes resting on the end of the bed.

Huh? They weren't there before.

I pick them up. A bright white button-up shirt and a pair of soft navy joggers. I inspect them. They are massive, far too big for me, which is a new experience. I glance over at my sort of see-through *Goonies* T-shirt and ripped grey jogging bottoms. The fresh, giant-sized clothes in front of me are the lesser of two evils and so I shrug and pull them on. The sleeves of the shirt fall down way past my arms, which makes me feel all dainty like Kylie, but isn't entirely practical, so I roll them up to my elbows. I do the same with the jogging bottoms, which luckily have elastic around the bottom and stay in place on my shins.

I can't find a comb in the room, and the only cosmetic I have with me is an iridescent lip gloss covered in handbag fluff. So I run my fingers through my towel-dried hair, pinch my cheeks in an attempt to put at least a little of the usual colour into my corpse-pale face and head out of the room to find Meg.

After an expedition that sees me making various false turns into a storage cupboard and a ladies toilet, I finally find my way into the main pub. There's no one about. It seems oddly quiet now that it's closed, like a ghost pub. I spot a fresh-faced Meg sat alone at a table by the bar, vehemently tucking into some scrambled eggs.

'Urgggh!' I groan as I approach. 'I feel very bad and sicky.'

'You look like crap,' she says kindly, biting into a thick piece of toast. 'Want some?'

'Yes. I could eat a scabby horse.'

I help myself to a piece of toast and take an enormous bite. Oh, yum. Hobbs thick farmhouse white, smothered in creamy butter – just how I like it. I pour myself a glass of fresh orange juice from the jug on the table and down it in one, not caring as it dribbles down my chin.

'Man, I'm thirsty!' I say, downing another glass.

'I've been up for ages,' says Meg brightly. 'I even went for a walk. It's gorgeous around here.'

'Good for you.'

How can she not be dying of a hangover? She drank far more than me and yet here she is, hair in a perky ponytail, looking all healthy and zesty and stuff.

'Where's your lovah?' I tease.

At this, Meg's face flushes.

'He works at the Hobbs factory up in the hills so left at stupid o'clock to go and bake bread.'

'You sound upset. Do you miss him? Do you lurve him? Do you wanna mawwy him?'

'As if,' she shakes her head. 'I was glad not to have to see him in the sober light of day. Oh God. I'm mortified at myself. At least I'll never have to see him again.'

'You slept with him then?'

She covers her face with her hands. 'I didn't even properly fancy him. Ugh. I'm such a big, fat hussy.'

'Of course you're not.'

She raises her eyebrows, questioning. 'Natty, do you think I'm a hussy?'

'No!' I say at once. 'See? The absolute truth!'

She looks mollified. That's the first time this stupid truth-telling has actually done some good.

'To be fair,' she reasons, 'I've not had sex in seven months, so I was due a blow-out.'

'So to speak.'

'Ew. I don't know what I was thinking. I don't think I was thinking at all. Anyway, let us never mention it again.'

'But—'

'Mr Francis in the Art Studio, Mr Francis in the Art Studio!'

'FINE! We shall never speak of it again.'

'Good,' she grins, finishing up her eggs. 'Nice outfit, by the way. Masculine, but cute.'

'It's my new look,' I say, fingering the soft Daz-white linen of the too-big shirt. 'It's from the man-dwarf chic collection at Sak's, New Yoik.

120

Thanks for leaving them on my bed. How did you get hold of them?'

'I didn't leave them for you.'

'Oh, I just assumed . . .'

'So you found them then?' says a deep Yorkshire voice from behind me.

I spin around and see Riley walking towards us holding a tray upon which lies a bright yellow teapot and all the related tea-making paraphernalia. His hair is still wet, presumably from the shower, and he's dressed in a soft chocolate-brown knitted sweater and worn pale blue jeans that stretch distractingly over his muscular thighs.

It suddenly occurs to me that it's his shirt and joggers that I'm dressed in.

'Oh. You put them there,' I say to him. 'Er, thank you.'

'No problem. I thought with the others being ripped, you know . . .'

'Yes. Of course.'

What a thoughtful thing to do. Or was it a weirdly *intimate* thing to do? I smile at him as he places the tray before us, but the smile turns into a grimace as my head throbs even harder. I root around in my bag for painkillers and neck two with some juice.

'I did ask Honey to bring some clothes over today,' he goes on, 'but she said that her stuff would be far too small for you.'

He innocently pours tea into cups, oblivious to the insinuation.

121

'Well. Of course. Obviously . . .' I mutter. 'Honey's teeny.'

'How long have you two been together?' Meg asks, helping herself to a cup of tea while Riley sits down at the table.

'She turned up in the village about six months ago looking for a job. We've been dating ever since.'

'Six months. Pretty serious then,' I muse out loud. 'Are you getting married? I'm getting married. In four weeks. Christmas Eve, actually.'

I'm not sure why I told him that. It seemed important to get it out there.

'To Olly,' he says, looking directly at me.

How does he know that? My face screws up in confusion.

'You told us last night,' Riley says brightly. 'You told us *everything*, remember?'

His eyes twinkle with amusement, and before I can respond he's standing up from the table and strolling off, taking his mug of tea with him.

Just before he reaches the doorway to the back room he turns around.

'Enjoy your meeting. I'll be in the kitchen cooking bland things with black pepper.' And with that he disappears.

Well.

How rude.

Talk about holding a grudge.

'Did he just say something about a meeting?' says Meg, passing me the last piece of toast.

'Yes, I think he did. He's odd, isn't he? Maybe meeting is, like, a Yorkshire term for breakfast or something.'

'Natty, we're in North Yorkshire. Breakfast is breakfast. I'm quite sure that meeting here means the same as it does back in Manc.'

And just as we're pondering what Riley meant, the door to the pub bursts open and in trail three of the locals who I vaguely recognize from last night, including Alan in his flat cap, and a wiry woman with her wispy grey hair scraped back into a bun and gold spectacles perched on the end of her nose. I don't recognize her at all.

'Hello, lasses. Glad to see you're up!' Alan bellows, instructing the rest of the newcomers to take seats at our table.

'Hello?' Meg and I chime, looking at each other, bewildered. I glimpse the clock on the wall. Hmm.

Isn't it a bit early to be coming for a drink? Is this a village of alcohol dependents?

'So,' says Alan, once everyone is seated. 'Shall we begin?'

'Um, begin what?' I ask, properly puzzled. What the chuff is he talking about?

Alan rolls his eyes at the others. 'Our meeting, of course. It's 11.30 a.m. Time to start Operation Locate Brian.'

It turns out that in the throes of my alcoholic stupor last night, I assembled a crack team of local pensioners to help with my plight. I must have

123

geed them up good and proper because they're very excited about the task in hand.

We've all reacquainted ourselves with each other, and by that I mean I've had to ask everyone's name again because I really don't remember a thing about organizing this.

And so Operation Locate Brian consists of Meg and me, ruddy-faced Alan, Mrs Grimes (the local shopkeeper and village gossip – she wasn't in the pub last night, but heard my tale and wanted to get involved) and Morag and Barney Braithwaite, a sweet retired couple in their late sixties.

While I was asleep, blissfully unaware of the hangover from hell creeping its way through my body, Alan, Mrs Grimes, and the Braithwaites were already on the case. They got up early this morning and searched Brian's house for clues.

'And the oddest thing was,' Alan is saying, tapping a fountain pen against a notebook, 'it didn't look as if Brian had gone away at all. The heating was on and there was a bottle of milk on the countertop.'

'That's strange,' I say. 'He definitely wasn't there?'

'We looked all around the house,' says Mrs Grimes gleefully, pushing her gold specs up her nose. 'He's got one of those bidets, you know? And his duvet cover has pink stripes!'

'But we couldn't see hide nor hair of him,' Alan interrupts, giving Mrs Grimes a disapproving glance.

'Then we thought, what if he's been murdered?' says Morag Braithwaite, a kindly looking woman with tight curly white hair. 'I thought it would be best to call the police.'

'But we couldn't,' adds Barney Braithwaite, patting his wife on the arm. 'After all, we had no business being in his house. We didn't want to get arrested.'

'You broke in?' Meg says, her voice perfectly echoing the shock that I feel. 'You didn't have a key? Brian didn't give you a key?'

Morag looks ashamed of herself, two spots of colour appearing high on her cheeks.

'We didn't steal anything,' Alan says gruffly. 'It wasn't a proper break-in. We just wanted to find some clues. But there was nothing helpful at all.'

'How on earth did you get in without a key?' I ask.

They go quiet.

'He once told me where he hides his spare key in case of emergency,' Mrs Grimes finally admits, her bottom lip wobbling with the guilt of it all. 'Under the fisherman gnome!' she finishes before clapping her hands over her mouth.

'No!'

'He's lucky it was only us who broke in, leaving a key under a fisherman gnome.' She tuts and folds her arms in a huff. 'What a cliché!'

Oh goodness. What have I instigated? Four pensioners, breaking and entering into someone's house, committing crimes.

'We're so sorry we haven't come up with anything yet, love,' says Morag, shrugging her shoulders sadly. 'But we do have another plan.'

The others nod, apparently excited.

'Which is?' I ask, feeling suddenly nervous.

'Well,' says Barney. 'We're going to do a media splash.'

'Excuse me? A media what?'

'On our radio station. Radio Trooley.'

'This place has a radio station?' says Meg in surprise. 'But it's so small!'

The locals look mildly affronted.

'I used to work for BBC Radio 2, I'll have you know. Radio Trooley has quite the following,' Barney grumps before turning back to me.

'I think your story is a real human interest piece, Natalie. The mystical hypnotism and your impending wedding, and a very unhappy groom . . .'

'Olly,' I mutter, nodding sadly.

'And we have listeners all over the North West of England *and* on the internet. If we tell your story on the air, someone in the know might be listening. Someone who knows where Brian is!'

The locals look very impressed with themselves.

I think about it for a moment. It doesn't seem like such a good idea. Once people find out that I'm a bonafide victim of hypnotism gone wrong, they'll probably want to know all about me. Scientists might want to experiment on my brain.

It'll be like in *ET: The Extra-Terrestrial*. Only without the flying bicycle, which is sad because that'd be really cool.

But then again . . . the quickest way to find Brian would be to have lots of people looking for him. And the only way to get lots of people to look for him is with publicity.

Maybe other people who have been the victim of his wayward brain control thingies will come forward. We could set up a support group . . . there could be wine and nibbles and—

'Natalie?' Meg nudges me.

'Can I think about it?' I say. 'And get back to you?'

'Oh yes. Of course, love.' Morag Braithwaite says kindly. Her husband Barney tuts and shakes his head.

'Thanks for the meeting,' says Mrs Grimes, getting up from the table. 'I must be off. Robbie's shirts won't iron themselves. Sons, eh? Lazy buggers.'

Beside me, Meg chokes on her tea. Robbie is this woman's son. And he still lives at home. Ha!

'I have work to do too,' Alan says gruffly, picking up his fountain pen and clipping it to his shirt. 'Great meeting. Thanks all.'

As the two of them wander away, I get the distinct feeling that they've done this before.

This place is so weird.

'Anyone for a very early lunch?' Riley says,

strolling in from the kitchen balancing a tray carefully in one hand.

A chorus of 'Oohs' go up around the table as the tray is placed in front of us. Riley removes a huge silver dish cover with a flourish, and there on a white saucer is an orangey pink blob surrounded by bright green bubbly liquid.

Morag jumps back as the blob wobbles around on the dish. She clasps Barney's hand in shock.

'What on earth is *that*?' says Meg, prodding the blob with her finger. 'It looks like it's breathing.'

Riley ignores her. 'Here we have a chicken parfait served with, um, pigs' trotters and a . . . sumptuous foam made from foraged pine.' He looks pointedly at me. 'Fresh, original and definitely *not* boring. Try it. You'll see. I think this one could go on the menu.'

'Not for me, thanks,' Meg says, not bothering to hide her disgust. 'I'm calorie counting.'

'I had a huge breakfast, love,' Morag pats her tummy for emphasis. 'I couldn't eat another morsel.'

'I just need to nip to the loo,' a pale-faced Barney says, rushing off to the men's.

'Dicky tummy,' Morag says apologetically before hurrying after him.

Which leaves just me.

'Natalie.' Riley smiles and nods to the blob on the table. 'You're the great culinary expert, seemingly. I think you'll agree that this dish is really something special.'

He hands me a fork, his face expectant.

I feel bad. If I try it and it tastes like it looks, then I'm only going to insult him again. Oh dear.

'Ah, go on,' he says, guiding my hand towards the plate.

I'm not sure what else to do without being horribly rude.

And so I taste it.

'It's . . . interesting,' I eventually say, struggling to swallow what must be the oddest thing I have ever put in my mouth.

'You have to ask her the question to get the truth,' Meg pipes up unhelpfully. 'She's trying to be polite.'

I scowl at her. She laughs at me.

Riley nods and takes a seat at the table, looking me straight in the eyes.

'How does it taste, Natalie?' he asks frowning slightly.

And I'm off.

'Individually, the elements aren't bad at all. But what on earth are you thinking serving chicken parfait with a pine foam? Are you on glue? It looks damn ugly, and if you're trying to be all trendy by serving pigs' trotters, then it isn't working. They're still pigs' trotters. You know? Feet of pigs! Pigs. Toes . . .'

I can feel myself getting all worked up. Who knew I was so passionate?

When I've finished my cruel analysis Riley runs

his hands through his hair, causing it to stick out at more bizarre angles than it was already at.

'This is never going to work,' he says, shoulders slumping. 'I'm starting to think this whole idea of turning The Old Whimsy into a gastro pub is just really dumb.'

He looks distraught, the sparkle in his eyes dulled. I feel truly awful that I've made him feel sad. It doesn't suit him at all.

'Why don't you just hire a chef to do the menu?' Meg says reasonably. 'Why are you trying to do it all yourself?'

Riley sighs long and low. 'I would, believe me. But we can't afford to hire anyone. Honey and I work for very little as it is. Alan helps out for free.' He gestures to the bar where Alan is methodically slicing lemons and limes while humming to himself.

'There's no way we could afford to take someone on right now.' He scratches the thick stubble on his jaw. 'That dick Jasper Hobbs is circling the place like a fucking vulture.' His eyebrows knit together. 'He thinks that if he throws enough cash at us, we'll give the place up and he'll be able to turn it into more Hobbs Bread offices. Fucking offices!'

He stops and looks up at us apologetically, as if his outburst has surprised him.

'I'm sorry. Inappropriate language for a Saturday afternoon. Or anytime really. Forgive me. I don't really know why I'm telling you this.' He exhales sharply, looking directly at me. 'I guess it's easier to tell the truth to strangers.'

My heart goes out to him. He's obviously really stressed. I can't help but think, however, that he is being a teensy bit dramatic.

Meg must be thinking the same thing because she brazenly says, '*Obviously* this place means a lot to you. But why don't you just take the money? If the Hobbs fella is throwing cash your way, then you could just buy a pub elsewhere.'

'Oh, Hobbs would love that.' Riley shakes his head. 'The Old Whimsy is the oldest building in Apperdale. Hell, it was here before the village was even a village. And it's been in my family – the Harringtons – for years. When you live in a place like Little Trooley, the age of a building carries status. Hobbs think that because they're such a big company now, Little Trooley belongs to them. And that includes this pub. They want an age-old Yorkshire build right in the centre of things to show off to their buyers. Well, I'm not going to give it to them.'

'But if you can't afford to keep it open . . .' I let my voice trail off when I see his face.

'You think I should just give up?' he asks, eyes flashing with frustration.

'No,' I say, truthfully.

We all go quiet. Riley thinking about the doomed fate of his pub. Me thinking about Brian, and Meg most probably thinking about her one night stand.

The silence is just on the verge of becoming

131

awkward when Meg says, 'Natty here is a chef, you know. Maybe she could help you.'

Riley's face lights up.

'Really? Ha! Are you really a chef?' He looks dead impressed. I quite like him looking at me like that. So much so that part of me wants desperately to lie and tell him that I'm a super amazing chef, Le Cordon Bleu-trained. But his question means I have to tell the much less impressive truth.

'I'm not a real chef,' I say. 'I did a year or so's training, but never got my qualifications in the end.'

This doesn't deter him.

'But you can cook? You know about food?'

'Yes. I suppose I can cook and I do know about food. I love food. I eat a lot of it.'

'She's excellent,' Meg says, nudging me with her elbow. 'She used to cook all the time when we lived together. Now she barely cooks at all. I have lost weight, though. I can't cook for toffee. Well, not unless you count heating up some Ambrosia rice pudding in the microwave.'

I giggle at Meg. She's right. I used to cook her all kinds of treats. The one time she cooked dinner for me, she served up burnt jacket potato with a processed cheese slice artfully arranged on the top.

'But . . . you could help?' Riley asks.

'Yes. But I'm not sure how long I'm here for. I've got to go back and track down Brian. And

I'm supposed to be babysitting my sister's dog tonight.'

I wave my mobile at them. It's been beeping away with frantic texts from Dionne since this morning.

'Babysitting a dog?' Riley asks incredulously before sniggering annoyingly.

'Yup,' I say. 'A poodle. It doesn't like being on its own.'

'Cancel it,' Meg says, rolling her eyes at the very thought of Dionne. 'She can miss one night out.'

'No,' I say shaking my head. 'I promised I'd be there. And I really need to see Olly.'

'Well, you've still got a good few hours before Dionne's expecting you,' Meg says, looking at a grandfather clock standing against the back wall of the pub.

Riley grins at me. 'If you've got a little time, I'd love for you to teach me just one dish. One teeny tiny little dish.'

His face is all pleading and boyish. I puff out my cheeks. I suppose I have got a few hours. And I haven't cooked anything in ages . . .

'Ah, all right then. Just one dish.'

I'm such a weakling.

Riley nods once as if he knew all along that I was going to say yes. Cocky git.

'Come on then.' He holds out his huge bear-like hand to lead me to the kitchen. Blushing, I studiously ignore the hand and turn to Meg.

'Will you be all right here on your own?'

'Oh yes,' she says cheerfully. 'I'll be fab, lady. I need to check my emails anyway.' She digs her BlackBerry out of her bag. 'Go on then,' she says, when she notices I'm still standing there. 'Go cook up a storm!'

I fold my arms and follow Riley into the pub kitchen.

CHAPTER 12

Text from: **Mum**
Where r u? When will you be back? Why
haven't you rung?

Pub kitchen is not quite how you would
describe this room. World's most gorgeous,
most spectacular kitchen may be more
apt.

I amble in behind Riley and do a little squeak
of pleasure.

The room is large and light with three huge bay
windows lining the back wall. The units are not
the expanses of cold steel you find in most service
kitchens but cream-painted oak, topped with a
silvery grey marble. Each cupboard is glass-fronted
and filled to the brim with both everyday and out-
of-this-world ingredients. A huge double fridge is
indiscreet in the corner and – joy of joys – a
Lacanche range cooker in Prussian blue stands
proudly to the left.

Be still my beating heart.

I stand in the centre of the room, by a gigantic

Victorian oak farmhouse table, expecting a band of angels to appear and sing a rousing chorus of 'Hallelujah'.

If I were to design a room to live in for all my days, then this room would be it. 'Wow . . . just wow,' I breathe, taking in every inch of the beautiful room.

'It's fantastic, isn't it?' Riley smiles, running his hand over the worktops.

'It's the most beautiful thing I've ever seen.'

'My mum designed it. A year before she died. She loved to cook. She was ace.'

'I'm sorry,' I say softly. 'That must have been awful.'

He hesitates for a moment. 'It was. But life goes on. It must.'

He obviously doesn't want to talk about it with a complete stranger, so I don't push the subject.

'If you like this,' Riley is saying more brightly now, 'then you'll love the greenhouse.'

If I had a tail, it would wag.

'You have a greenhouse?'

'Yep. Just outside. Alan looks after it. Do you want to—'

'Yes,' I answer before he can even finish the sentence.

He lumbers over to the faded blue back door of the kitchen and pulls it open, beckoning for me to follow.

We step lightly along a narrow bramble-lined

garden path, being careful not to slip on the icy trail, until we reach a huge glass outbuilding.

Riley thrusts open the door and I gasp again.

The harsh winter sun streams in through the glass ceiling, illuminating row upon row of fresh fruit, vegetables and herbs, all in precise, even lines. The colours are wonderful. The smell is incredible. I cannot believe they have all of this here. Right here behind the pub!

Without even thinking, I grab a floppy wicker basket from a small table beside me.

'I'm going to show you how to make a ratatouille,' I say suddenly. 'It's a brill place to start, I think. Simple and zingy and tasty. And it won't take long at all.'

Riley follows me as I stride through the greenhouse. He gives a little cough before speaking.

'I don't mean to be rude, but ratatouille isn't really the kind of dish people will travel far and wide to eat,' he says carefully. 'Perhaps you can show me, I don't know, a tartlet of quail, or a confit ravioli, or something with dry ice, you know . . . something more impressive?'

'Something poncy, you mean?' I scoff, pausing by a plot of carrots and feeling a rush of exasperation. 'People don't always travel far and wide to eat food made up of fancy names and endangered species. Sometimes they just want fresh, simple produce, cooked well – not fricking sunmagicked pink grapes hand peeled by baby orangutans.'

'But—'

'And seeing as you can barely knock together a tomato and mozzarella tart, I think no. No, I can't show you a tartlet of quail.'

I lift my head a little higher.

Riley is frowning, clearly not used to being told the truth. Serves him right.

'Look,' I say more kindly. 'It's probably best for you to start with the basics. Trust me.'

Riley reluctantly nods his assent and I continue my journey of discovery through the greenhouse.

I can feel the excitement bubbling through my body as I make my way, row by row, around my version of heaven. I pick out juicy plum tomatoes, and smooth-skinned, burgundy aubergines, plonking them haphazardly in the basket.

Meanwhile Riley straddles an upturned crate and watches me with a peculiar expression on his face. It occurs to me to feel awkward, but I really am too excited to care very much. I want to cook. My gosh, I want to cook. I want to take these beautiful ingredients and I want to cook them into something brilliant.

I smile to myself and gather sprigs of thyme from the terracotta pot in which they're growing. I bury my head into a large basil plant and inhale deeply before plucking a handful of leaves.

When I've finished my spree, I march back into the kitchen, Riley strolling behind.

'Right,' I say with a burst of confidence, the likes

of which I haven't felt in a long while. 'Hands washed. Apron on.'

'Yes, ma'am!' Riley laughs, doing a silly little salute.

We soap our hands side by side at the huge Belfast sink and Riley digs out a couple of starchy white aprons from a bottom drawer.

I practically dance my way around the kitchen, pulling out all the utensils and ingredients I need and lining them up on the oak table.

'So, the trick with ratatouille is this,' I say, handing Riley an onion to slice. 'You must cook each vegetable separately. People think ratatouille is like a stew – you just bung all the ingredients in, cook it for a bit and hey presto. But that's wrong. We're not looking for one flavour. We're looking for *layers* of flavour. Loads more interesting.'

'Layers of flavour. Got it,' nods Riley, sliding a huge knife through the onion.

As we stand alongside one another chopping up vegetables, I find my mind wandering away from the worry of Brian and Olly and the hypnotism. It's a welcome relief.

We sauté the aubergines and courgettes, and I instruct Riley on how to season the food correctly, and how he should make sure that each ingredient is cooked until it becomes a golden colour before being transferred to the cooking pot. While we're bustling about, Riley chats away about the pub and his efforts to keep it open.

As he speaks about it, I begin to understand why it's so very important to him. The Old Whimsy isn't just a pub. It's his heritage, the last link to his mother, and, really, the heart of the Little Trooley community. He tells me about the entire village getting involved in the cause. Mrs Grimes has even organized a fundraising barn dance for next weekend. A real live barn dance!

'You should come,' he says casually. 'It's going to be fun. And I'm sure the locals would love to see you again. Last night was a hoot for them. They've not had that much excitement in years.'

A barn dance sounds so unlike anything I've ever been to before, and one of those strange villagey-type things that I ought to see at least once in my lifetime. But I've already done enough skipping off from real life.

'That sounds lovely,' I say. 'But I've got lots to do at home. The wedding, and fixing things with Olly . . . and in the absence of Brian, finding another hypnotist to sort out my muddled brain.'

'Fair enough,' Riley shrugs. 'Thought it was worth a mention.'

'Well, thanks for the invite.'

'No problemo.'

'Yeah, thanks.'

'It's no problemo at all.'

'Who says problemo?'

'Me.'

'Right.'

And with that, the conversation ends. The ensuing silence is a tad awkward, so I take my mind back to the task in hand.

After about ten minutes Riley's deep voice bursts through the soothing sound of sizzling and stirring.

'What's that song?' he asks, watching as I transfer each cooked vegetable to a large teal casserole dish.

'What song?'

'That song you're humming.'

Huh? I'm humming. I didn't even realize.

'Oh . . . I don't know,' I say absently.

'Sounds like . . . wait . . . it sounded like a Phil Collins song.'

My face goes ruby because I realize that he's right. That's exactly what I was humming.

'Hmm,' I mutter, focusing my gaze on the ratatouille dish.

'Natalie,' Riley says with affected nonchalance. 'Was that a Phil Collins song you were humming?'

Stupid questions. Stupid truth-telling.

'Fine,' I hiss. 'Yes. Yes, it was. It was "Easy Lover" from the album *Serious Hits . . . Live*.'

So excruciating! I pride myself on pretty much impeccable music taste and somehow an errant cheesy song makes its way into my brain. Damn you, Phil Collins and your beguiling melodies.

141

Riley gives a sharp bark of laughter; it's so sudden that it makes me jump. I scowl at him but he doesn't even notice. His eyes are closed and he's grabbing onto his stomach as if he's afraid that the raucous chuckles are about to explode right out of his belly.

Well.

It's not that funny . . .

Okay, it's a *little* bit amusing, I suppose.

I keep a determinedly serious face but as I hear him heartily laughing, a giggle escapes.

'Shut up!' I say, chuckling reluctantly. 'It's actually a really good song. You know, I think it reached number one in the UK *and* American charts.'

'Oh, no doubt,' he laughs. And out of nowhere he starts to sing in a surprisingly tuneful voice.

'She's an easy lover. She'll get a hold on you, belieeeeeve it.' He pauses, face scrunched up. 'That's actually all I know.'

'Shame. I was so enjoying that.' I shake my head, dropping a few sprigs of thyme into the casserole dish and taking it over to the stove of dreams. 'So, *anyway*, you put this in for about seventy minutes. About gas mark four, I'd say.'

I fiddle with the dials until I get the right settings, before rinsing some basil leaves at the sink.

'You know you might want to write that down,' I say as I notice Riley peering off into the distance, not really paying any attention to what I'm saying.

I tut and continue to wash and then chop the basil.

'Natalie?'

'Yes?'

'Do you know all the words?'

'Excuse me?'

'To "Easy Lover". Do you know the words? Can you sing them for me?'

To my absolute horror, his questions flood into my brain and before I know it, my mouth begins to move, once more without permission, and I . . . Oh shit. I start to sing 'Easy Lover'. Making sure to enunciate every lyric for clarity.

Oh no. God.

It wouldn't be half as bad if I had a reasonable singing voice, but I really, truly don't. Modesty aside, I sound like Mr Bean. Mr Bean in a world of pain.

I croon away, red-faced and as quickly as possible so that I can get to the end of the song. But there are a million different verses my brain wants me to get out and I know all of them.

Riley is staring at me, mouth wide open in horror and, oh no, he's putting his hands over his ears. He tries doing it surreptitiously by leaning his elbows on the table and casually positioning his palms at the side of his head, but I know. I know he's trying to block out the sound of my foghorn voice.

And then, as the humiliation takes over my concentration on chopping the basil, I accidentally slice down onto the tip of my little finger.

The upside is that it shocks me out of the singing. Oh great. All I have to do to get the hypnosis to stop is injure myself?

'Ow, piss it!' I yell as my finger immediately starts to bleed. I dash back over to the sink, turn on the cold tap and run it over the wound.

Riley, fast as a bullet – given his bear-like size – rifles through a drawer, retrieving a packet of plasters.

'Are you okay?' he says, peering down at my bloody finger.

'No, I'm not. Holy focaccia, it hurts. That was your fault.'

'Was it?'

'Yes. It won't stop bleeding!'

I pull my hand away from the tap and inspect the cut. It's only shallow, but it stings like crazy.

Ugh. I feel all faint.

'You need to suck it,' Riley says matter-of-factly.

'What? That's rude!'

'You should suck your finger to stop it bleeding. Then I can put the plaster on.'

'No. Ew. I'm not . . . Dracula, you know.'

'Just . . .'

Riley takes hold of my hand and, eyes fastened upon mine, guides my finger into my mouth. My heart begins to gallop. This should not be sexy. It should *so* not be sexy.

But it kind of is. In a weird, vampirish, RPatz kind of a way.

When the bleeding stops, he wraps the plaster around the wound, but doesn't let go of my hand.

It's not uncomfortable at all. It should be but it isn't. Our eyes are locked onto each other's. I look up at his really rather outstanding mouth, and feel a dart of lust go through my tummy.

He runs his thumb softly over the palm of my hand, studying me with a weird, greedy look in his eyes. He smiles and shrugs slowly.

I. Want. To. Kiss. Him.

Olly!

'I must go!' I blurt suddenly and much too loudly, pulling my hand away and clutching it to my chest. 'I'm so late. I've got to babysit a dog! I have to get married! I'll miss *America's Next Top Model* if I don't get back at once! Thanks for the plaster. Don't forget, basil on the ratatouille in forty minutes!'

'Natalie, I—'

'Must dash. Ha ha, moustache! Yep. Bye now. Fabulous to meet you. All the best.'

With the thump of my heart pounding in my ears, I leave Riley behind and dart into the pub, where Meg is laughing with a handsome, important-looking man in a navy suit.

'Meg!' I yell in a wacky, overly cheery, sing-song voice. 'Time to go!'

'Whaaaat?' Meg blinks. 'But, I'm just—'

'Time to go home now. Really.' I grab her hand and march her towards the door.

'Goodbye, Jaaaassssper!' she cries out to the navy-suited man at the table as I drag her out of the pub.

And just like that, we flee the village of Little Trooley.

CHAPTER 13

Text from: **Stone Chutneys**
Good luck, kidda. Remember. The drugs
don't wrk, they jst make it wrse. But I know
I'll c ur face again. Keep me updated.

'What the buggering bugger was that
about, Natty?'

I'd like to say we're zooming down
the motorway headed for home, but the roads
are spectacularly icy so it's more of a leisurely
trundle than a zoom.

Either way, I'm glad to be out of that bizarre
place. What was I thinking? Getting all lusty and
dangerous with a stranger in a kitchen. Maybe it
was the kitchen. Maybe magnificent interior design
is a real turn on for me.

Oh dear.

I feel awful. Like a bad, terrible, hideous
person. Olly's probably sat at home in his pants
watching Dave Ja Vu and eating spaghetti hoops
straight from the tin – a sad and lonely vision
of handsomeness and heartbreak. And here I

am almost . . . well . . . almost kissing another man.

What is wrong with me? I haven't felt lust like that since the first time I saw Patrick Dempsey going shirtless in *Grey's Anatomy* (season one, episode one, about five minutes in). And now . . . now I can't stop thinking about that look in Riley's silver eyes. Like he wanted to take me roughly in the barn . . .

Meg's question filters through.

'I'm sorry. We had to leave . . . I – I've been unfaithful.' My voice is all wobbly.

'Wait, what?'

Meg makes a bizarre yelping noise and swerves over onto the hard shoulder, attracting the anger and beeping horns of her fellow drivers. She flips them a V and once we're safely at the side of the road, unbuckles her seatbelt and turns to me, eyes wide like they always get when she's about to receive some really good gossip.

'What happened?' she breathes.

'Well, we were cooking,' I say, lowering my eyes in embarrassment. 'And Riley made me suck my finger—'

'Ew! Gosh! I wouldn't have pegged him for a finger fetishist.'

'No, no, my finger was bleeding.'

'Ohmigod. A sadomasochist?!'

'NO! I cut my finger,' I say, showing her the plaster. 'And it wouldn't stop bleeding. He said sucking it would make it stop.'

'And did it?'

'Yes.'

'Ooh, I didn't know that. Isn't that odd?'

'Yes, it's odd. And then he looked at me funny.'

'Funny how?'

'Funny, sexy funny. You know.'

'Oh yes . . . I know,' she says, looking nostalgic for a moment. 'And then?'

'And then it went quiet and we were looking at each other for what felt like ages.'

'Yes?'

'And then . . . I ran away.'

'What? He chased you? Like role playing? Are you into that kind of thing, Natty?'

'No, you great pervert! I ran away from the kitchen and into the pub to get you.'

Meg's shoulders slump. 'So, you didn't have sexual relations with that man?'

'God, no! What do you think I am?'

'And you didn't kiss him?'

'No. Definitely not.'

'You daft bugger! What are you flapping about? That's not unfaithful. You didn't do anything wrong.'

Losing interest, she digs out the packet of half-eaten Maltesers from the dashboard compartment.

'I thought about kissing him. That's just as bad.'

Meg sighs.

'Nat, do you honestly believe that Olly has never thought about having sex with another woman?'

I ponder for a moment.

'Well, maybe that woman from *Mad Men*. The secretary lady with the—'

'Obviously her. But I mean women that he meets. At work, in the pub, the gym?'

'No,' I say immediately. 'He's not like that. He thinks I'm almost perfect.'

Meg rolls her eyes.

'Fine. What I'm saying is that thinking about something isn't the same as doing it.'

'No?' I say, still unsure.

'So you've done nothing wrong.' Meg folds her arms and nods decisively. 'And we've left now. It's not like you'll ever see him again.'

'Yes.' I nod, feeling suddenly bereft. 'I won't ever see him again. It's all good. It's fine.'

'All good in the hood,' Meg says, putting her seatbelt back on. 'Anyways, talking of sexual activity, did you see the man I was chatting to, the one you rudely dragged me away from?'

'Yeah. Sorry about that.'

'It was that Hobbs fella.'

Jasper Hobbs? The man who wants to buy Riley's pub?

'He was lovely. Lovely!' Meg is saying, a wistful expression crossing her face. 'Polite, funny, gorgeous.' She drops her voice and raises her eyebrows. 'Rich.'

'Hmm,' I mutter distractedly, wondering whether Jasper Hobbs is even allowed inside the pub or whether he just snuck in.

'He's very interesting, you know. He does music producing in his spare time. Like a creative hobby away from all the Hobbs businessy stuff. He knows so many people in the music biz. He's going to get in touch with this guy he knows, Ian. See if they can't get me a demo sorted.'

I turn to Meg in surprise. She's always talked about wanting to be a pop singer, for as long as I can remember. But I never really took her seriously. I just thought it was one of those things she chats about while pissed. She's never really done anything about it.

'Singing?' I ask.

'Yeah. I didn't say anything because you've got all this going on.' She waves her hands around as if my troubles are right here in the car. 'But I'm thinking it's about time I quit voiceover. Start, you know, chasing my dream.' She blushes as she says this.

Chasing her dream? We don't chase our dreams. We just talk about them and chicken out at a later date. That's what we do!

'Are you sure?' I say, shocked.

She shrugs. 'I just . . . I want to stop going on and on about how much I want to sing. I want to actually sing. In front of people. I want a bit more recognition. I want to be . . . a pop star. I want to finally go for it and make it happen. It's about time to make the big leap!'

151

Well, this is a turn-up for the books.

I feel odd. Not jealous but . . . I guess I always saw Meg's pop star dream like I see my restaurant dream. Something to fantasize about when life is tough or tedious. Nothing more. Not a real-life thing.

'Did you give him your number?' I ask, trying to be excited for Meg in spite of myself.

'Yep. And my work number. And your number too. And my BlackBerry pin. Just in case.'

'I hope he gets in touch, Meg,' I say, smiling at her and squeezing her hand.

'Oh, he will,' she says, grinning back. 'Course he will!'

It takes us another two hours to get back to Manchester. It's slightly disappointing to go from somewhere as beautiful and serene as Little Trooley to the high-rises and suburban estates of Manchester. It all seems a little greyer somehow.

Meg pulls up outside Dionne's terrace.

'Which one are you moving into?' she asks.

'That one.' I point at the top half of the house next door to Dionne's ground-floor flat.

'You weren't kidding when you said it was next door!'

'Nope. There it is. My marital home.'

'Dionne. Next door. All the time. Nat—'

'I'm going in – I'm already late. Do you want to come in for a brew?'

'Nah. As much as I'd *lurve* to spend time with your lovely sister, I have things to do, songs to write, plans to make.'

I lean over to give her a kiss on the cheek. It's nice to see her so excited.

'Right,' she says firmly. 'Enjoy your night with Jean Paul Gaultier. And remember, don't let Olly know you're back. At least not until we can contact another hypnotist to sort you out.'

'Okay. Yes.'

I plan to use the entire evening to Google local hypnotists and call each one until I find someone able to fix me.

Meg waits for me to get out of the car. But I don't. I sit there, worried.

'What is it?'

'What if Dionne asks me questions? Or Mum?'

'You love those guys. I'm sure they won't ask anything you wouldn't be happy to answer honestly.'

'I suppose. Thanks, Meg.'

'No worries. Love you. And remember . . . don't let Olly know you're back, not unless you want Disaster: The Sequel, 'kay?'

''Kay,' I say, grinning and getting out of the Beetle. I've hardly shut the door before she takes off down the road, leaving a puff of engine smoke behind her.

I shake my head and smile before heading down the front path of Dionne's house. Ignoring the 'Let' sign looming large in the garden of the house

153

next door, I pull the brass lion knocker and after a few seconds the door opens. Standing behind it, the remnants of a smile fading from his face, is Olly.

CHAPTER 14

Email from: sexyladydionne
To: nattyb
CC: alisonbutterworth
Subject: Re: Chatterley Wedding Checklist

Auntie Jan has given us a list of her songs. The following are her best vocals. Can you choose two, please?

'Up Where We Belong' by Joe Cocker and Jennifer Warnes

'I'm Not in Love' by 10cc

Titanic song by Celine Dion

'Bring It All Back' by S Club 7

Have found some shoes to go with your dress. They are on this website: www. brideshoessparkle4u.net. They are the ones with diamante hearts on the top. Are they too high? You need high shoes to make you look slimmer.

Irene from the corner shop has offered to do the evening buffet at a cut price. I have sorted out the menu. Nobody is coming who is allergic to nuts, are they? Oh well, too late now! Ha ha. JOKE.

Here is the link to the car we have ordered – it's amaaaaazeballs: www.fivestarlimousines.com/pinklimo.

* I was thinking I might wear a tiara as well. Do you mind? I've already bought it.

* Bull is going to be an usher. Don't worry, you'll probably meet him before the big day! I was thinking Jean Paul Gaultier could be one too – I've seen some really cute doggie tuxedos in town.

Don't worry – everything is under control, babe. Just keeping you updated.

'I haven't even got time to ask where the chuff you've been.'

To a blaring soundtrack of Lady Gaga, Dionne is using one hand to frantically hairspray her blonde beehive into place, and the other hand to simultaneously smoke a cigarette and swig from a bottle of red wine.

I resist the urge to tell her that hairspray and cigarette is a precarious combination, because she is already clearly unhappy with me.

'Thank God Olly was available,' she hollers over the music. 'Else I'd have been staying in tonight.'

She throws me a dirty look and then simpers prettily at Olly who is sat on her sofa, cross-legged and pretending to read one of her old copies of *Heat* magazine. He doesn't look at me.

'I really am so sorry I'm late,' I apologize for the gazillionth time. I desperately hope that she doesn't ask me where I've been and what I've been doing. I needn't worry, though. She has no interest in asking me any questions about myself.

I let her have her rant.

'I mean, you promised me you'd babysit Jean Paul Gaultier. I wouldn't have even minded if you'd have, like, let me know. A text! You could have sent a teeny little text. But nooooo. And here I am sorting out your whole wedding. Bending over backwards to make it as beautiful and as classy as possible.'

She takes another swig of wine, cursing as some of it dribbles down her chin and rolls down in between her massively pushed-up cleavage.

'Big dangly balls!' she cries, dabbing the wine from her breasts with a tissue. Olly eyes her furtively from behind the magazine.

Outside a car pips its horn. Three short bursts and then a longer one.

'That's Bull! My beloved!' Dionne slides her feet into some impossibly high-heeled shiny patent boots and pats her hair. 'Right. I'm off. Jean Paul Gaultier's upstairs somewhere. He's been fed. Make sure you let him out for a poo and a wee, otherwise he'll just shit and piss everywhere.'

She smiles again at Olly. 'Bye, Olly, sweet. And thanks for stepping in.'

Olly smiles back. 'My pleasure. Enjoy your

157

Madras. Jean Paul Gaultier will be well looked after.'

He turns back to his magazine, not once making eye contact with me.

I follow Dionne through the hall to the front door, and watch as she races to Bull's car – a yellow BMW with blacked-out windows – and slides in. I try to catch a glimpse of him but to no avail. Dionne is in the way. As the car is screeching down the road she winds down the window and yells, 'I'll probably be really late!'

Of course.

I wave her away and go back inside.

Walking back through the hall, I feel a sharp pang of jealousy that Dionne got to stay here in her own little place. She was supposed to be the one looking after Mum until I finished my course, but the night before she was supposed to move her stuff in she signed a six-month lease on this flat, claiming that I, as the more patient sister, would be able to handle Mum's moods better and that the rent on this place was too much of a bargain to give up. I meant to have it out with her, but in the end there was no point. The lease was signed and Dionne had called Mum to tell her I would be the one moving in. There wasn't a fat lot I could do about it.

In Dionne's small but tidy kitchen, I choose a bottle of white from the fridge, grab two glasses and join Olly in the boudoir-inspired living room.

I pour out two glasses, switch off Lady Gaga on the hi-fi and plop down onto the leopard-print sofa opposite him.

'No questions,' I say first. 'Please, Olly, don't ask me any questions because I don't want to answer any more.'

Olly looks up from the magazine, expression nonchalant. 'Go on then.'

I take a deep breath and attempt to explain.

I tell him the story so far, obviously leaving out the bit about Riley and the whole crazy finger-sucking, near kiss situation. When I'm finished, I take a slug of wine and tense up, waiting for him to get mad at me again. Even to my own ears, it sounds like the most ridiculous story ever invented. *And I know it's true!*

Olly doesn't get angry, though. He comes over to the sofa and sinks down beside me. Brushing my hair from my face, he kisses me tenderly on the head.

'Let me help you,' he says, concern clouding his perfect features.

Emotion sweeps through my body. Happiness? Guilt? Thankfulness? What a sweetheart. Offering to help after I said those awful things about his stamina and his taste in music. I love him.

'Thank you.' I look up into his earnest blue eyes. 'It's been a really odd couple of days.'

'I love you, Nat. I just want you to be okay.' He squeezes my hand.

'Excellent. Well, in the absence of Brian, I really

need to find another hypnotist; we can Google it, probably. Where is Dionne's laptop?' I look around the living room.

'Natty,' Olly coos. 'I meant help you mentally. Emotionally.'

'Okaaaaay?' I ask, totally confused.

'I spoke to my parents and they agree that perhaps you should see someone with the capabilities to deal with this. So I've made you an appointment with the GP for Monday morning.'

'What?'

'We think . . .' He sighs ever so sadly. '*I* think you might be . . . depressed. The stress of the wedding, not losing weight . . . It's the only way to explain your erratic behaviour. Why you're making things up about being hypnotized. It's such a bizarre excuse. I think maybe you're in denial.'

Is he for real? He really does think I'm crazy! A surge of anger zings into my chest. I've just spent half an hour explaining it all to him. Telling him exactly what I've been going through the past couple of days. And he thinks I'm depressed about the size of my thighs?

'Fuck, Olly, I'm not depressed. I've been hypnotized. I just told you! I need another hypnotist, not a doctor.'

Olly jumps back in his seat, eyes wide with shock.

'Listen to yourself! In all the time I've known

160

you, you have never shouted at anyone, let alone cursed like that. It's really unbecoming.'

'Cursed? Unbecoming?' I spit. 'Sorry – did we just get a DeLorean back to the 1950s?'

Olly looks at me as if to say that my retort is exactly what he's talking about. I will myself to keep calm – something I've never had a problem doing before – but it's like the truth-telling has unlocked a part of me I never even knew existed. An angry, feisty side that, when I think about it, could have been lying dormant for years. Because Brian didn't change my thoughts and feelings, did he? He just took away my ability to keep them in. It's an oddly releasing feeling. Like when water freezes in a pipe. Everything expands until the pipe can't take the pressure. And then BOOM! It explodes. Something like that.

I count to ten in my head, waiting for my heart to slow down its furious, indignant pounding, but it's no use. I'm angry. I know the whole tale of the past two days sounds far-fetched, but surely it's his job to believe me. To trust in me. I take my glass of wine and rebelliously down it in one. Olly draws back and gasps.

'That's full alcoholic wine, Nat,' he scolds. 'It's supposed to be treated with respect. And you tell me there's nothing wrong! The evidence is right here, clear as day!' He inhales sharply and starts gesticulating madly. 'I shouldn't even be surprised. I mean, look at your mother. Mental illness runs in the family. You were always going

161

to be susceptible to depression, darling.' He pats me on the shoulder.

And with that I do something that I will most probably be ashamed of for the rest of my life. I pick up Olly's untouched glass of wine from the coffee table, and I throw it in his face.

How dare he? How dare he jump on my mother's pain, on my past, and label me like that? It's one thing to criticize me, but another to make a comment about my family. Only *I'm* allowed to do that.

I glare at him, watching as he runs his shirt sleeve over his face, his lower lip wobbling. The wine drips off his exquisite eyelashes and then rolls sadly down to his jaw before plopping onto his chest.

I think he's about to cry.

I immediately feel guilty. What a mean thing to do to a person. He was only trying to help. I should have known that Olly wasn't the type of person to believe in anything so leftfield as hypnotism. And what he's saying isn't entirely wrong. My mother *is* depressed. Maybe I'm depressed . . . Oh God, maybe he's right.

'I'm so, so sorry,' I say, taking a step towards him, reaching my hand to his chest. But he steps back, widening the distance between us, his mouth set downwards in a frown Robert De Niro would be proud of.

'Olly,' I try, tears filling my eyes.

'See a doctor. See a – a hypnotist. Whatever.

Just don't talk to me until you are back to yourself. If you can't figure out how to do that, then
. . . then I'm calling the wedding off.'

He strides across the living room to the door. And right before he leaves he spins his head around, his face purple with constrained anger, reaches into his wallet and tugs out a foil wrapper, chucking it onto the floor.

'And to think I bought these for you!' he spits, before slamming the door behind him.

I shuffle over and pick up the foil packet. It's some kind of anaesthetic condom. As I hear his car drive off, Jean Paul Gaultier trots into the living room, gives a little bark of greeting and proceeds to piddle on my feet.

CHAPTER 15

Following a quick spell washing and sniffling in Dionne's power shower, I dress myself in one of her robes and spend the next hour simultaneously Googling and sobbing.

I Google the following:

Hypnotists in Manchester
Weird shaky breath thing you do when you cry
Amazing Brian Fernando
Jon Hamm. Nude.
Toning down orange hue in hair – tips
What to do when you are accidentally hypnotized and have upset your fiancé who might then bin you
Is it possible to unhypnotize yourself?
Depression genetic

Some of the internet searches have proved more fruitful than others. For instance, there are far more hypnotists in Manchester than you might think. The first three numbers I call don't pick up, which is understandable, it being a Saturday night and all. I imagine that they're all out together. Drinking cocktails and gleefully telling tales about whose minds they've messed up recently.

The fourth number I dial picks up after only one ring.

'Hello, Alice McKee speaking.'

Her voice is young and professional. I feel a glimmer of hope. As calmly as I can manage, I explain my situation to her.

'And so I need you to hypnotize me into not being hypnotized. If that's okay?' I finish.

'Oh. No, no, no,' she says in a voice that suggests I just asked her to do a naked samba outside Manchester Town Hall. 'I'm afraid I cannot help with that.'

'But why?' I ask, trying to disguise the hiccups that have now appeared, courtesy of all the crying.

'It just wouldn't work. Only the person who put you into a trance can take you out of it. That's the way it is.'

That can't be it? She must be able to do something!

'But can't you just say some stuff and . . . you know, clap me out of it?' I whine. 'It's ruining everything! Some charlatan has hypnotized me and it's destroying my life! Come on, Alice!'

'Try to stay calm,' she replies in a soothing radio presenter-type voice. 'You are feeling caaaalm. You are at the seasiiiide . . .'

I take in Dionne's animal-print-and-sequins-decorated living room. No. I'm definitely not at the seasiiiide.

'The subconscious part of your miiiiiind that is under hypnotic traaaaance will only respond to the voice that put you into that traaaaance. My voice, or anyone else's, wouldn't be able to terminaaaaate the suggestions locked into your braaaiiiin. And if we tried . . . it could just make things wooooooorse.'

Worse? Surely it's impossible for this to be worse.

'Worse how?'

'Well, complications can include side effects such as nausea, irritability, guilt, identity crisis . . .'

I can handle those! I *am* handling those!

'. . . vomiting, hallucinations, sexually acting out . . .'

Sexually acting out?

'I could go on?'

'No, no need. Thanks a million. Bye.'

I slam the phone down. Sexually acting out . . . I wonder what that involves. I think back to Riley in the kitchen. Shit. I wonder if that was me sexually acting out.

I wearily put my head onto the laptop keyboard. I can feel the keys pressing into my head. They'll probably leave a mark. Natalie Keyboard Head.

What the bloody hell am I going to do now?

I can't just sit around and wait for Brian to appear. What if he doesn't? My entire life is at stake. Telling people exactly what I think ALL the time is going to leave me with nothing and no one.

Exasperated, I click the search engine tab on the laptop once more. I'm about to do a search for 'sexually acting out' but without really thinking about it my fingers fly over the keyboard to type out 'Riley Harrington' and 'The Old Whimsy'.

The first result is a news article relating to the death of Mary Harrington. I click onto the item, my heart lurching with sorrow as I take in the details of how Riley's mother was killed two years ago in a car accident in Little Trooley. How awful. Poor Riley. I examine the picture of Mary in the article. She's standing outside The Old Whimsy and she's beautiful. Rosy cheeked and smiling, her wavy blonde hair plaited and tied with a bright red ribbon. Beside her are two young boys. One is skinny and dark haired; the other is chunky and blonde – very clearly Riley. He's shielding his face from the sun, but it's definitely him. Poor guy, losing his mum like that.

As I click off the computer, Jean Paul Gaultier trots over from the basket he's been lying in and licks my toes.

I smile in spite of myself, and pick him up, burying my face into his soft white fur.

And then the doorbell goes.

Olly! Please be Olly. I pull the anaesthetic condom from the dressing gown pocket and clutch it in hope.

I put Jean Paul Gaultier down and race to the door, pulling it open with a rush of optimism.

'So, the Queen of Sheba has returned.'

It's Mum. She's wrapped up against the cold in a huge hand-knitted mustard-coloured scarf and a long black wool coat. Her cheeks are flushed from the icy chill and her long dark brown hair is all messed up and windswept. It's not Olly, but the disappointment fades quickly. I realize I am pleased to see Mum. Mums make things better.

'Well, let me in then,' she tuts. 'We're just standing here like a couple of plebs!'

'No. I mean, yes. Of course. Sorry.'

I open the door and follow her through to the kitchen.

'Cup of tea?' I ask.

'I'll make them. Yours are too weak.'

I perch at the breakfast bar and wait for her to finish preparing the drinks. She lays the teapot out on a tray, and pulls a packet of biscuits from the cupboard, fanning them out onto a saucer Mum-style.

'Dionne texted me. Said you were here,' she says, carrying the tea tray into the living room. 'Down boy!' she scolds Jean Paul Gaultier, who is trying to climb up her leg with impressive commitment.

'Yes. I made it!'

'Only just, I hear.'

She leans forward and sniffs at my hair. 'You know . . . you smell like a Sunday roast. Have you been eating a Sunday roast? On a Saturday?' She gives me a disapproving glance.

'No, no Sunday roast.' I shake my head, thinking I wish I had been eating a Sunday roast.

She sniffs again. 'Well, what's that smell? It's like . . . rosemary and thyme. Have you been cooking?'

Rosemary and thyme . . . the shampoo at Little Trooley! I'd forgotten about that. 'No,' I say, running my hands through my hair. 'It's this fabulous shampoo I used. Some herby thing.'

'I don't like it. Where's Olly?' she asks. 'Dionne said he was here.'

'Oh. He left. We had a row. It was horrible, Mum.'

Mum shakes her head and tuts. It occurs to me to ask her not to ask me any questions. But knowing how she is, that'll only encourage her to ask more. It's fine. It's not like she's going to ask me anything that I can't answer.

'You need to be careful, love,' she says, stroking Jean Paul Gaultier, who has nestled comfortably in her lap.

'About what?' I ask, sipping my tea.

'Olly. You mustn't nag him.'

Nag him? My anger bubbles up once more, spitting and hissing like milk left for too long on the hob. She assumes it's *me* who's caused the problem, that a row with Olly must surely be my fault.

In this case she's right. But that isn't the point.

I decide not to reply. Just stare into my tea.

'Did you read the checklist?' she asks, breaking the silence.

169

This is safer ground.

I smile. 'Yes. Yes, I read it. Thanks.'

'Well? What do you think?'

'I hate most of the ideas.'

I cover my mouth with my hand. 'Sorry. Shit. Just kidding,' I say through my fingers, hoping this works.

'What do you hate?' Mum asks.

She's far calmer than I expected. Nevertheless, I feel terrible as the truth-telling does what it does best and causes me a whole heap of shit.

'The cake is going to be a replica of a sleeping swan. Do you not think that's creepy? It's *so* creepy. And I don't like the dress you chose. It's not what I wanted at all. I'm grateful that you bought it, but it's so far away from what I wanted, you may as well have dressed me in a sparkly pink catsuit and I'd be more comfortable in it.'

Mum stares at me, her mouth opening and closing like a stuttering guppy. But I have a lot more to say, it seems.

'I feel sad that you and Dionne are planning it all and I'm not involved. And I don't like diamante.'

Mum reels.

'How on earth can you not like diamante?'

'I don't. It's too shiny and distracting. Diamante is Dionne's thing. Not mine.'

Mum puts her cup of tea down on the table.

'Why the bloody hell didn't you say anything?'

This one takes me longer to answer. I'm not entirely sure why I didn't say anything. Because

I'm a wimp? Because I can't bear to offend anyone? The answer eventually comes out.

'Because you need this. You need something to do. After Dad.'

Oh dear. I sound like a patronizing bitch. I *am* a patronizing bitch.

Mum's face crumples, her chin jutting outwards with wounded pride.

'Let's get just one thing straight, young lady,' she sniffs, eyes steely. 'I might be having a bad time of it at the moment, but I do not need to plan my daughter's wedding to cheer me up. Believe it or not, I do have a life outside of this family. I'm a working woman with friends of my own. I don't need your pity.' She presses her hand to her chest and grimaces. Quickly she fishes an antacid tablet from her purse and chews it angrily.

'But . . .' my voice fades off. I don't even know what to say. I feel horrible.

Mum gathers her bag and her coat. And for the second time in one night someone I love leaves me behind.

CHAPTER 16

Email from: stone_chutneys
To: nattyb
Subject: Just Say No

Dear Natalie,
I tried to call the rehab clinic to check up on how you were doing, innit. They told me no one by your name was there, but they were probably just trying to protect you. They're very protective in rehab. I know from experience, kidda.
I just wanted to say that you can do this. You can beat the drugs. I'm rooting for you. When you make it out of the dark and into the light, your job will be waiting.
Best,
Stone.
PS Is Marie married?

The trouble with truth-telling against your will is that you can absolutely not trust in what you think you believe. Half of the truths that slip out of my mouth are a complete surprise to me. I think I'm in a relatively safe situation, a situation in which I've got nothing to hide – like a simple conversation with my mother – and then bam! I'm asked a question and out pops some horrible opinion of mine that is so far down in my subconscious that I didn't even know it existed.

And for this reason, until I can locate Brian, I have had to take it upon myself to become a complete hermit. I cannot trust myself not to say something that will either embarrass me or someone else or cause someone's feelings to get utterly trampled on. I've warned everyone off with a mass email giving details of a fake and very icky bout of the lurgy. And now I'm a prisoner in my own home.

The one time I dared venture into the outside world was to get a much needed bottle of milk from the corner shop. Only the shopkeeper, Irene, asked me what I thought of the jumper she was knitting for her husband and I told her that even if I was stranded stark bollock naked in deepest Alaska with only a perverted old Eskimo with skin disease to keep me warm through intimate cuddling, I would still refuse to wear it. To be fair, it had a Siamese cat knitted into it and its whiskers were actual pieces of silver wire sewn onto the cat's cheeks to look like real whiskers. But still. It was incredibly rude and clearly hurt her feelings. So going out? Not such a grand idea.

I've been a slave to my mobile phone. Waiting for someone from Operation Locate Brian to call and tell me Amazing Brian has returned and can't wait to unhypnotize me out of this mess. But the phone has been resolutely silent. Oh, except for on Wednesday afternoon when I answered my phone to a marketeer trying to sell me brand-new PVC mock-stained-glass windows. Now, I should first tell you that as much as I abhor telephone marketeers, my general thoughts on them as human beings has always been that they are unlucky to be in such an annoying job. And for that reason I usually feel bad for them and end up buying whatever it is they're selling – this is the reason why I have an extortionate mobile phone contract and am the adoptive mother of an African goat named Cujo. So it surprises me when my conversation with the telemarketer goes a little differently.

'Hello, my name is Steven from Wondrous Windows. I'm calling to offer you a very special, unprecedented discount on a set of windows for your home. With every set bought you get a free carpet cleaner. Would you like me to arrange an appointment to visit you to discuss your window needs further?'

'Oh, Steven. No. I do not wish to make an appointment. Why on earth would I invite you, a veritable stranger, into my home? I do not need new windows. The chances of you calling on the very day, the month even, that I naturally come to the decision to purchase new windows are ridiculously slim. Do you understand that, Steven?'

'Certainly, Miss Butterworth. Can I ask you when you are due to review your window situation?'

'Yes. You can ask me that, Steven. You just did. I think I'll next be reviewing my window situation around the time that I review the situation of my doors and the situation of my walls. Saves time if you assess all the situations together, I find. By the way, I'm being sarcastic. I don't think I'll ever review the situation. I'm sorry.'

'Um. It really is a very good offer, Miss Butterworth. Are you sure I can't persuade you to give me your address? Make an appointment with me?'

'No. I'd rather pierce my own tongue with a rusty nail. Now fuck off, Steven. *Zoo Vets at Large* is on and you're making me miss it.'

Mum has barely spoken to me since our conversation on Saturday night. She just wafts around the house sniffing and sighing as if I'm getting in her way. Plus, her eyes are permanently watering like she's about to start sobbing, which makes me feel horribly guilty.

I suppose the good thing is that she's not asking me any more questions.

So, yes. I've been locked in my house for an entire week, watching *Jeremy Kyle*, baking cakes and feeling very sorry for myself.

On Thursday morning Dionne insists that my (fake) lurgy is no longer reason enough for me to stay locked up indoors. She bursts into my bedroom, pulls open my childhood Care Bear curtains and bounces on my bed, prodding at my shoulders annoyingly.

'Wake up, biatch! It's snowing!'

'Gnahh.'

It's been about ten years since I was last excited by the snow. What is there to be excited about? It's just rain that's gone solid.

'Come o-on.' Dionne prods me again. 'I got the day off work. We have things to do.'

Hmm. I open one eye at this. Dionne never takes days off from her job at the travel agent's on the High Street. She loves her job.

'Olly rang me last night.'

Okay. This wakes me up completely. In the absence of me being able to fix my troubling brain flaw, he's probably decided to go ahead and cancel the wedding. I sit up, fear booting me right in the belly.

'I'm awake. I'm awake!'

'Nice hair. It looks like Shredded Wheat.'

I roll my eyes and pat down my erratic sleep hair.

'What did Olly say? Is everything all right?'

'I'm not going to tell you until you get up.'

'Seriously? I'm up now. Look.' I make my eyes wide. 'I'm wide awake. Timmy Mallett style.'

'You have to get up and get dressed. I don't know what's going on with you – you blatantly don't have a cold – but you're never going to sort things out with Olly if you just hide away like some kind of arachnophobe.'

'You mean agoraphobic?'

'Whatevs.'

She pulls at my arm, but I pull back.

'Dionne,' I say as sternly as I can manage this early in the morning. 'This isn't a game. Olly isn't some secondary school boy I kissed in the park last Friday after too much gazillion per cent cider. He's my fiancé. I need to know what he said.'

Dionne nods sincerely.

'Yes, I see what you mean . . . but . . . I'll tell you when you get up. Soz!'

She jumps off the bed and flounces out of my bedroom.

'Wrap up warm!' she sings from the hallway.

Aaaargh. Infuriating.

I pull myself out of the toasty bed and squeal as the cold air hits me. Jeez, it's freezing!

Following an uncomfortably chilly shower I dig in my wardrobe and select a rather fetching outfit of a vest, one woolly jumper (white) and a woolly cardigan (blue), my boyfriend jeans and my favourite pair of thick, polka-dot socks.

I attempt to dry my hair into some semblance of style, but Barbara's brutal haircut means it just falls straight back into the pudding-bowl bob. Pah.

I slouch downstairs to where Dionne is sat at the kitchen table, hands curled around a cup of coffee, Jean Paul Gaultier settled on her knee.

'Did you make me one?'

'No. Soz.'

I nod and spoon some coffee into the cafetière.

While I'm waiting for the coffee to brew Dionne chatters away.

'I don't even know why you argued, and I'm not that interested. But Mum is seriously mad at you. Not what I need right now, being chief wedding planner and all. I really could do with her help. I've got so much to do and the wedding is only two weeks away. Olly—'

'What did he say?'

'He called last night to see how you were.'

'And?'

'He said you were depressed.'

I sigh. I consider telling Dionne that I'm not depressed at all. But I realize that even if I wasn't before, I certainly am after this past week.

'He said something about you pretending to be hypnotized!' She squawks with laughter.

I take a breath. There is no point trying to avoid it anymore.

'Well . . . I *was* hypnotized.'

'Really?' Dionne looks up from her coffee. 'When did that happen? Was it to stop you from eating so much? Was it expensive?'

'It happened last week. No – it was to make me tell the truth whenever I'm asked a question. It was free.'

She doesn't even notice the strange way I blurt

out all the answers to her. But that's Dionne for you. In her own sparkly Dionne world.

'Oh, that's rubbish. They should have done it so, I don't know, you clucked like a chicken every time someone said Nando's or something. That would have been well more fun than telling the truth.' She shrugs. 'Anyway, Olly said I was to cheer you up.'

'Did he say anything else?'

'No.'

'Oh.'

Dionne notices my sad face and pats me lightly on the shoulder. 'He wants you to cheer up. He obviously still cares.'

I smile grimly. That's true, I suppose. If he truly hated me, he wouldn't give a crap if I was miserable.

'Also, he knows we're still planning the wedding. He hasn't, like, told us to stop.'

My heart leaps at the thought of this. Olly is many things but wasteful he is not. He couldn't bear the thought of money being spent on a wedding that wasn't going to happen.

Dionne grins, slurping down the last of her coffee. 'We're going out.'

'I can't go out.'

'Why not?'

'Well, because of the truth-telling thing. It's embarrassing. I'll embarrass you, I know it.'

'Are you on glue?' she frowns.

'No.'

'Dionne Butterworth does not get easily embarrassed. Now stop being such a drip and get your coat on.'

I obey. I'm sick of staying in. Dionne's right. There are only two weeks until the wedding. I have so much to do. Plus, she did take the day off.

'Where are we going?' I ask, pulling on an unflattering but super cosy puffa jacket while Dionne lifts Jean Paul Gaultier into her handbag.

'We're going to get you a pre-wedding makeover.'

That sounds easy enough. I smile and put on my hat. 'Brilliant. Let's go!'

CHAPTER 17

After a pit stop at the Trafford Centre so Dionne can get some 'fucking amazing' earrings she'd seen in Topshop, and a brand-new pair of furry knee-high boots, we arrive at the beauty salon, which is situated on an industrial park in deepest Salford. I balk slightly when I see the sign. 'Serious Beauty' is flashing in pink neon lights.

'This is the best place in town,' Dionne says, noticing my expression. 'Trust me.'

She pushes open the door and we enter one of the weirdest places I've ever seen in my life.

Seriously. It's like a spaceship. In the middle of the vast, factory-like room is a huge steel desk manned by a perfectly coiffed platinum-blonde lady in a red air hostessy uniform. The edges of the room are taken up by rows of large pods that look a bit like oversized portaloos. In the distance I hear the sound of a woman screaming.

'Bikini wax,' Dionne nods knowledgeably.

'What the hell is this place?' I hiss, as we walk to the front desk.

'It's a cutting-edge European concept. Serious beauty.'

'I'm frightened.'

Dionne laughs.

'Sonja!' She greets the blonde woman at the desk with a kiss. 'Here she is. My sister, Natalie!'

Dionne gestures towards me as if I'm a prize cow for sale. 'What can you do to help?'

'Dionne, darlink!' Sonja drawls before looking me up and down. 'Ah, I see vat you mean,' she says with a foreign accent and a look of deep sympathy. I bristle at her scrutiny and wonder what Dionne's been telling this woman about me.

'I think she is rrripe for the From Drab to Desirable programme.'

'That's, like, exactly what I was thinking!' Dionne nods earnestly.

Drab to Desirable? What am I? A chuffing living room?

Sonja reaches from underneath the desk and hands me a starchy white gown. It looks like a hospital nightie, a fact that doesn't exactly fill me with confidence.

I'm not really an expert on beauty salons, having only been to one three times in my life, but I'm pretty sure there is supposed to be champagne. And why is there no soothing music playing in the background? Where's the friendly lady who will chat to me about her children while doing my nails in pretty pearly pink?

'I don't know if I can afford all this,' I whisper to Dionne, as Sonja types my details into an expensive-looking computer.

'Oh, no worries. Bull knows someone. It's on the house.'

'Oh.'

A gangster salon!

'We are ready!' Sonja says brightly, clapping her hands. 'Natalie, if you could leave your belongings right here, I vill put them in the safe.'

I hand over my coat and handbag.

'Now, if you'd like to come vis me, I vill lead you to Pod Thirteen.'

'Dionne . . .' I yelp nervously.

'Don't worry. It'll be amazing!' she beams. 'See you in about, ooh, four hours.'

Excusez-moi?

'Four hours!' I bark, flinching as Sonja takes my hand and leads me, rather forcefully, across the huge room. I turn back as we march on, and see Dionne waving me off excitedly like a mother waving off her child on the first day of school.

'There is such a lot to do,' Sonja says. 'It vill be over sooner than you think. Come on now. Don't be a big, vat baby.'

I don't know if it's her Bond-villain accent or her tight grip on my arm that unsettles me most.

I collect myself. Stop being such big, vat baby, Natalie.

Okay. It's only a makeover. Just a friendly, four-hour makeover.

What could go wrong?

You think makeover, and what springs to mind is a facial, a bit of slap and maybe a massage if you're lucky.

It turns out that Serious Beauty is far more hard core than that. Over the past few hours five very serious, white-coated beauty technicians have tended to me silently and with incredible concentration. I've been massaged to within an inch of my life, wrapped up in sloppy bandages (apparently this tones up my flab), waxed more than the car in *The Karate Kid*, festooned with big spidery fake eyelashes, sprayed nut brown and adorned with more make-up than an entire branch of Boots The Chemist.

I am, surprisingly, very happy with the progress. Looking in the pod's mirror, I notice that my skin looks fresher, tighter, brighter. My eyes look wider. I am actually looking better than I have in years. I look . . . groomed.

'Finally, we will do your lips,' says the last remaining technician, a large, pretty woman with petrol-blue spectacles balanced upon her nose.

I nod dreamily. A bit of expensive lip gloss to finish things off. Perfect. This is all so much better than I thought it would be. Wait until Olly sees me!

I lean back in the chair and part my mouth, ready to be attended to.

'Fuck.'

I jump up as a sharp object is stabbed into my gob.

'What the hell?' I cry, clutching my hand to my mouth.

That is one seriously sharp lip pencil.

The technician startles at my shouting, and it's only when I go to apologize for swearing that I notice she is brandishing a needle. A huge, gigantic, industrial-sized needle.

'What. Is. That?' I say, pointing at the offending object.

'It is a Restylane gel filler. I know it hurts a bit—'

'A lot. It hurts a lot. Why in the name of all that is holy are you putting a gel filler in my mouth?'

The technician looks confused. 'It is a part of the programme . . . from Drab to Desirable . . .'

'No, no, no,' I say, sitting up, my lips all tingly. 'I did not sign up for this!'

'But I just said, miss. I said, "Finally, we will do your lips."'

'I thought you meant lip gloss!'

'No . . . Oh no.'

She looks mortified, her chin wobbling with upset.

'It's okay,' I say in a kinder voice. 'You only did a little bit. We'll just leave it there. I'll be going now.'

The woman looks uncomfortable.

'But I only did one side. It will be uneven.'

She passes me a compact mirror so that I can take a closer look. And sure enough, the left side of my top lip is all pillowy while the right side looks sorrily thin in comparison.

'Shit. Fine. Do the other side.'

'And I will have to do the bottom lip too now.'

I nod warily. What else can I do? Surely better to have colossal lips than uneven ones.

I sit back and brace myself for the needle. It stings but hurts slightly less now that I know about the impending stab.

When bespectacled lady is done she hands me the mirror once more.

My mouth is huge. The very definition of a trout pout.

'Okay, miss. Your lips will probably be swollen for about a week.'

'Wait . . . they will look like this for a week?' I say, dismayed.

'That is just a little swelling. It will soon go down.'

'And how long after that will I have oversized chops for?'

'It lasts for six months. You will love it! The boys . . . they love it.' She smiles and I notice that her lips are massive too. But on her they don't look so bad. She has the Slavic bone structure to carry them off. I can only produce

186

cheekbones on my extra round face if I'm sucking on a straw. And it's not like I can walk around with a straw in my mouth for the next half a year.

Or can I? It could be like one of those cool quirks, like carrying a parasol in the sunshine, or wearing kooky hats. I'd be . . . straw girl.

What am I thinking? Nobody wants to hang out with straw girl.

'If you would like to follow me then, I will take you back to your sister. She will be happy, I think.'

I get up and take one last glance in the mirror. Apart from the gob, I look rather good. Pretty, even.

I smile at myself but it hurts, so I shrug and follow the lady back out into the main room.

Dionne is at the front desk chatting away to Sonja. Shit, has she been there the whole time? I shouldn't even be surprised. Dionne standing gabbing for four hours isn't really a huge leap of the imagination.

But as I get closer, I realize that Dionne has had something done too. She definitely looks more tanned.

She notices me and smiles. Or it looks like a smile. It could in fact be a grimace.

Oh, I see. She's been Botoxed.

'You look fab, Nat!' she says when I reach her. 'Loving the lips. Look at my head!'

She points to her forehead.

'It doesn't move at all – how cool is that?'

'Dionne, you're twenty-five. You have no wrinkles.'

'Ah, it was included as part of the programme.'

'From Sexy Lady to Seriously Sexy Lady,' Sonja pipes up proudly.

Dionne looks weird. Like a wax model, or Dannii Minogue.

Well, I can hardly disapprove. I do have lips like a life jacket.

'And look at Jean Paul Gaultier! He's had a bow put in.'

She lifts Jean Paul Gaultier out of her handbag. He does not look impressed with having a green tartan bow in his hair.

'Here is your bag and big, vat coat,' Sonja says, handing over my puffa jacket and bag. 'I am glad you have enjoyed zis experience.'

She looks so pleased, I can't tell her that enjoyed isn't the exact emotion I would choose to describe the whole thing.

We leave the salon, and make our way to Dionne's car, which is now covered in a thin dusting of snow. I yawn as we climb inside, Dionne switching on the windscreen wipers to get rid of the snow.

Wow, I'm beat. All that primping has really taken it out of me. It's tiring being seriously beautiful.

'Shall we get some lunch? I'm starving,' I say to Dionne as she puts on her seatbelt.

'I'm not hungry. And anyway you should be dieting before the wedding.'

My phone beeps loudly with a text. I dig it out of my bag absentmindedly and take a look.

It's a number I don't recognize.

Text from: **Number not available**
Brian is back in Little Trooley. He is in The Old Whimsy. Hurry.

Oh my God! I check the number again. It's no one from Operation Locate Brian. I'd know because I stored all their numbers in my phone last week.

I indicate for Dionne to turn off the engine. She tuts but complies. Meanwhile I dial the number from the message.

'The person you are calling is not available. Please hang up. Please hang up.'

I hang up.

Shit. A rush of excitement courses through me. Brian is back! I'm finally going to be fixed. My life will not be ruined.

'Dionne, I need you to take me to North Yorkshire. Now!'

The urgency in my voice seems to fly right over her head.

'Hmm. Why?'

'Because the man who hypnotized me is there and I need him to fix me.'

She rolls her eyes. 'Are you still going on about

189

that? Like, how long will it take?' She could be sulking, but I can't tell with her whole face frozen. It *sounds* like she's sulking.

'Of course I'm still going on about it,' I answer dutifully. 'It's the worst thing that has ever happened to me!'

'Drama queen.'

'And it'll take about two hours.'

'Um. Nah. I'm not in the mood. My Botox hurts. And Jean Paul Gaultier is getting bored.'

I look towards the backseat where Jean Paul Gaultier is snug and sleepy inside Dionne's handbag.

'He doesn't look bored,' I try. 'Please?'

She huffs and glances at her Swarovski bejewelled watch.

'Jeez. No need to go on about it. Fine. But you owe me big time.'

'Thank you, thank you, thank you!' I lean over to give her a kiss.

'Ooh, your gob feels dead weird,' she shrieks.

'Does it?' I ask, putting my fingers to my mouth and pressing. My finger practically bounces back off the surface of my lips.

'Yeah. All mooshy.'

'Great.'

'Oh no. It's a compliment. They're like blow-job lips. They're the best kind. For men, I mean. Olly will be made up.'

I almost ask her to explain the concept of

190

blow-job lips, but worry that her explanation will be far more detailed than I can stomach. Instead, I smile with my new mahoosive gob and say, 'Step on it, sis!'

And she does.

CHAPTER 18

Text to: **Olly Chatterley**
Thanks for asking Dionne to cheer me up.
I love you. Please 4give me. I promise I
will sort this out! X

Dionne's Mazda (pearl pink with zebra-print interior), along with her complete disregard for speed limits, means that despite the steadily increasing snowfall, we reach Little Trooley in about two and half hours.

As we park up by the village green, I'm taken aback to find that I've missed this place. I've only been back in Manchester for a week, but seeing the beautiful honey-coloured stone houses and the tall trees again makes a wonderful sense of calm wash over me.

Dionne is not quite as impressed.

'Oh, my days. This place is, like, the middle of nowhere. I didn't even know places like this existed.'

I get out of the car and race out towards The Old Whimsy.

'Do you not think it's beautiful?' I ask, breathing

in the fresh air and waving my arms around. 'And the smell. It's so clean.' And then I realize that I'm talking to myself because Dionne isn't even there. I look back. She's still in the car. Arms folded and staring in front of her.

I scoot back over. 'Are you coming or what?'

'Nah. I'll wait here. I need to let Jean Paul Gaultier out for a wee anyway.'

'I'll wait while he goes. Come on. It's cold out here. You may as well come in.'

Dionne climbs out of the car, sets Jean Paul Gaultier on his lead and watches while he does his business on a patch of grass.

'I suppose I can have a swift half while I'm waiting. You're buying.'

So Dionne, Jean Paul Gaultier and I trot towards the pub. As we reach the door I feel a sudden flutter of butterflies in my tummy. And I hear music from inside. Wait . . . It sounds like . . .

'She's an easy lover. She'll get a hold on you, belieeeeeve it . . .'

And there, as I open the door, are Riley, baby-faced Robbie and two men I don't know – all doing a pretty good impression of a band. A band rocking out to Phil Collins.

I don't get time to register what I think about Riley strumming a guitar with his eyes closed. Or the fact that they're singing the song that I was singing the day Riley and I almost kissed, because there, popping out from behind Robbie, laughing

193

and overzealously bashing on a tambourine, is Meg!

What the heck! Without thinking about it I shout out 'Meg!'

It's more of a cry actually.

Meg startles as she notices us standing there. Her mouth drops open and she blinks a few times as if we are a mirage.

'Natty? Dionne?' she signals for the band to stop playing, which they do immediately.

Well, she's obviously been making herself very comfortable here.

She hurries over.

'Oh noes! Have you been punched? Did Marie hunt you down?' she asks, gawking at my lips in horror.

'No and no,' I answer immediately. 'I had them filled. I – I don't want to talk about it.' I cover my mouth with my hand. 'What are you doing here?' I ask more grumpily than I should. It's a free country. Why can't she be here without me?

'Sit down,' she says, leading me over to a table.

'I want a drink and some crisps.' Dionne yawns, holding her hand out for money. I hand over a note from my purse and she heads to the bar. Riley hurries over to serve her. I notice him glancing at me, a funny look on his face. A kind of smile, I think. He looks lovely in a pair of baggy cotton trousers and a white T-shirt. All fresh and tall and outdoorsy. I blush and turn to Meg.

'Go on then,' I say. 'Tell me why you're here.'

'Stop looking at me like that, Nat! I came to see Jasper.'

'Jasper Hobbs?'

'Yes.'

'Why? How long have you been here for?'

'Three days. I—'

'Why didn't you tell me?'

'I was going to but . . . to be honest, Natty, I didn't think it was a good idea to remind you about what happened when you were here last week. You know. You seemed so messed up and guilty about it.' She looks at me pointedly, postbox-red-painted lips pursed, and then glances over at Riley who is chatting to Dionne.

'Yup.'

She's right.

'When we got home I couldn't stop thinking about stuff,' Meg carries on, 'about what Jasper had said about his connections in the music industry. The more I thought about changing careers, giving up the voiceover stuff and taking the big leap, the more excited I got. I'm tired of waiting around. So I called him.'

'And?'

'He invited me up to record a demo in his studio.' Her eyes sparkle. She looks all energetic and new.

'Jasper has a studio?'

'At the family home up the hill.'

'He lives at that massive house?' I say, thinking

195

of the huge manor-type building up in the hills behind the pub.

'Yeah, that's Hobbs Manor! It was brilliant, Natty. I felt like a proper star. Jasper's friend Ian – you know, the music biz one – really thinks I've got something special. He said I was like a young Lulu.'

I nod, unaware of whether this is a compliment or not.

Dionne strolls over with a glass of lager and some prawn cocktail crisps. She brings me no change from the note I gave her.

'All right, Meg,' she says, opening the packet of crisps and handing one to Jean Paul Gaultier who is perched obediently beside her.

'Hiya.' Meg acknowledges her with a brief, not particularly friendly, nod.

I wish they got on a little better.

'That guy behind the bar is well fit,' Dionne says, nodding over towards Riley, who keeps shooting peeks over at our table. 'He looks like a hot woodcutter.'

Meg laughs in spite of herself and pokes her tongue out at me.

'*Anyway*,' I say, trying not to think about Riley as a woodcutter, naked and chopping up wood in the sunshine.

'Anyway,' Meg carries on. 'I'm going there tomorrow to put down the backing vocals. See? Check me out! I just said "put down the backing vocals". I'm like Mariah Carey.'

'What are you on about?' Dionne asks, mouth full of crisps.

'Meg is going to try to become a pop star,' I explain.

Saying it out loud, I realize how bizarre it sounds. So out there. I can't help feeling that she's setting herself up for a fall. I mean, who really thinks that they can simply decide to become a pop star and it'll just happen? And at twenty-eight, when you're almost old enough to be Justin Bieber's mother? It's silly. Of course, I don't tell Meg that. She seems so happy.

'You?' Dionne scoffs. 'And that band?' She smirks and looks over to the corner of the pub where Robbie and the other two men are messing half-heartedly with various instruments. Robbie appears to be banging the tambourine on his rotund bottom.

Meg rolls her eyes and scowls at Dionne. 'Yes, me. Not with them, though. That's just a mess about. They're rehearsing for Mrs Grimes's fundraiser.'

Oh yes, I remember Riley saying something about that. Though he never mentioned he could play the guitar.

'Ooh, I'd love to be a pop star,' Dionne says, sipping from her drink. 'I think I'd be dead good at it.'

'Hmm. You have to be able to sing.' Meg leans down to pat Jean Paul Gaultier, who growls at her.

'Um. No you don't. Look at The Saturdays. And what, you're the only one who's allowed to be a good singer?' Dionne grumps. 'I think—'

'Wait a second,' Meg interrupts, turning to me. 'Why are *you* here?'

Shit. Seeing Meg and Riley, I completely forgot about Brian.

'Oh crap!' I say. 'I got a text message from someone. Brian's back!'

'Is he? That's fabulous!'

'Well, yes, according to the text. So you haven't seen him?'

'No, not in here. Riley might have.'

Is it me or is she wiggling her eyebrows?

Well, I'm going to have to speak to him at some point. It would be rude if I didn't.

I leave Meg and Dionne to throw evils at each other and approach Riley behind the bar.

'Hello, Miss Butterworth,' he smiles when I get there. 'I didn't think we'd be seeing you again so soon.'

'Yes, yes. Here I am. Surprise!' I feel myself blush. 'I actually came to see Brian Fernando. I heard that he was back in Little Trooley, here in The Old Whimsy, actually. Have you seen him?'

He thinks for a moment. 'Nope. I'm pretty sure he's not been in the pub.'

Maybe the sender of the text was mixed up. He's here in the village, just not in the pub.

'Hang on a second,' Riley says before darting into the back. He returns a second later, his Uncle

Alan trailing behind in a pair of mud-stained blue overalls.

'Hello, lass!' Alan booms when he sees me, ambling around from the bar to envelop me into a huge muddy hug. 'Did you get yourself fixed?'

I hug back, surprised, but thrilled at his enthusiastic greeting.

'No, I'm afraid not,' I say. 'That's why I'm here. Somebody text messaged me to say that Brian was back. In fact, they said he was right here in this pub.'

I pull out my phone and show the pair of them the message.

Alan grimaces and shakes his head. 'Oh. I'm sorry, love, but we've not seen hide nor hair of him for weeks now.'

My stomach drops.

'Maybe he's at his house.' I try. 'I'll pop over. Have a look.'

Alan shakes his head again, this time putting his hand on my shoulder.

'I was there about an hour ago, love, watering his plants. He wasn't home.'

Oh no. What the hell?

'But the text message,' I say. 'Someone—'

'I think perhaps you've been the subject of a practical joke, lass.'

That can't be right. I can't have driven all this way to find out that he's not even here again.

The disappointment stings. I thought I was close to getting my life back. Who would joke about

199

that? *Why* would someone joke about that? It's really not funny. I could understand if it was amusing, but it really isn't. I look around at everyone in the pub, suspicion glinting in my eyes. Who was it? Who sent the message?

'Has anybody seen Brian Fernando?' I address the pub at large, my voice shaky but strident. But there's hardly anyone in here. Just the band and Dionne and Meg and Riley and Alan, and another two men who are playing cards at a table by the fruit machine. Most of them look at me like I'm mental. None of them answer.

So he's nowhere to be seen. Again. Great. I'm in exactly the same position as I was last time I was here. The only things that have changed are that Mum is mad at me now, as well as Olly, and I've accidentally had my lips inflated.

Shit.

SHIT!

What am I going to do? Olly said that if I didn't get myself sorted, then he'd call the wedding off. I want to get married. I want to start a family of my own and live happily ever after. And Mum. Poor Mum. I can't live my life like this. Letting everyone know my deepest, darkest thoughts. I'll have to live like a hermit forever. One week was horrible enough. But forever?

Oh God.

I feel dizzy suddenly. As if all the blood in my head has dropped into my feet. And I feel sick. And my lips hurt. They throb. Oh no.

'Oh dear,' I choke, as I realize I'm having some bizarre kind of panic attack. Zooming my vision in on the nearest chair, I wobble towards it before my knees buckle. But then everything blurs before me. Tables and people and bottles of alcohol swim in and out of focus. In my hazy vision I notice Robbie drop his tambourine, leap off the stage, run towards me and hold out his arms for me as I fall backwards. And then it all goes black.

I awaken in a dark room. In a bed with a soft woollen blanket wrapped around me. My head hurts. And, ouch, my mouth hurts. Jeez. It feels like I've been kissing a brick. A brick that's been chucked at my face repeatedly. What the focaccia have I been doing?

I press my hand to my lips and feel their swollen puffiness. Oh yes. My huge trouty mouth.

'Natalie? Are you awake?' comes a deep voice from across the room.

It's Riley. He's sitting cross-legged on a leather tub chair at the end of the bed, a newspaper folded on his lap. Has he been . . . watching me?

'Yeah. Er . . . where am I?'

'You're in . . . well, you're in my bedroom.'

What the what?!

'In The Old Whimsy. This is the only downstairs room. It was easier to carry you here.'

'Where's Meg?' I croak. 'Where's Dionne? What happened?'

'They're asleep in bed. In the guest rooms upstairs. It's about 2.30 a.m. You fainted.'

'I've been out all this time?' I squint towards the window. 'It's so dark outside.'

'We put you in here to rest,' Riley explains. 'You were a bit muddled and then you fell asleep.'

'Oh God. I'm sorry. How rude of me!'

'It's all right,' he says kindly. 'Your sister said that you had nothing to eat today and that you had a massage and, um, a lip filler injection. That might be why you were so tired and a bit woozy. Luckily Robbie is a qualified first-aider. He checked you over, said you were fine, probably a bit low on sugar. Do you not remember?'

'Vaguely.' I have a blurry image of Robbie checking my pulse while I was splayed out on the pub floor.

This is embarrassing, isn't it? Who *does* that? Who even faints nowadays? I'm like a Victorian woman with a too-tight corset. And who on earth goes to sleep at a pub? Oh yes. Hi there! I'll just have a little nap, now, *in your pub*! Sweet dreams, y'all.

I rub my eyes and jump as something drops off my face and onto the bed cover.

Oh. It's a strip of fake eyelashes. I peel off the other eyelashes, grimacing at the pain, and sneakily chuck them onto the floor beside me. Riley lights a candle at the end of the bed. I wonder if he's going to pray for my sanity.

Or . . . is he trying to set the mood?

202

'I keep meaning to fix the lights,' he clarifies. 'But the wiring's properly messed up in here and it's too expensive to redo at the moment.'

Ah. The lights are broken. *Obviously.*

As the candle illuminates the room slightly, I take a surreptitious look around. Riley's bedroom is . . . full of clutter. I sit up and try not to exclaim out loud as I take in the three huge bookcases stuffed to the brim with classic and contemporary fiction, as well as a load of dusty old reference books. The wardrobe doors are forced open by the one million shirts and sweaters and outdoorsy coats piled up in there. I rub my eyes. There's so much stuff! The wall opposite me is covered in photographs which, from what I can gather, span Riley's entire life.

I feel around my body to make sure I've still got my clothes on before getting out of the bed and shuffle over to take a closer look at the pictures. There are images of Riley at school, so much taller than the rest of the kids, his hair as messy as it is now, and one or two of him with Honey. She's looking at him with an intense, devoted expression, clinging onto his arms, while he looks sleepy and relaxed, grinning toothily at whoever is taking the picture.

Right in the middle of the wall is the photo of his mother that I saw on the internet. Next to it is a polaroid of his mother, laughing with a tall red-haired man and holding a new baby. On the white trim someone has written *Mary and Jack*

Harrington with baby Riley. I wonder where his dad is now?

While I gaze at the pictures, a strange aroma pervades the room. It smells like brandy. I sniff suspiciously.

'It's a stinky candle,' Riley says. 'I've already used all the normal ones. This one's the only one left. It's Christmas-pudding scented.'

'Hmm,' I turn back towards him and breathe it in. 'It's lovely.'

I perch on the end of the bed, not quite sure what to do with myself. I fiddle with one of the buttons on my cardigan.

'Oh no,' I blurt, as I suddenly remember Dionne. 'Dionne is going to be so mad at me. She has to work tomorrow. Did she have a tantrum?'

'She was a little . . . irate,' Riley says with a bemused expression. 'But she had no other choice but to stay here, regardless of your passing out. The snow is really coming down hard now. It would have been dangerous for you to drive back through it. Alan forbade it, actually.'

'Gosh. Well, I suppose it's good in a way that I fainted. I mean, if I hadn't, we might have tried to drive back and got caught in the storm with no way of escaping and we'd have had to eat each other like in that film *Alive*. Jean Paul Gaultier would be the first to go.'

I don't think I've properly come round. Riley kindly overlooks my wittering on about dog consumption.

'I hope you don't mind me being here,' he says. 'I thought it'd be best if someone kept an eye on you. You know, just in case.'

I nod, inwardly cursing Dionne and Meg for not insisting that *they* be the ones to keep an eye on me.

We fall into silence, Riley scanning his newspaper and me watching the candle flame dance and flicker in the dark. I have no idea what to say to him because this situation, let's face it, is utterly weird.

'Oh, you play the guitar,' I say when I can bear it no longer. I gesture over to the two acoustics propped up against a bookshelf.

Riley answers back super quickly as if he too had been waiting for something to break the silence.

'Yeah. I learned at school.'

'You took guitar at school? Lucky!'

'Well. After school. I was in a performing arts group.'

I can't help it. I laugh.

'What's so funny?'

'I can't picture you in a performing arts group. That's all. You're too gruff.'

'Gruff!' Riley raises a sandy brow. 'I've never been described as gruff before. Lanky, chunky, great big bastard always. But, oddly enough, never gruff. Is gruff a good thing?'

'Totally.'

'I'm glad.'

'So did you do musicals and stuff? Like *Chicago* and . . . *Annie*?' I giggle again at the very thought. Riley looks mildly offended.

'No way! We were cooler than that.'

'Yeah, it sounds like it.'

'We were! We did *original* stuff.' He gets up off his tub chair and plucks a photo from the wall. 'This guy here wrote the plays,' he says, pointing to a short, dark kid with long hair. 'And now he writes for *Coronation Street*.'

'Impressive.'

'You bet. And I wrote the songs.'

'You can do that?' I ask, impressed.

'Yeah.' He smooths back his hair and affects a smirk. 'I'm an exceptional songwriter – a genius, some might say. I have, in fact, been referred to as the new Bacharach.' He lifts his chin up and folds his arms.

'Write me a song then.'

He looks around. 'What, now?'

'Yeah, now, Mr Exceptional.'

He pauses for a second before shrugging. 'No problemo.'

I don't really expect him to write me a song but he hops over to his guitar, picks it up and starts to strum.

After a few moments he starts to sing.

'Natalieeeee, you are so cruel to meeee. You made me write a soooong, when I didn't have very looooong, erm, to prepare.'

'Genius,' I say, smirking.

'Hold on, I'm just getting started.' He coughs and plucks at the strings again. 'You say you're hypnotiiiized, but I think it's all liiiiies.'

I open my mouth in indignation.

'It's a good job you're so pretty, else I'd think you a teensy bit mean and . . . shitty.'

'Pretty?' I say, before I can stop myself.

'Um. Yeah.'

Awkward silence no. 37.

'Right. Good song.'

We go quiet again then because the atmosphere shifts. It's imperceptible, but it's there.

Things improve further when my stomach lets out an almighty growl.

Oh, nice one, Natalie. Real classy.

Riley grins and puts down the guitar. 'Food?'

'Yes, please. If that's okay? I don't want to put you to any trouble.'

'Oh, it's no trouble at all.'

'Really? Are you sure?'

'It's cool. We don't want you going hungry.'

'Thanks.'

'No problemo.'

We make our way to the kitchen.

He thinks I'm pretty.

When we get to the kitchen, the range is throwing out heat and fresh snow is stuck to the outside of the huge windows. It's bright, cosy and smells of buttery thyme-roasted potatoes. It's perfect really.

Apart from the hum of the lights and the soft

flutter of the snow outside, it's totally silent. So quiet that it's hard to believe that there's anyone else in the entire village, let alone the pub.

I take a seat at the huge table while Riley pulls open the fridge.

'How about a sandwich? Let's see . . . there's some cold roast beef left. And some horseradish cream. Will that do? We've got hot chocolate, if you'd like some of that? Or I can do you a cold drink?'

'Hot chocolate would be lovely. It all sounds lovely. Thank you,' I say graciously.

He gives a single nod and pulls out the sandwich ingredients before slicing up thick doorstops of bread.

I notice that the bread is Hobbs rye bloomer.

'I thought you hated Hobbs?' I say, getting up from the table to warm some milk for the cocoa.

'Nah. I don't *hate* Hobbs; I'm no fan of Jasper Hobbs, though. The bread I have no problem with. It's good bread. We get it at a discount.'

'Ohmigosh, lucky you!'

'Yeah. My mother was great friends with Alfred Hobbs, Jasper's dad. He continues to honour the agreement that we get all of his products at a third of the price.'

'That's nice of him,' I say, thinking that in fact it is more than nice. If someone offered me the entire Hobbs range at a third of the price, I would eat nothing but toast for the rest of my life.

'So,' I say, watching over the warming milk. 'If

Alfred Hobbs was such good friends with your mum . . . why is he letting Jasper get away with all this buying up the pub malarkey? Surely your mother wouldn't have been happy about that?'

I can see Riley's shoulders tense as he lays the roast beef on the bread.

'Because Jasper is heir to the Hobbs throne. Alfred retired a couple of years back and while Jasper doesn't actually do much *work* at Hobbs, he still has a majority say in every major decision. Alfred is kind of a recluse. I haven't seen him in well over two years. Nobody has.'

'Is he dead?'

Why did I say that? Oh God. Riley's mum is dead. Why am I talking about people being dead? Total foot in mouth, Natalie.

But Riley laughs. 'No. He's not dead. People catch glimpses of him every now and then. It's a running joke around here. Seeing Alfred Hobbs is akin to spotting Bigfoot.'

I giggle at the thought of the locals taking binoculars and cameras up on the hills Alfred-watching.

'And what about his wife? Jasper's mum? Surely she's not that chuffed to be married to a recluse?'

'Oh, Mrs Hobbs left years ago, as soon as Jasper turned eighteen. She was a model before she married Alfred. Turned out a life in the sticks was more than she could bear and she divorced him. I guess it didn't help that Alfred was a bit of a ladies' man back in the day. And I reckon he

209

always had a thing for my mum. Last I heard, Mrs Hobbs is living in Monte Carlo with another woman.'

'Gosh. And now Alfred hides away in his massive mansion.'

'Yep. Since my mother died, he's completely dropped out of society. It's funny. He has this helicopter. The Hobbscopter. He sends it out with his pilot, Carlos, all over the country so that he can still have access to everything he used to enjoy in the outside world.'

'How decadent! Like, what kind of stuff?'

'According to Edna Grimes, meals from posh London restaurants, French champagne, tailors and barbers flown in. All sorts.'

'Sounds a bit excessive.'

'He's a very rich old man. He can afford it.'

I finish making the hot chocolate and take it over to the table, where Riley joins me with a platter of delicious-looking roast beef sandwiches.

'So . . .' I ask, curiosity getting the better of me. 'If your mother and Alfred Hobbs were close, then you know Jasper quite well? Surely you can reason with him about The Old Whimsy? Talk to him and tell him how much this place means to you?'

Riley doesn't speak for a moment.

'I'm sorry,' I say quickly. 'I'm being nosy.'

'No. No, it's fine. You're right. I did know him well. We were friends. Not best friends, but I've had my fair share of pints with the guy.'

I think of Riley, scruffy and boisterous looking,

and then Jasper, the slick, suited man I saw only briefly in the pub last week. They don't look like two men who would ever be friends.

I bite into my sandwich. Oh man, it's delicious. I sigh in delight.

'Is that good?' Riley asks.

'Orgasmic,' I say at once, the hypnotism doing its work. 'You can't cook but you make a mean sarnie.'

In the space of a sentence I've talked about sex and insulted him again. I'm on fine form today. Where are you, Brian Fernando? Come back and save me from this.

'Orgasmic,' Riley repeats, a smile playing around his eyes. 'I do like to please.'

Argh! Is he just being friendly, or was that completely flirty? I try to shake off the dart of excitement that pierces my stomach.

'So why did you stop having pints together then?' I ask, desperate to move away from chatting about orgasms. 'Was it because he wanted to buy the pub for office space?'

'No,' Riley says, biting into his sandwich. 'Mmm. Orgasmic indeed.'

I blush.

'No. Jasper and I don't get along because I believe he's the reason my mum died.'

He says it so simply and without emotion. Like he's just told me he's nipping to the shops.

My eyes widen at this revelation. 'What happened?'

Riley takes a sip of his hot chocolate and shrugs.

'She died in a car accident. It was two winters ago and snowing out. You'll probably have already noticed that the roads around here aren't the safest. Scrap that – it's a death trap if there's ice.'

I nod in agreement. The roads here are skinny and winding. Not safe, especially in winter.

'Mum was a careful driver. I used to make fun of her for how she always indicated early and never, ever exceeded the speed limit. The night it happened, she was going to see Alfred for dinner at Hobbs Manor. They'd been spending a lot of time together and I remember her asking me which earrings she should wear. And then, as she was driving up the hills, she full on collided with a speeding car. The driver of the other car was Jasper Hobbs.'

'Shit. What happened?'

'He'd just got a new sports car and thought it'd be a good idea to treat Little Trooley like his own personal racetrack.' He runs a hand over his stubble and frowns. 'Showing off to some girl he'd picked up in London. Mum didn't stand a chance.'

Gosh. No wonder he doesn't like Jasper.

I think about the article I saw online. It mentioned nothing of Jasper Hobbs.

'Was Jasper arrested?' I ask.

'Yeah. But he was cleared of dangerous driving. The whole thing was blamed on the icy roads and his entire involvement was hushed up. It's sickening what being rich can afford you. But I'd been in cars with Jasper before; I knew how reckless he was. Growing up with money has led him to believe he can do exactly what he likes without any consequences. But then it cost my mother her life.'

'Jesus,' I say softly. Poor Riley.

'And now he wants to take away my pub.' He spits. 'My mum's pub.'

'I'm sorry,' I say, reaching over to squeeze his shoulder.

'Cheers,' Riley says, blinking hard. 'I can't seem to let it go. I've tried, but . . . it's fucking difficult.'

'And what about your dad?' I ask, though I suspect I already know some version of the answer. The pain in his eyes is starker than I've ever seen in any person before.

'He died when I was one. Heart problems. My mum always said his heart was too big.'

He gives a half-hearted laugh.

'Oh God. Riley.'

'It's okay. I was too young to know what it meant. It being just Mum and me was the only life I knew. Us against the world and all that. I always felt I should have missed him more. But . . .' And then, as if that conversation never happened, he takes a deep breath and changes the subject.

'So, Natalie Elspeth Butterworth. You know I'm actually rather glad you're back here.'

Wow. What does *that* mean?

'Your ratatouille was a huge success.'

Oh.

Pleasure warms my body despite my embarrassment at thinking that he might just have meant something else.

'It was incredible. I've never seen people react that way to food before. They were sharing it with each other, asking for seconds and thirds, ordering some to take home to their wives and husbands. It was mad.'

His face lights up at the memory. It occurs to me that he may just be saying this stuff to be nice, but no, my ratatouille is that good, I'm sure of it.

'That's fantastic,' I laugh. 'I'm so glad I could help.'

'You did,' he nods and drains the last of his hot chocolate. 'But, if it's not too much trouble, I'd like to bend your ear some more. Your ratatouille has made me rethink the whole menu. The whole focus of what I'm trying to do.'

'Of course I'll help,' I say, covering an errant yawn with my hand.

'Great. Tomorrow then, before you leave. It shouldn't take long.'

He gets up and takes the sandwich plates over to the sink.

'Right,' he says, once he's rinsed them off. 'Well, you should probably get some sleep.'

'Yep. Defo. Thanks for the food.'

'My pleasure.'

'Oh, wait . . . where are *you* going to sleep?'

214

I'd forgotten I was taking over his room. I wonder if he's going to stay in there with me. On the floor, of course.

'Honey lives up the road. I'll sleep there.'

'Oh yes. Obviously,' I say, not entirely comfortable with the jealous sensation that prickles me.

'Well,' I say, brightly. 'Goodnight, Riley. Thanks for the song.'

'Goodnight, Miss Butterworth.'

I do a stupid little wave. And without looking back, I plod off to bed.

CHAPTER 19

Dionne is not happy. *Really* not happy. I haven't seen her this angry since Adam Rickitt left *Coronation Street*.

She storms into Riley's room early the next morning, Jean Paul Gaultier tucked under one arm, the other arm on her bony hip.

'We're fucking snowed in,' she fumes. 'Snowed. Fucking. In!'

I wipe away the sleepy dust from my eyes.

'Pardon?'

'Did I stutter? It's been snowing like a mother-fucker all night. And now we are stuck in this godforsaken village. I've had to phone work. They were *not* happy. I'm supposed to be seeing Bull tonight an' all!'

Oh no.

I scramble up on the bed and peer out of the window above the headboard.

Jesus Christ.

It's like Narnia out there. Every inch of land is covered in a thick layer of snow. And it's still falling.

'I'm so sorry. Are you *absolutely* sure you can't get the car out?'

Dionne huffs. 'Oh yes, I'm sure. I've been out there with a bleeding spade. A spade! It didn't do anything. I managed to clear the snow around the car. So, yes, I can drive a few inches back and a few inches forward. But other than that we're stuck. *I'm* stuck. Why did you have to faint? Why did you do that to me?'

Jean Paul Gaultier gives a little yelp as if confirming her speech.

'I didn't do it to you. It just happened. I don't know,' I answer truthfully. 'Calm down,' I try, rubbing my eyes and sipping from a bottle of water that's been put out on the bedside table.

'I've called Bull. He's working on it. Seeing if he knows someone. But your mate, the old dude with the red cheeks and the cap—'

'Alan?'

'Whatever. He says it won't clear for at least the next few days.'

'Oh. How does he know?'

'He says this happened before, two winters ago. That this place is one of the highest points in England. That it's too cold for the snow to melt and that no one can drive anywhere. I've not even got any fresh clothes with me! I probably stink.' She sniffs dramatically at her armpits. 'I *do* stink! Maaaaan.'

Oh crap. My stomach begins to churn uncomfortably as I realize the implications of being stuck here. I haven't got three days to waste. I need to sort out my wedding. And, you know, make friends with the groom. Plus, I need to sort things out with Mum.

'Shit.'

'With extra shit,' Dionne agrees.

The door bursts open once again. This time it's Meg, not looking at all troubled by the situation. In fact, she looks as happy as I've ever seen her.

'Isn't this exciting!' she trills, moseying over to sit on the bed.

'About as exciting as herpes,' Dionne huffs, throwing her a dirty look.

'You'd know,' Meg throws back before turning to me. 'It's like a film. There's a big commotion and everyone's here in the pub already. Get up! Get up and dressed! It's so romantic . . .'

'Is drinking really the answer?' I say worriedly, a sudden vision of the locals gathered around the bar doing absinthe shots in distress.

'I'm pretty sure it is for me,' Dionne pouts, storming out of the room, Jean Paul Gaultier in tow.

'They're not drinking, silly,' Meg giggles. 'They've all turned up to discuss a plan.'

'A plan?'

'Apparently Wonky-Faced Joe has a tractor—'

'Which one's Wonky-Faced Joe? I must've been pissed. I don't remember a Wonky-Faced Joe.'

'You do! Joe. Wonky face. Wonky-Faced Joe?'

'Oh, yes.'

'Well, he has a tractor.'

'Right?'

'But it's broken.'

'Oh.'

'And he knows someone who has a gritter.'

'Great!'

'But he can't get in touch with him.'

'Not so great.'

'So until the tractor is fixed or he can reach his mate with the gritter, and they can drive to the next village for supplies, they're planning for survival.'

'Ooh, that does sound exciting,' I say in spite of myself. 'Do they think we'll all die?'

'No one knows,' Meg says seriously. 'The snow doesn't look like it's stopping anytime soon.'

'What about my wedding?' I say in a small voice.

Meg ponders. 'It will definitely be cleared by then. I'm sure of it. And even if it's not, Wonky-Faced Joe's tractor will be fixed, and they'll be able to drive us home.'

'Hmm,' I say, not entirely reassured. 'But I still have lots of planning to do!'

'Not that much. It's pretty much finished, and your mother is taking care of the rest. Or we can do it online. God bless the internet.'

I sigh.

'Come on,' she chides. 'I brought a suitcase of clothes with me. Get a shower and I'll put you out an outfit. Hurry, we need to find out what we should do if we're going to beat this blizzard and stay alive!'

I use the en suite shower in Meg's room, delighted to find some of Mr Harrington's shampoo made from scratch. This time it's basil flavour. It's delicious. My hair smells like Italy.

Drying myself off, I look at the outfit Meg has laid out on her bed for me.

It's a dress. I haven't worn a dress since I was ten and was forced to wear one for the junior school maypole dance. My backside does not work in a dress.

I find Meg's suitcase and dig through it in the hopes of finding some trousers. But there are none. Just lots of dresses and skirts and sexy tops.

I sigh and pick up the dress from the bed again. It's actually one of my favourites. Well, when Meg wears it, of course. It's an emerald-green jacquard shift dress. It was all the rage last year at the fashion shows. Not that I know anything much about fashion, but it was hard to get away from this dress. It was the 'It' dress and in all of the shops. It's perfect for *Meg*. The cut of it accentuates her milkmaid curves beautifully.

I pull it on and look in the mirror. I look like an emerald-green sausage. I take it off immediately and decide to stick to the jeans I was wearing yesterday, but with one of Meg's very tight, very white T-shirts – the best of a slutty bunch.

I dig into her make-up bag and dash on some mascara and cheek stain. I fully ignore my lips. They are so gargantuan they need no highlighting at all.

I don't bother doing anything with my hair besides a quick comb through. There's no point. It's determined to look bad whatever I attempt. Stoopid Barbara the hairdresser.

I pull on my woolly blue cardigan and my trainers and, with a quick spritz of Meg's Ralph Lauren Romance, make my way downstairs to the pub.

Meg was right. This is a commotion if ever I saw one. And it is rather exciting.

The pub is chock-a-block with locals sipping on cups of tea and nattering away. It's buzzing. Meg is chatting animatedly to Morag and Barney Braithwaite and, from behind the bar, Alan is holding court while Riley hands out toast and juice to whoever wants it.

'Those of us who have wood-burning stoves would be best to invite those with oil-burning stoves over to stay,' Alan is saying, much to the approval of the rest of the people in the pub.

'Hear hear!'

'My oil will only last another day!'

'We have two spare rooms at our house. But men only, please!'

I smile at the fact that it's only the first morning of a snow-in yet the village are thriving on the notion of pulling together, of being a real community. It's heartening.

'I have lots of tins of tuna!' someone in the crowd calls out.

'I can knit extra blankets!' adds a gruff voice.

'I too have tuna to spare!'

'I can cook!' I call out, completely unaware until I hear the sound of my voice echoing back to me.

It's very infectious, this pulling together stuff. From her table Meg raises her eyebrows at me, laughing.

Someone prods me on the shoulder.

I turn around to see that it's Dionne, dressed in a stylish denim jumpsuit and a fur cape. Behind her, looking gorgeous and surprisingly friendly, is Honey.

'This is Honey,' Dionne says. 'She lent me some clothes. We're, like, exactly the same size.'

'We've met.' I smile warily at Honey. She smiles back but it doesn't quite reach her eyes.

'It's soooo good to see you again,' she says, twirling her wavy red hair around her finger.

'Oh. It's good to see you too,' I say, wondering what has brought about her apparent personality transplant.

'Yah, Riley said you were back,' she says in a southern, high-pitched tone. 'He said you fainted, you poor, poor thing.'

Her expression doesn't equal her words. She looks about as sympathetic as a wooden spoon.

'Um, yes.'

'It's a jolly good job he's so big and strong. Having to carry you to bed like that.'

She laughs. It's an irritating scratch of a noise.

I don't quite know how to respond to that. What she's saying isn't exactly rude, but it still bristles.

Honey turns to Dionne and blows her a kiss.

'I have to work now, sugar. But just pop by if you need anything at all. Bye-bye, dear Jean Paul Gaultier.' She wiggles her fingers daintily in an impression of a wave and floats off.

Dionne beams, staring with heart-shaped eyes as Honey saunters off to the bar.

'She's amazing,' Dionne sighs in admiration. 'I was outside, crying in the car, and up she comes like a tiny fashionista angel. Offers me the use of her clothes. Just like that.'

'That's nice.'

'And she goes out with that woodcutter lad, Riley. She told me he's great in bed – an animal, in fact! She said that when they're together, she—'

I feel sick as an unwelcome vision of Riley and Honey flashes into my head. I do not want to know this information. I do not want to know about them doing rude stuff to each other.

'Look, Dionne,' I butt in, my voice weirdly strangulated, 'I have to nip to the loo. Why don't you get us some tea and toast, find us a seat. I'll meet you back here in a second.'

And before she can answer I run to the ladies room, leaving her to stare after me.

223

I stand in front of the mirror and take deep breaths.

What is wrong with me? I'm about to marry the man of my dreams and here I am getting jealous over some guy I barely know. Some guy who has a girlfriend, no less.

And why the hell don't I know the answers to my own questions? I certainly know the answers to everyone else's!

I splash some cold water onto my face before going into a cubicle, pulling down the loo seat and sitting down.

Is it nerves? No, it can't be. I can't wait to marry Olly. The idea of sleeping with only one man for the rest of my life has never bothered me. I like the idea, the security. The comfort of knowing that one person is yours forever, and you are theirs.

Hmm. I wonder if the hypnotism made me into a sex maniac. That woman Alice said on the phone that sexually acting out was a very real and possible symptom . . . No. That can't be it. I don't fancy anyone else.

But I fancy Riley.

I fancy the spectacularly muscular arse off Riley. There.

I said it.

As I'm pondering this unsettling revelation there's an impatient knock on the cubicle door.

'Let me in!'

It's Meg.

'Oh noes.' She frowns when she sees my face.

'We're not really going to die, Natty. There's enough tinned tuna in this village to last seventy gazillion years.'

'Is that an exact number?' I ask, a slight grin lifting the corners of my mouth.

'It is. Really, Natty. What's wrong?'

'I fancy Riley,' I blurt out in answer to her question. My face contorts into a shamed grimace.

Meg is unperturbed.

'So what? He's hot! It'd be weird if you didn't fancy him!'

'So what? *So what?* I'm marrying Olly. I love Olly. I can't fancy anyone else.'

Meg crouches down so that her face is level with mine. She brushes her fine blonde hair out of her eyes.

'I've said this before and I'll say it again, pet. There is nowt wrong with being attracted to someone else. Loads of married couples probably have crushes on other people. You don't have to do anything about it.'

'But it's weird. I'm not used to feeling like this.'

'That's because you're lovely and loyal. It's only a crush.'

'A massive crush,' I correct.

'But you love Olly?'

'Yes.'

'See. That's the truth. That's the only thing that matters. As long as you love Olly, you're not going to act on a little crush. Stop fretting.'

She's right. I obviously do love Olly. The

truth-telling says so. And I'm excited about our wedding. About our life together as a family.

'You're right,' I say to Meg, feeling stupid for getting into such a tizz. I'll just stay out of Riley's way. Wait until the snow clears, go home and forget all about him.

'I'm always right. Anyway, come on.' She takes my hand. 'We don't want to miss all the free cups of tea.'

'No.' I follow her out. 'We definitely don't.'

CHAPTER 20

Text to: **Olly**
Thinking of you. Please text back. X

'We were so disappointed when you left the last time, duck. We had the whole media splash planned out!'

It's midday and the pub has emptied considerably. Mrs Grimes and the Braithwaites have gathered around a table with me and Meg. It's Operation Locate Brian reunited. Well, apart from Uncle Alan, who is off tending to his vegetables in the greenhouse.

Dionne has gone for a lie-down with all the stress of being snowed in and Barney Braithwaite is talking about putting me on the radio.

'I think it's your only hope now, love,' he says earnestly. 'Brian might be listening, or someone else who could help you.'

'We could put it on our site too,' Morag says, eyes alight. 'Little Trooley dot online dot co dot uk.'

'Oh yes. And I can do a video on my iPhone,'

says Mrs Grimes. 'My son could put it on YouTube. See if we can't get it to catch a virus!'

'It's viral, Edna. It's called going viral,' says Barney irritably. 'But she's right,' he says, turning back to me. 'You need all the publicity you can get, young lady. The more people who know about the hypnosis, the better chance there is of finding someone who can help you.'

Hmm. I don't really like the idea of going on the radio or on the internet, especially not in my dangerous state of mind. It's one thing to embarrass yourself in front of a few people. But loads of internet viewers and large radio audiences? That's quite another.

'I'm not sure there are any other options,' Meg shrugs. 'Brian really is nowhere to be found. Olly may be peeved at you right now, but there is no way he'll call off the wedding. You know that. And when you get to the church, you need to be able to take your vows with a completely clear head. You can't do that under mind control.'

'Oh yes. Vows are very important,' Mrs Grimes nods, glancing at Meg with approval.

'And worse,' Meg continues. 'What if the vicar asks you a question and you do the truth-telling bit and say something you regret?'

'I won't,' I answer at once.

'But you said to me that sometimes you don't even know what you think until it comes out of your mouth. The vicar might say, "Do you promise to love him in sickness and in health?" and you might say something daft, like, "Only in health – he's a real pain in the arse when he's got man flu.'"

It's supposed to be funny, but I don't laugh. Because as silly as it sounds, saying something like that is a very real possibility. Olly is horrible when he has man flu. Grumpy and groaning and shuffling from room to room, bumping into furniture. I could very well say that. It would ruin the entire day and our wedding memories would be forever tarnished.

'Okay,' I say, knowing that I have few or no alternatives. 'I'll do it.'

A little cheer goes up around the table.

'Good girl.' Barney rubs his hands together. 'The public will love it.'

What have I let myself in for?

Staying away from Riley is about as easy as threading a needle in boxing gloves. Especially since I agreed to let him bend my ear about his plans for serving food at The Old Whimsy.

While Meg is trekking through the snow to Hobbs Manor to do pop star stuff, and Dionne is talking Honey (I can only hope) half to death in the pub, Riley and I are sitting in the kitchen of dreams with a bottle of Barolo, a stack of battered-looking cookbooks, his mum's recipe notes and the scent of the beef stroganoff, which

Riley prepared earlier, wafting out from the oven and under our noses.

'And the thing is,' Riley is saying, 'your ratatouille made me realize that I was thinking in completely the wrong way. Yorkshire is stuffed full of poncy gastro pubs, with foams and jus and quenelles of everything under the sun. But it's also stuffed full of pubs that serve basic home-cooked pub grub. No taste and no flair. I was thinking I'd like The Old Whimsy to be somewhere in the middle.'

I take a sip of my wine and try not to think about how delicious he's looking today. That white T-shirt clings to his torso and arms. Revealing not a sculpted body like Olly's, but a strong, natural muscle definition. His slate-grey eyes are glowing with excitement at his plans.

'So somewhere in the middle. But a bit different, if you know what I mean. What do you think?'

He eyes me hopefully.

'I think it's a great idea,' I say at once. 'Home-cooked food with an indulgent twist.'

'Yes! The dishes people have grown up with, but taken to a new level. A bit more sophisticated.'

'I like it.'

'Really?' he asks, grinning madly.

'I do. But . . . are you sure you can take that on? I mean, it's hard enough to get basic dishes right. Putting a twist on them takes training.'

His smile falters. 'I was worried you might say that.'

Well, he did ask the question.

'I *have* been practising. Ever since I saw people's reaction to that ratatouille, I've been practising new dishes every day, you know.'

He gets up from the table and, putting on some flowery oven gloves, takes the stroganoff out of the oven. He sets it down in front of me and hands me a fork.

'What do you think?'

I pull a face, not happy at his blatant questioning.

'I'm sorry, I'll stop with the questions. I'd like to know what you think. No questions. I promise.'

I take a forkful of stroganoff, blowing gently first to cool it down.

I chew and taste, examining the flavours on my tongue. Hmm. It's meh. What a shame. I was so hoping it would knock my woolly socks off.

'The mushroom sauce is fine, though it could stand to be a tad creamier,' I say carefully. 'And the beef is a little bit sinewy . . . I can't taste any gherkins.'

'Gherkins?' he looks horrified.

'Yes! You must have gherkins in stroganoff. It's a definite improvement, though. You know, on the pigs' trotters.'

'But it's still not amazing.'

He doesn't say it as a question, so I don't have to answer. But looking at his face, disappointed after he's been trying so hard, I speak without thinking, and it's nothing to do with the hypnotism.

'Let me help you. I want to help.'

'Really?'

'Yeah, really. I don't know how long I'll be here for but your Uncle Alan says it will be at least three days before we can leave. It's not like I have anything else to do and I wouldn't mind the distraction . . . so I'll teach you.'

'In three days?'

'Sure. I can teach you a few of the recipes you want on the menu. It would be intense, but it's possible.'

'I can do intense,' he says, widening his eyes into a silly intense stare.

My heart flips.

'At least you'll have a good basis to be getting on with.'

'Thank you, Natalie,' he says sincerely. 'But . . . I'm afraid we can't afford to pay you. Except in beer. I could probably pay you in beer. Or bread.'

I nod slowly, thinking. 'All right. I'll do you a deal.'

'Go on?'

'I'll teach you six dishes in three days. And in return, you let Meg, Dionne and me stay here for free.'

'Done,' he says at once.

He holds out his hand for me to shake. I think

about last time we held hands when I cut my finger. Not a good idea.

I grab onto my wine glass and hold it up in a stupid toast instead.

'Done.'

CHAPTER 21

Email from: alisonbutterworth
To: nattyb
Subject: Re: Chatterley Wedding Checklist

Natalie,

You've buggered off again. I wish you would let me know when to expect you. It's like living with a fifteen-year-old again.

Dionne texted me to say that you were stuck in Yorkshire. How the bloody hell did that happen? I tried to ring you but for some reason I cannot get through.

Anyway, I just wanted to say that everything is on track for Christmas Eve.

I've thought long and hard about what you said. I'm afraid it's too late to change everything about the wedding now. You should have said something earlier – not blurted it out like that last week. It's your own fault.

I'm sure on the big day you will only notice Olly and not the decor which you might not like. If you don't, then tough. You'll just have to deal with it because I cannot face any more stress.

I have picked up your tiara, and your shoes have arrived. They are lovely, but you'll probably whinge about them too. There is just no pleasing some people.

All that is left to do is for you to choose a DJ as Mickey McCann who I had booked has been sent down for burglary.

I must go now as I am busy with the girls. We are playing bridge tonight, so lots to do.

From,
Your Mum.

I have never been so cold in my life. Seriously. Brrrr.

I'm trudging over to the Braithwaites' house, and while it's supposed to be only a five-minute walk, snowfall up to my knees and a whining Dionne are doubling the time it takes to reach their house on the other side of the green.

It's 6 p.m. and the village, though mega cold, is looking spectacular. Since I was last here a mammoth Christmas tree has been erected in the centre of the green. It sparkles with crystal-clear fairy lights that reflect gorgeously off the frozen pond and light our way. Most of the huge houses are now decked out with lights and decorations in time for Christmas. Actually, decked out is an understatement. Each stone house is festooned with holly wreaths and nativity scenes and lights in every shape, size and colour. It's truly magical.

Although it's a Friday evening, the hazardous weather means that most of the locals are tucked safely away inside their houses or the pub. Warm and snug.

I'm beginning to think that that's exactly where I should be, rather than out here in a pair of borrowed wellies that are two sizes too big and with a little sister who doesn't know when to shut up.

'My Uggs!' Dionne is squealing. 'My poor, poor Uggs. Ruined, they are. Do you know how expensive Uggs are? I'm so sorry, darling Uggs.'

'No, I don't,' I say, stomping through the snow. 'I appreciate you coming, but you didn't have to, you know. I'd have been all right on my own.'

Dionne pulls her scarf a little more snugly around her neck.

'I had to come. I can't have you going to some old stranger's house on your own.'

'It's Barney Braithwaite, Dionne!' I scold. 'He's got a wife. And probably loads of grandkids. And he used to work for BBC Radio 2.'

Dionne snorts. 'Well, I can be your agent then. I don't want them taking advantage of you on the internet and radio. And it's not like Meg is here to help, is it?'

'No,' I shrug. 'It's not.'

I haven't seen Meg since this morning. She's been living it up at Hobbs Manor all day. Lord knows what she's been doing all that time. I mean, how long does it take to 'lay down backing vocals'?

Do you know what? I bet she's shagging Jasper Hobbs. He *is* her idea of a perfect man, after all. Rich and typically handsome and with a recording studio in his massive house.

I make a note to myself to tell her what Riley told me when she gets back. Not that I want to put a dampener on things if she is embarking on a brand-new relationship. But I'm her friend. I should tell her everything I know. And what I know is that Jasper Hobbs doesn't sound like a particularly nice person.

We reach the Braithwaites' house, a beautiful chocolate-box cottage with twinkling star-shaped Christmas lights in every window.

I don't even get a chance to reach out to the gorgeous old-fashioned pewter knocker because the door is pulled open and Morag Braithwaite is standing there, red-cheeked and very happy to see us.

'Come in, come in, ducks,' she says warmly, waving us through to the living room. 'What a darling dog!' She reaches into Dionne's handbag and gives Jean Paul Gaultier a friendly ruffle. He eagerly licks her hand in a return greeting.

'Hi,' I say, noticing that she appears to have

done her hair differently. The curls are a little neater and it looks like it's been blasted with so much hairspray that five hundred high-powered wind machines would struggle to shift it.

The Braithwaites' living room is warm and cosy, full of low beams, rich colours and nooks and crannies. Christmas cards are propped up on every available surface. Brass ornaments hang off the walls and there is the most wonderful smell of cinnamon in the air.

'Take off your shoes, lovies. I'll put them in the airing cupboard. See if we can't get them dry.'

Dionne and I do as she says. I check my socks. Phew, no holes.

'I hope you like apple pie? It's my speciality.'

'Mmm, I love apple pie,' I say, beaming at such hospitality.

'Do you have vanilla ice cream?' Dionne asks. 'I like my apple pie with vanilla ice cream.'

'Ooh yes!' Morag clasps her hands together. 'Of course, petal. Whatever you like. Oh, this is exciting. It's been a while since we've had any young'uns up here!'

Dionne and I take a seat on the plump, pale blue sofa, while Morag bustles about pouring tea and slicing up apple pie.

'Barney is just upstairs in our media room. Getting things ready for you.'

Dionne sniggers at the very thought of there being anything as high-tech as a media room in this house.

As soon as Morag goes to the kitchen to fetch the ice cream she's forgotten to bring in, Dionne leans over towards me and whispers, 'Did she say media room?'

'Yes.'

'I bet it's, like, a tape deck and a Commodore 64. Ha, or a gramophone!'

'Shh!' I hiss, as Morag returns with the ice cream.

'There you go,' she says cheerfully, spooning some out into Dionne's dish. 'Enjoy!'

We tuck in. Oh yum. This is amongst the most delicious things I've ever had in my mouth.

'It's scrumptious!' I say, mouth still full.

'Mmm-hmm,' Dionne chimes in, looking even more pleased than me.

'Oh, it's an old family recipe,' says Morag, flushed with pleasure. She drops her voice. 'A dash of whisky in the apple sauce!'

I nod with approval. Whisky!

'Morag, dear! Send them up, please!'

It's Barney, his voice coming from somewhere upstairs.

'He's ready,' Morag says. 'Eat up now and I'll show you girls to our media room.'

Dionne and I scoff the remainder of our pie and follow Morag up some creaky stairs. Tons of photographs are hung up neatly above the banister. At each step Morag explains who the picture is of.

'And that's our daughter Amy, with Barney, of

course. Amy lives in London. She's very clever. A bigwig in a bank.'

Next step.

'And this here is our old cat, Paws. She passed three years ago.'

Next step.

'Here we are at our holiday apartment in Paris. We don't get to go as often as we'd like. Barney's always so busy.'

'It looks lovely.'

And this is Barney with the editor of the *Daily World*. He used to work there!'

'Morag!' comes Barney's voice. 'Are you showing them those bloody photographs? Let them get up the stairs, for chuff's sake!'

Morag chuckles and turns to us. 'We best get up there then.'

The stair/photograph tour comes to an abrupt end as Morag leads us through a flock-wallpaper-decorated hallway, up a couple more steps and to a cream-painted door with a sign that says, 'MEDIA ROOM. PLEASE KNOCK BEFORE ENTERING'.

Morag knocks three times. Beside me Dionne giggles quietly. I nudge her and frown, though I must admit that it is a little funny.

'You may enter!'

Morag pushes open the door with a flourish. And oh my! It is actually a media room.

Next to me I hear Dionne gasp.

Morag smiles proudly.

'It's rather snazzy, isn't it, ducks?'

'We're going to record *as live.* Which means that the listeners will think it's live. But it won't be. It will be *as live.* It will actually go on air in the morning. It gives us a chance to edit things a little.'

I'm sat on one of those leather twisty chairs at Barney's control desk, still in shock at the fact that this room exists in this traditional cottage. There are three – three! – flat-screen computer monitors lined up on a long, pale, curved desk, wires and headphones everywhere, and even an orange light on the wall. Apparently when we're recording it will go red. The walls are hung with pictures of Barney, obviously once quite a successful journalist. There's a picture of him with Shirley Bassey. And, bloomin' heck, one of him with Phil Collins and Cliff Richard!

Wow.

Morag is busy typing away at one end of the desk, ready to transcribe my interview on the radio for her Little Trooley blog site, and Dionne is sat on a brown leather sofa on the other side of the room, texting on her phone.

'So . . . obviously I'll be asking you some questions,' Barney is saying, fiddling with dials on the computer. It's odd. He looks different in here. Like a mogul! It's comforting that he obviously knows what he's doing.

'Please don't ask me anything . . . private,' I say, fingering a stray piece of wool on my cardigan. I have to make sure that this interview isn't just another opportunity to embarrass myself, to get myself into more trouble.

'He won't, love,' Morag says kindly.

'Of course I won't,' Barney shakes his head. 'I'll just ask you questions about what has happened to you. And why you want to find Brian. Don't worry, lass. It's all under control.'

'Okay.'

'And we'll be filming the interview for YouTube, too.'

He gestures to a top-of-the-range camcorder propped up on a tripod and pointing directly at me.

'Oh. Won't that be a bit boring?' I ask, curious. 'The same thing on the radio, website and on YouTube?'

'Of course not! The medium is the message, Natalie.' Barney rolls his eyes.

'Oh yes. The medium is the message, Natalie,' Morag agrees, nodding fervently.

'The medium is defo the message,' Dionne pipes up, looking knowledgeable for a brief moment.

I have absolutely no clue what that means, but it's obvious that they all think I should know that the medium is the message . . . so I nod along like I get it and pat my hair in an attempt to get rid of any remaining snowflakes. I *am* going to be on the internet after all.

242

'Oh dear,' Morag says suddenly. 'You'll need make-up for onscreen. We don't want you looking ghostly!'

'Oh, I'm fine,' I say quickly, absently touching my ginormous lips and thinking about the last makeover I had.

'No. No. We must. Just a bit of powder to stop the shine, my love. And perhaps a little rouge.'

A bit of powder? Rouge? I can live with that.

I nod my agreement and Morag hurries out of the media room to get her make-up bag.

While she's gone Dionne puts her phone back inside her bag and says, 'So when is it all going to be on then?'

I don't know if it's my imagination, but I'm sure Barney looks irritated for a second. He has already told us it will all go out tomorrow morning after editing. I tell Dionne this and she shrugs, taking her phone back out of her bag and starting to text again.

I do an apologetic face at Barney, but he's too busy fiddling with the computer again to notice.

'Here we are!' Morag scuttles back in.

I sit patiently while she dabs a musty-smelling powder over my forehead and nose. She takes out a peach-coloured panstick and rubs it into the apples of my cheeks.

When she's done, Barney hands me a pair of massive earphones. They feel heavy on my head. He nudges one of the microphones on the desk over to me, flicks a switch on the camcorder and

243

then something on the computer screen. He wheels around on his chair, facing me now with a wide, eager smile.

'Let us proceed.'

I'm aiming for somewhere between Terry Wogan and his silky smooth radio voice and Sarah Cox with the whole carefree, cheeky northerner thing. But I'm so nervous that I start doing this curious posh accent. And my voice is dead high. I'm pretty much landing somewhere between Joanna Lumley and a whistle.

It's a good job this is all going to be edited. Barney asks me far more questions than I expected, and much more probing ones too. The interview starts off simply enough, but goes downhill when Barney asks me to tell the audience *exactly* what happened with Olly. Dionne sits there agog as I blurt out everything in my new plummy accent. I explain how he was bad at sex and how his cooking skills were no better. I confessed that I wished he was taller and that I hated the perfume he got me for my birthday. Everything.

After Barney asks me what my worst habit is, whether I give to charity and why it's so important for me to marry Olly, I'm exhausted.

As if that isn't enough, Barney asks me what I like best about Little Trooley, which you'd think would be a pretty straightforward question. Only it isn't.

'I like the people,' I squeak. 'In particular Riley from The Old Whimsy. He's very handsome. I'd like to have sex with him.'

Dionne laughs her head off at this, but I'm mortified. I know it will be edited out but I can't believe I said it out loud. In front of Morag!

Aware that I'm still being recorded, I do a cutthroat motion with my hands. I'm ready to stop answering questions.

Barney nods curtly and wraps up the interview by asking the audience to get in touch if they have seen or know Brian Fernando, or think they might be able to help me.

He switches off the record buttons on the camera and computer and removes my headphones.

'You did very well, love,' he says.

'You will edit out the bit about, um, Riley and Olly, won't you? And when I said I don't care about the Queen or *The X Factor*? That has to go, else I'll be lynched.'

'Of course, of course,' Brian nods, patting my knee. 'We'll make it very sympathetic.'

Phew. Sympathetic is good.

'Can we go now?' Dionne stands up and stretches. 'That was *so* funny. You really do have to tell the truth! It's amazing.'

I ignore her and follow Morag, who hands me my wellies and Dionne her Uggs and sees us out.

'It'll be on the air at 9 a.m., sweethearts, and on the website a little later. Thanks for stopping by. It's been a pleasure to have you here. I'll see you both in t'morning.'

'Thanks for the pie!' I say, as Morag envelops me and then Dionne into a lovely warm hug.

'Yeah, the pie was cracking,' Dionne grins.

And we leave, making our way back across the snow-covered green and back to The Old Whimsy, our way lit by the twinkling Christmas lights of every house in the village.

CHAPTER 22

Email from: stone_chutneys
To: nattyb
Subject: (No Subject)

Hiya kidda,
  I'm guessing you're feeling like shit right about now. Probably climbing the walls and wishing that you had never been born. Detox is a bitch like that. I wanted to let you know that I am cheering for you and I was also wondering if you knew what Marie's favourite perfume is?
  Good luck.
  Best,
  Stone.

The next morning there's a real buzz in the air. Not only is it the night of Mrs Grimes's barn dance fundraiser, but before that I'm going to be on the radio!

I'll be honest. I'm quite excited at the prospect of hearing myself on the airwaves.

Of course, it's only a local station, and there'll

be hardly anyone listening, but it's still the radio! I feel like a little celebrity. Not to mention the fact that the chances of finding Brian after the media splash are greatly increased. That's the most exciting thing of all.

My thrill of being on the airwaves is enhanced by the fact that Dionne and Meg, Morag Braithwaite, Mrs Grimes and Uncle Alan are all gathered around a pub table, a portable radio pride of place in the middle.

'It's time!' Morag chirps, switching the radio on and turning it right up. As the end of a Duran Duran song plays out, Riley hurries in from the kitchen with a bowl of warm popcorn and takes a seat at the table.

'Hurry up, Duran Duran!' Dionne tantrums.

'Shh!' Meg hisses at her. 'It's on!'

Barney's voice blasts out through the speakers.

'And now on Radio Trooley we have a very interesting guest . . . Natalie Butterworth . . .'

It's funny how everyone stares at the radio as my interview begins, like it's a TV.

As my voice comes through I feel a thrill. I don't sound as squeaky as I thought I would. I sound rather nice! Nice and friendly and proper. Morag beams at me, a mobile in hand, ready to take calls from any listeners with potential leads.

'You sound really posh!' Meg laughs.

'Ooh, that was me coughing in the background!' Dionne cries. 'I'm famous!' She does a royal wave at the rest of us.

I start to relax as the interview continues. I'm actually coming across really well. I'm clear about my plight. I'm not stuttering. I feel a little glimmer of pride. Maybe cooking is not the only talent I have . . .

But the interview continues and I realize that NOTHING has been edited. Nothing at all. Out come the questions about Olly and, with them, my answers. My own treacherous voice, discussing mine and Olly's sex life. The sound of my incessant truth chatter echoes in my head.

My heart starts to hop like a Mexican jumping bean.

'What's your worst habit?'

'I pick my toenails. I find it therapeutic.'

Oh brother, how embarrassing! Dionne and Meg crack up, while Mrs Grimes glances at me with ill-disguised disgust. Riley appears to be stifling a chuckle.

But my toenail confession is nothing compared to what happens next. It gets a whole lot worse.

'And what do you like about Little Trooley?'

Oh. My. God. Barney! Don't ask it! I will myself not to answer but it's pre-recorded. I already *have* answered. What's gone wrong? He agreed to edit it!

I reach out for the radio to switch it off, but Mrs Grimes snatches it up and clasps it to her chest. 'It's not finished yet,' she tuts.

My voice no longer sounds nice and friendly on the radio. It sounds perfidious and humiliating.

'The people. Especially Riley from The Old Whimsy. I'd like to have sex with him.'

A small gasp goes up around the table. Mrs Grimes turns off the dial in a flash.

'Well, that's quite enough of that!'

Morag is red-faced. 'Dear me. There's obviously been some kind of *technical* difficulty. I'm going to find out what's going on, love. I'm ever so sorry.' She scuttles off out of the pub.

I can hear the blood rushing into my ears. Shit.

Meg grabs my hand and squeezes. I can't even look at Riley. He must sense my acute embarrassment because he lumbers back to the kitchen without a word.

My God.

'Oh Balls,' Dionne whispers.

I look at her. She looks all pale, like she's going to be sick. Jesus. She's really embarrassed for me.

'It's all right,' I say, putting my arm around her instinctively.

'No, it's not,' she says, tears flooding her eyes. 'I texted Olly last night from the Braithwaites'. Told him to tune in so he would hear that bit you said about how much you loved him.'

'What?' Now my face drains, my hands begin to twitch.

'I thought they'd cut the other stuff out. I thought it would help. I'm so sorry,' she pleads. 'Natalie . . . I think Olly heard everything.'

I don't know what to say to that. I can't say anything. My vocal cords have stopped working.

250

My mouth has gone dry and my eyes start to blur.

I grab my bag and run out of the pub.

Please don't let Olly have heard. Please let him have been out. Please let him not have been able to tune in to the Little Trooley frequency.

I'm standing by the pond on the green, getting some air, when my phone beeps with a text.

> Text from: **Olly Chatterley**
> Nice interview. Enjoy long-lasting sex with the barman. I can't do this. Wedding off. Olly.

I stare at it. Not entirely sure that it's real, that this is actually happening. My knees wobble precariously. I rush to a bench and sit down, unbothered by the snow that seeps in through my jeans. I'll probably get nappy rash. I don't care.

I hold the phone in my shaking hands; it feels heavy and clunky, like a phone from twenty years ago.

Should I ring him?

No. I can't. It will only make things worse. I can't trust myself to speak to Olly until Brian comes back. And the chances of that happening before Christmas Eve are slim to none. What was I doing? Thinking that an interview was a good idea? That people could be trusted?

Anger washes over me, stinging my skin and

pulling and tugging at my lungs so that it gets harder to breathe.

What the fuck was Barney doing? He promised me he would edit it. He promised.

I put my phone back into my bag and march furiously through the snow to the Braithwaites' house.

Morag opens the door, her face all flushed.

'Oh, love. Oh, poor love. I'm ever so sorry.'

Barney appears from the hall. He doesn't look in the least bit sorry. In fact, he looks positively thrilled.

'What on earth happened?' I ask, my voice trembling.

'Oh, lass. Don't get so worked up,' Barney dismisses. 'This is just the nature of news! You have to give the public what they want.'

His voice has a patronizing edge. He no longer looks like a cuddly old Yorkshire man. He looks like . . . he looks like a shark.

'You did it on purpose?'

'Ah, don't be so naïve. This way the story will get lots more attention. It'll probably get picked up regionally, nationally even! Far more chance that someone will find Brian.'

I start to sob openly. I'm pretty sure that there's a snot bubble poking out of my left nostril.

'I don't need Brian anymore!' I half shout, half bawl. 'Thanks to you, Olly has called off the wedding. He's called the whole thing off! It doesn't matter what happens now!'

A flicker of guilt flashes over Barney's face. Morag shakes her head sadly.

'Come in, love.' She opens the door wider. 'Let's sort this out. There've already been some phone calls. Barney might be a git, but . . . he might also be right.'

I shake my head. I don't want to sort this out. There is nothing to sort out.

I kick at the snow roughly and turn on my heel. Fuck this.

I've been stomping through the snow for half an hour. And now I'm lost. It wouldn't be so bad, but everything is covered in white. There are no distinguishing features around. No buildings, no postboxes, nothing.

I stand in the middle of nowhere and glance around at my surroundings. I'm getting cold now.

I shiver and look behind me. Where did I turn? Which way did I come from?

I feel like Dorothy from *The Wizard of Oz* as I struggle to make the decision to turn left or right. If only there was a creepy scarecrow to assist.

I sigh and decide on left.

After another ten minutes I realize that left was wrong. I come to an area full of gnarled-looking bare trees. I stride along, fighting my way through branches and twigs. A few of them poke through my cardigan. No doubt they'll leave a scratch.

All of a sudden I come out of a clearing and

arrive at what looks like a waterfall. Only – oh my goodness – it's frozen.

I amble over slowly, taking it all in. Oh my gosh. It *is* a frozen waterfall!

It's incredible. Solid and crystal clear, as if someone pressed pause on the water flow and it has been flawlessly captured in its descent.

I have a memory of looking on the map the first time Meg and I were driving here. There was a waterfall . . . what was it called?

Truth Springs. That's it. How bloody apt.

That seems like so long ago now.

I stand in the bitter cold, the complete lack of noise hurting my ears, and wonder whether to make a wish.

Can you even make wishes on a waterfall? Surely it's just wishing wells and fountains, but right now I could really do with a wish. And this here is a frozen waterfall. It's not every day you get to see a frozen waterfall.

Pulling my blue Aran cardigan more tightly around my shoulders, I brush some twigs off a crooked overturned log and sink onto it. Exhaling long and loud, I watch as a misty cloud forms in front of me and then dissolves as if it were never there.

I've managed to stop crying, which is a good thing. I've never shed so many tears in one sob session before. Any more and I'm pretty sure they would have started to freeze into icicles.

I tremble slightly and gaze at the frozen

waterfall, taking in the way the formations of ice look like turrets on some kind of enchanted ice castle. Wow.

I close my eyes and I wish.

I wish that Olly would forgive me for the awful stuff that I said.

I wish that Barney Braithwaite could be trusted.

I wish that Brian would come back and fix what he has broken.

I wish that I'd never said those horrible things to Mum. My poor mum.

I wish that it will all be okay.

I wish that my hair was better.

I cross my fingers and I wish and wish with all of my weary heart.

In the moment that I make my wish, a tiny robin redbreast flies out from the trees, sails across the waterfall and lands swiftly on the log beside me.

'Hello,' I whisper, not wanting to frighten it away. I stare as the robin shuffles its wings and dips its head down to taste the snow.

'You're a handsome fellow,' I murmur, jolted by how the sound of my voice seems to muddy up this clean, untainted silence.

My heart quickens and trips over itself as the robin scoots further along the log and then hops up onto my knee. Its head twitches as if it's listening out for something. I listen hard too, but there's nothing. It's completely, utterly still.

I look around, willing someone else to materialize and witness this . . . this miracle!

Maybe it's a sign, I think to myself. A sign that everything *is* going to be okay. That my life might be in complete ruins right now but it might just figure itself out.

'Are you a sign?' I whisper again, not feeling quite as daft as I thought I would, you know, having a natter with a bird.

Quite unexpectedly, the robin cheeps. It's a high-pitched, clear, beautiful sound.

It hops off my knee and darts behind me. I spin around to watch it. It pauses for a second, twitches its head back at me, and then flies upwards, circling for a few moments before disappearing into the leaden sky.

'Bye then, Mr Robin.'

I get up from the log and stretch out my legs. Tentatively, I step into the area of woodland that the robin has just flown away from. I cast a glance over my shoulder and take one last long look at the waterfall. It may have stopped for now, frozen and stuck right in the middle of its journey to the river, but soon spring will arrive and the waterfall will flow again, naturally confident of its purpose, where it's going and where it's supposed to end up.

I wonder if spring will come for me too.

Where will I end up?

I walk forward, through the tall, barren trees. One hundred per cent sure that a solitary little robin has shown me the way to get home.

★   ★   ★

I don't speak to anyone for the rest of the afternoon; I just sit in my room at The Old Whimsy (I've moved from Riley's bedroom to upstairs), look out at the snow, reread Olly's text message over and over, and get irritated at the fact that I'm unable to sleep – the only thing I actually feel like doing.

At about five o'clock Dionne and Meg burst in, looking to stage some kind of cheer-me-up intervention.

In the middle of them listing all the reasons why it's not all bad, I silently take my phone from beside me on the bed, find the text message and hand the phone over to Meg. That pisses on their chips.

Meg puts her hand to her chest while she's reading Olly's message.

'Shit. Oh, Natty.'

Dionne grabs the phone from her. 'Gimme!'

Her eyes widen and she tuts. 'He can't do that! He can't call off the wedding!'

'He did,' I say wearily. 'And he had every right to.'

'But . . . but all my hard work! All Mum's hard work!'

I glare at her, willing her to hear the stupidity of what she's just said, but she doesn't.

'It wasn't even that bad, what you said on the radio. I mean, obviously he's, like, embarrassed or whatever, but to call everything off! What a selfish git. Does he have any clue how much time

257

I've spent on this? How long it took Bull to find that swan cake? What I had to do to—'

'Shut Up, Dionne!' I cry, unable to take anymore. 'Just . . . shut up!'

She jumps like I've punched her. I've never raised my voice to her. No matter how many times I've wanted to, I never have. To her credit, she shuts up at once. I instantly feel bad. I should apologize, but I don't get the chance.

'I can see I'm totally not needed here,' she pouts.

'Dionne, I'm—'

'No. No need. I'm, like, out of here.'

She stalks out of the room, slamming the door behind her.

'Aaaargh!'

I put my head in my hands and exhale slowly.

I'm so, so tired.

'Come on, now,' Meg says, putting her arms around me and pulling me into a hug.

'It's all ruined,' I cry. 'It's finished. I'm stuck here. Olly's dumped me. I just continue to upset people and Brian's still missing. It's all sodding ruined.'

Meg places her hand under my chin and gently lifts my head up.

'It's ruined today. That's all. Just today.'

'What am I supposed to do?'

She puffs her cheeks out. 'I honestly don't know, pet. Wait it out . . . Wait for him to cool down . . .'

'What if he doesn't?'

Our whole relationship, just . . . poof! Dissolved because of a stupid radio interview. That can't be it.

Meg shrugs again. 'I think you need a drink.'

That observation is the most appealing thing I've heard all day.

'I think I do.'

'It's the barn dance tonight.'

'Oh crap. I agreed to help Riley with the food. He must be wondering where I am. I'm such a bloody let-down!'

'He'll understand, I'm sure. Come on. Come up to my room, have a shower, we'll get dressed all sexy and do our hair. And then we'll go to the barn dance and drink lots and let loose a bit.'

We look at each other for a few moments, the very notion of what is happening – the fact that my wedding has been called off, we're stuck in a nowhere village and are now attending a barn dance – too peculiar to bear.

Then Meg does this huge, overexaggerated sad shrug. Like she's at an absolute, complete loss for what to say or do in this, the most unexpected of life situations.

The expression on her face is ridiculous, and despite the fact that I want to bawl and blub, a little laugh trickles out instead.

Meg jumps at the noise, pressing her hand to her chest in fright. And then she laughs too. It comes out like a horn, in one loud blast. Her face creases with mirth, her eyebrows dropping low as she cracks up. That sets me off properly and I snort. We look at each other again and before I know what's happening we're rolling around on the bed, spluttering with laughter. There are tears streaming down our faces.

'Oh nohohohohoh!' I collapse, clutching my stomach. 'This is just tooooo weird!'

As we laugh like loons, the door bursts open and Dionne comes back in, her hair in rollers and her face as much like thunder as it's possible to get with all that Botox in there.

'Well, I'm glad you find this all soooo hilarious,' she snarls, before storming out.

And that makes us laugh even harder.

CHAPTER 23

Text from: **Mum**
Olly is in bits. What have you done?!

I'm in somewhat of a reckless mood. It could be to do with the double vodka and cranberry juice I'm currently sipping on, but it's more likely the fact that I've been dumped by my fiancé that's making me feel like I could do just about anything and it wouldn't matter. It's a bittersweet mixture of pure abandon and a deep ache in the pit of my stomach.

It's not like I have anything to lose now, anyway.

After many years of her trying and failing to get her hands on me, I've finally agreed to give Meg complete control over my 'look'. Everything. Hair, make-up, outfit, shoes, jewellery . . .

It's an effective distraction: the excitement that I might *not* come out of her style renovation looking like a drag queen and the fear that I most probably will.

Meg's face is full of concentration as she wraps strands of my hair carefully around a set of curling tongs. Her tongue pokes out of the side of her mouth as she focuses on not burning herself.

'Are you sure it won't look funny curled? It's so short.'

'No. Trust me.'

I have no other choice but to trust her. She's covered all the mirrors in the room with pillow-cases, which (apart from being super creepy) makes sure I have no idea whether the curls she's putting into my hair are Meg Ryan or Justin Timberlake circa 1998.

Speaking of bands . . . 'Are you doing the rude stuff with Jasper Hobbs?'

'Nat!' She pulls my hair with the tongs.

'What? I can't be the only one blurting things out about my sex life around here. Fess up.'

'He's nice. Lovely. But no. I'm not doing the rude stuff with him.'

'Really?'

'Really. Not through lack of flirting, mind. He's got a girlfriend. It's annoying because he's the perfect man.'

'That's not what Riley thinks,' I say, thinking back to his tale about Jasper Hobbs in the car two years ago. I consider telling Meg the story, but decide against it. It's kind of sensitive. And I've already blurted out enough secrets around here. Besides which, there's no point in warning her off if there's nothing going on. 'Have you met his girlfriend?' I ask.

'No. She's never around . . . I wonder if she even exists. Maybe she doesn't. Maybe Jasper made her up to stop me from coming on to him. Oh jeez. I bet that's it. I'm vile.'

'Shut up. Robbie fancies you.'

'Oh God, I know. He won't leave me alone. He's always hanging around trying to do things for me. You know, yesterday he brought me hot water with honey in case the cold weather affected my voice!'

I laugh. 'He's cute. Do you not fancy him?'

'Nope.'

'But you—'

'I know. I was very drunk. He's definitely not my type. He's a friend type of bloke. It was kind of sweet with the honey water.'

'Very sweet,' I say, thinking about Robbie and his cute baby face. 'He really is cute. And he was great singing in the band. AND he caught me when I fainted. He practically saved the life of your best friend, Meg. I could be dead if not for him and then where would we be?'

'Natty. I see what you're doing. Stop talking. Time to do your make-up.'

After an hour of having my face painted, the vodka cranberries I've been sipping at are not doing quite enough to keep me from getting antsy.

'Are you nearly done?' I whine. 'I want to go to the dance.'

'Stop moving your mouth, Cinderella,' Meg scolds. 'It'll make your eyeliner wobbly.'

I harrumph as motionlessly as I can – no one likes wobbly eyeliner – and within a minute or two Meg announces that she is done.

'About time.'

I stand up from the chair and shake out the pins and needles in my legs; the sudden movement after being sat down for so long makes my eyes go bleary.

'Whoa!' I say, flopping back into the chair.

Meg takes the vodka glass away. 'Don't go so fast! You'll have no room left.'

I sulk.

'Let me see then!'

'You're not dressed yet.'

'Oh yeah.'

Meg hurries over to the closet and rifles through, eventually pulling out one of her dresses.

'It doesn't fit me very well, but it's probably perfect for you,' she says, handing it over.

I've not seen this one before. It's short and black with delicate beading running through the material in loops. I hold it out in front of me. The top half has a high neck at the front and a low back. The waist is nipped in and the skirt is flippy. It's lovely. Sexy. But not something I could get away with.

'Do you have something a bit more . . . .'

'Nope. That's the only one. At least try it on!'

Well, I suppose I did agree to relinquish all control over to Meg.

I pull the dress over my head. It doesn't feel

tight, which is good. Meg zips up the side panel for me and ties the dress at the back of my neck.

'Wowsers,' she beams, standing back to look at me.

'Wowsers, I look like a chump?'

She ignores me and pulls out a pair of silver shoes. Dangerously high and a size too big.

'They're too big!'

'Beauty is as beauty does,' she says solemnly.

I don't think she's quite got the hang of that saying.

'You can't wear your trainers,' she continues. 'You can put your wellies on to walk over to the barn, and then switch into these.'

'They'll fall off!'

'We'll stuff the toes.' Meg hurries over to her make-up bag and pulls out a couple of new foundation sponges from a pack. She grabs the shoes and pushes the sponges into the ends.

I try them on again. I do a miniature walk across the room. Little shuffling steps. That's not bad at all.

Meg hands me a pair of silver drop earrings in the shape of snowflakes before declaring me done.

She positions a mirror in front of me and after counting to three, pulls off the pillowcase with a flourish.

Oh. My. Gosh!

I gaze at my reflection, a slow smile creeping across my face.

I look hot.

My hair isn't curly at all. It's in a kind of bouffant at the top and flipped out at the ends and Meg has zigzagged the parting so that the tabby cat stripes are only half as obvious. I peer at my face. My eyes look big and dramatic; the eyeliner wings out and my eyelashes look all fluttery. My mammoth lips actually look very sexy, lined in a way that makes them look slightly smaller, and dabbed with clear lip gloss so that there's the merest hint of shine.

And the dress! It flatters my modest cup size, skims softly over my hips and . . . and I have a *waist*!

'You are GOOD!' I hug Meg, who is clapping with glee.

'Told ya! You look like Brigitte Bardot.'

I turn back to the mirror.

'You know what? I actually do!' I chuckle with excitement. Whoa.

'I'm afraid it isn't *quite* barn dance attire,' Meg apologizes with a giggle.

'No, it isn't,' I agree, patting my newly shiny locks. 'It's way better!'

Unable to drive anywhere in the snow, I throw on some wellies and my puffa jacket and trundle alongside Meg, halfway up the hill where Mrs Grimes's barn is. We're carrying a huge rainbow-striped golfing umbrella to protect our outfits and hair from the flurry of snowflakes that are still falling thick and fast.

Meg looks gorgeous. She's donned her favourite cherry-red tea dress and put her hair in a sophisticated marcel wave. Her lips are painted in the same red as her dress and she's brought a black faux-fur shrug to put on once we get inside and take our coats off.

As stunning as she looks, I find myself, for once, not feeling like the less impressive sidekick. The feeling of abandon flickering away inside of me, and the fact that I know I have never looked as put together as this, gives me a sense of confidence I've never had. I am rather enjoying it. I'm Audrey Hepburn, graceful and poised. Ooh, or Jessica Rabbit, ginger and sultry. No. Jessica Rabbit is a cartoon. I'm Beyoncé, a veritable firecracker of . . .

I'm a bit tiddly, I think.

There's a tent erected outside of the barn where Meg and I change out of our wellies and coats and put them on one of the designated hangers, manned by an old lady reading a Mills and Boon.

Slipping into our high heels, we totter across from the tent to the barn and open the door, being careful to shut it again just as quickly so that the blizzard doesn't enter along with us.

So, this is what a barn dance looks like.

The party is already in full swing. People are

milling about with pints of amber-coloured ale; some are dancing on a makeshift dance floor in the centre of the room. Ohmigosh, over there is a group of blokes dressed kind of like Morris men, bopping about with swords.

I look around, impressed with what Mrs Grimes has put together. The crooked beams on the ceiling are strung with colourful lanterns and fairy lights, casting a warm, jovial glow upon the room. Chunky bales of hay are dotted haphazardly here and there, tables from the pub are covered in fresh linen and surrounded by chattering locals and right at the front is a big handmade banner, carefully stencilled in electric blue paint and reading, 'Save The Old Whimsy Barn Dance'.

In front of the blue banner the band is playing. It's the same band I saw in The Old Whimsy. Robbie, some short red-headed guy I don't know, and a hairy bass player. They're playing some kind of upbeat folk song and look like they're having a hell of a time, dancing and stamping their feet as they play their instruments. Riley isn't with them and I instinctively glance around the room trying to spot him.

There he is.

He's stood behind a long wooden table, carving up a smoky hog roast for hungry dancers. He's clearly busy and doesn't notice me come in, which is exactly as I want it to be.

Obviously.

After what I said on the radio, I suspect any interaction with him would probably cause me to spontaneously combust with pure mortification.

I ignore that distressing train of thought and follow Meg to a rough-and-ready bar area – a table, a few barrels, buckets of beer, bottles of wine and lots of paper cups – and help myself to a cup of wine.

'The band is brill,' Meg shouts over the noise. 'I'm going to dance!'

I don't quite feel like being left alone yet, but Meg looks very keen to bop. I wave her off and lurk at the edges of the room, jigging a little in time to the music.

The buzz of partying people and deafening music isn't doing as great a job of distracting me as I'd hoped, and as I stand on the fringes of it all I find my mind drifting to Olly.

It's almost as if the whole thing is yet to sink in properly. An entire relationship just vanished with a text message. My stomach lurches as I think about the fact that the brand-new perfect family I had been counting on having with Olly, the escape I've been wanting for so long, has just slipped away. It surprises me that I'm surprised. Experience tells me that men leave when the going gets tough. That's what they do. Why should Olly be any different?

Now I'll be stuck. Stuck living with Mum until I can save for a place of my own. Stuck in an everlasting childhood. Getting up, going to work, going to bed. Over and over and over.

Oh shit. Mum. All her hard work has been for nothing. Damn it.

My thoughts echo back through my head and it occurs to me how weak I sound, like an anti-feminist. But when you've spent so much time with an idea, an expectation stuck so firmly in your head – *I am going to be married, I am going to have a family of my own, I will be a grown-up* – it's bloody hard to take when that notion has disappeared. You're left not knowing what the hell is supposed to happen to you next.

I think about Brian, wherever he is, doing whatever he's doing, with no idea that he has taken an innocent woman's life and sent it into free fall. I try to send a message to him telepathically.

What? You never know. Hypnotism, psychic abilities – they're all the same jurisdiction. Kind of.

I close my eyes so tightly that I can see imprints of the barn lanterns on my retinas.

Brian, if you can hear me, please come back. Please come back and fix me so I can have my life back.

Hmm. Actually, politeness has not been working well so far. I close my eyes again.

Brian, you bastard. You better come back and sort this out. Or else I will . . . I will be very mad. I'm unstable enough as it is at the moment. Who knows what I'm capable of doing? If you get this message in your brain, I strongly suggest that you come back from wherever you are and fix me at once. At once!

I open my eyes and half expect the doors to burst open, Brian lumbering in wearing his jumper and announcing that he is going to make everything better. But he doesn't. Of course he doesn't.

I go to drink my wine and notice that the cup is already empty. God. Everything is going wrong!

I wander back over to the bar area to get some more and catch my reflection in the silver beer pump. Oh. That's right. I look hot tonight. Nothing at all like a woman who has just been dumped, whose very future has just been snatched away. In fact, I look like I'm very put together. A woman in control of her life, a woman who does not get dumped but who does the dumping.

Looks are so deceiving.

I pour myself another drink, lift my head up a little higher and make an executive decision to try to have fun.

Okay. Fun.

Fun, fun, fun. Fun times.

I should bolster myself up for all this fun I'm about to start having but, honestly, I'm at a bit of a loss.

It's not like I can go over to random villagers and start off some witty repartee, is it? No doubt I would just insult someone else with the

271

truth-telling. I mean, I would almost certainly tell that man over there that when he dances he looks like a cockerel. And that woman by the food table? I would likely let slip that that particular shade of custard yellow she's wearing makes her look very pasty-faced indeed. I would almost certainly do that.

And so I drink. I drink because I want to fuel this burgeoning feeling of recklessness inside my tummy. I drink so that I no longer care about this worrying situation, what I might say or do. I drink to let loose. To relax. It's par for the course after a break-up. Aren't them the rules?

I drink because it's not like I have much else to do.

I'm just pouring my third paper cup of wine when the barn doors swing open and the resulting blast of cold air sends a collective shiver around the room. The new arrivals are Dionne, who is wearing a pair of tight leather trousers and has her platinum hair scraped back into a high pony-tail, Jean Paul Gaultier on his lead and wearing his tartan bow, and Honey, petite and beautiful in a pale pink, expensive-looking chiffon dress. They look stunning, linking arms and laughing together like BFFs.

Apparently oblivious to the admiring and curious looks they're getting, they saunter through the room, Dionne towards me and Honey making a beeline for Riley.

'You look nice,' Dionne chirps, her face flushed prettily from the cold.

'So do you,' I say absently, peeking over to where Honey has draped herself across Riley, shooting me 'hands off' glances and nibbling his ear. Is it me or does he look irritated by her attention and the ear nibbling? But then he is trying to carve up a hog roast, which isn't easy at the best of times.

'I told Mum about what happened,' Dionne says. 'She cried. You should ring her.'

'I will,' I sigh, thinking that being on the other end of one of Mum's meltdowns is the last place I want to be right now. I don't think I could cope. 'I'll do it tomorrow.'

'Good. You also need to, like, cancel everything. Mum's going to email you the details. She said she's well too embarrassed to do it herself.'

'Of course. I understand.'

Dionne switches Jean Paul Gaultier to her other arm, a sour look on her face. '*Of course, I understand?*'

'Yes?'

'That's it? You're just going to give up? Just like that. The wedding's off. "Oh well. All that hard work down the drain. No more Olly"?'

'Yes, I'm going to give up.' I look at her, answering at once. 'What else am I supposed to do? I can't force him to do anything he doesn't want to do. Can you really see me dragging him

273

down the aisle by his ear? "You WILL take this woman to be your wife, Olly. You WILL!"'

'Olly's just mad, yeah. You can at least try to sort it out.'

'Dionne, I can't even talk to him. A simple conversation is out of the question because I don't know what I'd end up saying to him. I have no clue what horror is about to pop out of my mouth. I'd make things worse and he'll hate me even more than he does now.'

'Hmm,' Dionne considers. 'Maybe I can talk to him.'

I don't want this conversation. I don't want to talk about Olly right now. I just want to forget. Just for tonight I want to forget. So I change the subject to something that will distract Dionne enough not to force this conversation.

'Your make-up looks ace.'

It does. She has gold sparkles all over her eyelids. It's very funky.

'Honey did it,' she beams, thankfully taking the bait. 'She's, like, totally amazing. These are her leather trousers too. I feel like Sandy at the end of *Grease*. You know she's not even mad at you.'

'Who? Sandy?'

'Honey, duh. After what you said on the radio about Riley. About wanting to bonk him. She said that you're nothing to worry about.'

Oh.

I'm nothing to worry about.

She's probably right. I glance over towards the food table again, but Honey's not there. She's dancing, her arms waving around delicately to the music. She looks like a French ballerina.

Dionne follows my gaze. 'Oh, look. Honey's dancing! She's so awesome. I'm going to dance too. Here.' She bundles Jean Paul Gaultier into my arms and struts over to join her new best friend forever on the dance floor.

I gaze into Jean Paul Gaultier's big soulful brown eyes. He huffs grumpily.

'I know how you feel, Jean Paul Gaultier,' I say, hugging him close. 'I know just how you feel.'

CHAPTER 24

Text from: Mum
Will you answer your blasted phone!

By about quarter past ten the alcohol is starting to take effect. I'm feeling nicely warm and relaxed. Jean Paul Gaultier's attached to his lead beside me and we're dancing away in our own corner of the room.

The party has revved up a few gears too. There's been a display of long-sword dancing by the men in the Morris-type outfits. Apparently it's a traditional Yorkshire dance and the Little Trooley team are national champions. The dance was both peculiar and entertaining, especially to Dionne who, watching the men in their short pants and funny hats, clinking swords and hopping, failed to cover the tears of laughter running down her face. I'll admit I had a sneaky giggle too. And there's a tombola in which a bottle of vintage champagne was won by Barney Braithwaite. Hello? Are you there, karma? It's me, Natalie.

The lights have dimmed now and the band has started to play songs that I recognize. Robbie really is a wonderful singer, blasting out a Sam Cooke song through the microphone, tunefully and with astonishing soul.

With almost everyone full up on hog roast and apple sauce, Riley has finished his stint at the food table and is up on the stage with the band, engrossed in his guitar playing with a dozy smile on his face.

I don't quite know how to feel about the fact that he doesn't appear to notice I'm here. You know, I bet he probably has noticed me, but has been scared shitless by my declaration of amorous feelings towards him on the radio. He probably thinks that if he chats to me, or even glances my way for a second, I'll start salivating like a rabid, sexed-up bitch on heat, and pounce on him, tearing off his cashmere sweater and his undies with my teeth.

Mortifying.

'Come and dance, you boring git. You've been stood there all night. The point of this thing is to have fun.'

It's Meg. She must have danced with every man in the place by now. Her cheeks are shiny and pink, and her hair has loosened out of the marcel wave. She looks brilliant.

'All right,' I acquiesce, tying Jean Paul Gaultier's lead to the foot of the chair next to me and following Meg to the dance floor.

The band segue into a fantastic, bass-heavy version of 'She Wants to Move' by N.E.R.D, and though the rest of the villagers don't seem to have ever heard of it, everyone cheers and starts to dance like maniacs.

I jump about, absorbing the deep vibrations of the music through my feet, and occasionally look up to where Riley is playing. Man oh man, he looks sexy with that guitar.

Dionne and Honey are across from us on the dance floor. They look like they too have been drinking and are now exhibiting some sort of sexy dancing duet, much to the disgust of Mrs Grimes whose eyes are on stalks as she waltzes by with Alan.

I glug the rest of my drink and gesture to Meg that I'm going for a refill.

'Get me one!' she shouts, swaying to and fro in time to the song.

I stumble over to the bar and check on Jean Paul Gaultier. He's sipping from the water I got for him earlier and being fed hog roast by everyone who passes by. He's one very happy poodle.

'So, you must be Natalie. The girl with the curious truth-telling problem,' says a smooth, well-to-do voice from beside me.

I turn around and recognize Jasper Hobbs smiling a rather friendly smile as he helps himself to a bottle of beer from a metal bucket.

'That's me!' I say, not quite sure how to behave towards a man I'm supposed to hate, but don't really know.

Jasper holds out his hand. He's very handsome.

278

Not particularly tall, but well built and wearing an exquisitely cut navy blue suit. His teeth are white and his skin tanned, his dark hair artfully foppish. He looks expensive.

'You shouldn't be here,' I find myself saying. 'You'll probably get into trouble.'

His expression is amused.

'I suppose you're right. I *am* the big bad villain of this entire drama.'

'Well . . .' I shrug uncomfortably, and as if to confirm his statement a few people end their conversations, look over to cast him the stink eye and start whispering behind their hands.

From the dance floor, Mrs Grimes spots Jasper and does a tiny 'O' shape with her mouth. She marches over, a massive scowl on her thin face.

'Oh no. Busted,' Jasper says, in a mock shaky voice. A wayward chuckle escapes my mouth.

'Mr Hobbs,' Mrs Grimes sniffs, her bottom lip wobbling. 'It is not appropriate for you to be here.'

Jasper looks at me, eyebrows raised, before smiling toothily at Mrs Grimes.

'Oh, come on, Edna. It all looks like such fun. You've done a marvellous job. I've only come for one teeny tiny little beer.'

'But this event is only *on* because of you,' Mrs Grimes replies, putting her hands onto her narrow hips. 'Because of your dastardly plans to take over our pub. It's *you* we're trying to stop. You've got a flaming nerve, young man.'

'It's a board decision, Edna. It's not entirely my

fault.' Jasper holds up his palms, the universal signal of innocence.

'It's Mrs Grimes. That charm won't work on me, Jasper, lad. Believe me. I'm immune.'

'Really? I always thought you were rather fond of us Hobbs men.'

At this, Mrs Grimes flushes and seethes.

Meg, having spotted Jasper, hurries over, beaming.

'Hello Jasper!' she says, fluttering her false eyelashes.

'Meg!' he kisses her on both cheeks, equally delighted to see her. 'What an utter pleasure to see you, and looking so beautiful too.'

Meg spins around in her dress, leaning over slightly so that her boobs look as big as possible.

'I think you should leave,' Mrs Grimes says to Jasper, studiously ignoring Meg's escaping bosom.

Jasper rolls his eyes comically, putting his hand to his chest.

'Mrs Grimes, you are *breaking* my heart. Let's see. How about if I donate one thousand pounds to your cause. Would you let me stay then?'

Mrs Grimes looks as confused as I feel. Why on earth would he donate a thousand pounds to the very cause that is opposing his plans to buy out The Old Whimsy.

'But why?' I begin, before it hits me.

Of course. He knows that a thousand pounds, or however much money raised tonight, isn't really going to change anything. It isn't going to make a dent in the cost of keeping the pub open. A thousand pounds is nothing to him. He's pretty much mocking the whole event. He knows that he's going to take over the pub no matter what happens.

Mrs Grimes appears to struggle with the offer, frowning and twisting her hands together in distress.

'Oh, go on, Mrs Grimes,' Meg pleads. 'He only wants one beer!'

'Two thousand pounds. And one drink,' Mrs Grimes says eventually, lifting her chin up and glaring at Jasper through her spectacles.

Jasper chuckles and pulls out a chequebook from the inside pocket of his suit jacket, as if this is the early nineties and people carry around chequebooks on nights out. I wait, expecting him to produce a Filofax too. He doesn't, of course. 'You drive a hard bargain, Edna. Father always said you were a feisty lady.'

'Oh, I know what you're doing, Sonny Jim,' Mrs Grimes spits. 'But if you want to throw your money away, then that's fine by me. And don't think it won't make a difference to our cause, because it will. We'll save The Old Whimsy. Don't you worry about that.'

'Whatever you say, Edna,' Jasper grins, handing over the cheque to Mrs Grimes, who snatches it and stalks off.

'Wow!' Meg says, looking at Jasper with reluctant admiration.

I have to admit, it is kind of exciting, the way he just paid that much money for a bottle of beer. But also, I don't know, a bit vulgar.

Jasper swigs from his beer, eyeing the room. His gaze rests on Dionne and Honey, who – oblivious to anything else that is going on – are now grinding dirtily in the middle of the dance floor.

Meg follows his gaze and frowns.

'Come dance with Natalie and me!' she says suddenly, grabbing his hand and then mine and dragging us to the dance floor.

She gives me a look, her grip on my arm tighter than Russell Brand's trousers. I have no choice but to follow.

I'm not a particularly good dancer. All right, I'm properly shit. So shit, in fact, that I got kicked out of ballet school as a kid for having a sickle foot and 'about as much natural grace as an over-boiled stem of broccoli'. So while Meg is shaking her bum at Jasper, and Jasper is half dancing and watching Meg's bum, I'm sort of hopping from side to side and clapping in time to the music. I look like a PE teacher.

Suddenly the tempo of the music changes and the band begin to play 'Will You Love Me Tomorrow' by The Shirelles.

Meg makes a swift move towards Jasper in an attempt to get a slow dance, her eyes alight at the very thought of getting up close and personal. But before she can reach him Uncle Alan appears, grabs a hold of her hand and starts to spin her around the dance floor. As he waltzes her off into the crowd I'm pretty sure I see her crying out. It looks like she's saying, 'Nooooooo.'

'Dance with me.' Jasper holds out his hand.

I glance up at the band and see Riley eyeing us while he strums his guitar.

Oh. So he's paying attention now, is he?

My common sense is likely skewed because of all the alcohol, and despite the fact that I find this man to be arrogant and a bit smug, I smile back at him and say, 'I'd love to dance with you.'

As we move across the dance floor, passing Dionne who is slow dancing with an elderly local, and Honey, whose eyes linger on us for a curiously long time, we reach Meg and Alan spinning wildly on the floor. She catches my eye and grimaces before Alan twirls her off into dance floor oblivion.

'You think I'm a prat, don't you?' Jasper announces out of nowhere, his plummy voice at odds with the broad northern accents I can hear conversing around me.

The forceful fizzing in my tummy urges me to answer his question.

'Yes. I think what you're doing is prattish. The whole hostile takeover of The Old Whimsy. It's uncalled for.'

He looks delighted with my straight-up honesty, but then it occurs to him what I've just said and he pulls a face.

'You know, you shouldn't believe everything you hear, Natalie.'

'No?'

'Not at all. Riley is behind on every one of his bills.'

'How do you know?'

He smirks. 'Oh, I have ways. And frankly, if I don't force the takeover, his obstinacy means he'll go bankrupt.'

God. That's awful.

'But why can't you just keep the place as a pub? Why do you have to turn it into offices?'

Jasper strokes his perfect goatee for a moment before shrugging.

'I did offer. I offered to buy The Old Whimsy and give Riley a job as the manager. He turned it down flat.'

I can't believe it.

Riley said nothing to me about this. In fact, I doubt he's said anything to anyone about this.

'He's very stubborn,' Jasper continues. 'He blames me for what happened with Mary, his mother. He'd rather go bust than let me help.'

'But if you don't like him, then why do you want to help him?'

'It's important to my father. He was very close to Mary. Father doesn't wish to see Riley lose everything because of downright obstinacy.'

I think about this new information, trying to process it through the wine-induced haze.

'So . . . why don't you just buy the pub and, I don't know, give it back to him?'

Jasper laughs. 'Because that's bad business. If Riley is refusing to manage the pub, then I need to recoup on the investment somehow, and the best way to do that is to use the building for offices. It's quite simple.'

So Riley lied. He was offered a way to save the pub. He's just too stubborn to take it.

'Everyone thinks he's a saint,' Jasper is saying now. 'But I've known him for years, and after hearing what you said on the radio . . .'

I blush.

'I think you should know that he has quite the temper on him.'

Riley? With a temper?

'I don't believe that.' I shake my head.

'I'll show you,' Jasper says strangely, a small smile on his face. And before I can ask him what he's on about, he pulls me to him and plants his mouth on mine.

CHAPTER 25

Is this real? What the hell is he doing? I yank away from him sharpish, untangling his arms from their grasp on my waist.

'What the holy focaccia do you think you are doing?' I hiss, my face aflame. Jeez.

Jasper doesn't seem at all perturbed by my rejection. He stands back and folds his arms as if he's waiting for something. Suddenly the music stops and Riley is at our side.

'You've had your beer, Jasper,' he says in a strange, steely voice. 'Time to leave.'

I stand back as Meg hurries over, nose scrunched up in confusion.

Jasper holds up his bottle, seeming to enjoy the quiet that has swiftly descended on the party. 'I still have a little left, Riley,' he says, putting the bottle to his mouth.

Riley steps closer and takes the bottle from Jasper's grasp.

'I think you're finished. Now leave.'

Jasper looks around at the crowd and rolls his eyes.

'All right, all right, don't make such a fuss about

'nothing.' And then ever so quietly, so quiet that I'm not sure I hear correctly, he leans towards Riley and whispers, 'Again.'

In a flash, Riley has dropped the bottle on the floor and has dived at Jasper, pushing his fist into his face with an almighty thwack.

A cry goes up around the room as the two of them get into a brawl, wrestling on the barn floor.

The men from the band and a few locals leap forward, trying desperately to pull them apart, but it's all going so fast they don't seem able to do much.

'Get off him!' Honey cries, floating over at speed. 'Get off my boyfriend!'

'Stop it!' I join in, tempted to wade in and try to pull them apart, but deciding against it for fear of my life.

They continue to tumble around, cursing at each other and grunting, their faces dark red with fury.

'Make them stop!' Meg cries out.

I look around at the locals, each of them trying their best to pull the men apart but none of them able to. Wow. They really hate each other.

'This is your fault,' Honey hisses at me, tears running down her face.

She's right. I have to stop this.

Before I even think about it I run up towards the stage area, wobbling drunkenly along the way. When I get there I grab the abandoned microphone that Robbie was using. I tap to make sure that it's on. It is.

Okay. I have the mic. I have to say something. Cripes. What the hell am I supposed to say?

I take a deep breath.

'Stoooooooooooop iiiiiiiiiiiiiiiit!' I bawl into the mic with all my might. But I must be standing too close to the speakers because they suddenly emit a toe-curlingly high-pitched screech.

Feedback. Oh dear. I hurtle, with the mic, to the other side of the stage area, but it doesn't make a difference. The noise just keeps on wailing out, setting my teeth on edge and making the hairs on my arms stand up.

It stops the fight, though, because Riley and Jasper pull apart, primitive instincts telling them that their hands would be better used protecting their ears than throwing punches at each other. The rest of the villagers do the same, grimacing at the noise and covering their ears, all of them looking up to see who is making such a racket.

'Sorry!' I say into the mic, causing it to screech again. I swallow hard and fumble for an off switch. I can't find one!

A chorus of jeers and shouts comes from the locals, all of them staring at me like I'm really stupid, which I obviously am. I sway to the side and try to keep my focus. Bloody hell. I didn't realize how drunk I was.

Then, to my horror, I hear a few of the crowd start to ask me what the hell I'm doing? What is wrong with me? Why does the microphone keep making horrible noises?

The copious amount of alcohol combined with all of the questions produces the biggest, fizziest urge in my tummy. I notice Robbie out of the corner of my eye hurrying forward and fiddling with dials on the PA system trying to stop the feedback. 'Hold on, Natalie!' he calls, concern in his friendly brown eyes. 'Cover your ears!'

I ignore him and bring the mic up to my mouth, unable to help but answer the questions.

'What am I doing, you ask me? I'm trying to stop these boys fighting before they cause each other serious, deathly injury. What is wrong with me? Well, many of you already know that I was hypnotized by your neighbour, Amazing Brian.' I spit his name out and shake my head sadly. The room spins a little in front of me.

'Since then, many things have gone wrong. My wedding has been called off, I've argued with everyone I love and my boss thinks I'm on drugs. Then, to make things worse, you—' I jab my finger in the vague direction of Barney Braithwaite '—you lied to me and said you were going to help me. You're a mean, mean man. And your comb-over looks stupid. Why on earth would you let everyone know how much I wanted to sexually act out with Riley Harrington? Can you imagine what AAAARGH!'

Out of nowhere, someone leaps onto me and pushes me over. The microphone rolls away from me and off the stage. I scrape my knee.

What the fuck?

'Sorry, sis.'

It's Dionne. She's lying by my side, breathing hard. 'I had to dive on you. It was the only way to, like, stop you talking. You were making a fool of yourself.'

I look up into the crowd and see Uncle Alan and the hairy bass-player escorting Jasper out of the barn. The rest of them are peering up at the stage trying to figure out what's happening. I try to spot Riley, but he's nowhere to be seen. He must have left.

Shit.

'Natalie! Oh my God. Are you okay?'

It's Meg. She's climbed up onto the stage.

'Yeah. I'm fine. So fine. Ha. That was funny, wasn't it?'

'How much have you had to drink?' she asks, while Dionne helps me up onto my feet.

'Dunno. Possibly a lot. Cups upon cups of wine, I think. I didn't mean to kiss Jasper. I mean. He kissed—'

'Shh. It's fine.' Meg brushes the hair out of my face. 'It's all fine.' She makes a weird face at Dionne and together they help me down from the stage area.

The three of us walk across the barn. I'm sure that everyone is looking at us as we go, but I don't care.

I'm so drunk.

Out in the tent, Dionne helps me on with my

coat while Meg replaces my high heels with the sensible wellies.

'What a palaver!' Dionne exclaims, linking my arm into hers.

'I know,' Meg says, linking the other side. 'Time for bed, I reckon.'

Yes. Definitely time for bed.

CHAPTER 26

Text from: **Mum**
Irene from the shop said you were on YouTube. I looked and there you were. What are you playing at? Turn your ruddy phone on.

I awaken with a start, the pervading thought in my head that I must have fluids right now or else I will crumble and die a dry and dusty death. I reach across the bedside table for some water, but there is none. Fancy drinking that much booze and not taking a glass of water to bed.

I rub my eyes and peer at the plastic clock beside me. Oh, hello 4 a.m., you cruel bastard. I sit up in the bed, expecting a headache of monster proportions. It doesn't come. I do a half-hearted air punch of joy, but then it occurs to me that I'm probably still a bit drunk.

I need water. No. I need Coke. Full fat Coke, with ice and lemon. And food. I'm starving. I rub my belly. I'm so hungry. Have I *ever* been this hungry before?

I really don't want to get out of this snugly warm

cocoon, foraging for sustenance in the dark, but I know that there's no way my body is going to allow me to get back to sleep without it.

I scramble out of bed reluctantly. Shit, it's freezing. I shiver, making an actual 'brrrr' sound for the purpose of feeling sorry for myself. Looking down and noticing that I'm wearing one of Meg's skimpy, frilly nightie affairs, I grab the blanket from the bed and wrap it around me tightly, tucking it in under my chin.

Slightly wonkily, I creep across the room and out into the corridor.

It's dark and deadly quiet. I try to avoid the creaks in the floorboards while making my way to the kitchen, all the while thinking about what food I'm going to eat when I get there.

Bacon. Definitely bacon. A massive salty, smoked bacon sandwich with a ton of red sauce. Or brown sauce. Maybe one of each.

Coke. Lots of Coke. I'm so thirsty.

Actually . . . not bacon.

I know! I'll make some mashed potato. All creamy and buttery and carby and with cheese and fresh chives mixed in. Can I be arsed with the effort of making it? Not really, but it will *so* make me feel better. Man, I'm ravenous.

I get to the kitchen, pushing open the door slowly so that the old wood doesn't groan and I don't end up getting discovered looking like a still tipsy lunatic in a too-short nightie and wrapped in a blanket that belongs in the 1970s.

My slow door opening doesn't matter much, though. Because someone is already in the kitchen.

Of course.

It's Riley.

He's sitting at the kitchen table cast in the moody shadows of a couple of candles and holding a bag of something frozen to his cheek.

Maaaaaan.

I take a few steps backwards, figuring that I'd rather die from lack of fuel than embarrass myself in front of him again. But it's just my luck that while managing to avoid all the creaky floorboards on my way here, Sod's Law ensures that right now I step onto what must be the loudest, creakiest bit of floor in the whole building. Maybe the whole world.

I jump back as I hear Riley's chair scrape across the floor. And then footsteps coming towards me. He's coming to investigate the noise.

Shit. If I run back to my room, he'll just follow and see me lumbering down the corridor. He'll probably think I was spying on him.

I have no other choice but to give myself up.

'Hello there,' I say, walking into the kitchen, the blanket positioned carefully to protect my modesty, of which there is very little in the teensy nightie. 'It's only me, just creeping around your house in the middle of the night! Quick! Hide the silver!'

He doesn't laugh. I wouldn't have done either. 'Sorry,' I try again. 'I've just come to get a drink really.'

Riley nods, gesturing for me to sit down. 'I'll get it.'

'Thanks,' I say, taking a seat at the table and enjoying the delicious heat bursting out from the Aga. 'Um, Coca Cola please. With ice. And, um, lemon.'

He raises his sandy eyebrows at me before taking a bottle of Coke out of the fridge, pouring some into a glass and adding a load of crushed ice.

I can feel my mouth watering. He hands me the glass and I down it in one. Oh, sweet, sweet cola.

'Another?' he asks when I'm done. I nod, discreetly wiping the drops of Coke currently making their way down my chin. Super classy.

'Thanks. I'm dehydrated, I think. How's your cheek?'

I notice that the space under Riley's eye is coloured with a deep purple bruise. Wow, Jasper must have really swung for him.

'It's fine.'

I feel guilty, like it's my fault. But I know it's not. Not really. From what I can gather, the pair of them have been building up to fisticuffs for years. I just don't understand why it was me who ended up as the catalyst. Unless . . . unless Riley was jealous? No. Of course not. He just didn't like Jasper being there. Telling me about his private business.

I finish my drink and decide I should probably leave Riley to it – he's obviously not in a very good mood and I'm probably the last person he wants to see right now. Sexed up, truth-telling, secret-blabbing fight-starter that I am. But . . . the thing is . . . I'm still really hungry. I'm starving. But it somehow doesn't feel like the right thing to do to start flouncing around in Riley's kitchen cooking mashed potato when he is so clearly fed up.

Riley is now sitting on the table top pressing the freezer bag back against his cheek. I peer closer. It's a bag of frozen raspberries.

'Peas,' I say suddenly.

'Excuse me?' Riley says.

'You need frozen peas.'

I stalk over to the freezer and pull it open. I root around until I find a full bag of petit pois.

'I think the point is that it's something frozen,' Riley says, a tad grumpily.

'Nope,' I say, switching his raspberries for the peas. 'Peas are the thing. That's what they always tell you to use. Like, on the telly and in the movies. Probably even says peas on the NHS Direct website.'

Riley shrugs and then stiffens as I press the peas to his cheek.

I can see a ghost of a smile playing around his mouth. 'Ah, yes,' he says. 'That's much better. Magic, medicinal peas.'

I adopt a serious expression and nod as if I am the fount of all medical knowledge. He lifts his hand and places it over mine so that both of us are holding the peas to his cheek.

The touch of his warm hand over my cold one sends a bolt of desire straight through me. I think I actually jump slightly with the power of it.

Gosh. I must still be completely legless.

My heart starts to beat loudly in my chest.

Shut up, heart.

I sneak a peek at Riley, mortified that he can probably hear it thumping away. I think he can hear it because he's looking at me with a very peculiar expression on his face.

'Man alive! These peas are dead cold, aren't they?' I say, in an uncanny impression of a complete idiot.

'I think you're lovely,' he says, so quietly that I'm not sure if I imagine it.

Is he on glue? I probably still pong of alcohol, am bundled up in a flowery blanket and no doubt have major panda eyes from the mascara *I know* I won't have removed. Perhaps he's concussed from the thwack on his cheek.

I laugh nervously, but stop after one high-pitched chuckle. Because Riley doesn't seem to find it funny at all.

I look at him anxiously, not sure what else to do. And then, all of a sudden, his lips are on my lips.

Zing!

The bag of peas drops onto the table with a crackly thud as Riley cups hold of my face. His kisses become more urgent.

I press my hands to his chest, kissing back eagerly.

This is delicious.

This is different.

This is not at all like Olly.

Shit. Olly!

I jump back as if I've been burned, my cheeks flushed, my whole body tingling.

We stare at each other, assessing, examining, our eyes narrowed. Riley is breathing fast, but doesn't say anything. It's like he knows that I'm weighing this situation up.

I mean, I have a fiancé. Oh, wait. No. I don't. He dumped me.

So . . . technically I'm allowed to kiss someone. It can be a rebound thing.

But no. Riley has a girlfriend. I don't like her one bit but that doesn't matter. It's such bad form to kiss somebody else's boyfriend. Totally unacceptable.

'Riley . . .' I say.

'We broke up,' he returns firmly, his voice hoarse. His pupils have dilated so much that they make his eyes look completely black.

'When did—' I start but don't get a chance to finish because his lips are on mine again. And it feels so amazing, so right, and I'm still drunk and I no longer have a fiancé, and Riley had a fight, and Mum hates me, and I've been hypno-tized, and have bad hair, and this really does feel exquisite. Like little sparks of lightning hitting each and every one of my erogenous zones.

Riley stands up from the table and pushes me against the door, his colossal body pressing against mine. I run my hands up through his hair, which feels cold and soft between my fingers. The blanket falls away, puddling down onto the floor and leaving me naked apart from Meg's scrap of white chiffon.

I don't care, though. I don't feel self-conscious. It's impossible to feel self-conscious when the only thing I care about right now is how brilliant *this* feels.

We sink down onto the blanket and when Riley takes off his shirt – revealing a gorgeously built torso with a very testosteroney spattering of hair – and starts to kiss my throat, I can think of nothing else.

This time there's no doubt about it. I am absolutely, definitely sexually acting out. And it feels brilliant.

Forty minutes later we lie on the kitchen floor, breathless and dazed. Riley doesn't ask me how it was for me. It would be impossible for him not to know that something incredible has just happened to both of us.

'We fit,' he says, lilting his voice up at the end like he's surprised. He pulls me to him and I nestle in under his huge arm, still trying to catch my breath.

I keep quiet, not trusting myself to speak coherently, but I know exactly what he means.

He kisses the tip of my ear before untangling himself from the blanket and standing up.

'I'm just going to . . .'

He trails off. It's obvious that he's going to the bathroom, but it doesn't seem right to say it out loud. Such a plebeian notion after something so amazing. 'I'll be back in a second,' he grins.

I smile and wave him away, wrapping the blanket snugly around me while he pulls on his boxers and leaves the room.

It only takes a few seconds of being on my own before the endorphins start to ebb and the guilt begins to flow.

What have I just done?

I have just had sex with someone I barely know. Amazing, exciting, lusty, best ever sex. And I've not even been split up with Olly for a day.

I attempt to justify it by telling myself that I'm incredibly confused right now, that I've been through a lot and am not entirely responsible for my actions. Also, I'm not fully sober.

But I know that's a lie. I knew what I was doing. I couldn't stop it, but I knew exactly what I was doing. Funny how I can't lie to anyone else, but I can lie to myself so easily.

It's only rebound sex, anyways. Everyone is allowed rebound sex . . .

Riley comes back into the room carrying a long

navy combed-fleece dressing gown, which he hands to me. I take it gratefully and put it on.

'Are you hungry?' he asks, opening the fridge door.

'Ravenous.'

'What do you fancy?'

You.

I think about it. What would I like most in the world right now?

'Mashed potatoes.'

He laughs. 'That's specific.'

I shrug, embarrassed. 'That's kind of what I came in here for. I was dreaming about mashed potato.'

Shouldn't we be feeling guiltier than this?

Riley pulls on the rest of his clothes and looks out of the window at the snow.

'I'll just nip to the greenhouse for spuds,' he says.

'Okay. Um, I'll boil some water.'

'Great.'

Okay, this is awkward again now. We've just been doing very rude stuff together and now we're talking about potatoes. SO weird.

Once Riley leaves, I tighten the belt on the dressing gown and get up to find a pan. I find a fab orange Le Creuset in one of the cupboards and put some water on to boil.

When he returns, we peel and chop potatoes in silence, then put them on to cook.

After too long of not speaking, I bite the bullet and ask.

'Honey—'

'It's over,' he says at once, like he knew I was going to ask. 'It's been on the cards for a while. I told her at the barn dance.'

So he's only just split up with her. In fact, it's probably just a fight. They could easily get back together.

I tell him that once the snow clears I'll be leaving. He is undeterred.

'I've never felt anything like that,' he murmurs. 'I don't want you to go.'

'I have to go. We don't really know each other. My life . . .'

I trail off.

He looks me in the eye and my tummy flips again at how easy it is to drink him in. The way his face is put together, the exact positioning of his features is so very attractive to me.

'I can't force you to do anything,' he says. 'But surely it's impossible to experience what we just did when you're supposed to be in love with someone else.'

I think about Olly and how much I love him. Regardless of how amazing Riley is.

'I think you're wrong,' I say firmly. 'It's just sex.'

But even as I say it, I know that it's not true. This is something more than sex. But it's new and confusing and really badly timed. It shouldn't have happened at all, but it did.

Riley comes closer, an indiscernible flicker in his eyes.

'Was that just sex?' He asks the question brazenly, cockily.

'No,' I answer at once, the treacherous truth-telling doing its work. 'No. It wasn't.'

He nods, satisfied.

'Would you like to do it again, Miss Butterworth?' he asks, this time a mischievous grin lighting up his face.

Oh my God. The fizz is strong and I answer clearly.

'Yes, please.'

He dives on me again, lifting me up onto the kitchen table as if I weighed nothing, undoing the dressing gown, biting my bottom lip.

My body responds like I'm under a spell, the protests from my brain fading with every kiss.

I'm an actual hussy.

Behind us the potatoes bubble over and start to burn. Neither of us cares.

CHAPTER 27

Text from: **Mum**
Have you or Olly cancelled arrangements
yet? I refuse to do it. It's time you grew
up, love.

I've had sex with someone else. I've had sex
with someone who isn't Olly. I've had sex with
a stranger. These are my first thoughts when
I wake up. And while my head is clear in terms
of hangover, it's not so clear in terms of, you
know, life.

After Riley and I did IT again last night, we
made some more food and agreed it would be
best to go back to our own beds. Despite the fact
that what we have done is clearly wrong, I can't
help but feel excited. I feel a bit like a child who's
just discovered popping candy for the first time
– it's incomprehensible, and pretty brilliant, but
if you eat it before your dinner it'll make you feel
sick.

I check outside the window to see if the snow
has eased off at all. It's still falling but a lot lighter
than yesterday, and the sky doesn't look quite as

leaden. In fact, the sun might even come out to say hello. And then the snow will melt. And then I'll be able to go home.

Home to Manchester.

Jumping into a hot shower, I push away that thought. I wash my hair and concentrate on ridding my head of all thoughts of Olly. But it's impossible. In the sober light of day I no longer feel the sense of abandon I did last night. As I pour out the conditioner, I get loads of flashbacks to memories of me and Olly.

The day we met in Chutney's. How gorgeous I thought he was.

The time he asked me to be his official girlfriend after he'd taken me to my first ever boxercise class.

Proposing to me at the vegan restaurant, his eyes shining with excitement and love.

Remembering this particular memory hurts the most and I sink down onto the floor of the shower cubicle, rest my head against the tiles and have myself a little cry.

When the soap suds on my head are beginning to itch, I stop crying and rinse them out. I must pull myself together.

I clip my hair away from my face because I'll be cooking today. Before I left for my own room, Riley pointed out that I'd be backing out of my promise if I didn't help him with the menu. And so I said I'd help him. And if there's one thing that will make me feel better, it's cooking.

In the pub I discover Meg and Dionne already having breakfast. They're scoffing omelettes and chatting away as if they don't hate each other. It's very disconcerting.

When they see me walking over they startle a little. As I reach the table they start talking about nail polish – to be specific, their favourite colours of nail polish. If I didn't know any better, I'd say they had been talking about me.

'Hiya,' I say, looking curiously at each of them and taking a seat.

'Hi!' they both say extra brightly.

'I was just saying to Meg how awesome it looks when you paint your nails white. Like Tippex but not skanky, because it's really nail polish!'

'It's very interesting,' Meg says, with barely contained enthusiasm.

This is weird. Are they *getting on*?

'What's happening?' I ask, pouring myself a cup of tea from the pot.

'Nothing!' They say, looking most suspicious. 'Nothing at all!'

'Um . . . did you sleep well?' Meg asks, in an obvious attempt to change the subject.

'Nah. I barely slept at all. I had sex with Riley.'

Jesus. I'd almost forgotten about my treacherous truth-telling gob! And now, in less than five minutes, I'm asked a question that leads me to blurt out something I'd have much, *much* rather kept private.

The pair of them stare at me shocked. Dionne

gasps, her hand shooting up to her mouth in dismay.

'But . . . Honey!'

I put my head in my hands. 'I know.'

'You're a bitch!' she says, anger crossing her features. 'He's a rat. You're a pair of . . . bitch rats.'

I'm stupidly surprised that Dionne's so mad at me. But then I remember that back when she was twenty-one, one of her friends slept with her then boyfriend. She was heartbroken for weeks.

'Please don't tell her,' I plead. 'It was just a one-off. They've broken up and we were drunk!'

'It's no excuse,' Dionne cries. 'And Olly! He's not even cold.'

'He's not dead!'

'You know what I mean,' she hisses.

'Please don't tell her.'

Dionne fumes at her cup of tea, while Meg remains mute. Shocked silent? Angry silent? I'm not sure.

Dionne pulls out her phone and fiddles with it absently.

'I don't even know where she is anyway.'

'What do you mean?'

'I went to Honey's house this morning to see if she was okay after last night—'

Oh nice! No bothering about whether I'm okay after pervert Jasper lunged at me. I dismiss my irritation. I have absolutely no right to be feeling irritated right now.

'—and she wasn't there. And she won't answer her phone,' Dionne finishes.

Oh God. I hope she's all right. What if she's been kidnapped? Or is dead? And I was there shagging her one and only true love?

I shudder at the very thought and tell myself I'm being stupid. Honey will be fine.

'Please don't tell her when you see her.'

Dionne slams her hand down on the table.

'I'm going to take Jean Paul Gaultier for a walk.'

She gets up and, after casting me the worst stink eye she may have ever cast at anyone, she stalks out of the pub to fetch Jean Paul Gaultier from her room.

'Jesus, Natalie,' Meg whispers as soon as Dionne's gone.

'I know,' I say, embarrassed.

'Was it good?'

Typical!

'Yes,' I say, unable to help the grin that creeps stealthily across my face. 'Incredible.'

'Well, as I always say, the best way to get over someone is to get under somebody else.'

'Meg!' I admonish.

'What! It's not like Honey is anything other than a complete bitch. I wouldn't feel bad.'

I shrug. I do feel bad, though.

'Anyway, speaking of getting under people, I'm off to record!'

I chew on some toast and look at her.

'With Jasper? After what he did last night?'

Meg looks nonchalant.

'It's not a big deal. You were both crazy drunk and we've all kissed someone we didn't mean to before.'

'But—'

'Oi, you. Don't be taking the moralistic high ground.' She frowns slightly.

I back down because she's right. She's allowed to spend time with Jasper. Just because I don't like him doesn't mean he's a bad person.

'I'll probably be back late. I'm going to jam with Robbie later.'

She looks embarrassed as she says it. I laugh out loud.

'Wit woo!'

'He's a good singer. And he plays guitar well. He's going to help me to write a song.'

'Fair enough,' I say, wondering why she would ever fancy Jasper when Robbie is clearly her perfect match.

'What are you going to do?'

I sigh. 'I've got to look into cancelling the wedding arrangements. Mum and Olly are refusing to do it, which is fair enough . . .'

'Oh, Nat. That's shitty.' She puts her hand over mine.

'S'all right,' I say, in a voice that belies how rubbish I feel about it. 'Anyway, I can't do it until later – I promised Riley I'd teach him another dish today.'

Meg shakes her head. 'You're a naughty girl, Nat. You've turned into a very naughty girl.'

'I know.'

The kitchen is gorgeously light and warm, the snow on the windows enhancing the brightness of the sun shining in. Riley is sitting at the table with a pot of coffee and is reading the newspaper. He's dressed in a pair of baggy black combat trousers and a snugly fitting charcoal cashmere sweater. My knees wobble slightly.

I really didn't think this through. It's been years since I've been in a morning-after situation. What's the etiquette? Do I acknowledge it? Say something jokey like 'nice shag last night'? Or do I excuse it by diving in there with red-faced mutterings about how I was so totally, horribly drunk last night?

In light of the wholly inappropriate situation, Dionne's dismay at my behaviour, and the fact that I'll be leaving here very soon, I decide to affect an air of complete professionalism and act as if nothing has happened. If he wants to bring it up, then fine. But I won't.

'Hi there.' I am brisk. I am professional. I am cool. The coolest.

Riley looks me up and down and beams.

'Hello,' he says in a low voice. A voice that makes me feel sensations far too rude for this early in the morning. Is it hot in here? Is the range on too high?

The coolest? Wow, I'm delusional. I've got no chance.

'Here I am!' I almost shout, willing my voice not to betray me by shaking or squeaking or saying, *I like you far more than is necessary. I can't believe we had sex last night. Let's do it again.*

'Yes . . . here you are.'

Riley doesn't mention what went on in this very room last night, but the tension is so tangible that I can hear it crackling like a bowl of blummin' Rice Krispies. I take a seat, plonk down the notebooks and pens I've bought from the post office and pour myself a coffee. It's hard to concentrate, though; my hands are actually trembling as I recall what went on just over there on the floor. And over there up against that cupboard. And here on this very table . . .

'Natalie?'

Riley is looking at me, puzzled.

Oops. Got a bit carried away with the flashbacks there. I shake my head in an attempt to clear it, pick up a pen and tap it manically against the table.

Grinning, Riley takes the pen from me and places it back on the table.

How can he be so calm and normal? How can he be so calm and normal when *my* brain is taken up by images and whispers and filthy flashbacks from last night?

Does he not feel the tension? Oh shitbags. Maybe he doesn't. Maybe I'm imagining it. It's all one-sided, and last night for him was just, let's face it, an easy lay, and he only said that stuff about us fitting so he could get into my pants again. And it worked, because he *did* get into my pants again. Fabulous. It's all in my head. Like the time I was a bridesmaid for Auntie Jan when I was fifteen years old and I thought everyone was looking at me because I was wearing a peach satin dress and looked really pretty, when actually they were all looking at me because I had a porridge stain right in the middle of my boob area.

Fine. *Fine.* Why am I even worrying about it? It's not like I want anything more with him anyways. I'm soooo not ready for anything more. I still love another man, for Pete's sake!

I sip at my coffee, willing myself to get focused and stop being such a flake. I'm an adult. A grown-up, adult woman. I had ill-informed sex with a man. It happens. It's normal. It's fine. Doesn't mean I have to freak out and start *analysing*.

I clear my throat. 'Okay.' I pick up the pen again and pull the lid off, open a notebook and write 'MENU' in big capitals at the top of the page, underlining it four times. 'Okay. Right. So, the food people know and love but at its very best.'

'Yup. The very best they've ever had,' Riley cuts in.

I stop short. I don't think that was a double meaning, but the way he said it, his voice low and growly. I glance over at him but his eyes are

312

focused on the notebook in front of us, his face the very picture of innocence.

'Um, yes,' I carry on. 'So I was thinking we could both offer our suggestions for starters, main courses and desserts, decide on a shortlist and try cooking some of them. Then maybe tomorrow we can do a tasting session for locals in the pub. See what they think?'

See, that wasn't so hard. I'm as professional as a . . . professor.

'Sounds grand.'

'Right. Well, let's get to it. Chop chop! The sooner we get your menu decided, the sooner I can create some initial recipes and the sooner you can start serving to the public.'

And so we get to it. To a Spotify playlist of mid-nineties R&B, we drink coffee and scribble down ideas in the notebook. Riley suggests favourite dishes; I suggest how we could make them more exciting, the logistics of serving them every night, sourcing ingredients, how easy or difficult they are to perfect. Talking about food is one of my favourite things to do and Riley is obviously passionate about the pub so there is no awkwardness. In fact, the conversation flows and trips over itself in the loveliest of ways. But still neither of us mentions last night.

We've managed to shortlist the menu choices to five classic pub dishes for each course. Based on what we've been able to forage from the larder

313

and the greenhouse, I've decided to show Riley the recipe for Granny's Soup – my nan's actual recipe – and concoct new, more appealing ways of doing steak and chips and an egg custard dessert. The exciting thing is that though every dish sounds the same as any other pub fare, we're going to put little twists into them so that each dish is tastier and more interesting than initially expected.

We've donned our aprons and are preparing our vegetables for the Granny's Soup. As we chop the holy trinity of carrots, celery and onion, with the music blasting out into the room and the sun sparkling through the huge snow-dusted windows, it's difficult not to be overcome with a feeling of utter well-being. Something about this situation, where I am at this very moment, feels good. And it's for that reason that when Riley starts showing me the official dance to 'I Wanna Sex You Up' by Color Me Badd, I join in, asking him to teach it to me.

'Put down the knife then!' he laughs, eyeing the massive vegetable knife in my hand with a comedy horror expression.

He picks up a couple of unchopped carrots from the table and hands me one of them.

'Your microphone, Miss Butterworth. I'll be Sam. You can be Kevin.'

'I can't believe you know their names!' I chuckle. 'No one actually ever knew their names!'

'I think you're underestimating the number of

Color Me Badd fans out there, of which I was numero uno.'

'Loser! All right then, which one is the lead singer? I want to be that one.'

'That's Sam. I'm being Sam. I bagsied Sam.'

I tut. 'But—'

'*I'm* teaching you. *I* get to be Sam. Come on. The song'll be over soon.'

And so, with carrots as microphones, Riley and I sway and twist and, on occasion, thrust our way through 'I Wanna Sex You Up'. Riley's size doesn't quite lend itself to graceful movement and it's already common knowledge that my dancing is really crap, so we just end up tripping up and laughing hard at each other's dud moves.

The playlist runs into three more nineties R&B songs, each one having a very specific dance according to Riley. He teaches me the moves to 'Jump' by Kriss Kross, 'Hold On' by En Vogue and 'This Is How We Do It' by Montell Jordan. I'm aware that he's making each dance up, and something about his camp moves and willingness to embarrass himself in order to make me laugh just endears me to him even more.

'You daft sod,' I chuckle, brushing the hair from my face.

'*You* joined in!' Riley admonishes, shaking his head.

The song changes. It's the super sexy, slow 'You're Making Me High' by Toni Braxton. The mood changes instantly. I try to jolly it back up

315

again by singing along in my terrible voice but it doesn't work and Riley is looking at me with that desirous expression in his eyes.

Like peculiar human-shaped magnets we edge towards each other.

Are we really going to do this?

That question, alongside *Has he sorted things out with Honey?* and *Which knickers do I have on?*, are jostling for attention inside my brain, willing me to pay them attention, but I'm unable to focus on my brain. I can only focus on my body. My body that's already singing like a canary.

'Again? Now?' I manage to choke out just before Riley's hands weave up into my hair, sending a sweet shiver down my spine.

He answers me with a half grin and starts to pull up my top. Dazed by his touch, I reach behind me to lock the door, and there by the fridge without any consideration for what is right and wrong, we make love.

CHAPTER 28

Text from: **Meg**
Grt time recording. I've got something to
tell you. I know this is a tease but wait until
you hear – you won't believe it.

I'm in the bath. I'm having a bath and considering the fact that it has taken only one day for me to become a woman of loose morals. There is no question about it. What I am doing is sexually acting out. Sex three times in less than twenty-four hours is something I have never done in my life. Cripes, sex three times in a *week* was an occurrence as regular as a solar eclipse. And the worst thing about it is . . . I want more. Man oh man. I want more of this sex with Riley, because – and I've never really known this before – it really is bloody marvellous. Everything is louder and brighter and in sharper contrast. I almost feel sorry for myself that I didn't know about this earlier!

Riley's back in the kitchen clearing up the pots and pans from what ended up being a most distracted cooking session in which only one dish – the Granny's Soup – was finished. And even though my hair is full of foam and the bath water has left mascara streaks down my face, I'm trying to send him a telepathic message.

'Come to my rooooom . . . join me in the baaath . . .'

Jeez.

I don't know. Perhaps the horn attacking Riley and me is purely circumstantial: I'm stressed about my break-up and the whole mind control thing, and Riley is stressed about the pub. Maybe what's happening is that we are recognizing that stress in one another and using sex as a distraction technique.

I ponder this for a few seconds before realizing that it's bullshit.

The simple truth of the matter is this: We Fancy Each Other. I've never fancied anyone so much in my life. And the way he looks at me? I'm pretty sure he's never fancied anyone this much either. It feels good. Even the truth-telling feels good right now. Like I'm free. I can't hide anything anymore so why even try? It could be rather a lot of fun this way . . .

I giggle to myself and duck my head underneath the water. I burst back up when I hear a knock on the door.

I jump out of the bath, gleefully ignoring the tidal wave that slops over the sides of the bath, and wrap a fluffy blue towel around myself, leaving my hair to drip water sexily onto my shoulders.

318

What?

Meg's recording with Jasper and Dionne's not speaking to me – it's got to be Riley.

I drop the towel slightly so that it reveals a bit more of my glistening skin and pull open the door with what I hope is an alluring grin. Only it's not Riley. It's Honey, and before I have chance to haul the towel back up, say hello or blink even, she leaps into my room, slams the door shut behind her, takes a run-up and punches me in the neck.

Ow.

I'm having a fight. After twenty-seven years of successful conflict avoidance I am now having a real, authentic fight. I've only ever seen real fights on *Jerry Springer* or once in Asda when these two women went into combat over the last reduced-price cinnamon swirl, so I don't quite know what I'm supposed to do.

After grabbing my arm and performing an unfeasibly painful mini pinch-twist with her pincer-like fingers, Honey grabs onto my hair and pulls. Only my hair is wet and her hand is unable to get a grip and slithers away. She stumbles backwards with the force of the botched hair yank and bounces off the wardrobe, snarling with sound effects. Oh crap. What has happened to her? Her floaty, tranquil composure has done a runner. She looks feverish. Her perfect hair is all messed up and

I'm quite sure that that is spittle resting at the corner of her mouth.

Balls. I knew she was a lunatic. The signs have been there all along. While Honey recovers from the wardrobe bounce I see an opportunity for escape. I waddle very quickly backwards and reach out for the bathroom door behind me. My heart pummels loudly in my ears as I push down the handle and dive inside, noticing Honey's look of surprise as I do so. I lock the bathroom door behind me and rest my head on the tiled wall.

The bathroom is so steamy that it's impossible to see anything, but even without looking in the mirror I'm pretty sure that my expression is one of simple, unadulterated terror. Man, I'm a yellow belly.

'Come out of there! I know what's been going on.' Honey yaps from the other side of the door. 'Come out and face the music, you sneaky bitch.' This time her growls are accompanied by the sound of tiny fists pummelling at the door.

Jeez. I *have* to open the door. This is stupid. I can't stay locked in the bathroom. But I don't want to go out there either. I'm scared!

'I'll come out,' I call, my voice all wobbly. 'But you have to promise, no violence! Violence is not the answer.'

There are a few minutes of silence and then, 'Fine. No violence.'

Hands shaking, I pull open the door and step

out. Honey is sitting on the end of my bed, her hands folded gracefully in her lap.

'Put some clothes on, sweetie,' she says, looking me up and down disdainfully.

'I'm so sorry,' I say, shame colouring my cheeks. 'I know you've only just split up and—'

'Split up?' she hisses. 'Riley and I are as together as ever.' She pats her hair and smiles serenely.

My stomach lurches.

'Um. What? No, he told me—'

'He lied. He's so stressed right now. He doesn't know what he's saying.'

'No, he defin—'

'Oh, Natalie. Natalie, Natalie, Natalie.' She gets up and starts to walk around the room. It's creepy. Why is she saying these things about Riley? He very clearly told me he had split up with her. That it had been on the cards for a while.

'You're lying,' I say, lifting my chin up stubbornly.

For a moment I kid myself that if he'd still been with Honey I wouldn't have done anything with him. But deep inside I know that's not true. I couldn't help myself.

'You're as stupid as that sister of yours. Though she does have her uses, telling me all about you and Riley. Idiot. Can you believe she felt bad for me?' She rolls her eyes, giving a tinkly little laugh.

'Yes, I can believe that, so shut up,' I snap. No one talks about my sister that way.

'You *really* think he wants you?'

'Yes,' I say at once.

'A meek little nobody who thinks she's under a magic spell? A girl who wears those horrible cheap trainers and a puffa jacket?'

'Yeah. He said that we—'

'He's using you, sweetie. Can't you see?'

I fiddle with the corner of the towel, wishing desperately that I had some clothes on.

'What? How? I don't know what you're talking about.'

Honey's eyes glint maliciously. Wow. She is horrible! Clearly unhinged in some way.

'He needs a chef.'

'So?'

'He needs a chef who will stick around here and work for free.'

I screw my eyes up. What is she going on about?

'Deary me!' She rolls her eyes. 'Sweetie. All Riley cares about is his precious little pub, *the only legacy his family has*. He'll do anything to keep it. Including sleeping with a skank so that she'll stay and do his bidding. He thought he'd hit the jackpot when you wandered in here with your slutty friend.'

I shake my head, unable to believe that she's spouting such ridiculous lies.

'I knew about it,' she says, taking a pot of vanilla lip balm from her cardigan pocket and dabbing it on. 'Please, I helped him to plan it. I just didn't expect him to go as far as to sleep with you. But that's for Riley and me to discuss. He really does *love* The Old Whimsy. It's worth an awful lot of money, you know.'

I don't know what to say to her. I can't help but tell the truth but my bullshit detectors are apparently weaker than Charlie Sheen's morals.

'You don't believe me?' she says, her perfectly shaped red eyebrows arching upwards.

'No.'

I don't believe her. What's been happening with Riley may be 'just sex', fair enough. But that 'just sex' was real. I didn't imagine his desire for me. I'm sure of it.

Honey giggles, the tickling sound of it scratching my eardrums. 'You poor, poor thing.'

And without another word she floats off out of the room, leaving behind only the sickly sweet smell of her Chloé perfume.

Shudder.

I curl up on the bed for ten minutes waiting for my heart to slow down its frantic racing. What is happening to my life?

I dry my hair and get dressed. I need to speak to Riley right away. I need to know what the bloody hell is going on and why his ex – is she even his ex? – has turned into a complete nut job.

I hurry down the stairs and into the kitchen, trying my best to hold back the tears. But I get there just in time to see Riley and Honey engaged in a very intimate-looking hug. Riley is oblivious to me standing in the doorway, his eyes closed as he and Honey embrace. But Honey notices me standing there and gives me a slow 'I told you so' smile.

Of course. Honey's right. Why would he want messy, weak-brained me when he's got beautiful, elegant (slightly crazy but maybe in a glamorous way) her.

I'm such an idiot. I'm such a gullible idiot. A strangled sob escapes me.

This place is crazy. I've got to get out of here.

On my way out of the pub I notice Dionne who is chatting away to a local while Jean Paul Gaultier drinks from a bowl of water at the side of the bar.

She catches sight of me and waves.

'I had to tell her, Natalie,' she shrugs. 'Honey's become a friend. Why should she have to be sad about breaking up with Riley when he totes is *not* sad about it? You don't, like, have a monopoly on telling the truth.'

Jesus.

'You're my SISTER!' I blast out so loudly that the entire population of the pub stops what they are doing to gawp at me in horror. 'It doesn't matter what I've done, whether it's wrong or right,' I say, ignoring the whispering and offended tuts going on around me. 'You're my *sister*. You're supposed to be on *my side*.'

Dionne's cheeks colour.

'You're mad at me?' she asks.

Oh hell.

'Yes!' I cry at once. And then it all comes

tumbling out. 'You walk around in Dionne World, giving your loyalty to new friends who you've known for less than a week and who, by the way, don't give a shit about you. You stick your nose in where it doesn't belong. You make everything about you! You don't know when to shut up.'

'What are you on about?'

'Telling Olly about the radio, telling Mum about Olly, telling Honey about Riley and me!'

Alan comes out from behind the bar. 'Now, now ladies. That's quite enough.'

Dionne starts to cry. Big fat tears plopping down onto her chin. 'I was trying to help.'

'No, you weren't,' I scoff. 'You like the drama. You're *a gossip*, Dionne. It's all a load of fun to you! Well, I'm not laughing anymore.'

And then, once I've said my piece, I flee the pub.

CHAPTER 29

Snow can kiss my larger-than-average arse. I'm on my way to find Meg and am halfway up the hill between The Old Whimsy and Hobbs Manor when it occurs to me that making this journey on my own, wearing trainers instead of wellies and without a coat, isn't the shrewdest thing I've ever embarked upon. But then again neither was coming back to Little Trooley, agreeing to appear on the radio when my brain is totally compromised, or having kitchen sex with a virtual stranger. So, freezing to death out here would be just about what I deserve for managing to get myself into such a gigantic, shitting mess.

In another genius move, I'm finding my way to Hobbs Manor by the power of moonlight. I've been walking for fifteen minutes and didn't think about the fact that December weather means it goes from daylight to night-time at precisely five o'clock. It's now five fifteen.

I shiver and push on up the hill, focusing on the warm yellow lights in the distance.

I pull out my phone and try ringing Meg again to let her know I'm on my way. But there's no answer. Totally frustrated, I can't help but have another little cry. The floodgates have opened. I have now become one of those girls who cry all the time. I feel like Gwyneth Paltrow. I don't think I'm just upset about the Riley thing. It's not like I love him. Obviously. But the being lied to is not nice at all. I feel like an idiot. It's like the universe is telling me to stick to what I know. I knew karma would get me. The one time I decide not to be completely responsible and it comes to bite me on the arse.

I think about Olly. Olly wouldn't have lied to me. Olly *loves* me. I bawl even louder at the thought of him. My phone jingles in my bag. It's Mum. Shit. I still haven't spoken to her since Olly called off the wedding. I consider not answering again, but she's only going to keep trying.

'Hiya, Mum,' I say, sniffing and shivering.

She doesn't say hello, just gets straight to the point as usual.

'I've just had a phone call from your Auntie Jan telling me you're on the telly. I thought she'd forgotten to take her medication but I switch it on to Channel Manchester and she's right. There you are on the telly. What the bloody hell are you doing on the telly?'

I'm on the telly? Why the . . .? Oh, wait . . .

My stomach drops as I think about the YouTube filming of my interview with Barney. Well, he's obviously kept that end of the bargain up, getting local media to pick up the story, something I only agreed to when I thought he was going to edit out all of the embarrassing stuff.

'Shit, Mum. It's the radio interview I did. I'm so sorry. How embarrassing. It's only Channel Manchester, though, Mum. It's cable. No one watches it.'

'Well, I bloody did! You look ridiculous. And you sound ridiculous. You know they interviewed your boss? He seems to think you are in rehab for drug addiction. And Olly! They've been hounding him, as if the poor lad hasn't been through enough.'

'Oh God. Stone. Shit. I'm so sorry, Mum. Shit. What am I going to do? I don't know what to do!'

I start crying again.

'What am I going to tell the women at bridge? My daughter has gone mental? My daughter has gone mental and then broadcast it on the telly? You've got yourself into a right flaming mess. No wonder Olly doesn't want to marry you. You're obviously having some kind of crisis—'

Suddenly, I stop walking. I can't believe what I'm hearing. Mum is exactly the same as Dionne. They're cut from exactly the same completely selfish cloth. How is this about *her*? Why is that all she's worried about? What? She can't cope being on her own, and she thinks I can't either?

'—I had to tell them that I no longer get to be mother of the bride. You have no thoughts for anyone else. You're just like your dad, Natalie. Self-centred.'

'Mum, I'm sorry. I am. But now is really not a good time to have this conversation.'

'Do you think it's a good time for me? I've had a terrible time of it. I'm weary and heartbroken. The only shining light was your bloody wedding! And now . . .'

She goes on. And on. And on.

And then something odd happens. She doesn't ask me a question so I don't have to tell her the truth. But I'm so angry. It feels like an unbearable churning in my chest and stomach. I've never felt so angry. I'm stuck on a massive hill in the middle of nowhere in the freezing cold, in need of a little comfort, and here she is telling me off, telling me what a bad daughter I am. So even though the hypnotism doesn't force me to tell her the truth, I do anyway.

'You're the selfish one!' I cry out in anguish. 'You say I'm a bad daughter. But you're a bad mum. You made me leave my life! Dad has gone, Mum, and you need to get to grips with it. You're better off without him. I was happy at catering college and living with Meg, and you demanded that I come back and—'

'I did not, Natalie.'

'You did. You said that you were worried what you might do if you were alone. What was I supposed to do? What choice did I have? That's so much to put on one person.'

'Watch your tone, young—'

'No. I won't watch my tone. I'm twenty-seven years old. I'm a grown-up. And I was happy to be there for you. Always. I love you. But all you do is get at me! You've got to understand that I have my own life to lead!'

'I'm looking out for you! That's all I've ever done. You ungrate—'

'You're looking out for yourself,' I yell into the wind. 'Making sure we're all as fucking miserable as you are.'

Silence for a moment.

'Right,' Mum whispers. 'Of course.'

And ever so gently she clicks the phone down.

Fuck.

Fuck.

What have I done? I go to ring her back immediately to apologize, but then stop myself before I've finished dialling the number.

No.

I will *not* feel guilty. I will not. She can't keep treating people like that. She can't treat *me* like this.

But you didn't have to be so harsh.

Whatever.

I shake my shoulders and concentrate on

ignoring the annoying guilty voice that pipes up in my head.

I'll just phone her later when I've calmed down. It'll be fine.

Close to hypothermia, I finally reach the gates of Hobbs Manor. It's the grandest house I've ever seen. The same caramel-coloured bricks as the rest of the village houses, but these bricks are massive, each one about half the size of the door. And it's an enormous door. Black and shiny. I knock on it and almost laugh when it creaks open at my touch. It's like something from a scary movie.

'Hello?' I shout, popping my head in. 'Um, Jasper? Meg? I'm here. I mean, it's Natalie. I'm coming in!'

I tentatively take a few steps in and gasp at the huge entrance surrounding me. Directly in front of me lies a gorgeously ostentatious staircase that separates into two more staircases at the top. I look up towards the highest ceiling I've ever seen. Wow. This really is like something out of a film. I step further in, wondering where everyone is. Shouldn't there be an old butler or something? I'm not quite sure what to do. If I go any further into the house, I'm technically breaking in. But . . . the door is open. Oh gosh, what if the door is open because someone is robbing the place, or someone is in here murdering Alfred Hobbs for his shitload of money? Oh man, what if Meg has become caught up in the crime and is tied up with lengths of thick rope in the drawing room?

I click the door shut behind me and venture past the staircase and down a red-carpeted corridor. I pause when I hear voices. Or is it one voice? I walk in the direction of the voice and stop when I reach the room it's coming from. It sounds like Jasper. I'm about to knock on the door when I realize that his low voice sounds highly agitated and so completely different to the smooth, calm composure I heard at the barn dance. The nosy cow in me puts an ear against the door and listens hard.

'You should have left it alone. You're going to ruin it all!'

Ooh, this sounds interesting. Who is he talking to?

'That idiot wasn't supposed to . . .'

Who is he talking about? I listen more closely.

'Yes, well, now we're going to have to go on with Plan B. But that means that we cannot afford for anyone to find out. I know. Dionne . . .'

Did he just say Dionne? Or is he talking *to* Dionne? And what does she have to do with Jasper? I can't hear properly. It's not clear enough. I sigh in frustration. What is he saying? I read somewhere once that one's senses are more powerful when other senses are compromised. So I compromise my sight by squeezing my eyes tightly shut, and my smell, by holding my nose. Then I press my ear up even closer to the door. I knew there was something fishy about Jasper Hobbs.

'I've just hidden it. He won't be coming back . . .'

Oh my gosh! Who won't be coming back? What is he planning? What did he hide?

I jump out of my skin when someone standing right behind me does a gentle cough. 'Ballbags!' I cry frightfully.

My shriek echoes around the gigantic building.

Ballbags, ballbags, ballbags.

I turn around and see a tall, thin old man with a long white beard, dressed in a maroon smoking jacket and slacks. He looks like Dumbledore! Maybe this is the butler.

'Hello, dear. Welcome to my home. Who are you and how can I help you?' He raises an eyebrow suspiciously.

Oh God. This isn't the butler. This is the reclusive, mega rich Alfred Hobbs. The man in charge of all the Hobbs bread in the world! I don't get time to ponder what it must be like to have access to all that bread because his question sparks off the truth-telling . . .

'Hello. Yes, I think you can help me. I'm looking for my friend, Meg. She should be here recording music with your son, um, Jasper. I'm Natalie and I'm having the worst week of my entire life.'

Alfred chuckles and holds out his hand. 'I'm Alfred Hobbs, dear.'

As he touches my hand he shivers. 'My my! You're colder than a witch's tit!'

I blink. Did he just say 'witch's . . . tit'?

'What on earth have you been doing?' he continues, frowning.

'I've walked up from The Old Whimsy.'

'Dear child, you'll catch your death. Come to the den. The fire is alight. I'll prepare us some tea and then we can address your problem.' I nod emphatically, quite scared to disagree with this imposing and eccentric-looking old man.

At that very moment Jasper appears.

'Father,' he says irritably. 'What are you doing now? I thought I told you—' He stops abruptly when he spots me and arranges his face into a less annoyed expression.

'Natalie Butterworth!' he says, kissing me on each cheek. 'Whatever brings you here?' He scratches his perfectly straight nose.

'I'm looking for Meg,' I answer.

'Yes, of course. Meg's not here, I'm afraid.'

'Oh,' I say. 'But she told me she was coming here to record some music?'

'Yes, she was. Robbie came for her about an hour ago.'

Robbie? Oh yes. I totally forgot. She said she was going to jam with him.

'How long have you been here?' he asks, coughing. He looks twitchy.

'Long enough to hear you talking on the phone, though I didn't hear everything you said.'

Oh gosh, how embarrassing. Stupid truth-telling. I can't hide anything! Jasper frowns for a moment before snapping himself out of it.

'I'm sorry for your trouble. I can walk you back if you'd like?'

'Nonsense,' Alfred Hobbs hollers. 'The girl will not be going back out into the cold until she's at least had a cup of tea.'

Jasper nods reluctantly. 'Yes . . . yes, I suppose you're right, Father.'

'Take her to the den, Jasper. I shall prepare the tea.'

Jasper sighs before gesturing that I should follow him back across the hall and into what must be the den. It's another huge room with high ceilings; den isn't really appropriate for it. It's still completely grand. The sofas are old and worn, but clearly expensive. Hanging from the ceiling is a gigantic antique crystal chandelier. Completely at odds with the fifty-billion-inch widescreen telly set up in the corner. At the centre of the room is a huge fireplace with a fire blazing brightly inside the hearth. I head straight for it.

'I'm freezing!' I explain, kneeling in front of the fire and putting out my hands to warm them. Jasper doesn't answer. After a few moments he comes up close behind me. He's so close that I can feel the heat of his breath on the back of my neck. I shudder and move away. Talk about invasion of personal space!

'What *exactly* did you hear out there?' he says, running a tanned hand through his foppish black hair.

Jeez. Paranoid or what. But of course the truth-telling does its work.

'I heard you say that you'd hidden something and that you wanted to go to Plan B. Did you mention my sister's name? I'm sure I heard you say Dionne. You sounded angry.'

'You are mistaken.' He swallows hard. 'And it's bad manners to listen in on other people's private conversations.'

I lower my eyes, ashamed. He's right. Earwigging is totally rude.

'My father would like you to stay for a cup of tea, but as soon as you are done I will walk you back to the village. In the meantime, I would quite appreciate it if you didn't mention anything about business.'

I raise my eyebrows questioningly. Why the bloody hell would I talk to Alfred Hobbs about business?

Jasper huffs. 'I mean about the business with The Old Whimsy. I prefer not to bother him with small troubles.' His tone is abrupt.

There's no reason why it should unsettle me – it's not like he's really a baddie or anything – but he definitely makes me feel uncomfortable.

'Tea!' Alfred Hobbs announces, hobbling into the den carrying a silver tray.

'Let me know when you are done and I shall take you back,' Jasper says, not quite looking me in the eye.

'You're not staying for tea?' Mr Hobbs asks his son. 'But we have a guest, Jasper.'

'I'm busy, Father.' And with that, he walks out of the room.

Okay, this is weird. This is one weird arse village.

Mr Hobbs carefully pours out the tea into two delicate white china teacups. There's no milk or sugar on the tray. Maybe this is how posh people have their tea.

'Thank you.' I smile at him as he hands over a cup.

Taking a sip, I try my best to hide the splutter that follows. This tea has got brandy in it!

I cough, my cheeks burning with the heat of the alcohol.

Alfred Hobbs chuckles. 'A little medicinal brandy to prevent a cold, dear.'

I smile weakly. He watches, nodding at me to take another sip. I'm too polite not to. Ick.

'Please excuse my son's behaviour,' Alfred says, handing me an icing-sugar-dusted chocolate from a little glass bowl on a side table by his armchair. 'Champagne truffle – my favourite. He's a busy man. I'm sure he doesn't mean to be impolite.'

'Oh, it's okay. I understand.'

Alfred smiles.

'So you're young Megan's friend then? Her mentally unwell friend?'

I almost choke. 'No. Not mentally ill. But, yes, Megan's – Meg's friend.'

'Dear girl. Very pretty.'

I smile. 'Yes. Gorgeous. And lovely with it.'

Alfred sips from his own tea and sighs with pleasure. 'And you. You are less . . . gorgeous. And far more beautiful. What a wonderfully plump mouth you have!'

'Um, thank you,' I say, fighting the urge to laugh. Of course I don't tell him about the accidental lip injections. I'm pretty sure he wouldn't understand.

'Yes, yes,' he says, slowly looking over my face as if I'm a painting to be studied. 'You remind me of an old love of mine. Mary was her name.'

Mary? As in Riley's mother Mary?

'Are you talking about Mary Harrington?' I ask.

'Well, yes, dear, I am! You have the same . . . kindness about you as she did. Serenity. An inner radiance.'

Me? Serene? Radiant. Gosh, this man is nuts. Sweet, and very good with the flattery, but totally nuts.

'So you were friends with Mary then?'

'Friends? Oh, we were more than friends. My dear, we were at it like rabbits for years!'

I choke again. Drinking tea around this man is a constant choking hazard. I put down the cup.

'That sounds . . . fun.'

Alfred chuckles, topping up my tea cup and handing me another chocolate.

'We had a lot of love for one another.'

I wonder if he was having an affair with Riley's mother when she died? Riley did say they'd been seeing a lot of each other. Wow.

'I'm sorry for your loss,' I say, patting him sympathetically on the arm.

'Thank you, dear.' He smiles lightly and holds my hand for a moment. 'You know it wasn't my first dalliance with Mary. I dated her in our younger days too. Until Edna put a stop to it.'

Edna? I'm sure I know of an Edna. I rifle through my brain trying to place the name.

Edna. I have a flashback to the barn dance. Edna is what Jasper was calling Mrs Grimes!

'You mean Mrs Grimes?'

Alfred nods and grins.

'Oh gosh, that makes her sound ever so old. But I suppose you would know her as Mrs Grimes. Yes, I was also having a rendezvous with her. They were both such beautiful women but in very different ways. I could hardly choose between them. And they were the very best of friends, of course. In the same class at school, and at secretarial college together.'

He shrugs, his blue eyes twinkling. He's

handsome for an old guy. I can imagine him playing the womanizer as a lad.

'It was quite the scandal. But then we were quite a scandalous group of friends.'

'Friends?' I ask, intrigued.

'Edna and I, Mary Harrington, her brother Alan, Barney and Morag and Joe . . .' He looks off into the distance as if remembering some cracking nights out.

'Blimey!'

'You'd never have thought it, but I disliked Mary for such a long time. She was much younger than the rest of us. By seven years. But Alan had to drag her along on our adventures in the way that big brothers ought to. By golly, she was irritating.'

He laughs at the thought.

'But then before I knew it she had grown into the most wonderful woman. Bright and funny and beautiful. So many admirers and not one of them good enough for her.'

Man alive! Talking to Alfred Hobbs is better than an episode of *EastEnders*!

Needing to zone out for a bit, enjoying the heat of the fire and the heat of the brandy and Alfred's company, I lean back into my chair and tuck my cold feet up underneath me.

'Tell me more, Mr Hobbs.'

'And then the police came and we had to make a run for it. Alan lost his trousers. It was a very good job it was dark, I say!'

'No way!' I laugh as Alfred Hobbs tells me another story from his youth. It turns out that he, Mrs Grimes, Alan, Barney and Morag Braithwaite and Riley's mother Mary were a real gang in their younger days. Alfred Hobbs was the rich kid in a small village and the aforementioned were the only ones not intimidated by or envious of his wealth and his family name. Alfred and Alan were even pilots in the RAF together during their twenties. They were best friends. It seems so sad that they haven't spoken in two years.

Jasper has been in a number of times, itching to walk me back to the pub. Each time Alfred has waved him away with a stern telling off.

I really should get back, though, not least to find out where Meg is. But I'm having rather a brilliant time, plus as much Hobbs toast as I want, which is just what I need after the day I've had. The fifth time Jasper comes in looking at his watch and declaring that he has to go to the village so I need to go with him now or else I'll have to walk back on my own in the cold weather when it might be icy and I might slip and die, Alfred suggests that I stay the night instead. He has plenty of spare rooms and it means we can continue with our chat and perhaps have some dinner together.

Jasper is wary. He sighs and looks at me suspiciously as if he thinks I'm going to rifle through his underwear drawer or something.

I nod my agreement eagerly. I can easily call Meg from here and I really don't want to go back to The Old Whimsy tonight. I don't want to see any of them right now.

'I'd really like to stay if I may,' I say. 'To be honest with you, I haven't really got anywhere else to go.'

'Well, then. It's decided,' Alfred declares, clapping his hands together gleefully.

'But Father, I think—'

'It's decided, Jasper. Don't you have business to attend to?'

Jasper rolls his eyes and leaves the room.

After a tour of the extensive and beautiful Hobbs gardens, Alfred's purpose-built gymnasium and – oh my gosh – his personal aircraft hangar in which he stores his OWN helicopter, we settle down to a slightly unorthodox but lovely dinner of fancy cheddar cheese on Hobbs toast with the most wonderful vintage champagne. When we have finished eating Alfred pats his napkin to his lips and says, 'I seem to have monopolized our entire conversation. Now tell me, dear, why are you so sad?'

Do I look sad? Is it so obvious? It's such a grand question, it takes my brain about thirty seconds to gather all of the information I need to answer. Of course the need to tell all is as strong as ever and the answers float on out.

I tell Alfred all of the things that have happened.

He listens attentively and when I'm done he nods and simply says, 'It will be okay, my dear.'

The knowledge that it probably won't be and the hope that it will bring a surge of tears to my eyes.

'Why are *you* so sad?' I ask, the champagne loosening my tongue. 'And why are you a recluse?'

As soon as I've said it I feel bad. Way to be tactful, Stupidhead. *Why are you a fricking recluse?* My cheeks colour.

Alfred looks sad for a moment and shrugs. 'I enjoy my own companionship, I suppose.'

'But you've enjoyed mine,' I say. 'I'm sure your old friends in the village would love to see you.'

He frowns. 'I know that to be untrue, my dear.'

'Why?'

'There was a lot of bad feeling after Mary's death. I'm not welcome there.'

'But that was ages ago.'

'It's quite all right, dear. I'm happy here. Most of the time.'

Poor Alfred. He doesn't look happy at all.

I'm about to say that he's not really helping matters by trying to turn The Old Whimsy into offices, but then I remember what Jasper said. Business is a no-go topic because of Alfred's blood pressure.

'Time for bed, I think,' Alfred says, kindly patting my arm.

'Yes,' I agree. 'Where should I go?'

'It's at the top of the stairs, fourth door on the right.'

'Thank you,' I say, standing up from the table.

We smile at each other, and in spite of the disappointments of the day, I feel like I've made a new friend.

CHAPTER 30

I 'm having the weirdest dream. I'm at a wedding. Dionne's wedding. She's getting married to a snowman and Amazing Brian is the vicar, only his jumper doesn't have AB on it. It says HA! instead. I'm a bridesmaid but I've eaten too much bread and my dress won't button up. I'm sumo wrestling with Honey, who is wearing a fur coat and singing Duran Duran songs. And someone is laughing – tinkling little giggles that are as irritating as a tap that won't stop dripping.

I wake up with a start. Sitting up in the vast guest bed in Hobbs Manor, I swivel round and look at the old-fashioned alarm clock on the bedside table. It's two in the morning. I sigh. I hate it when that happens. You full on wake up thinking it's the morning and it turns out to be ages away and you've got to try to force yourself back to sleep. It never works.

I lean out of the bed and click on the glass lamp beside me. Once again my breath is taken away by the grandness of the room I'm in. When I first saw it last night I danced with delight, though of course that could have been something to do with the vintage champagne I'd been chugging. The bed is an actual four-poster bed. The most mahoosive bed you've ever seen, with thick million-gazillion-thread-count blankets and pillows like feathery clouds. The carpet is this luxurious garnet-red pile and all of the furniture is expensive, glossy walnut. I feel like I'm in a castle or something.

I get up out of the bed – having to jump down a bit because the mattress is so high – and groggily pull on my clothes. I totally need a wee. Just as I'm fastening up my trousers I hear a giggle. It's the giggle from my dream. That giggle woke me up! Is that . . . Meg? Has she come back to perform a secret middle-of-the-night seduction on Jasper? Ew. I hear a short sharp shush and a deep, muffled cough. Well, that has to be Jasper. Unless Alfred Hobbs has a booty call coming to visit. I highly doubt it. The man hasn't left his estate in two years.

I wonder who Jasper has with him. If not Meg, then it has to be someone from the village. The whole place is snowed in so it's not like it's someone from more than ten feet away.

When whoever it is has gone I shuffle to the door and pull it open slightly. I *really* need that wee now. I try to remember where the loo is. Alfred told me, but this house is so big, and it's so dark and it has more doors than a chuffing advent calendar.

A cold shiver creeps down my back. Shit. Did he say left out of the bedroom or left from the stairs? He must have said left from the bedroom, two doors down. Or was it three? No. It was definitely two.

Okay. I'm just going to go for it. I turn left and feel along the wall for the second door down. I pull on the handle and open it tentatively. It's so dark I can't see a thing. Man, that wee *really* needs to happen. I cross my legs and feel around for the light. Aha! There it is! I switch it on and almost jump out of my skin when the first thing I see is *not* a lovely expensive loo but a tanned, muscular bottom pumping away on top of a person. The someone underneath is squealing with pleasure.

The tanned bottom is attached to a man. A man who whirls his head around and looks over his shoulder in fright.

It's Jasper Hobbs. He is not happy. Well, he was happy about thirty seconds ago. But he's definitely not happy now.

Whoever he's entertaining has yanked the covers up over their head and has gone stock still.

How embarrassing.

'Fuck,' Jasper shrieks, grabbing a pillow and using it to protect his modesty. 'Get the fuck out!'

For some unknown reason I stand still. I'm so mortified that I can't seem to move!

'Get out, you idiot! What are you *doing*?' Jasper cries, his eyes bulging, his face crimson with sexual exertion and fury.

'I don't know,' I reply to his question. 'I seem to be watching you! I'm sorry. I'll go!'

Aaaargh.

'I really am ever so sorry,' I say once more, my face aflame. I turn to leave the room. I want to find that bathroom NOW, not only for the purposes of weeing, but because I need to scrub my eyes out with soap. But on the way out I stumble, tripping over something soft on the floor. I glance down quickly and notice, trapped under the door, a tight emerald-green shift dress.

Meg's dress.

CHAPTER 31

Why hide it from me? I know it's embarrassing when your best mate walks in on you with your legs in the air, but to actively hide? Meg's never been secretive about anything with me before.

I kind of expected her to come to my room shortly after, to laugh about the whole mortifying incident. But I stayed awake for the rest of the night and she never did. She's probably still doing IT with Jasper Hobbs.

I feel a prickle of disappointment. I told *her* about Riley. I mean, I couldn't help but tell her about Riley what with the whole inability to keep ANY secrets. But I still told her. We tell each other everything.

I may not even like Jasper. But if she likes him, which she *obviously* does, then I'm totally happy for her.

I pour myself a cup of tea in the vast Hobbs kitchen. It's crazy early so no one else is awake. I feel like all I do these days is sneak around in other people's houses, drinking their hot beverages.

I wonder if Meg's still here. I'll give her a bell and find out.

Urgh. My mobile is dead and I have no charger.

I sigh to myself, scratch my head and look around.

After about five minutes I decide that I'll just use the landline here. I'm desperate to find out what's been going on. And to tell her about my fight with Honey.

I wander out into the hall, looking for a telephone table. There's nothing of the sort. Surely all posh houses have telephone tables?

Oh, wait a second . . . wasn't Jasper on a phone yesterday? In that room down the corridor? I lumber down to the room Jasper was in. I expect it to be locked but it isn't. I push open the door to find a large office. There's an antique-looking bureau with one of those green desk lamps like they have in lawyers' offices and American libraries. On the wall are a number of pictures and certificates. Jasper Hubert Alfred Hobbs BSc Management.

Jackpot! There'll definitely be a phone in here.

I shuffle over to the desk and peer around. It's covered in paper. Wow. Jasper Hobbs is messy! I move the papers about, hoping to God that it's nothing important I'm reshuffling.

Bingo! A phone. It's not the landline I was expecting to find but a sleek, smaller-than-my-hand, silver mobile phone. I pick it up, a frisson of guilt spiking through me. I tell myself not to feel bad. It's probably not a personal phone. Who leaves their personal phone hanging about for all and sundry to find? I pat my own mobile, snug and safe in my pocket.

I press the on button of the silver phone. Nothing. Oh crap. The battery on this phone is dead too. I'm having no electrical luck at all today.

I suppose I could just go upstairs and talk to Meg in person . . .

I get a vision of Meg and Jasper in an even less restrained position than last night and decide against it. I'll phone her first, to give her a bit of warning.

There must be a charger somewhere around here. I drag open a couple of drawers and root through among the standard fare of notepads and pens and elastic bands.

No charger. Humph.

I run my eyes along the skirting boards, searching for plug sockets in case a charger has been left in. But nope. No luck.

What I do spot, though, the corner of which is sticking out from under a filing cabinet, is an envelope. This wouldn't be very exciting except for that it has HARRINGTON scrawled on the front in thick black ink.

It's none of my business.

It's wrong to snoop.

But it says Harrington, which must mean Riley.

My nosiness gets the better of me and I creep over to the filing cabinet.

What? Sleeping with Riley might have been a huge mistake but if there's a secret file about him and The Old Whimsy, then I want to know about it, not least because it might be important info for all the nice people I've met who are working so hard to save the pub.

I check that the door is definitely closed before I open the filing cabinet. I pull the envelope out with a swift yank.

It's sealed.

An annoying goody-two-shoes voice inside my head tells me that it's soooo not on to open a sealed envelope. It's against the law or something. If I'm caught and arrested, I won't even have the power of lying to wriggle my way out of it. I'll get a criminal record. I could end up going to jail and having to develop a new persona. The persona of a woman not to be messed with because jail is dangerous. I'd probably have to shave my head and get a tattoo. I find my mind wandering briefly into the realms of tattoo designs I might consider and then realize where I am and what I'm doing.

I turn the envelope over in my hands. I should put it back. I'm going to put it back and get out of here. I'm treading a crazily fine line between curiosity and crime.

I bend down to shove the envelope back under

the filing cabinet, but then I hear a shuffling noise outside. And then some footsteps.

Balls! Someone's coming!

I run around in a semicircle, the envelope in my hand. Eek! EEK! Just as the door opens I panic and shove the envelope down the back of my trousers.

'Natalie!' It's Jasper, looking astonished and unimpressed that I'm in his office.

He shakes his head and blinks hard as if he can hardly believe I'm here. I can kind of understand his grievance with me. I must be really starting to get on his nerves.

Damn. He's going to ask me what I'm doing in here, and then I'm going to have to tell him the truth: that I'm snooping and stealing stuff from him. He'll probably call the police. But then the police won't be able to get here because of the snow. And Jasper will have to sit on me until the snow melts and law enforcement arrives. That sounds horrendous. Before I get myself into even more of a mess by getting arrested, I make an executive decision. There's only one thing I can do.

Leg it.

I jog right out of the office, down the corridor, through the amazingly grand entrance hall and out the front door of Hobbs Manor. I don't even get time to say goodbye to Alfred Hobbs or wait for Meg. I run – with an envelope tucked down by my arse – all the way back to the village.

★   ★   ★

Unless you count the fact that I ran all the way back here, slipping three times in the snow, and have numb feet and an inability to breathe properly because of poor fitness levels, I reach my room back at The Old Whimsy with no problems.

It's still early so thankfully there's no one around to bother me.

I get to my room and pull off my clothes, changing into the navy dressing gown Riley lent me. As I pull it on I catch the scent of washing powder mixed with Riley's aftershave, which is some kind of sandalwood and spiced orange combination. My tummy flips as I inhale it. Mmmmmm.

NO! Do not think about that. That is over. That was a one-night stand. Or a one night and one afternoon stand. Whatever. It's done.

I take the envelope from where it lies beside me on the bed and, heart galloping at super speed, I gently tug it open, being careful not to rip the paper.

What kind of a person have I become?!

I empty the contents onto the blanket beside me. It's a load of letters and pieces of papers and, ooh, a few photographs.

I go straight to the photographs.

The first one is of two toddler boys. One with messy blonde hair and one with close-cropped dark hair. They're sat on a chequered picnic blanket in the sunshine and are eating biscuits.

It's clearly an old photograph, the image slightly softer than photos nowadays, and with a sepia tint to it.

I flip it over.

Riley and Robbie, August 1987

What? Why the heck has Jasper Hobbs got a picture of Riley when he was a kid?

I rifle through the other photos. There's one of two women and a bloke. The guy is clearly Alfred Hobbs – even back then, without the long dramatic beard, he still had that aura of power and charisma. He has his arms around two women, one blonde and chubby, one slight and brunette. I turn it over.

Mary and Edna and Me, 1982

Hmm. That's definitely Mary Harrington. I remember her face from the picture on the internet.

I shuffle through the rest of the photographs. There's one of a glamorous, tall, pregnant woman wearing a silver dress with big puffed-up sleeves. She looks like something out of *Dynasty*.

Anna pregnant with Jasper, 1987

So Anna must be Jasper's mother.

I pull open a piece of folded paper. It's not as thin and delicate as the others. It's thick white paper. Fresh paper.

Oh. It's a photocopy of Alfred Hobbs's will. I scan through it. Of course, it leaves everything to the rightful heir, Jasper Hobbs.

And then I pull open a letter. The bottom of the paper is torn off. The handwriting loops and swirls elegantly across the page in black ink. I read what's left of it.

> *Dear Alfred,*
> *I am three months pregnant with your child. I understand that this is not what you want to hear, having only just got married to Anna, but I feel it is something you need to know.*
> *I am perfectly happy in my new relationship and lord knows what I was thinking three months ago at the barn dance. Perhaps I wasn't thinking. Nostalgia and scrumpy turned me into a fool and I do not wish for anything to change. Heaven knows it took you almost forty years to find and marry the perfect woman for you, and I would hate to ruin what you have with Anna. Please extend me the same courtesy by not mentioning our dalliance to Jack. It's early days, I know, but he's a good man. A solid man.*
> *I do not wish for you to be in my child's life. It would do nobody any good. I do not ask for any money from you. We have all we need. If m*

And that's where the letter is torn.

Oh my gosh. I sit there staring into space as the photos and the stories about Mary Harrington and

356

the letter, surely written by Mary, spin around inside my head and then settle into place.

I can't believe what I've found out.

Riley is Alfred's son.

CHAPTER 32

What the frick am I supposed to do with information like this? The more I think about it, the more I realize the implications of what I've just discovered.

If Riley is Alfred's *first-born* son, then surely he is entitled to make a claim on the Hobbs Estate?

I take a deep breath.

This isn't any of my business.

Mary obviously didn't want Riley to know that Alfred is his real father. She would have told him if she did. She clearly didn't want anyone to know about her affair with Alfred. It's not really my place to share that, is it? Not when she can't even defend herself . . .

What on earth am I supposed to do?

I don't get time to figure out the answer to that because the door knocks, and in bursts Meg.

Our conversation is awkward to say the least, neither of us willing to ask about what went on last night.

After an exchange about the weather (still snowing but less so), Honey (Meg feels that having a fight is a rite of passage and agrees with me that Honey is the loopiest, meanest, prettiest girl either of us have ever met), and the smell of my hair (must be a brand-new shampoo in the shower – this time it smells like apple and cinnamon), I bite the bullet and ask her outright.

'Why aren't you telling me about last night?' I demand, folding my arms. 'I saw the pair of you *in flagrante delicto*! I know the truth!'

Her face goes absolutely bright red and she gasps.

'What? I didn't do anything!' she sits down on the bed, not meeting my eye.

'I walked in on you, Meg! Why are you denying it? I saw you with your legs in the air. I saw your dress on the floor! Didn't you know it was me?'

Meg shakes her head. 'Shit. I must have been too distracted to notice anyone coming in. I thought we were the only ones in the house.'

Why is she acting weird? Is she embarrassed? Everyone's allowed to have sex. Sure, I walked in on her and stood watching for a few seconds longer than necessary, but that's no reason to act like a lunatic.

'I really like him.' She shrugs, smiling more to herself than to me.

'But I thought you'd decided not to bother in the end?' I say.

'I did. But we've been getting closer and closer, bonding over the music. I couldn't help it! I didn't *want* to help it!'

'Blimey. Great!'

'Oh, Natalie. He makes me laugh so much, and he's so sweet and he seems to really like me too. He makes me feel like the me I always wanted to be. Like I can really be somebody. Like I can make it as a singer!'

Wow. I don't know whether to be more surprised that this is evidently more than a sex and massive recording studio thing for her or that Jasper can be described as funny and sweet. Well, they do say you don't *really* know other people's relationships. Maybe he does all the funny and sweet stuff in private?

I peer at her. She looks truly happy. Flushed and relaxed and giddy.

'I'm happy for you,' I say. I am. If my best friend has found love, whoever it might be with, then I'm happy for her.

'Really? Are you?' she asks, though it's not that she doubts the truth, just that she wants to hear me say it again.

'Really. Truly.'

'Please be my friend again. I'm sorry.'

It's Dionne. After Meg left to get some food, she blasted into my room and is staging a sit-in on my bed until I forgive her. Part of me longs to do what I would normally do and roll my eyes, give her a hug and agree to forget about it because we're sisters. But I don't know. This past week, I seem to have become harder. No, harder isn't the right word. More assertive, that's it. I'm not feeling the overwhelming need for peace. It's like it's only just occurred to me that sometimes you can be mad at people. Sometimes you can fall out and it's okay.

'Dionne, I really don't want to talk to you right now. Please leave.'

'But . . . Jean Paul Gaultier misses you.'

I sigh, glancing over as Jean Paul Gaultier pokes out his tongue, desperate to lick me. I hold my hand out to him, ruffling the soft fur behind his ears.

'Look, Dionne,' I say. 'I'm mad. I'm allowed to be mad at you.'

'But . . . you're never mad.'

'Well, now I am. Please leave. I'll talk to you when I'm ready.'

And then her attempt at making up reveals itself to be as flimsy as I suspected and her face drops.

'I don't believe you! You have no right to be mad. It's your fault that I'm stuck here. You haven't given a thought to how this, like, affects me. *Oh, poor Natalie. Poor hypnotized Natalie.* And Olly! What must he be feeling right now? You don't give a shit. You're changing. It's like this past week you've become someone else. You're selfish! You're . . . hard.'

I've had enough of this. I don't need it anymore; I don't have to put up with it.

I stand up and, taking Dionne firmly by the hand, march her out of my room, slamming the door behind her.

'I'm staying in my room and I'm not coming out. Please leave me alone. I do not wish to talk to you.'

I hear her cry in protest. I don't care.

I manage to lock myself in my room for a grand total of one hour and thirty minutes before getting claustrophobic and making a bid for freedom. Not that I've ever had a problem with claustrophobia before, but pretty much as soon as I announced to Dionne that I planned to lock myself in my room, I wanted to be anywhere other than my room.

Also, I'm hungry.

I make my way down to the kitchen, head down, eyes to the floor. I cross through the pub where there appears to be another meeting going on about the state of the snow. I decide that I definitely do not want to talk to any of the locals right now and try my best to sneak around the back of the crowd to the kitchen, when somebody grips my arm very firmly. It's Morag Braithwaite.

'What are you doing?' I grump, as she pulls me out of the main pub and into the corridor.

'We've done it, Natalie. Your tape has gone viral. *Yorkshire Tonight* has contacted us and wants to do an interview with you. Over the phone or webcam, obviously – there's not a cat in hell's chance they're getting here in the snow – but still, they'll put it on the telly proper and we'll—'

'Have they found Brian?' I interrupt, my heart leaping.

'Um. No.'

'Has *anyone* found Brian? Was there any point at all to the media splash?'

'Well, yes. I mean, no one has found him. Not yet. But once *Yorkshire Tonight* is involved, they'll be sure to come up with a lead. Everyone watches *Yorkshire Tonight*.'

'Sorry,' I say, shaking her off. 'Not interested. I'm not making that mistake again.'

I turn on my heel and stalk off. The cheek!

I get to the kitchen to see Riley dashing from worktop to table to cupboards and back again. The smells emanating from the stove are surprisingly delicious. Not that I care. I'm just here to grab myself a quick something to eat before I leave again.

'You're here!' he says brightly as I enter the room. 'I didn't see you for the rest of last night. Figured you'd gone straight to sleep.' He raises an eyebrow. 'You certainly tired *me* out . . .'

Why is he acting so normal? Like he's not cheated on his girlfriend? Like he didn't use me? What an arrogant prick.

I'm about to tell him this when he asks me a question and I'm forced to answer. It's getting really old now.

'Here, what do you think of this?'

He's proffering a small plate with a slice of tart on it. Oh no. Another tart.

I take the fork he's holding out and grumpily taste the mouthful of the food resting upon it.

Oh.

Oh!

Plum tart. With . . . aniseed? Yes. Aniseed.

Yum.

And double-cream ice cream.

Very yum.

'Delicious,' I declare, as soon as I've swallowed. 'I'm impressed.'

I hate the fact that the truth-telling means saying something nice to him. I fold my arms and scowl.

He doesn't seem to notice. Just smiles madly and runs his massive hand over his eyes.

'I've had about two hours' sleep!'

Oh God. He's not going to tell me that Honey kept him up all night, is he? Would he really be so cruel?

'After you and I . . . you know . . . I was inspired. I tried getting to sleep but my mind began to come up with all of these recipes. I got up and made them. Of course I got a little help from my mother's cookbooks, but the twists and turns, they're all my work! It was fun. I'm going to send a few of the final choices out into the pub this evening, see what the reaction is. We can do this! I'm not great, obviously not as good as you, but I think with the stuff you taught me too, we really have a fighting chance.'

I get a flashback to the look of pity on Honey's face as she told me that Riley was only looking for a gullible chef to make him some money. I look at him. He lied to me. Olly would never lie to me.

'There is no "we", Riley.'

'Natalie!' he half laughs, unsure if I'm joking.

'Look, Riley. Let's not get too deep into this. We had a . . . a *casual shag*, and it was nice and all, but I think we both know there's nothing more to it. At least not for me there isn't.' My voice shakes a little. I swallow and it hurts my throat. 'I'm not wasting any more time in this tinpot town. Good luck with the pub. I really hope it all works out for you.'

I hug him quickly, tears blurring my eyes. And then before he can ask any questions and I end up blurting out my discovery about Alfred Hobbs and his mother, I dash out and leave him behind.

CHAPTER 33

Email from: stone_chutneys
To: nattyb
Subject: Drugs or no drugs?

Where are you, kid? The news people told me you were not in a detox unit but stuck in a village in Yorkshire. I didn't believe them. I didn't believe you would lie to me, after I rooted for you. I rooted for you so hard.

I broke into the rehab centre and looked in every room for you. The police tackled me and locked me in a cell. Marie had to post bail. Needless to say you were not in the rehab centre. I found out that you were never there. I soon realized that you are not on drugs at all.

I have spoken to Marie about this and she thinks that I should fire you. I am in love with Marie so this means that I mostly have to do what she says.

I have posted the stuff from your locker to your home address, innit.

Best of luck with everything, kidda.
Stone.

The snow might be starting to ease off, but what has already fallen is frozen solid, making it difficult to go anywhere that isn't in this damn village.

At a loss for where else I might find some peace and quiet, a place to feel sorry for myself, I find myself sneaking into The Old Whimsy's greenhouse.

I plonk myself down beside a large crate of tomatoes and think.

I need to get out of the pub. I can't stay here anymore. Not with Riley and Honey going on right in front of me. Not that I have any real feelings for him beyond lust. Obviously. But still. It's awkward. And as vile as she is, it's hardly fair on Honey.

But where else would I go? Everyone else is already bunking up with one another in order to make village supplies last until this volatile weather settles. I can't go to the Hobbs's. Not now I know such sensitive information about Alfred Hobbs and Riley and Jasper. That combined with the truth-telling would be an unmitigated disaster!

I pull an empty hessian sack from the wooden stack shelving to the right of me and bundle it up. I put it under my head, using it as a makeshift pillow. It scratches. I take off my cardigan and use it as a blanket. It only covers my belly.

Well. This is shit.

What the hell happened to my existence? It's three days before Christmas and instead of singing carols and baking mince pies and preparing for the wedding I've dreamed of all my life, I'm locking myself in a greenhouse that isn't even mine, with only a muddy sack for comfort.

I want to go home.

'Bloody Nora, you gave me the fright of me life!'

I wake up with a painful crick in my neck. I'm still tucked away beside the tomato crate. I must have dozed off. I rub my bleary eyes and see Uncle Alan looming large over me, a basket of overflowing herbs in each of his hands.

'You're a popular one, you are. The entire bloody village has been in the pub looking for you. I've not had a moment of peace. "Where's Natalie?" "Have you seen Natalie?"'

'I'm sorry.' I stand up and brush down my now dirty trousers.

'Oh, I don't mind, love. Not at all. Seems to me a lot of people want a little piece of you at the moment. You're welcome to hide out in here any time you like.'

'Thanks.' I grin sheepishly. 'What are you doing?' I nod at the basket in his arms. 'Are you cooking? Would you like some help?'

'Oh, this. No, love. I can't cook for toffee. I'm making my cosmetics.'

I look at him blankly. The very picture of this

burly, red-faced man in his wellingtons and the word 'cosmetics' are at odds with each other.

'The shampoo, love,' he says, in response to my befuddled expression. 'The one you've been using to wash your hair since you got here. Don't think I don't know you've been using it all. I can smell my shampoos anywhere.'

'The shampoo is yours?' I laugh. 'You made it?'

Of course. Mr Harrington's Shampoo. Alan Harrington. Duh. That should have been more obvious.

'Aye. It's mine. Just a hobby. For our B&B guests.'

'It's wonderful stuff. You should sell it.'

'Oh no, love. I don't know if anyone would buy it. It's just a bit of fun.'

I can't believe him!

'You should! It's really wonderful. Apart from the terrible cut, my hair has never been in better condition. And the smells! The smells are amazing.'

Alan's eyes twinkle with pleasure.

'Do you really think people would buy it?'

'Yes!' I cry. 'And you know for a fact that I can only tell the truth. I'm not just being polite.'

Alan chuckles and looks down into the basket of herbs.

'Aye. Aye. Maybe I'll look into that. A proper business, like.'

'Mr Harrington's Shampoo Made From Scratch!'

We hug and Alan marches off to his shed, a spring and a new sense of purpose in his step.

I stretch and peer around at the colourful greenhouse. You know, if all this crap wasn't going on, Little Trooley wouldn't be a bad place to live at all. But for now, it's time to face the music.

The pub is even busier than it was this morning. People are grouped around the little tables, wrapped up against the cold in colourful woolly hats and gloves. Christmas classics provide a festive soundtrack and the lights from The Old Whimsy's Christmas tree twinkle jauntily in time with the music. The festivities only serve to make me feel even sadder about my situation. Things are so rubbish that I can't even get excited about Christmas, my most favourite holiday.

I don't get a chance to order myself a drink and a packet of cheese and onion crisps before I'm hounded. It's Morag Braithwaite again and this time Barney is with her.

Why won't they just leave me alone?

'Hiya, love. It's me again,' says Morag.

'I know. I can see you.'

She looks taken aback by my abruptness. It even surprises me how forthright I've become this past couple of weeks.

'I thought we could have another chat about *Yorkshire Tonight*. You see—'

'I'm not interested, Morag. I'm sorry to disappoint you but I'm having a rubbish day and really could do without anything making it worse.'

370

She nods understandably and casts a glance at Barney who is lumbering shiftily in the background.

'Come on, love,' she says to him. 'Let's leave the poor lass alone.'

I smile at her gratefully.

Then it occurs to me. I said no. She didn't ask me a question and I was still able to say no. And it was okay. No one died. This is progress.

'You take care,' I say, turning back to the bar to get served, a small smile of victory on my face.

But I still don't get to order my drink because all of a sudden Barney takes a fancy-looking flip video camera out of his back pocket and holds it up right in front of my face.

Oh my gosh. He's *filming* me?

'Stop that!' I scold, waving away the camera.

'Stop what?' Barney asks, his eyes glinting.

'Um. Stop filming me!'

This is weird. I get a glimpse into what life must be like for Lady Gaga or Jedward, constantly hounded by the paparazzi. It's very uncomfortable. I shudder and shoo Barney away.

'You're being silly, Natalie,' he urges. '*Yorkshire Tonight* is the *big time*. You could be a star. You only need to answer a couple of questions. Just a couple.'

'That's what you said the last time!' I admonish. 'Anyway, why are you so bothered?'

'I'm trying to help you, love.' He looks wistful

for a moment. 'Of course, I won't deny that it would be nice to have one of my stories in the national press once more. I used to work at BBC Radio 2, you know? I was friends with Phil Collins!'

'Yes. You said.'

'I was a real somebody. Everyone who was anyone in radio knew my name . . .'

His eyes are glassy with the ghosts of unfulfilled dreams. Morag shakes her head and looks at me with an apologetic expression, but Barney shrugs her off and forces the camera nearer to my face. He advances towards me, asking questions, licking his lips at the very thought of snaring his juicy story.

'What are you most afraid—'

'Shut up!'

'What are you most afraid of, Natalie?'

The urge ripples through me and before I can get away from him I have to answer.

'Being alone,' I squeak.

How embarrassing.

Is that really what I'm most afraid of? I thought it would be poisonous snakes or Simon Cowell's hairy hands.

Before he can ask me another question, I spin on my heel and frantically push through the busy crowds so that I can get away.

But I don't get to walk the distance of the bar before once again I'm stopped in my tracks.

This time it's Jasper Hobbs. And he looks so

angry that I can practically see the steam shooting out from his ears.

Oh boy.

I should have thought this through. I should have stayed in that bloody greenhouse until the snow melted. It would have been fine there. A bed made of vegetable sacks and enough food to sustain me through the cold snap. A huge skylight just like I've always wanted in my dream house . . .

'Thief,' Jasper hisses at me, snapping me out of my ill-timed dream house fantasizing. He grabs my hand and pulls me into a secluded corner of the pub behind the chubby Christmas tree.

I should say something to him. But I don't know what to say. He's right. I am a thief. I have no excuse. There is never an excuse for thievery.

'Give me back those papers at once. Give them back to me and . . . I won't press charges.'

Jesus. They really are that important to him.

'No,' I say firmly, surprising myself.

God. Why am I getting involved in this? It's none of my business. I don't even know why I'm saying no.

'No?' Jasper repeats incredulously. 'NO?'

'No,' I say again. 'NO!' I shout.

We sound like a couple of parents telling off a wayward toddler.

'You have to tell him,' I say, my face going pink with embarrassment at the fact that I am even having to take part in this conversation. 'What you are hiding is . . . fraud!'

I lift my chin up. Looking at his oily hair and fake tan, I feel a wave of repulsion. What the hell does Meg see in him? The mean, sly look on his face helps me to make a real decision about what I'm going to do with the information I am now privy to.

'He deserves to know,' I say with a confidence I don't feel. 'I have to tell Riley, not because of the money, but because he deserves to know who his father is!'

Jasper grabs my arm and pinches.

'You have no fucking clue what you are getting involved in.' He bares his perfectly capped teeth.

I prise his hand away from me. He really is a nasty piece of work.

I don't know why I even doubted telling Riley about the papers. It may be none of my business, it might mean that his mum lied to him, but she obviously had good reason. He might be hurt, but he deserves to know that his father is alive and living less than ten minutes away. Also, he's rich. He should know how rich he is.

'I'm telling him!'

I dart out from behind the Christmas tree towards my room. I need to get the papers before Jasper. God knows what he'll do. He'll probably burn them. Light a fire and chuck me on too. I half walk, half jog as he follows me, hissing curse words underneath his breath but not so loud as to draw any attention to us.

'Ow!' I yell suddenly, as someone stamps on my toe.

Jesus *Christ*.

I turn around and intend to give the clumsy oaf a very disapproving look before continuing the dash to my room. But I halt when I catch a glimpse of the toe stamper.

It's Meg. And she's . . . whaaaat? She's snogging someone up against the jukebox. What is with her and snogging people up against things?

Huh? But Jasper?

I huff out loud and tap her on the shoulder.

She glances backwards and beams at me, as if Jasper is not standing right here, watching her kiss – oh man – Robbie?!

'What's wrong with you?' she says, taking in my expression of horror and confusion. 'You've got a face like a slapped arse.'

'I'm so confuuuuuused!' I say, helpless as my mouth does all the work.

'Natty?'

She eyes me like I'm crazy. Maybe I am. Maybe the hypnotism has finally addled my brain and turned it into mush.

'You're kissing Robbie,' I say in a puzzled voice, 'but only last night I saw you having sex with Jasper!'

'What?' Jasper seethes, as if he can't quite get over how much he hates me for spilling all of his secrets.

'What?' Meg laughs, squinting at me like I'm mental.

'What?' Robbie frowns, backing away from Meg.

'What?!' spits Honey who seems to have appeared from thin air.

Where did *she* come from? That woman is so creepy.

And – oooooooh – she is also wearing a green dress.

A green dress exactly the same as Meg's green dress . . . And then it kind of falls into place. It wasn't *Meg* in bed with Jasper. It was *Honey*. I KNEW there was something off about her. She's sleeping with all of them!

It seems that I'm the only one who has figured out what the hell is going on because what happens next is an almighty brawl.

Honey dives onto Meg, screeching and pulling her hair, while Jasper tries, unsuccessfully, to pull her off.

'You cheated on me?' Honey howls at him. 'You cheated on me with her?'

'Cheated!' Jasper sputters. 'What makes you think it's any of your business what I do and with whom? I've only shagged you four times, Honey, and last night was the last time. Nobody tells Jasper Hobbs what to do. No one.'

Robbie grabs his pint from the bar and downs it in one before resting his chubby-cheeked head in his hands like a kid who's just figured out that there's no Father Christmas; it's actually a drunken Uncle Jim in a Santa outfit.

Meg is trying to untangle Honey's tiny hands from her hair and I can only join the rest of the pub in looking on with befuddlement.

When Honey draws back with a hefty chunk of Meg's hair in her hands, I decide that enough is enough. I boldly ignore my quivering insides at the very thought of another violent altercation with Honey, step in and lift her up under the arms. She weighs nothing. Good for her. I carry her through the pub and deposit her outside the doors in the snow.

'Thanks,' Meg says when I return. 'That girl is a nutter. And strong. Ouch. And you're a bloody nutter too, saying that about Jasper and me.'

'I made a mistake. I really thought—'

'Are you sleeping with Jasper Hobbs?' Robbie asks Meg, ashen-faced.

'God, no!' Meg says. 'I promise!'

'But Natalie said . . .'

'I was confused,' I say to Robbie earnestly. 'It was actually Honey in the sack with Jasper last night. Honey and Meg have the same green dress. God. I wonder how long *that's* been going on. I wonder if Riley knows.'

'Huh!' Robbie looks mystified, running a hand through his dark spikes.

'Don't worry, Robbie,' Meg soothes. 'I didn't sleep with Jasper. I would never do that to you!'

'Blimey, I'm glad,' Robbie says, taking Meg's hands in his own. 'Because Meg . . . I know it's only been a few weeks . . . but I think you're the best person I've ever met. You're so gorgeous and talented and . . .' he coughs, his cheeks bright red, 'sexy. And I don't know what I did to deserve you walking through that pub door and into my life, but I'm right glad that you did. Right glad.'

Ohmigosh!

A gasp goes up around the whole room. A few people clap. One person asks whether this is a pub theatre performance that is occurring and how long it's going to go on for.

I fully expect Meg to shrug Robbie off, pat him on the shoulder, and tell him he's a doll. Robbie, with his normal-person job and his sweet, chubby face, is the very opposite of what Meg has always said she wanted. He might be lovely, but he's not quite the Adonis Meg's been holding out for. So what comes next is a bit of a shock.

'Oh, Robbie. I can't believe it, but I think I'm falling for you.'

She clasps his hands to her chest. Robbie beams.

'I can't give you riches and grand houses and clothes,' he says, staring deep into her eyes. 'But you don't need me for any of that anyhow. I can promise that I'll always look after you. And that life with me will always be an adventure.'

A collective aaaaaah goes up around the room. Me included. This is super sweet.

'And that's why,' Robbie continues, 'I'd like you to come on tour with me.'

'Tour?' Meg breathes.

'Yeah. We're so good together. I want us to go on the road. Perform music all over the country. We'll have to sleep in the van and eat Spam straight from the tin.'

'I don't care,' Meg coos, her eyes sparkling with delight. 'I quite like Spam.'

And with that they embrace and snog noisily. I wipe an unexpected tear from my eye. Well, this is a turn-up for the books! Meg peels herself off Robbie and gives me a hug.

'This is awesome,' I say, squeezing her tightly. 'Puzzling, but awesome.'

Meg woops and dances off to the bar.

'I'll be back in a second,' I call over to her, thinking of Riley and the papers in my room. 'There's something I have to do.'

She waves me off and I think I'm *finally* about to make it to my room when I'm stopped once again. This time by Riley. He's already holding the stolen papers in his hands.

CHAPTER 34

'I was looking for you and I found these, Natalie.'

He holds up the envelope with the letters, his face stony. 'What are they and why on earth do you have them in your room?'

'I was just about to tell you,' I say at once. 'That's exactly what I was just doing, coming to find you.'

'What are those?' Barney Braithwaite is suddenly there again with his video camera, pointing it at the brown envelope in Riley's hands.

'Secret documents,' I snap. Why won't he just bugger off? 'Please shut off the camera,' I ask him as politely as I can manage.

He ignores me and presses the zoom button.

'Riley,' I say, aware of everyone around me listening intently and wondering what is going to happen next in this ridiculous spectacle. 'I found them. I'm sorry I didn't say sooner. I was at Hobbs Manor last—'

'Hobbs?' Riley says, anger darkening his bright features. 'One snog from this slick git and you're on his side? What an idiot I am.'

'No,' I plead. 'I'm so sorry. I found them in Jasper's room.'

'Jasper's room?' Meg's eyes pop out of her head. 'What on earth were you doing in Jasper's room?'

'Do you really need to ask?' Riley spits.

Oh gosh, he's mad. I'm about to explain myself again, apologize *again*, when it occurs to me that here Riley is acting like he's the very model of morality and *I'm* the liar when, in fact, he's just as bad! I put my hands on my hips and step closer to him.

'You have no right to talk to me like that,' I say. 'Not after the way you've treated me.'

'Excuse me! What are you talking about? I welcomed you into my home. I – we—'

'You lied to me. You seduced me so that I would stay here and cook for you. For free! So that I would help to save your pub and I would be too lusty for you to say anything about it!'

Riley goggles.

'Are you kidding?' He rubs the back of his neck as if he's in pain. 'What went on with us was *real*. I've always been honest with you, Natalie.'

'Honey *told* me. She told me you planned it together. You haven't even split up with her! I saw you together in the kitchen, hugging and smooching. You've not been honest at all, Riley. You lied!'

'I wasn't smooching. Jesus. I was hugging Honey because she was upset about our break-up! I swear to you.'

381

'Oh.'

We're both standing there feeling awkward and utterly confused as to what's going on when Honey barges back into the pub. She has snow in her hair, her lipstick is smeared across her face and her eyes are glinting with fury.

'Riley, she's lying. I never slept with Jasper.'

'What are you on about?' Riley opens his arms in a gesture of complete confusion. 'What the hell is anyone on about?'

Honey doesn't seem to get it.

'Take me back, Riley. Don't make me leave. They all make me leave!' she cries, her face red and crazy looking.

Oh my goodness! She's acting like this has happened to her before – the whole sleeping around, stirring, making trouble in a small village thing. However much I dislike her, though, she's really very upset and for a moment I feel bad for her.

'Honey, are you okay?' I try, because she clearly needs some assistance. 'Why don't we just—' I make to take her by the arm and sit her down but she slaps me away with her tiny hand.

'Why won't you just fuck off!' she hisses at me. 'You've ruined everything.'

'But I—'

'I was fine. I had it all and you ruined it. He would have fallen in love with me eventually! Now I'll have to move *again*!'

She breaks down into a heap of noisy sobs.

Mrs Grimes hurries forward and takes her hand. 'Come on, love. Time to get you home.'

Honey's sobs quieten down into soft sniffles while Mrs Grimes gently eases her out of the pub. My goodness.

Riley looks stunned. He blinks and sinks slowly down onto a stool, pulling out the picture of his mother from the brown envelope.

'They don't belong to you.' Jasper appears and snatches the papers out of his hands.

Riley stands up. 'They're about me. About my mother. *My father.*'

Jasper's fists are curled, his face red. 'You're not entitled to anything! It's my money. Don't think you can go getting your grubby, common hands on it. I'm the one who's looked after that stupid old man for years on end. It's my money. I fucking earned it.'

'I don't care about the money, you moron.' Riley grabs the papers out of Jasper's hands. 'I care about the fact that I have a dad and no one bothered to fucking tell me.'

'I promised your mother I would never tell.' A voice comes from the door of the pub. It's Alfred Hobbs.

'Alfred?'

'Alfred Hobbs is here!'

'Isn't he dead?!'

'A recluse, Wonky-Faced Joe. He's a recluse!'

'Not anymore. He's here! Alfred is here!'

Alfred gestures that everyone should calm down.

His impressive height, carrying voice and the understanding that he's about to say something really juicy and important means everyone shuts up quite quickly.

'Leave the lad alone, Jasper. He's had a shock, can't you see?' Alfred roars.

Riley is just stood there. His hands are shaking. His eyes are filled with tears. He keeps looking down at the picture of his mother. He doesn't look at Alfred.

'I had to keep my promise, son,' Alfred says, approaching Riley. 'I never wanted to. But . . . now you know . . .'

Riley says nothing. He drops the photograph. As it flutters gently onto the floor, he turns on his heel and walks out of the bar.

'Riley,' I call, going after him. But a strong arm grabs hold of me and pulls me back.

'Natalie! Natalie!'

I wheel around at the distressed voice calling my name. It's Dionne and she's crying hysterically, a snot bubble forming at her nose.

'Olly just called. It's Mum. She – she's in the hospital. She's had a heart attack.'

And everything goes silent in my head. Nothing else matters now.

CHAPTER 35

You know how in films when something tragic happens to a character and suddenly everything they hear sounds all muffled and gloopy, like they're underwater? Well, that's not just a made-up special effect. That's actually what happens. That's what's happening as Dionne sobs in front of me. Her mouth is moving but I haven't a clue what she's saying.

Mum.

My mum.

I get a sharp picture of her, sad, alone, deathly pale on a hospital bed. I snap out of my daze.

'We need to get out of here,' I mutter. 'We need to get to her.'

'But we can't!' Dionne bawls. 'The snow. We're stuck! What if she dies?'

Meg hurries over when she sees my face.

'What is it, Natty?'

'My mum.'

'What's happened?'

'She's had a heart attack. She's . . . it's my f . . . it's my . . .'

'Wonky-Faced Joe,' she calls out immediately.

385

'Is your tractor fixed? We have an emergency. Natalie needs to get home right now.'

'No,' he says, looking embarrassed. 'It's nearly there. Maybe in another day or two.'

'What will we doohoohoo?' Dionne croaks.

'I don't know.'

My poor sister. My poor mum.

And then I remember.

I march over to where Alfred Hobbs is sitting in the corner of the pub, fiddling with a bar mat and avoiding eye contact with everyone.

'I'm sorry to interrupt,' I say, my voice shaking with the tears I'm trying not to let fall, because if I let them fall then they won't stop, I'm sure of it.

'What is it, dear?' Alfred looks up. His expression is kind.

'Mr Hobbs, I'm sorry to interrupt you when you obviously have so much going on at the moment. I know you're waiting to speak with Riley . . . but this is urgent.' I swallow hard. 'You know that helicopter you've got at home?'

'The Hobbscopter?'

'Um. Yeah. The Hobbscopter.'

'Of course, dear.'

'I kind of need to borrow it. There's been an emergency in my family and I need to get home right away. But the snow means no one can drive.'

'Oh dear.' Alfred puts his hand on my arm. 'My pilot Carlos usually flies the helicopter and he's in Pittenweem for Christmas with his family. As much as I would love to, I'm afraid I can't help.'

This is not good enough. We need to get back to Manchester. Oh God. This cannot be happening.

'But can't *you* fly it?' I try. 'You used to be in the RAF, didn't you? You told me so! Please?'

Alfred looks at a loss. 'Dear, I'm far too old to pilot now. At least not on my own. I'd put everyone in grave danger.'

No!

'You bloody scaredy cat,' says a gruff voice coming from my left. 'The Alfie Hobbs I knew wouldn't let a thing like being an old git get in the way of helping a lady in need.'

Uncle Alan is at my side. He eyes up Alfred with trepidation.

Alfred's eyes widen. 'Alan? Alan Harrington?' His bottom lip trembles slightly.

'If you're worried about a co-pilot,' Alan goes on, 'I've got a few hours spare, like.'

We both look at Alfred. My heart is about to stop with nerves and hope.

After what seems like an age, Alfred gives a firm nod of agreement.

'Thank you. Thank you so much,' I cry, gesturing to Dionne to get Jean Paul Gaultier.

Okay.

We're going home.

CHAPTER 36

I'm in a helicopter. I'm in a helicopter being flown by two old-aged pensioners who have not handled even a toy aircraft in at least ten years.

Our trip up to the helipad at Hobbs Manor was quiet and quick. Alfred and Alan are trying to tone down their excitement at seeing each other and flying a helicopter again out of respect for Dionne, who continues to sob loudly, and me who, to be honest, is still in an utter daze.

It's weird looking out of the window and seeing the snow-covered hills of Little Trooley become smaller as we get higher and farther away.

Goodbye then.

My legs feel like jelly. I feel sick.

Heart attack.

The whirring sound of the helicopter engine should be doing a better job of drowning out the horrible thoughts going through my head.

It's your fault, Natalie.

You should never have left. She couldn't be alone.

You're selfish for leaving. She needed help.

She's going to die and the last thing you said to her was that she was a bad mother.

I hold Dionne's hand and squeeze tightly as we soar across the sky. I vaguely hear Alfred organizing to land at the helipad at Manchester Royal Infirmary, but mostly I just think about getting to Mum in time to tell her I'm sorry.

We arrive at the Royal Infirmary within the hour. I briefly thank Alfred and Alan before grabbing Dionne's hand and racing down to the accident and emergency ward.

'Ladies! No dogs in here!' A podgy blonde nurse shouts at us, looking horrified as Jean Paul Gaultier jumps up at her knees in the lobby.

She's right. We can't bring a dog into a hospital. Fuck. We haven't got time to waste finding somewhere safe for him.

'Here. I'll take him.'

I spin around.

It's Olly! He looks tired and handsome in his work suit. I feel a pang of something indiscernible in my chest. Dionne bundles Jean Paul Gaultier into his arms.

'Your mum's in cubicle ten,' he says, running a hand through his hair. 'She's okay. She said she just wants to see her girls.'

I give Olly a swift hug before racing off to cubicle ten.

I pull open the curtain and enter the makeshift

hospital room. Mum is propped up against two crisp white pillows. She's hooked up to all kinds of monitors and machines. Her face is grey and sweaty and her lips are pale pink. But she smiles when she sees us.

And that's when the tears I've been holding in all day start to fall.

'I'm fine. I promise,' Mum reassures us as we fuss over her. 'It wasn't a proper heart attack. It was angina pectoris.'

'What's that?' Dionne says, her voice still shaky.

'It means that not enough oxygen was getting to my heart. At least they know now. There's medication I can take. I'll be fine. It sounds much scarier than it is.'

I know exactly what angina is. I watched plenty of *Emergency Doctor* during my week of hermitdom in the house. I know that angina can be caused by emotional stress. The kind of emotional stress you get when you, say, argue with your daughter and she's a complete bitch to you.

I plump up the pillows behind Mum and take hold of her hand.

Now we've established that no one's death is imminent, everything goes quiet. This is the first time we've spoken or seen each other since our fight, or since the wedding was called off.

Dionne, in a surprising show of diplomacy,

announces that she's going to go and get us some coffee and give Bull a ring.

Mum and I are left alone.

'I'm so sorry,' I say at once. 'I didn't mean any of what I said. I've . . . just been going through a weird time.'

We both know that I must have meant what I said during our argument because it came out when she asked me a question. Thankfully she doesn't bring that up, just gives me a watery smile.

'It's all right, love.' She waves her hand dismissively. 'You're back home now. Things can go back to normal. Did you see Olly?'

'Yes.'

'You know he loves you very, very much, Natalie.'

I sigh. 'Yes. I know.'

'I think he loves you enough to forgive you too.'

I expect a surge of hope at her words, at the possibility that things *can* go back to normal. That Olly and I can work it out. That everything can be fixed. But it doesn't come.

'I think I might have met someone else,' I say suddenly. I put my hands to my mouth in surprise that I've just said that out loud to my mum. It's not even like it's worth mentioning. Riley thinks I'm a liar. It was just a one-night stand.

'Olly's a good man,' Mum says steadily, looking deep into my eyes and holding my hands in hers. 'Reliable and honest to boot. Now those qualities might not be glamorous and exciting, but they're the qualities that make for a successful marriage.'

I take in what she's saying.

'You're almost thirty, Natalie.'

'I'm twenty-seven!'

I feel the tears well up again and feel my stomach clench as they spill over and trickle onto my cheeks.

Mum grabs my hand and squeezes gently.

'You're just nervous. That's all.'

I nod. She's probably right.

'Time to grow up.'

Dionne returns and I leave because I'm desperate for a wee. I must turn a wrong corner or something because I end up on a long, dimly lit corridor.

There must be a loo somewhere along here, I think. I turn another corner and pause at what appears to be a ward. There's a glass window looking in upon two rows of beds. Two blue-uniformed nurses are gossiping at a station. Great! There'll definitely be a toilet in here.

I'm about to go in and ask when—

'I know you, lass. I never forget a face!'

Oh. My. God.

I spin around, my heart pounding so fast I fear it's going to explode.

There in the very first bed, with his leg in a huge white cast and grinning nonchalantly, is Amazing Brian.

That bastard!

CHAPTER 37

'Yooooou!' I snarl, marching over to Brian's bed and slamming my hand down on his hospital table, causing a bowl of grapes to topple over onto the floor. 'You! You ruined my life.'

The two nurses at the station, spotting a mad woman about to commit murder on a patient, make a lightning-quick move towards me. One takes out a walkie-talkie and calls for back up. I'm sure the other one cracks her knuckles as if preparing for fisticuffs.

Brian stops them.

'It's fine, Nurse Gilda, Nurse Maud. I know this lass. She's all right. She'll be quiet.'

The nurses narrow their eyes at me, not sure whether to trust what Brian says or rugby tackle me to the ground and sit on me until hospital security arrives.

They look at each other and eventually back away, the more muscular of the two growling at me to keep my voice down or else there will be consequences.

'They're like my bodyguards, those two. God love 'em,' Brian laughs, all bright and breezy.

'What happened to your leg?' I say, curiosity getting the better of me.

'I bloody slipped on some ice about, hmm, three weeks ago . . .'

'Oh.'

So *that's* where he was. Seems stupid that I didn't check the hospitals. They always check the hospitals when a person goes missing!

'So. You were saying?' Brian grins.

'Oh, right, yes. You. Ruined. My. Life,' I spit once more, carefully keeping it to a stage whisper. I pull up a pink visitor's chair and plonk myself onto it.

'Did I?' Brian asks, nodding at me to pass him the glass of Lucozade on his bedside table. 'Did I really?'

I hand him his drink. I might be mad at him, but I'm not going to deny a sick man his fluids. I'm not a complete cow.

'Yes, you did, you . . . bastard. You hypnotized ME, you daft git. Three weeks ago at a pub in Manchester—'

'The Pear and Partridge, yes?'

'Yes, the Pear and Partridge! You were supposed to hypnotize my friend—'

'Meg—'

'Yes, Meg! But you hypnotized me. And now I can't hear a question without answering with the absolute truth, which might sound like it wouldn't be that much of a problem but actually it is. It turns out that I'm a great big liar. I've been going around for *years* never telling people what I really think and now all I can do is tell people what I really think and it's not pretty.'

'Oh, lass, it can't have been that bad, surely?'

Not that bad? *Not that bad?* I resist the powerful urge to slam my hand down onto his broken leg.

'Since you hypnotized me, Brian, you great bastard, my wedding has been called off, the man I love dumped me, I got snowed in in Little Trooley . . .'

'Oh, that's where I live!'

'That's why I was there, stoopid. Continuing the list of bad things that have happened to me since I met you, I got fired, I upset my mother so much that she had an angina attack, I slept with a stranger, ate some pigs' feet, got cosmetic surgery injections in my lips, took a helicopter ride with two old blokes, had my first ever physical fight, discovered some heavy-duty secrets and hurt some people I really care about.'

I take a deep breath and stare at Brian. I hope he feels bad about this.

'That's terrible, love. Sounds like you've had a right time of it.'

'Yes. Yes, I have,' I say, feeling very sorry for myself.

'Would you like me to stop the hypnotism now?'

Oh yes.

I've been so concerned with being angry at Brian that I'd forgotten the entire reason I needed to find him!

'Yes. Yes, please. Then everything can go right back to normal.'

'Which is a *good thing*,' Brian says, patting my arm.

'Yes . . . which is a very good thing,' I nod defiantly.

Brian sits up further against the pillows. I see that his pyjamas are the same design as the jumper he was wearing at the pub. Blue with the initials AB in red.

God! What an egomaniac.

'Right then. Let's get to it.'

I shake my shoulders ready to be put into a trance, to be taken into a deep slumber so that Brian can access the deepest recesses of my mind and fix what he ruined.

'AWAKE!' he shouts. It's so loud that I jump and my eyes fly open. Next to us an elderly woman screams. As soon as Brian makes eye contact with me he leans forward and claps. Three times. Right in front of my face. The sound of the claps echo around the hospital room and around my brain.

I go hot for a moment and slightly dizzy.

'There you go,' Brian says brightly. 'All done.'

I blink. And then again. 'What? Just like that? So quickly? So *easily*?'

'Yes, love. That's how it works.'

'Oh.'

I can't help but feel a sense of anticlimax. After four weeks of having my brain not do what I want it to do, the whole stressful search for Brian, the worry that my life was all but ruined. After all that, it took only four seconds for my brain to return to normal.

Normal.

I'm fixed.

'You need to be more careful in the future,' I say sternly to Brian.

'I always am,' he says, his eyes twinkling as if he knows a secret that I don't. 'I know exactly what I'm doing.'

'Well, obviously not,' I scoff and stand up from the chair. 'I hope your leg feels better soon, but I still hate you.'

'Bye, Natalie Butterworth. Good luck!'

'Yeah, bye Brian.'

I walk up to the tall nurse at the nurses' station.

'Ask me if I like your shoes,' I say, peering down at her feet and the ugly white and fluorescent yellow trainers she's wearing.

She frowns quickly and then shrugs, obviously curious to know what I *do* think of her shoes. 'Okay. What *do* you think of my shoes?' she asks.

'They're gorgeous,' I say easily. 'The nicest shoes I've ever seen. All my life I have longed for shoes like that!'

I lied!

Hurrah!

I look over at Brian and do a thumbs up. He returns the thumbs up, shrugs and goes back to his newspaper, as if this whole bizarre episode was just a normal occurrence in the life of the Amazing Brian.

What an odd character.

As I leave the ward I wonder how Brian knew that my last name was Butterworth. I don't remember telling him that . . .

I finally get to the loo and end up asking two women in there to ask me a question. And then I ask a porter and a doctor to also ask me questions. And I can lie. I can lie *so well*! I tell one of the women that I was born to a family of Eskimos, and I tell the porter that when the clock strikes midnight I sprout wings and fly over Greater Manchester for a few hours before I go to bed.

It feels wonderful to finally have control over my brain. Control over my life!

As I make my way back to Mum's hospital room, I think about Riley. I've checked my phone a few times to see if he's been in touch but there's been not a beep or a jingle. Why would he get in touch? He's got far more important things on his mind than the girl he had a one-night and one-afternoon stand with. But still, I check my phone, just in case.

★ ★ ★

After another half an hour with Mum, in which Dionne regales her with dramatically embellished tales of our snow-in and the helicopter ride, the podgy blonde nurse comes in to tell us that it's time to leave. Mum needs to rest, but will be able to return home tomorrow.

We meet Olly outside where he's been waiting on a bench with Jean Paul Gaultier.

A car screeches up in front of us. It's yellow and shiny and loud.

'Bull's here,' Dionne says. 'I'm going to go straight to his. Olly, you'll give Nats a lift back, yeah?'

'Of course,' Olly says, handing over a sleepy Jean Paul Gaultier.

I try to peek into the windows to get a glimpse of the enigmatic Bull, but they're blacked out.

Dionne gives me a terse hug, tinkles her hand in a wave, jumps into the car and zooms off into the night. It's weird, but as soon as she's gone I start to miss her.

'Come on then, sweetness,' Olly says, throwing an arm around me. 'Let's get you home.'

We drive to Olly's apartment in relative silence. I think that perhaps he's afraid to say anything in case I tell the truth and cause another argument. For some reason I don't tell him about the hypnotism being fixed. And even if I did, it probably wouldn't matter. He never believed in the hypnotism anyway.

Once inside his house I take a shower and get changed into a pair of his pyjamas. I'm drying my hair when my phone flashes with a message.

Text from: **Riley Old Whimsy**
How is your mum? How are you?

Reply to: **Riley Old Whimsy**
She's fine now. Thank you. Are you okay?
Did you speak to Alfred?

Text from: **Riley Old Whimsy**
Not yet. Need time.

And then I pluck up the courage to ask what I want to know.

Reply to: **Riley Old Whimsy**
Were we just a one-night stand? Did I imagine that we were something more than that?

I lock myself in the bathroom and wait for his reply.

It doesn't come.

It's weird. Everything seems unusual and quiet. There's an empty, hungry feeling in the pit of my stomach, like the feeling you get when you come back home from an amazing holiday abroad and it's almost as if it never actually happened.

But things have happened. Things have changed.

And even though I'm back in the same place I was before any of this happened, I feel like a completely different person.

I must fall asleep on Olly's sofa because I wake up at around midnight absolutely freezing.

I sit up. Olly is lounging on the chair opposite me.

'I was just about to wake you,' he says softly. 'Tell you to get into bed.'

I nod, wrapping my arms around myself.

The television is on mute but the bright colours cast flickering shapes over his handsome face.

'I'm sorry,' I whisper. 'I'm so sorry I hurt you.'

He rises from the chair and is at my side within seconds.

'I didn't cancel the church, Natalie,' he says fervently.

'Huh?' I ask, rubbing my eyes.

'I cancelled the other stuff. The flowers, the food, everything. But I kept the church. I just couldn't bring myself to cancel that.'

I stare at the face I know so well. The face I love. The person I always anticipated spending my life with. The steady, secure, reliable man who will always look after me. He's already my family.

Olly takes hold of my hand and squeezes it.

'I love you, Natalie. I'll forgive what you did. We can forget all about it . . . Just say you'll marry me on Saturday?'

I get a brief flash of Riley singing the Colour

Me Badd song in the kitchen. Of his face when he thought I'd been lying to him. I push it away. What does that matter now? It was a fling. A rebound. I don't even know Riley. I know this man here. The one right in front of me, who is asking if I'll spend my life with him.

'Yes,' I whisper eventually. 'Yes, I will.'

CHAPTER 38

Mum is back from the hospital the next day, and despite strict instructions from the doctors and me and Dionne not to get too excited, she is throwing herself into making sure that this wedding happens properly.

With the nuptials taking place tomorrow and with only one day to sort things out, she has set up a command centre from her bed. She's already managed to sort out flowers, catering (Irene from the corner shop is going to do a pie and peas supper) and someone to come to the house to do our hair and make-up in the morning. The reception was less easy to reorganize so we're now having a party for family and close friends at The Trap Inn, our local pub, and one of Olly's workmates is doing the music.

Dionne has managed to get Bull to sort out a cake, and while the glittering sleeping swan cake I desperately didn't want is the one I'm now going to have at my wedding, I don't really mind anymore. I'm just grateful that it's happening at all.

Dionne has been wonderful, actually. I'm thinking that maybe telling her the truth about the way she was behaving was actually for the best. Not only has she been mad helpful in getting the wedding sorted, but she's been sure not to overtake the situation and make it all about her. I know it can't have been easy for her, but she's letting me have my moment in the spotlight. And besides, after what happened to Mum, we've both realized that there are more important things than arguing and getting at each other. Family is more important.

Text to: **Meg**
I'm getting married in 6 hours. Can't sleep! Will u b here? Please say u will. Need best mate. X

Text from: **Meg**
Am still trying! Bet you're excited? You love Olly so much. Don't you? X

Text to: **Meg**
Of course I do, silly. Did you tell Riley? X

Text from: **Meg**
Yeah. Mentioned it tonight. He didn't say anything. Not seen him since. Why do you ask? X

Text to: **Meg**
No reason. X

I'm getting married! In a few short hours I will be Mrs Natalie Chatterley.

It's impossible not to be excited. Mum's house is buzzing. Dionne's turned on some music and is already handing out champagne while Auntie Jan practises her scales for the song she is going to perform in the church (we decided on 'Up Where We Belong'), and in a few minutes the hairdresser will be here to help make me look beautiful and groomed.

Everything is going to plan. I'm back where I belong, I'm marrying the most handsome man in the world, and my brain is fixed. It's all great. Everything is great.

I'm having my face moisturized by the make-up lady when Mum shouts downstairs for someone to answer the door.

'The hairdresser is here! Let her in!'

No one else seems bothered about the continuously ringing doorbell so I apologize to the make-up lady and plod to the door myself.

Oh balls. I've seen *this* hairdresser before.

It's Barbara. From fricking Hair Hackers.

Oh no, she didn't.

'Calm down!' Mum scolds, as I have a mini panic attack in the living room. In the grand scheme of things that have gone on in my life recently, bad hair isn't really one to worry about, but the hideous haircut Barbara gave me does not bode at all well for what kind of wedding updo she'll adorn me with.

'Barbara was the only person available at such short notice,' Mum shrugs.

No wonder. She's shit.

'But . . . But . . .' I start, but Mum shushes me and plonks me down in the chair. Dionne hurries over with a glass of champagne. I neck it in one.

'Okay. A simple chignon,' Dionne says slowly to Barbara. 'That's what you want, isn't it, Natty?'

'Yes. Just simple,' I echo, throwing Dionne a grateful look.

'Not what I'd go for but . . . it's Natalie's day.'

Barbara puts her hands on her ample hips. 'I don't know why you're fussing. She runs her fingers through my locks. 'This here is a top-class haircut.' She huffs. 'A bloody chignon. Easy peasy, flower.'

Once Mum and Dionne have established that Barbara will indeed be able to put my hair into a simple chignon, they leave again to pretty themselves up.

'It's grown out a little bit, hasn't it? I can cut it again now for you if you like?'

'No!'

'Why not? You loved your hair the last time I did it!'

It's my first instinct to lie, to be polite to this

woman and agree that, yes, I did love my hair the last time she cut it. But something happens. I *want* to tell her the truth.

'I didn't love it. I think you rushed it, actually. The colours were horrible, and you charged me too much. I should have told you at the time but I was too afraid of hurting your feelings.'

Barbara goes quiet for a moment.

Shit. I've upset her.

She strolls over to where her kit bag is on the dining room table and digs inside.

What is she doing? She's probably getting out her largest pair of scissors to stab me with. Or worse, her electric razor so that she can shave my head and I'll have to be a bald bride.

But she does none of those things. She pulls out a big wad of twenties and peels off five notes.

'Love, my feelings are not easily hurt. I'm sorry you didn't like the job I did. You should have told me. Here's your money back.'

And then she hands me a hundred quid.

What? Just like that?

I look at her. She doesn't appear to be upset. Or have hurt feelings. In fact, she looks like this is something that has happened to her before which, let's face it, probably has.

'Oh,' I say like an idiot. 'Well, thanks. I'm glad that's sorted.'

'Can I do your bloody chignon now?'

'Yes. Thanks, Barbara.'

* * *

The chignon turns out to be exactly what I wanted. Twisted elegantly at the nape of my neck and with a few beaded clips dotted here and there. It's a shame I'll have to ruin the effect with the dress of horrors, but that's what you get when your wedding is called back on at the last minute, I suppose.

When I've done up my bra, I slip on my dressing gown and call out to Mum, who's been waiting outside the bedroom door with my dress, that I'm ready to get changed.

She comes in, her face flushed with pleasure, and unzips the huge garment bag she's holding.

I get the shock of my life when what she pulls out isn't the dress of horrors, but an elegant corseted dress with a soft flippy skirt and lace sleeves.

'What . . . How . . .' I gasp, unable to take my eyes off one of the most beautiful dresses I've ever seen.

'It's the same dress!' Mum bursts out excitedly, like she's been waiting to show me for ages. 'I adjusted it.'

'Adjusted? Are you mental! This is a complete overhaul!'

I can't believe it. The diamante has been unstitched and replaced with tiny glass beads; the top is still corseted but a brand-new sweetheart neckline has been added. The reams of netting underskirt have been totally removed.

Mum blushes and brushes her fringe out of her

eyes. 'Well, I had a little think and I realized that maybe we were a bit pushy with the dress. You were right. It really wasn't you. Dionne maybe. But definitely not you. I've been working on it day and night since then. You know. Just in case . . .'

I do a little jump up and down. I can't believe I'm going to get to wear this dress.

'Thank you, Mum,' I say, leaning in to give her a squeeze.

'You're welcome, darling,' she says, squeezing back just as tightly.

Bull is driving us to the church in his flashy yellow car with the blacked-out windows. Now, the only thing I know about Bull is that he's a bit of a gangster with fingers in many dodgy pies and contacts with some of the most dangerous criminal masterminds in the country. So I must admit I'm surprised to find that his appearance is less Jason Statham and more Pee-wee Herman.

Bull is a geek. No two ways about it. He's dressed in a black tuxedo with a yellow cummerbund and a matching bow tie. Dionne flings herself at him and smothers him in kisses. He blushes, but kisses her back all the same, commenting on how wonderful she looks in her black tutu. They are a very cute couple.

'Hello, Natalie,' Bull says in a softly spoken cockney twang. 'You look beautiful. It's nice to meet you. Your sister says nuffink but great things about ya.'

'She does?' I chuckle, as Dionne pokes her tongue out at me. 'It's good to finally meet you too.'

'What are we standing here like buffoons for?' Mum interrupts, bustling out of the front door behind us. She looks lovely and bright and decidedly unfrail in a deep purple shift dress, matching jacket and hat. I feel a glimmer of pride.

'Come on then, everyone. Let's get this show on the road!'

CHAPTER 39

It all seems to have happened so quickly. I can't quite believe that this is it. I'm getting married!

We stop outside the church for a few moments while Irene-from-the-shop's husband Bob takes some photographs of me, Mum and Dionne.

I take a deep breath, reapply some lip gloss and then it's time to go.

I get to the entrance of the church and Mum hurries in before me. I hear her saying hello to all the guests.

Oh God. This is it.

Dionne is next to me, looking exactly like the Black Swan from *Swan Lake*. She straightens my dress and pats down my hair.

'You're gorgeous,' she says.

'Thanks. Have you got a tissue? I'm sweating.'

Dionne pulls a hanky from out of her cleavage and hands it over. I dab at my forehead.

We stand there and wait for the music to start playing, my cue to walk down the aisle to Olly.

'I can't wait until I get to do this with Bull!' Dionne beams, her eyes sparkling at the very thought.

'He's lovely,' I say approvingly. 'Not at all what I expected. You go very well together.'

'I know,' Dionne says, making heart eyes. 'We're soooo in love.'

All at once I stiffen.

My stomach drops and my ears ring.

'W – What did you just say?' I ask, feeling the colour drain from my face.

'Um. We're soooo in love?'

Oh God.

'Ask me if I'm in love with Olly,' I say, my heart speeding up.

'What? Why?'

'Because no one asked me that when I was under the truth-telling spell. They all asked me if I loved Olly. And of course I do. Of course I *love* him. But no one asked me if I'm IN love with him.'

'Calm down,' Dionne scolds. 'This is classic cold feet. Besides, it doesn't matter if I ask you – you're not hypnotized anymore. You don't need me to ask you the question to know the truth.'

She's right. But . . .

'Just do this for me, Dionne. Ask me. Please!'

She sighs and rolls her eyes.

'Are you in love with Olly?'

The answer comes back at once. Not forced through my mouth because of a spell cast upon me by some crazy old man with weird powers. But in my heart. And I'm sure. I've never been more sure.

'No. No, I'm not in love with him.'

Dionne gasps. I gasp.

And then the organ strikes up with the wedding march.

Massive balls.

What is someone supposed to do in a situation like this? I don't know how it works. They don't tell you about this in the wedding blogs and magazines.

I can't marry Olly. I can't marry somebody I'm not in love with.

Dionne does a squeak and pushes me further towards the church entrance.

'You're being silly. You don't know what you're talking about.'

She pushes me again. I stumble forward and then I'm inside the church. Crammed full of guests of whom I only know about half.

Shit. I have no choice. I can't back out now. Not after I've messed everyone around. They've all put in so much effort. I feel like I'm in a bad dream. The worst dream.

I start to walk.

There's Auntie Jan, looking resplendent in her brand-new burgundy trouser suit; she's supposed to be singing later. And Irene from the shop who worked through the night to do pie and peas and some egg mayo sandwiches and spring rolls for a buffet.

I carry on walking.

414

There's Barbara from Hair Hackers, who decided to support me at my wedding even though we don't know each other and I called her a bad hairdresser.

And Meg! There's Meg in the front pew, looking windswept and happy, Robbie by her side. She made it! Behind her sit Alan and Alfred. They must have flown her over in the Hobbscopter. Ha ha!

I spot Mum. My mum. Who truly believes that Olly is the right man for me. Who has a frail heart and has been looking forward to my wedding for so very long.

And finally, there's Olly.

Lovely, sweet Olly. Who forgave me my behaviour and still – after all this shit – wants to settle down with me.

Settle down. SETTLE DOWN.

But . . . But . . .

I'm not ready. I haven't lived! I *can't* settle down yet. I can't settle down when I've never ever been up. I can't settle down for the rest of my life when I haven't lived!

And Olly. I know in my heart of hearts that he's not right for me. We're not sexually compatible. He wants me to lose weight and stop dreaming about being a chef because being a counter assistant is perfectly fine.

I halt. Right there on the aisle. Dionne bumps into me.

'Natalie?' Olly says, eyes narrowed. 'Come on!'

415

He laughs nervously and rolls his eyes at the crowd as if I'm being silly.

Silly Natalie.

From behind I feel Dionne push me a little further forward. I stand my ground.

I have to tell the truth.

I glance at Mum, fully expecting her to have a face like thunder, or worse, another angina attack. And though she looks disappointed, she shrugs and smiles sadly at me.

'I love you,' she mouths.

Her blessing gives me a fresh burst of confidence.

'I can't do this,' I say to Olly quietly.

His face crumples.

'What the fuck?' he hisses.

'Mind your language,' the vicar frowns, tugging uncomfortably at his bedazzled dog collar.

'I'm so sorry, Olly,' I say, as clear and calm as the frozen waterfall in Little Trooley. 'But . . . I'm not in love with you.'

Oh goodness, I feel awful. But surely it's *more* awful to lie and to let him marry someone who doesn't want to spend their life with him?

His eyes water and he furiously blinks away angry tears.

Oh God. What have I done to him?

'You selfish cow.'

He spits it with such venom I have to take a step back.

'Now now.' Alan from Little Trooley stands up. 'You do not talk to a lady that way.'

Alfred pulls him back down.

'Olly, I'm so—' I start.

'You know how lucky you are to have me?'

'I kno—'

'You think you can treat me like this after all I've done for you?'

I start to cry.

'I can't lie to you Olly! I just couldn't—'

'You'll never find anyone else like me, Natalie. Someone who'll put up with your huge arse and your battleaxe misery guts mother and—'

'Olly, stop this!' I plead. 'You're being horrible!'

'No wonder your dad left. Maybe you're actually doing me a favour.'

I look at him shouting, his face red, and suddenly he's not quite as handsome as I always thought he was. He's mean. Olly is mean. And weak. And controlling. And he is too short. And BAD in bed. He's soooo not the one.

'I'm sorry, Olly. I am. I've got to go now.'

'You what? You're not actually going to leave – you bloody—'

'Oh, do shut up, Olly!'

It's my mum. She stands up from her place in the front pew. Alan from Little Trooley rushes over to take her arm and hold her steady.

'Natalie.' She turns to me and does her most stern teacher voice. 'If you don't bugger on off out of this church right now, I will be very upset indeed. Do you hear me?'

I smile at her. I never could argue with my mum.

417

And so I do as she says.

I go.

I spin around and, ignoring the shocked murmurs and wailing echoing around me, I leg it out of the church and into the sunshine.

I stop my escape totter when I get out into the church grounds. Partly because I need to catch my breath but mostly because I just want to look around to see if anyone has followed me out. I kind of expected that they would, but no one has.

'You didn't go through with it, then?'

It's Riley.

He looks a bloody mess. He's panting and red-faced like he's been running. He's wearing a thick green snow suit, there are scratches on his face and his hair is all over the show. I don't understand.

'What are *you* doing here?' I cry, my knees wobbling precariously. 'How the hell did you even get here?'

'On Wonky-Faced Joe's tractor,' he says. 'It kind of took me all night.'

'I thought it was broken?' I say, fighting an ill-timed urge to laugh.

'It is. Hence the all night thing. I broke down four times and got stopped by the police twice.'

'Why are you here, Riley?' I ask. 'What do you want?'

'I. Um. I was kind of coming to stop your wedding.'

What the fuck?

'Stop my wedding?' I echo disbelievingly.

'Yes. I was going to break in and make sure you didn't marry Olly.'

'Well, you're too late. I've already not married him.'

I stalk off across the grass of the church grounds and then stop and turn back.

'You didn't reply to my text message,' I say, grumpily.

'I'm replying to it now.'

'Oh?' I raise an eyebrow. It's probably both eyebrows.

'I wanted to tell you in person.'

'Wanted to tell me what?'

He edges closer, takes my hand and leads me to a quiet corner of the church grounds shaded by shrubs and trees.

'Natalieeeee,' he starts to sing, his voice cracking with nerves. 'I want you to come back with meeeeeee . . .'

'To Little Trooley?' I interrupt.

He nods and stops singing. His voice becomes serious.

'I like you. A lot. A very lot. Pretty much more than I've ever liked anything else in my whole life. *Even more* than I like Colour Me Badd.'

Oh my gosh.

I can't help the grin that stretches across my face. It makes my cheeks ache.

'I like you a lot too,' I murmur, my heart leaping

419

with pleasure at his words. 'Even more than I like bread.'

He laughs gleefully, pulling me to him. He places his lips softly on mine.

Zing!

This is how it should feel. It should feel amazing. It should feel *unquestionably* right.

'But . . .' I say, reluctantly breaking the kiss.

'But?' he asks, frowning.

'I'd love to come to Little Trooley with you, Riley. I would. But . . . I kind of have to do something first. And it might take a while.'

'What is it?' he asks, looking really, really confused.

I take a deep breath and exhale steadily.

'I want to live a little,' I say simply, truthfully.

And then, not entirely sure whether running away from the man I AM in love with is the new most ridiculous thing I've ever done in my life, I hitch up the skirt of my wedding dress and I run out of the church grounds and far away.

It feels like flying.

CHAPTER 40

Two Months Later

I'm in Paris. Can you imagine? Me. Natalie Butterworth – the homebody of all homebodies – in Europe's most exciting city!

After the wedding of disasters I decided I needed to get away from everything. Figure things out. Figure me out.

I went back to Mum's from the church, packed a suitcase and headed straight to the airport. From there I called the Braithwaites. Morag was only too happy to lend me the use of their holiday home here for as long as I needed. Her way of apologizing for Barney, I suppose. So, still in a daze, I booked a ticket, got on a plane and I've been here for two months.

'Natalie! Le cheesecake pour la table deux!'

The voice of Maurice, my boss at the restaurant I'm waitressing in, interrupts my thoughts.

'Oui, chef!' I call back, picking up a slice of cheesecake from the counter and taking it over to the customer.

Working at Le Café de Maurice is great. My French isn't wonderful, but I'm learning, and the people here are nice. We socialize and it's fun getting to know everyone. Despite the language barrier, I'm starting to make some new friends.

'Merci, Natalie,' Maurice calls from the kitchen, his caterpillar eyebrows knitting together in a grin. 'Dépêchez-vous maintenant ou vous serez en retard.'

He just said, 'Thank you, Natalie. Now hurry or you will be late.'

See? My French is getting rather good.

I smile back at him and untie my apron before collecting my bag from the cloakroom.

'Au revoir!'

'Au revoir, Natalie! Bonne chance! Good luck!'

I wave and leave the cafe, setting off down the Rue Saint-Honoré towards Avenue de l'Opéra, which is where I need to be.

I take off my cotton scarf, enjoying the chilly February wind against my face. It's refreshing after the hot atmosphere in the cafe. I walk at a steady pace, in time with the queues of people going in the same direction as me. We all have places to be.

You know, I heard from Amazing Brian one last time. At the airport after the non-wedding. I was getting a sudden attack of the jitters about upping and leaving my life without any real

422

plan about what I was going to do. I almost turned back when my phone beeped with a text.

Text from: **Number not available**
Bonjour Natalie. Paris is waiting. AB

I'm not sure how he got my number, or how he knew I was at the airport and wondering whether I should go to Paris, but the text did make a few things clear to me.

1. Amazing Brian was the person behind the text message that sent me back to Little Trooley.
2. Amazing Brian is a total lunatic.
3. Maybe magic is real and somehow I've been lucky enough to have had a little sent my way.

I've not heard from Olly at all. I tried to call him a few times when I first got here but he won't answer. It's still raw, I suppose.

I understand that.

Dionne tells me that he's started seeing a girl called Bunny, a personal trainer at his gym. I hope it works out for him.

Dionne and Bull are engaged! They're getting married later in the year and I'll be going back to be her chief bridesmaid. I'm thrilled for her. I've been getting to know Bull on Skype and his gentle, intelligent nature couldn't be a more perfect fit for her. He's even managed to convince Dionne to let me choose my own bridesmaid dress – no diamante included. What a guy.

I've been in touch with Meg religiously. She's doing a tour of Europe with Robbie and is having the time of her life. Apparently there's a huge buzz about their band and a record is even in the pipeline. She really is going to be a pop star! The next stop on their tour is Paris, so I'll get to see her in a few short weeks. I can't wait.

Things have been better with Mum. We speak to each other on the phone every day and it's never awkward. In that sense the truth-telling worked wonders. I no longer feel the need to lie to her. I told her the truth about my feelings, about our childhood and about not wanting to be tied to home for the rest of my life. It was hard at first, but she's coming round. In fact, I think she's a little bit proud of me. Proud that I've taken the plunge and left Manchester on my own. She says I'm brave. That makes me happy. And she's happier now too. She's got an admirer in the shape of Riley's uncle Alan. He sends her his shampoo (soon to be available in Harrods!) and boxes of vegetables – his version of an over-ture, I guess – on a regular basis, but Mum says she's taking a leaf out of my book and learning to be independent. I don't know how long that'll last for, though. From what she's told me, the chemistry between them is smoking hot! Eeeeeeew.

I get to where I need to be and take a deep breath. The building is huge. A masterpiece of French eighteenth-century architecture, the Hôtel du Rêve, which literally translates as Dream Hotel, is imposing and breathtaking. Maybe I should have got changed. Too late now.

I push open the door and stop for a second, marvelling at the crystal chandeliers overhead. I gulp. I can't believe I'm here.

I stride over to the reception desk where a stylish woman with cropped black hair asks what she can do for me.

'Hello,' I say nervously in French. 'My name is Natalie Butterworth. I'm here to begin my cooking diploma.'

The woman smiles and replies in English. 'Welcome, Natalie. Here are ze directions.'

She points me down a long hallway and tells me to turn left at the bottom. I thank her and walk over the thick carpet down the corridor.

My heart begins to thud as I reach the kitchens. I push open the door.

It's massive! Huge, long steel tops and silver chairs. At least eight stoves!

I notice that everyone is already dressed in their whites. A chubby woman points me in the direction of the changing rooms.

He heee!

I put on my whites and examine myself in the mirror.

My eyes are sparkling. I look like a chef. An actual chef!

And then:

'She's an easy lover. She'll get a hold on you, belieeeeeve it . . .'

I freeze.

What the pickle?

I turn around, and nonchalantly standing there against a locker is Riley.

My Riley.

'Your lips have gone down. I was starting to like them all puffed up.'

My heart leaps into my throat. I want to hug him tightly; I want to kiss him hard and repeatedly. But I haven't seen or talked to him in ages.

'What – what are you doing here?' I breathe, unable to get over the sight of him. I giggle girlishly. I can't help myself.

'Well, a very beautiful girl once told me that my cooking was shit. I thought it was about time I learned how to do it properly.'

I laugh out loud. 'A very beautiful girl, eh?'

'Amazing, actually.'

'You're doing the course too?'

He nods once, staring at me with those delicious eyes, the cutest grin fixed upon his face.

I take him in. He looks taller, if that's even possible. And tanned and, well, perfect actually.

Riley.

I can't believe it.

'But what about . . .'

'The Old Whimsy? Jasper's left the family business and is gallivanting somewhere in Thailand so the pub is safe. In fact, Alan and Alfred are going to run it for a while. They told me to bugger off. Apparently you're not the only one who needs to live a little.'

I nod, unable to take the smile off my face.

'And Alfred? You've talked?'

'It's weird. But we're getting there. Getting to know one another.' His voice breaks slightly and he coughs. 'It's not easy, but he's a good man. And he really loved my mum. He's got some great stories about her.'

'I missed you,' I say, as I drink him in.

'I can go one better than that.'

'Oh yeah?'

'Yeah. I love you, Natalie Elspeth Butterworth. I should have said it at the church that day because I felt it then, but—'

'Come here, Riley.'

We fall into each other's arms and kiss long and hard. My eyes flood with tears because I know that right here, right now, with him, is exactly where I'm supposed to be.

We pull back and look at each other, noses nuzzling.

'We're going to have the best time,' Riley says, his voice husky with emotion.

'I know. I'm so totally in love with you.'

'Truly?' he says, raising a sandy eyebrow comically.

'The absolute truth,' I return, taking his hand. And then it's time to cook.

TIPS FOR A SUPER SEXY WEDDING BY DIONNE BUTTERWORTH

It's your big day, ladies, and you will be playing the part you were always meant to play: the centre of everyone's attention. That's why it's important that everything about your wedding is ridiculously hot. Hot enough to make all your friends hate you, all your exes rue the day they ever decided to cheat on you with Lindsey Trippett from the Spar, and all of the guests who you don't really know wonder, *Who is this smoking hot woman and how has she pulled off the best wedding of ALL TIME?*

Here are some top tips from me to you:

Hair

• The bridal magazines may use words like 'soft', 'feminine' and 'simple' but they are barking up the wrong tree. The word you need to keep in mind is 'glam'. GLAM!

• Glam hair can be achieved in many ways, but the most effective way is with hair extensions. The human hair ones are best (try not to think too much about the fact that it is a stranger's hair). If you buy the clip-in ones, you can even take them out halfway through the day to change your look!

• Bigger is better when it comes to weddings – when it comes to everything really. Except mobile phones and knickers. Use a massive styling wand to create bouncing waves. Top off with your diamante tiara.

Make-up

• Once again, it's really important not to listen to those people who tell you to go for the 'natural look'. They are the same people who do sad face emoticons on Facebook, or watch *Dickinson's Real Deal*: losers. It's much better to go intense, so that your features do not disappear on the photographs and your head doesn't end up looking like a blurred thumb with amazing hair.

• Eyebrows can really make a statement on your wedding day. By plucking them extensively before-hand you can draw them in a little higher to create an expression of pleasure. This way you will look happy throughout the whole wedding day, even when your groom does his ugly cry face.

• Get your lips plumped. Obvs.

• Fake eyelashes are vital. Anyone can be trans-formed from Ugly Duckling to Sexy Swan with the right set of lashes. The Girls Aloud Cheryl ones are my own personal favourite, but they're

430

always the first to run out in Superdrug. The Kimberley ones aren't bad if you have no other choice.

Wedding Dress

• Pink sparkly dress or white sparkly dress? A truly tough choice and one I can't help you with. Soz.
• A corseted dress will really enhance your boobs to perfection. The higher up you can get them, the better! If the rest of the day goes tits up, an outstanding cleavage will help to make the wedding memorable for your guests.
• You might want to be 'unique' and go for a slinky, straight skirt, but trust me: everyone at your wedding will be disappointed. Your skirt should be so big that it knocks at least one person over during the day. Preferably Lindsey Trippett from the Spar.

Venue

• Pick a theme for your venue and decorate it in this style to create an air of fun. Some really hot ideas for themes are 'Ibiza in the 90s', 'Las Vegas Showgirls' or 'Diamante'.
• Intimate weddings are for people who have no mates and this makes for sad wedding pictures. Invite everyone you know and some people you don't, just to be sure.
• While a Scottish castle is clearly the best case

scenario, sadly it's not always affordable. My handy tip is to hire a local nightclub instead. Not only will it have good-looking bar staff, but the disco lighting will make for a really funky and sexual atmosphere.

Congratulations on your Super Sexy Wedding. Everyone on Facebook will be so jealous!

NATALIE'S RATATOUILLE
OR NATATOUILLE

The secret of this dish is to start cooking the ingredients separately first, before then bringing them together and baking them in the oven. It's also important to get the best vegetables that you can, especially the tomatoes which should be lovely and ripe. Each part of the dish is seasoned separately, so do it lightly in order to emphasize the flavours of the vegetables.

Ingredients

1 large onion, chopped
2 green peppers, peeled, deseeded and sliced
4 cloves of garlic, crushed
2 aubergines, thickly sliced
3 courgettes, thickly sliced
4 large fresh tomatoes, peeled, deseeded and chopped
2 sprigs of fresh thyme, the leaves stripped and chopped
1 handful of fresh parsley, chopped
1 handful of fresh basil

433

Olive oil
Salt and pepper
A pinch of dried saffron

Method

Heat some olive oil in a frying pan and sweat the onion with the green peppers on a low heat until tender but not brown. Add the garlic and cook through. Lightly season with salt and pepper before placing in the bottom of an ovenproof roasting dish.

Lightly season the aubergines then fry them in a generous amount of olive oil on a medium heat until lightly golden. Add them to the oven dish and sprinkle over some thyme and parsley.

Do the same with the courgettes in the same pan, using more oil if needed, then add them to the roasting dish, sprinkling over some more thyme and parsley.

To peel the tomatoes, dip them in boiling water for 10 seconds then remove the skin by hand. Slice in half then squeeze over a bowl to remove the seeds and juice, using a spoon if necessary. Chop the tomatoes finely, season lightly with salt and pepper, and mix with the saffron and remaining thyme and parsley. Spoon over the top of the vegetables in the oven dish.

Bake at 180°C/gas mark 4 for about 70 minutes, stirring only the top layer of tomatoes after thirty minutes.

Serve alone in bowls with delicious crusty bread, or as a side dish to meat or fish. Garnish by tearing up the basil leaves and sprinkling on top.

Voila!

LITTLE TROOLEY RADIO INTERVIEW TRANSCRIPT: BARNEY BRAITHWAITE TALKS TO NATALIE BUTTERWORTH

Barney: And now on Radio Trooley we have a very interesting guest . . . Natalie Butterworth.

Natalie: Hi there. Hi. It's a pleasure to be here.

B: Welcome. We're so pleased you're with us today. Now, you have a great . . . I mean, a very tragic story. Can you tell us, Natalie, about the terrible thing that happened to you?

N: Yes, I can. I was hypnotized by a man called Amazing Brian, who, let me tell you, is not amazing at all. Now I can only tell the truth when anyone asks a question. It's awful. It's ruining my entire life.

B: That sounds like a very tricky situation, Natalie. And why can't you just get unhypnotized?

N: Because Amazing Brian has gone missing. I need the public's help to find out where he is!

B: And that's why you're here today, of course, on 97.8 Radio Trooley – *Small Village, Big*

Voices. Just to help our Radio Trooley listeners to get a clear picture of how terrible this is, can you tell us what happened with your fiancé?

N: I *can* tell you. I told him he was bad at sex and bad at cooking. I told him that I wished he was taller and that I hate the perfume he buys me. I love him, so it was *horrible* to say those things to him.

background giggle from Dionne Butterworth

B: And then what happened?

N: He walked out. And now he won't speak to me and we're supposed to be getting married in a couple of weeks.

B: Oh dear. How rotten for you. Now, can you describe Brian Fernando for our listeners?

N: Yes. I only met him once, but he had a white beard and was chunky. Not fat, but sturdy, you know. Chunky. He looked quite serious in an accountant kind of way, but he had twinkly blue eyes. Oh! And a jumper that had the initials AB knitted in.

B: For Amazing Brian?

N: Yes.

B: Natalie?

N: Yes.

B: What is your worst habit?

N: I pick my toenails. I find it therapeutic. Oh God. Sorry, everyone.

background snort from Dionne Butterworth

B: Do you give any money to charity?

N: Yes, but I pretend to give fifty pounds a month when I only give thirty. Isn't that what we all do?

B: Why do you have to marry Olly?

N: Because he's almost perfect and he thinks I'm almost perfect too.

B: What do you like about Little Trooley?

N: I like the people. In particular Riley from The Old Whimsy. He's very handsome. I'd like to have sex with him.

B: Gosh. And—

N: STOP!
   sound of microphone clatter

B: Right. Well. Natalie has somewhere to be now so we have to wrap this up! Please, listeners, get in contact with any leads on Brian Fernando AKA Amazing Brian. You can call us at the studio on 01555 787 555 or visit our website at www.littletrooley.online.co.uk. And now for a little something from a dear friend of mine . . . Shirley Bassey.

N: God. Please will you edit out that—
   abrupt cut to 'Anyone Who Had a Heart' by Shirley Bassey